Torn Slater—
On The Warpath!

Rounding a sharp bend in the canyon, Ghost Owl and Geronimo saw them. A line of a dozen troopers riding high-stepping bays. They were hard-looking men with sabers and pistols. Springfield rifles were held at the ready.

Colonel Stark rode out in front of his men and gruffly demanded of the woman: "You the translator?" She nodded. "Then tell this bronco renegade that I'm bringing him in."

"You lied to us?" Ghost Owl asked matter-of-factly.

The back of Stark's hand whipped against her mouth, his West Point ring cutting her lip.

"I don't need a flat-back blanket-headed squaw telling me—"

"Sir!" a voice barked out behind him.

Colonel Stark turned to look.

Up the pass, behind the soldiers, was a tall white-eyes dressed only in a breech-clout. He was mounted on a big, deep-chested Appaloosa. Red and yellow war paint streaked his cheeks and forehead, and a dazzling yellow sunburst was painted on his broad, bare chest.

There was no mistake about it—**Outlaw Torn Slater** was going to war!

Novels by
JACKSON CAIN

Hellbreak Country
Savage Blood

Published by
WARNER BOOKS

SAVAGE BLOOD

JACKSON CAIN

WARNER BOOKS

A Warner Communications Company

This novel is a work of fiction. Names, characters, dialogue, places, and incidents are either the product of the author's imagination or, if real, are used fictitiously.

For my editor,
Ed Breslin,
who steers with care.

I am indebted to Robert Gleason and John Kelly for permission to quote from their songs, "Ghost Owl" and "Yuma Jail," © 1983, on pp. 103 and 305. Their work has provided the basic text for J.P. Paxton's "The Ballad of Outlaw Torn Slater" and has been a constant and unending inspiration to me throughout the writing of these books.

What if a weapon had done this deed? What if I held in my hands the evidence of antique murder committed with a deadly weapon a quarter of a million years before the time of man? What if the predatory transition should be susceptible to proof, and accepted as the way we came about? Could we afford to surrender in such desperate hours, as those we now live in, our belief in the nobility of man's inner nature?

I asked Dart how he felt, from a viewpoint of responsibility, about putting forward such a thesis at such a time. I said that I understood his conviction that the predatory transition and the weapons fixation explained man's bloody history, his eternal aggression, his irrational, self-destroying, inexorable pursuit of death for death's sake. But I asked would it be wise for us to listen when man at last possessed weapons capable of sterilizing the earth?

Dart turned from his window and sat down at his desk; and somewhere a tunnel collapsed, a mile down, and skulls jiggled. And he said that since we had tried everything else, we might in the last resort try the truth.

—Robert Ardrey, *African Genesis*

BOOK I

Sir, when I shoot Torn Slater—the most wanted desperado in thirteen states and territories—I'm taking more than that twenty-thousand-dollar reward. I'm taking his head. I'm bleeding it like a stuck pig, putting it in a barrel of water, then mixing in a large flask of concentrated formaldehyde. I shall put Torn Slater's head in a clear glass crock and take it across the country in my Wild West Show. I shall build that show around Slater's head, and around the live-on-stage reenactment of how I killed Slater. I shall perform for millions. I shall make tens of millions. I shall be rich. All of you—who will, of course, be actors in my Wild West Extravaganza—shall be rich. We shall be bigger than Halley's Comet.

—J.P. Sutherland, Wild West Impresario

PART I

1

The canyonlands of the Great Sonoran Desert. It is noon, the sun at zenith, the temperature a hundred and eighteen degrees. Inside the canyons it is hotter. The walls reflect and retain the thermal energy, turning the interior into a cauldron. In this inferno, life grows up hard. To subsist is to fight. Survival is struggle, and nothing in the canyons is safe—nothing.

Until it is dead.

Unimaginably ancient, the gorges stretch out in all directions. The dun-colored hardpan and crimson standstone were gouged and chiseled by long-forgotten rivers into an infinite maze of twisting arroyos, now waterless as sun-bleached bones. This endless succession of winding chasms is broken only by scattered alkali flats, arid as brick, hot as the devil's own frying pan.

Here, everything that lives must tear and scratch. Even the plants must fight, and in the canyons there are forests of hooks, needles, and knives. Flat-padded prickly pear; the squat, round barrel cactus with its big, curved spines; and the imposing saguaro, rising to over eighty feet, its many arms arching out and upward, high overhead. The pointed mesquite, the spiky maguey, the ten-foot-tall yucca with its base of razor-sharp, bayonetlike leaves.

Here is the land of the rattlesnake—two dozen varieties in all. And the scorpion, tarantula, the blood-sucking beetle called the Walapai Tiger that attacks you in your sleep and leaves you at dawn, your body covered with pus-seeping sores. Above the land the vulture wheels, keeping his lonely death watch. With blood-crusted beak, black, snaky neck, and spread wings, he glides on thermal drafts, describing wide, lazy circles in the cloudless turquoise sky. Here, the hawk shrieks, winging over the rimrock, a diamondback dangling in its talons. The spotted owl hoots its mournful cry, which some say portends death. The coyotes bark and squall and yap. The nighthawks and bullbats swoop and plunge and soar. The locusts drone and shrill and scream even in the midday heat. The flies keen, and in the distance, up in the rocks, the puma roars.

Land of the Apache. Their trade is theft, honor their plunder, their rule sustained by fear. What can be said of men who bury people up to their necks, then jerk their heads off with ropes? Who cut off your eyelids, then stake you, face to the sun? Who stake you out on cat-claw and cactus, over ant hills and termite mounds, maguey juice dripped over genitals and eyes? Who skin you like a rabbit? Who hang you by the heels over slow-burning fires, roasting you to death for days at a time, with meticulous care, infinite lassitude? Who cut off your genitals? And feed them to you while you're still alert, still alive?

Canyonlands. Moon shadows of an impossibly ancient time, infinite chaos of lost chasms, endless arroyos, a trackless wilderness, remote as the bottom of the sea, vast as hell's abyss.

Canyonlands. No trees. No water. No farmhouses with smoke curling up the blue, flawless sky. Nothing. In all that aching emptiness.

Nothing.

2

It took Deacon a full half hour to scale the canyon's hundred-and-ninety-foot wall, and the work was hard. He was over sixty now, gnarled, burned brown as a hide from too many years in the desert, and not up to the climb.

When he reached the top, he pushed his brown, sweat-stained Plainsman's hat far back on his head, revealing a matted forelock of iron-gray hair, and a wet, dirty forehead. He pulled himself up over the canyon's rim, and untied the red bandana. He wiped off his face, his gray, drooping gun-fighter's mustache, and the back of his neck. He drew a deep breath. He took the bag of Bull Durham and papers out of his shirt pocket and began rolling a quirly. Twisting the ends, he put it in his mouth, flicked a phosphorus-tipped Lucifer with a thumbnail, and lit up. Exhaling a long stream of blue smoke, he sighed. He stared at the land around him.

This far up on the rimrock, he had an open view of the Sonoran Desert. The endless maze of tortuous canyons, grotesque rock sculptures, dried-up gorges. Staring out over the vast waterless wastes, he felt as though he had wandered onto the moon. What was he doing here in this silent ocean of mesas and buttes rolling in all directions to all horizons? Here you felt no soft caress of comfort, heard no sound save the dry moan of the wind, witnessed no vision save the narrow band of blue, winding above the canyon walls, or the blindingly bright sun at zenith. What was he doing in this no-man's-land, this blistering inferno of snakes and buzzards and scorpions?

And Apaches.

He stared west into the glimmering heat waves and the dancing mirages playing late-afternoon tricks, changing shapes and forms in the blazing sun. He studied these Western sierras. They floated in the shimmering haze like ships. Sometimes they seemed so near he could reach out and touch them, even though he knew them to be a good hundred miles away.

As he squatted on the canyon's rim, a scorpion approached. The arched tail was poised, tipped with the bulging bulb of poison and the curved crimson stinger. It crab-walked closer and closer to Deacon on clawlike legs. Deacon carefully removed his battered Stetson, and, with the brim, knocked the scorpion over the edge of the gorge a hundred and ninety feet down into the camp beneath.

As the scorpion tumbled into the abyss, Deacon stared down into the camp and wondered how the hell he had fallen in with this hopeless horde of fuck-ups. The whole outfit appalled him. Here they were—a dozen packhorses, a remuda of two dozen saddle ponies, enough grain and water lashed to those cross-buck packsaddles to provision General Crook's entire army for the duration of his Apache campaign.

And all for what?

To catch one lone man.

Outlaw Torn Slater.

At the far end of the camp, he caught a blur of motion. He glared at the frenzied activity. It was Sutherland's eighteen-year-old trick-shot artist from Cody's Wild West Show. Kid Colt was a blond-haired, blue-eyed farm boy from Iowa who was an uncanny pistol shot and a very fast draw. He was now practicing his swift. Diligently. In fact, the Kid was working up a sweat. Deacon watched incredulously as the Kid went through his whole repertoire of draws-and-rolls, poker-chip draws, cross-draws, road-agent-spins, border shifts, left to right and right to left. He watched him fan, thumb, and slip-hammer the empty guns.

By consensus they forbade the Kid from using ammunition during his practice drills. The boom of his Colts in those closely confined canyons was not only ear-cracking, it was singularly inappropriate to the purpose of the trip—namely, surprising Slater and killing him unawares.

Deacon tried not to look at the rest of the camp, but he did pause to take in Mangas, the Pima tracker. He was decked out in greased braids, a buckskin breechclout, and thigh-high moccasins curled up at the toes. His buttonless, floral-patterned brocade vest covered his bare chest, and his black stovepipe hat was adorned with an ostrich plume. The clothes were plunder, no doubt taken in a raid on civilians. The plume could only have been lifted from one place—the campaign hat of a dead cavalry officer.

The tracker's chest and neck were festooned with Navaho jewelry of hammered silver and turquoise, a gold rosary— booty from a raid into Mexico—little bits of lightning-blasted wood, and small leather sacks filled with sacred pollen and owl feathers. The Pima believed these objects holy, good-luck totems, medicine gifts, the grace of the gods.

He glanced down at the Mexican packer. Eduardo had just finished rubbing down the pack stock. He had been working over their lathered, saddle-galled flanks and withers with an old sack and a curry comb, and was now into the graining and watering.

Deacon skipped over the hired guns, perhaps seeing too much of his own early youth in their angry faces. He also tried to ignore Sutherland, but somehow his eyes took him in anyway—the dapper limey in the red bowler with the silver and turquoise hatband. The rich bastard was putting on a fresh, ruffled silk shirt, tucking the tails into his red whipcord jodhpurs. The dandified riding pants bloomed outrageously around the thighs, then tapered tightly against the knees, where they were tucked into black, thigh-high riding boots of imported calfskin. He carried a black British swagger stick under his arm. He was smoking his fruity-smelling, tailor-made cigarettes. He made Deacon sick. He always made Deacon sick.

His eyes paused over the woman, Judith J. McKillian. As much as he or any man might desire her, she made him sick, too. The way she went swinging her ass and flashing her snatch all over hell's creation might have gone in a Denver brothel, but not out here on the trail. These men seldom mingled with women, and then invariably with the middle-aged whores who plied their shopworn wares in the upstairs cribs above barracks post, mining camp, and cow-town dead-falls. These men weren't accustomed to an emerald-eyed, milky-skinned, upper-class courtesan with a long mane of flame-red hair coiling over her shoulders and halfway down her back.

As J.T. Cross, a hired gun from Tascosa, Texas, had remarked about Judith McKillian's presence the night before:

"These men ain't used to high-grade whore-ladies. They sure ain't used to a first-class snatch walkin' 'round here in them butt-tight jeans, swingin' their fuckin' ass like it was a diamond mine, decked out in that China-silk shirt with nuthin' underneath 'cept a pair of righteous lungs. They can't handle that. They can't handle red-haired, green-eyed bitches with them big, black Stetsons pulled down over their eyes, turnin' up their noses at 'em. She gonna flaunt that pussy and swing that ass like she's peddlin' it, mister, she *is* gonna peddle it."

If that wasn't enough, up the pass was Torn Slater. He was the most wanted desperado in the history of the West—wanted in thirteen states and territories. He was a real gunman—a man who had ridden with Quantrill, Bloody Bill Anderson, and the James-Younger gang. A man who twenty years ago had been raised by the Apaches and who was now struggling to return home after two decades of crime, followed by three years on the Yuma rock-pile. And, most recently, a trio of Arizona bank heists—Tucson, Flagstaff, Prescott—under his belt. Torn Slater with a $20,000 price on his head, and God knows how much gold and silver in his saddlebags.

Yet even with all that potential loot in the offing, Deacon wanted no part of it. The outfit was too damn crazy—a keg of dynamite on a short fuse, and that McKillian woman was just the phosphorus-tipped Lucifer to set it off.

He was sorry now he had accepted Sutherland's money and agreed to ramrod this job. He was sorry with all his heart. That gaggle of fools was simply no match for Slater, a man the Denver papers called "a veritable gold rush of grue, gore, torture, and death."

If he strung along with them, these fools would get him killed.

Deacon stared up the pass. Far off in the distance, several days' ride away, was a towering obsidian needle called "the Black Beauty." This jet-black, volcanic monolith rose five hundred precipitous feet straight up out of the desert pan. Several million years ago, an outcropping of basement rock had exploded out of the Great Sonoran shield, and this soaring spire of blackest, sheerest, bottom stone was some of the oldest rock on the continent.

Deacon checked his bearings. Yes, they were headed straight for this volcanic needle. About five days' ride, he figured. Slater was headed there, too. Of that he could be sure. Because aside from being the oldest outcrop on the Sonoran shelf, the Black Beauty had one other inimitable feature.

Alongside the great black rock was a sweetwater spring.

It was the only reliable hole within a hundred-mile radius.

Deacon stared at the monolith, and his eyes narrowed. They could still turn around. It would be tough, but they could still get back. Another day, however, and they would pass the point of no return. They would have to make the hole.

And there they would find the man they'd tracked through five hundred miles of scorching desert.

Wearily, he started back down the canyon wall.

He did not believe they could reach the hole.

And he knew they could not take Slater.

3

It was night.

Two men were standing guard at opposite ends of the canyon. The rest of the group—nine men and one woman—were squatted around the campfire. They sipped Arbuckles and Old Crow bourbon.

Any fire in a slick-rock canyon gives off brilliant illumination, and the light glittered wildly up and down the draw. Grotesque shadows of the men, and woman, and the horses danced and flickered on the canyon walls, and the heat cut through the nighttime chill.

As they watched the fire, they also listened to the desert. They listened to the droning whine of the locusts and to the whistling whoop of the nighthawks. Off in the distance, a mountain lion roared, and her cry was greeted by a hoarse chorus of coyote barks. An owl hooted close by. The Pima tracker began mumbling protective incantations and fumbling his buckskin medicine bag filled with *hoddentin*, the sacred pollen, bits of lightning-charred wood, and the tail feathers from a horned owl. The small sack was an amulet, a charm against evil, and the nearby screech owl was evil indeed. A potent ghost from the Spirit World come to spoil his medicine or even snatch his soul. The Pima shuddered violently. No Pima shaman was present to propitiate this ghostly bird.

Deacon was not amused. He thought Mangas was right. The place was full of bad omens, which was partly why he made camp so far up the gorge. There was plenty of cover if things got rough.

He watched the light flicker eerily on the talus slopes of the gorge, and on the clumps of jumbled boulders—some as big as barns, others the size of freight wagons—strewn along the canyon floor. The big gorge was nearly two hundred feet high and twice as wide. And with all that room and all those boulders, Deacon thought they could hold this pass. A dozen gun-hands, lots of supplies, countless weapons, a ton of ammunition, and plenty of cover.

Yes, they could hold this pass, if their medicine held.

They could hold it against the *federales*.

They could hold it against the Apaches.

But could they hold it against *him*?

Against Outlaw Torn Slater?

4

After most of the men had turned in, Deacon approached
Sutherland. The Englishman was standing in front of the fire,
a mess cup of Napoleon brandy in his hand and a fruity-
smelling, tailor-made cigarette, stuffed into the end of a
long-stemmed holder of carved teak, clenched between his
teeth. His hips were canted. The red twill jodhpurs bloomed
around the thighs. Deacon felt Sutherland's disdain.

"Sir, we really gotta talk about this Slater business."

"Yes?"

"We been on this trail a hell of a long time. We crossed
the border nearly two weeks back, and we be deep into
Mexico, ass-deep. We still ain't up to him, not halfway up.
And the further we move into these here canyonlands, into
'Pache territory, into the desert, the less I like it."

"Mr. Deacon," Sutherland said, "what is it you want?
More money? Or maybe you would like Mr. Slater to simply
give himself up? Or would you prefer to turn back?"

"Maybe he wants his mama to tuck him in," Kid Colt
cracked, his tone matching his employer's.

Deacon ignored Colt's sarcasm, but fixed Sutherland with
a hard stare. "I ain't askin' for no more money. Them 5,000
gold simoleons you put in my Denver bank done just fine.
Nor am I suggestin' Slater give up. That just ain't gonna
happen. I am suggestin', though, that it's about time you
filled us in on why exactly you got eleven grown men and
this very fancy lady-friend of your'n goin' to so much trouble
and expense over a man like Slater."

"I'm a hunter, Deacon. Slater's game. Big game. The
biggest game."

"That still don't figure. Oh, I can see how a man like

you—bein' an international big game hunter and all—might go into the wild for a week or two. But from here on out this thing is gonna get real bad. 'Paches swoopin' down on us, lots more heat, no water to speak of, and 'bout this time Slater'll be gettin' a little pissed, us bangin' around all over his back porch and all. That happens, and he'll make them heathen 'Paches out there look like women in bonnets. You ain't got no better reason than baggin' game, then you're right. Yeah, we best call it quits. Piss on the fire and call in the dogs. 'Cause this hunt's over.''

It would occur to Deacon later that this was the longest speech he had ever made in his life, and it impressed Sutherland. An old, hard-bitten, trail-wise, taciturn man spitting out more words in two minutes than he'd spoken on the whole trip. Now it was Sutherland's turn to fix Deacon with the hard stare.

''Gentlemen, Miss McKillian, I may as well put the pistols on the table, as you sons of the sagebrush phrase it. I have hunted everything on God's good earth. I have shot, killed, mounted, and hung big game the world over. I've hunted everything that crawls, walks, swims, and runs. Men included. What is less commonly known, however, is that I was also a silent partner in Buffalo Bill Cody's Wild West Extravaganza. At least, I was until Cody resigned. So, gentlemen, what you see before you now is a circus impresario without a circus. Gentlemen, I am the creator, backer, and promoter of a Wild West legend, and I have lost him.''

''Sir,'' J.T. Cross said from across the campfire, ''Slater may be a legend, but he ain't no fuckin' sideshow.''

''He will be when I get done.''

''How? You gonna put him in a cage like an ape? Mount him on a fuckin' wall?''

''Not quite.'' Sutherland pointed across the campfire to a cross-buck packsaddle lying on the ground. A dozen more were scattered around it. This one differed in that alongside the pack the ends of a six-foot steel tube jutted out of the tarp. ''Inside that tube,'' Sutherland continued, ''is a six-foot longbow of the finest osage orange. It has a seventy-five-pound pull. It is inset, backed, and bellied with ivory. The arrows are of seasoned Norwegian pine taken only from the oldest Norseland shipwrecks. They are fletched with the finest eagle feathers, and the tri-bladed broad-heads are of *Kruppwerk* steel, honed to a razor's edge. The telescopic scope which I have also packed in the tube is five-power, and when slipped into place above the grip will give me a range of up to one hundred yards. In short, I am as accurate with that osage longbow as you men are with your Winchesters. Furthermore, I can nock arrows as quickly as you can lever rounds. Gentlemen, let me assure you I am no novice with this weapon. I have killed snow leopards, Bengal Tigers, and Kodiak bears with that bow. And I've killed men. In the Franco-Prussian War. And I can kill Torn Slater.''

"I still don't get the point of it," Deacon said.

"Let me put it this way: the last time I built a Wild West legend, Bill Cody, he got away. He ran off with some old cronies, rejoined the Army as a scout, claimed he liked the money but not what they termed my 'fraud and deception.' This time, gentlemen, I plan to find a bona fide Wild West hero with no such scruples. I shall create a legend out of the man who killed Outlaw Torn Slater with only the help of his osage longbow and his trusty sidekick, Kid Colt. Men, my next and newest Western hero shall be none other than James Sutherland. Gentlemen, the hero shall be myself.''

5

Standing in the flickering glare of the canyon fire, watching the grotesque shadow-figures dance on the far walls, Deacon knew it was time to leave. The water was low. The Apaches were near. Slater was closer still.

And Sutherland was clearly mad.

Still Deacon pressed the issue. "Sir, I just ain't sure no more how you plan to do this. This here last year in the Sonoran Desert's been drier'n a nun's cunt. Them last three so-called water holes was just plain dead. We dug till we hit hell, and still we didn't find no water. Now you wanna bet your hide that sweetwater spring by the Black Beauty's still gushin', you be my guest. But I don't want you bettin' mine. We still got enough water to get us back to so-called civilization. And I ain't dyin' out here of 'Paches, Slater, and dehydration. Not for no sideshow.''

''You said the Black Beauty hole was reliable, Mr. Deacon.''

''That was before we started, before we saw them last three. But I also told you that in the desert here, there ain't no guarantees. Nuthin' here is dead-solid certain. The Black Beauty spring? After the way them other holes dried up, I ain't bettin' on nuthin'. I say piss on the generals, and call in the troops. This war's over.''

The five of them stood there in silence. Kid Colt was fingering the turned-out butt of his .45, glaring at Deacon. Judith McKillian stood there, hips aslant, Stetson pulled down low over her eyes, looking.

J. T. Cross, the experienced, hard-nosed gun-hand from Tascosa, Texas, just stared up the canyon into the Apache country, his eyes, cold, indifferent, uncaring. Sutherland continued to study Deacon, cigarette holder still clenched in his teeth, the bowler fixed firmly on his head, the vague hint of a smile playing on his thin lips.

''Mr. Deacon,'' Sutherland finally said, ''have you known the Black Beauty spring to dry up before?''

''Ain't never seen these canyons so dry before.''

''You haven't answered my question.''

For a long, hard moment Deacon thought of lying to Sutherland, of saying, Yes, I've seen it dry before, drier'n a cinderblock. Instead, he was silent. He listened to the night-time drone of the locusts, a pair of barking coyotes whose squalling sounded like a whole pack of hounds. He listened to the whooshing swoop of the nighthawks. And when in the midst of all that desert night cacophony an owl hooted, he actually shuddered.

''Mr. Deacon, I asked you if you'd ever seen or heard of the Black Beauty drying up.''

''No sir.''

"Then I say we push on. Unless there's any other recommendations? Colt? Cross? Judith?"

"Yeah, I got a question." It was J. T. Cross who spoke, the veteran gunman with the drooping mustache, the hound-dog eyes, and dead-flat Panhandle drawl. " 'Cause Deacon's right about one thing: we been runnin' this fox from hell to breakfast. And we still ain't got him treed. So, yeah, I got a question. Let's call it 'methods and procedures.' 'Cause we need a new method. This present one ain't workin'."

"Noted and observed." Sutherland's voice was terse. "Mr. Deacon, any revision in plan?"

"Sir, as I been sayin' all along, we be overloaded. *If* we find water at the spring and *if* we continue on, we gotta lighten up. We got all them pots and pans and ladies' garments, all them barrels and cameras and stuff. Even a lotta extra guns and ammo. We got everything 'cept the Egyptian pyramids. And every pound of gear we pack takes water. Water we ain't got."

"But Slater ain't hurtin' like us. Slater don't need water, I suppose?" Kid Colt sneered.

"He don't need much. Slater travels like an Apache. A blanket, guns, a knife, a handful of jerky. He'll kill his meat on the way and eat it raw. He'll suck out the juice to cut down on the need for water. His stock'll get by, too."

"His stock needs grain and water, same as ours," Colt pressed.

"No sir. *We* picked ours"—Deacon fixed Sutherland with a hard sarcastic stare at the word *we*—" 'cause they was Morgans and Tennessee Walking horses, 'cause they was gentle and took good camera pictures. *We* wasn't plannin' on ridin' 'em this far. Not Slater. He picked his stock 'cause they was tough and could live off the land. While we're luggin' half a ton of grain, his stock'll feed on mesquite and prickly pear. While we haul all that water, he gets half his moisture from raw meat, half of it lizard. Whatever water he's carryin', hell, he probably gives to his animals."

"He really eats raw snakes?" Judith McKillian asked, amazed.

"Ma'am, he'll eat sticks and rocks like a hydrophobic dog," said J. T. Cross.

"But his stock can't live off the land, not forever," Colt said.

"Oh, he'll keep them goin' a piece," said Deacon. "He'll work them till their ribs and hip joints stick out like a rack of bones, till they be goose-rumped and cow-hocked. When they be so whipped down they can't get up, he'll just kill 'em, skin 'em, and jerk their meat. He'll make seventy miles a day on foot. Ma'am, I know Torn, known him twenty years. He ain't no ordinary man."

"And that may be the trouble with you," Kid Colt said with contempt. "You've known too many men, too many years. You lived too many years. Why ain't someone buried you by now?"

"Kid," J. T. Cross said softly.

"Don't 'Kid' me. I've watched this old man when he talks about Slater. Talks about him like Torn Slater was some sort of devil's spawn, hatched in hell, bigger'n Beelzebub and howlin' for our hides. Like he was some sort of fiend from Hades who's cloaked himself in human flesh, like he was tryin' to throw a scare into us or somethin'. I'll tell you what I think. I think we ain't found Slater yet 'cause this here ramrod is too yellow. He don't want to find Torn Slater. Afraid Slater'll take his guns away and spank him with them. Or maybe he's afraid he'll find that Torn Slater ain't shit. Just another tired old man like himself who's outlived his time. Like all you fools who rode with Quantrill and Bloody Bill. It's time someone threw some dirt in all your faces."

No one had ever talked to Deacon like that. And lived. Nor would Kid Colt have survived the next five seconds had not J. T. Cross of Tascosa, Texas, cut in. He snapped:

"Shut up, Colt. Them ain't wrinkles on that old man's face. They be a war map. He's holed a hundred punks like you. And don't talk so smart about Slater, neither. I don't say fear him, but I say respect him. 'Cause like Deacon, I seen him do some things, some terrible things."

Kid Colt slipped the thong off his hammer and loosened the big .45 in his holster. He turned toward Cross.

"Just talk, Cross. And talk don't get it done."

"Now boys," Sutherland was saying softly, attempting to quiet the waters. "Let us not forget the primary purpose of this little *business* venture. This *is* a business venture. We are not here to murder each other, but to track down Outlaw Torn Slater and make a great deal of money in the process. For not only do I plan on building a fabulous Wild West Show around this little expedition, I want each of you—Judith included—to perform in that show. But in the meantime, we do have to catch and kill Mr. Slater. Mr. Cross here has correctly suggested that we consider a change in procedure, which I have approved. Mr. Deacon was about to expand upon the suggested change."

The loquacious speech calmed the waters. The endless torrent of oily words quieted even Kid Colt.

"First you gotta understand that in Slater's eyes he ain't the hunted," Deacon said. "You can see it from his trail. Hell, Slater was raised 'Pache. He's a man who, if he wants, don't leave no track. He probably don't even cast no shadow. The way Slater sees it, his track works in reverse. He sees his track as a long rope lashed around our necks—each of our necks—and he sees himself as draggin' us along after him. When the time comes, he'll just jerk us down one by one."

"I don't get it," Sutherland said. "Aren't we clearly the cat and Slater the mouse?"

"Not in Slater's eyes. If that was true, he'd just go to ground. Hell, this is his ground, his blood-ground. He was born here. Raised here. He'd climb into a hole and pull it in after him. We wouldn't find hide nor hair. We'd give up and head back home."

"Why doesn't he do that, then?" Sutherland asked.

"In Slater's eyes, us stalkers is the stalked, us hunters the prey. This is a game of cat-as-mouse. And when you play Slater's game, there's a difference."

"What difference?"

"You're goin' after Slater like you was Ulysses S. Grant takin' Richmond. You think you're gonna run your prey, chew at his heels, and when you finally catch up, tear him to pieces. You'll worry your kill like dogs on a grizzly. But Slater won't sit still for that kind of fight. Hell, no. He was trained by the 'Paches and by Quantrill. And he'll stalk *you*. He's stalkin' you right now. He plans to hit you where you ain't lookin'. He'll let heat and fatigue and desert terrain do the rest. He'll hit and run like an Apache. He'll surprise you to death. And some of his tactics'll be so terrible they could frighten you to death.''

"You seem frightened to death already," said Kid Colt.

"I got cause. I seen him fight. In the Rebellion. We was under Quantrill and Bloody Bill. I seen him do some hard things. Cross seen him, too, up Tascosa way. He's all outlaw— the double-tough, case-hardened, triple-distilled essence of outlaw. I don't know how else to put it. But he's bad, very bad.''

6

It was only the next morning, after the Mexican mule packer had thrown the last diamond, wrenched the hitch tight, pulling the tarp-covered pack together, that Deacon noticed Kid Colt was gone. His absence was easy enough to spot. J.T. Cross, who was roping mounts out of the remuda, had the saddles all lined up and ready. Only Kid Colt's was missing. As Deacon glanced around the camp, it was easy to see they were also missing the Kid.

Deacon searched for the Kid's bedroll. He seemed to remember that it was laid out behind a jumble of boulders just north of the camp. Without raising a fuss, Deacon quietly walked over to inspect it.

At least, he inspected where the Kid's bedroll had been. The ground on which he'd spread his roll was scratched and chewed up rather badly, as though a couple of randy horses had pawed on it half the night. Furthermore, Deacon noted a few strands of white silk thread and a mother-of-pearl button on the ground.

A certain woman had been in too much of a hurry to get her blouse off.

He pocketed the thread and button, and on the way back noted the dainty boot prints of Miss Judith McKillian trotting to and from Colt's bedroll.

Christ, he thought gloomily, every form of print 'ceptin' pecker tracks.

He motioned Cross and Sutherland away from the remuda. When he got them alone, he said:

"Colt's gone."

"What?" Sutherland said, shocked. He seemed unaware of his lady friend's liaison.

"That talk I had last night, the one that was supposed to advise caution—seems it had the opposite effect on Colt. His tracks are leadin' up-canyon."

"Well, I'll be damned," Sutherland said.

"We all will. But if it's any consolation, this idea of Colt's ain't half bad. Right now, we're too many and too few. Takin' on Slater is a job for a few good men or one whole army."

"Oh yeah?" Cross said. "I've seen some good men go up against Slater. Come to think of it, I never seen none of them around later."

"Well, Colt is fast," Sutherland said. "Fast and accurate. Maybe he'll get lucky."

"I just hope he remembers to load them damn guns," Deacon said grimly.

7

A man lay prone on a canyon wall ledge nearly a quarter of a mile above the gorge. It was hot. As he slipped out of the collarless tan shirt, the massive back muscles rippled smoothly, revealing blocklike shoulders, large, heavily veined biceps, and an astonishingly narrow waist.

Torn Slater was uncomfortable on the narrow ledge—and irritable. He had wasted half a day scaling this god-awful canyon wall just to get a look at the scalp-hunters dogging his trail. He did not fear the men below. He merely resented their existence.

He lowered the fourteen-power scope. It was almost too powerful to examine the man riding up the canyon on the big deep-chested gray. That man especially irked Slater. Here it was, high noon in the desert, and that shorthorn fool was cantering the hocks off a perfectly good horse, all in hopes of catching up with Torn Slater ahead of his friends. Slater raised the scope. The horse was drenched in lather along the saddle's edge and was blowing foam.

Slater pointed the scope on down the canyon. Nothing. Nothing. Nothing. At last he came to the long line of pack mules, twelve in all. They were led by a dozen men on horseback.

At present, Slater was safe. While the straight-line distance between Slater and the main posse was only three thousand yards—only ninety yards through the scope—it was a good two days' ride through those winding gorges. Maybe longer, when you pulled a jerk-line string. Even so, he knew they would close the gap near the Black Beauty. There, Slater would have to rest his horse and his mule near the spring to rehydrate them, or they would die. And he needed them to get to Geronimo's stronghold.

Geronimo.

His blood-brother.

That was another problem. He stared at his long, jagged palm scars. These were the lines that united him and his friend. They had been gouged into his hands twenty years ago by Cochise, the Apache leader who had been his *hunka,* or spiritual father. Cochise had carved identical wounds into Geronimo's hands, then lashed the palms together with rawhide thong. Their blood had commingled, and the bond was sealed.

Yes, Geronimo would take him back. Unless, that is, he committed some grave offense to the Apache nation. He could think of very few which might render him unacceptable.

But one offense would be to lead a band of white scalp-hunters to the secret Chiricauhua stronghold.

Then there was Slater's pride. As much as he hated to admit it, these white bounty-hunters, who tracked him for the price on his head, had finally gotten on his nerves.

He put the scope back into its tubular metal case, twisted the ends of the tubes together, and shoved it under his belt.

He picked up his collarless tan shirt and slipped it back on. He eased himself down over the side of the canyon ledge and then paused. Three hundred yards up the canyon rim, in a clump of boulders, was a puma—a huge tom—guarding the female's den.

The puma.

The animal the late Cochise had called his "medicine cat." Once during a hunting trip Cochise had flushed a puma his way. The puma had come down a steep slope like a bullet straight at Slater and Geronimo. Geronimo had turned and fled, but the young Slater, instead of panicking, had coolly raised his bow and fired the nocked arrow straight at the rocketing cat. The big Folsom broad-head had struck the puma in mid-leap, straight through the heart, and when the hurtling painter had crashed into Slater, bowling him over, the creature was inert, stone dead.

Cochise had proclaimed this shot the greatest hunting feat he'd ever seen. He later said that great medicine existed between Slater and the puma, that Slater could compel the beast to do his bidding.

And as Slater stared at the puma in her den among the rocks, scrupulously guarding her cubs, he wondered if once again the old man might not have been right.

Because high above the lion den was another ledge, one from which . . .

He stared down into the canyon. Off in the distance he watched the roiling dust of the lone man cantering up the canyon in the hot desert sun.

The man who was trying to take Torn Slater alone.

The man who was obviously very, very foolish.

8

They rested at noon near a bend in the canyon which had plenty of boulders for cover in the event of an Apache attack. While the men sipped their water ration and chewed on jerky and hardtack, Sutherland and his whore ate daintily from tins of smoked fish and caviar. They split what appeared to be a bottle of good French wine.

Deacon watched the whore with the long, flame-colored hair, the bosom bulging under the sheer, red blouse, and the equally protuberant ass almost bursting through the taut Levi's. Why on God's good earth had Sutherland taken her along? Deacon did not even believe they screwed. Long ago, Deacon had dismissed Sutherland as some sort of weird deviate.

She was trouble, all right. And they would pay for her presence in blood before this trip was done.

If Kid Colt had not paid for her persuasive charms already.

After Sutherland and the woman finished their delicacies, he strolled over to a bit of shade for a nap. Deacon took the opportunity to approach Judith McKillian.

The one the Mexican mule packer called a *puta*—a whore.

The one Deacon thought of as a *bruja*—a witch.

They had talked before, and the contempt had been mutual. Judith McKillian saw in Deacon a Puritan righteousness which she instantly construed as hypocrisy. After all, he was a man who made his living with a gun. He saw her sexual license as perversity and degradation.

To some extent, they were both right.

He caught her alone leaning against a boulder near the north canyon wall.

"God only knows what Slater will do to Colt when he catches him."

"Drop it, Deacon. The boy did what he did."

Deacon stared at the wealthy *puta*. She was so damn cold, so damn sure of herself—and so attractive. He stared a brief moment at his dusty boots, canvas pants, and his collarless brown shirt. He took off his tan, sweat-stained Plainsman's hat and beat the dust out of it against his leg. He knew he looked like hell.

Judith McKillian, on the other hand, after nineteen days and nights on the trail—the last ten without bathing—looked immaculate. Not one strand of her long, red hair was out of place. No bead of sweat on her cheek or brow. The ruffled silk shirt and the skin-tight Levi's were inexplicably neat. She was so damn cool, so damn detached he wanted to kill her.

He felt her mocking gaze appraising him. "What's wrong, Deacon?"

"You. What you did to Colt over behind them rocks. What Slater will do to Colt when he catches him."

"Don't be so sure, Deacon. That Kid, he was one *macho hombre*."

"Like hell. He weren't supposed to take off like that."

"What he did, he did."

Deacon looked away.

"Don't take it so hard. Suppose he makes it? Think of all the blood and lives he'll save. Think of him as a brave man, a hero. And all for such a noble cause."

"Yeah," Deacon said, staring pointedly at her crotch. "I can understand that cause. I wonder what he will think of that noble cause when Slater has him."

"He admired it greatly last night."

"But now? Today?"

She gently touched Deacon's cheek. "Ah, my puritanical friend, in the morning many people have found many things different. Perhaps, sometimes, even you."

"Yeah, but I never got myself tortured or killed over it. Not over no piece of ass."

"Maybe you did not love the woman enough. Maybe you did not love any woman enough."

He watched her laugh lightly, turn, and walk away. Straight back, long strides, swinging her ass like it was the Comstock Lode. She stopped by the remuda and waited while Cross roped out her big black gelding. He bridled it for her. Afterward she swung onto the black Texas saddle, lavishly inlaid with turquoise and silver. Cross pulled the cinch tight, notch after notch after notch.

Deacon walked over to the remuda and roped out the bay.

When they were all mounted up, Deacon yelled: "Line 'em up and head 'em on out!"

They headed up the canyon, Deacon and Cross in the lead, Sutherland and Judith McKillian close behind.

Deacon could not help wondering if the whore was right. Perhaps he had never loved a woman enough.

9

Judith McKillian was not thinking of love.

She was thinking of the Kid.

Had she really seduced the boy into sneaking off after Slater? From her point of view, the answer was no. Seduction was a two-way street. She had simply inflamed his libido, just as he had aroused her. They had satisfied each other.

But was the seduction really so even-handed? No. With a small, private smile, she recalled that even as her tongue stroked the underside of Kid Colt's member, she'd also teased him, whispering how weak and unmanly these so-called *pistoleros* were. She told the Kid that if a dozen men were needed to take Torn Slater, then the West must truly be lacking in *cojones*. As she kissed and fondled his virility, she had also goaded him on and on, saying that all these gun-slingers were good for was whoring and drinking. And mostly for drinking. She cursed men everywhere—all save Kid Colt.

She said she was going after Slater herself. Alone. That night. She would come back, get Kid Colt, and they would ride off with all of the $20,000 bounty. To hell with the rest! She and Colt would take the reward and the others—especially that sonofabitch, Sutherland—be damned!

She'd kissed him excitedly. She kissed his cheeks, hair, throat, chest, worked her way slowly down his stomach, languidly luxuriating at his navel, then down across the groin. She'd taken his tremendous cock just a little at a time. First the tip, teasing the sensitive underside subtly with the tongue, gradually easing her way down the whole tingling length, taking his entire member in her mouth. She sucked it slowly, softly. She gyrated her head and rotated her tongue, teasing and tantalizing. Soon she'd sensitized every nerve ending till his whole member was throbbing, hot, and engorged. Still she teased, still she tantalized. She waited him out, torturing him, waited until he whimpered. Only then did she increase the pressure of tongue and lips, only then increase the gyrating pump of her mouth and head. She did this with precision. Gripping the head of his member in her lips, she clamped them shut at the base of his cock with her fingers, all the while massaging the sensitive underside of his prick with her tongue.

And he came. God, how he came! Over and over and over and over. Into her mouth, down her chin, over her cheeks. Most of it she saved in her mouth, tried to spill it back out onto the sensitive tip of his penis. And when his prick was covered with his come, she gyrated her lips and face around the milky fluid, massaging the sensitive member, covering her lips with a dripping froth of translucence, the ring of cream on her lips in alabaster contrast against her tanned skin and flame-red hair.

Perhaps it was the sight of her—his come so starkly white on her mouth—perhaps that was what drove him on, would not let him stop, would not let his member go down.

His sperm still wet on her cheeks, she grabbed him around the neck and crushed his lips against hers. Now the Kid was coated with his manhood, and that sight of him smeared with his come made her nipples stand hard and erect. And when he did not wipe it away, but instead eased a palm across her breast—one nipple first, barely touching one, then the other, his fingers cupping each breast as he did so—that, too, aroused her.

Now she was breathing hard, fighting against her desire, wanting desperately to control the situation, whatever the consequence, even at the cost of her own pleasure and satisfaction. But she could not do it. Now her breasts were rising and falling in the bright moonlight. Her own blood was up, and she knew she would play out the hand, play it to the hilt, right there in the desert, moaning her pleasure. In the mesquite, not on satin sheets in her Denver hotel, but on rough wool army blankets in the Mexican chapparal.

They were both naked, and he rolled over onto her, and then she could feel the whole delicious length of him pressing against her. And then once more, against her will, she was hot, open, and wet, and he was entering her, his stiff prick inside her, all the way.

She'd heard that men in danger, men on the brink, were more passionate than in moments of safety. And she'd sometimes believed she'd experienced that. But it was never like this. This time there was a finely drawn tension to the act—a tautness, a suspense.

She felt his fingers reach around the small of her back, under her ass, and then felt the electric shock of a rude middle finger force its way into her anus. She, in turn, gripped him by the buttocks and painfully impaled his own ass.

By now he was thrusting wildly, and she accommodated the driving thrusts with the easy roll of her own gyrating hips, bringing their groins up tight, holding them there. Her eyes were shutting, and she cursed herself softly before succumbing to her desires.

Inch by inch he increased the length of his stroke. First just the tip of his penis had been in her, but then, slowly, every inch an agony of pleasure, he let himself sink in, his hardness cutting through her softness, her body clinging to his, until he was jamming his cock into the base of her spine.

Then he stopped. He held her there for what seemed a full

five minutes, her cunt impaled on his prick, two fingers violating her anus, probing the thin wall between her anus and vagina, touching through the folds with the very tip of his member. He held her there immobile for what seemed an eternity, sunk all the way into her, crushing pelvis against pelvis, as her body tingled and quivered.

Her head began to roll from side to side, and her soft, wet mouth opened and moaned. Then again he slid halfway out, held her there, balanced in agony on arching backs and groins. Again he sank, and again the groan rose in spasms, reflexively, from her body. Again he rose, again he fell, now faster, faster, increasing the stroke, accelerating the thrust.

Then she was drunk with desire, out of her head—damn him!—the violent drunkenness of her pleasure raging out of control. She was losing consciousness of everything, except the hot piston pounding inside her, thrusting and thrusting. Somewhere in the dim abyss of her brain she heard a soft *oh!* and then another *oh!* and was stunned and angered to realize it was her own voice. Then he was bucking above her, but instead of lying passively on the block, she assisted in her own execution. With each buck, her pelvis charged into his, pounding uncontrollably. The small of her back then shuddered and shook. She cried again, gripped him with her fingers, gouged her nails into his back and buttocks, cried out over and over. Again, they bucked, bucked and shuddered, crying angrily. She jammed her middle finger deeper and deeper into his anus, wrenching at it violently, wanting only to hurt him, humiliate him for what he was doing to her, for making her succumb to her needs and passions like an animal, a common whore, a bitch in heat.

Then it was as though she was transformed, transcending the flesh, the burning cunt between her legs a thing apart from the rest of her. She was raised up to him, virtually levitating off the wool blanket, every inch of her—his! his! Gyrating and thrusting, impaled on his pumping member, a raspy wail tore out of her throat, splitting the midnight darkness apart. His, all his. Her very soul was tumbling down a long, black, bottomless abyss, lost and out of control. Shuddering, shuddering—lost.

And when she came to, climbed back out of the long, black hole of unconsciousness, a whimpering little cry wrenching from her lungs, half whispered, half moaned, he was gone. On his horse, up the canyon, after the outlaw. To kill Torn Slater and take the bounty.

Gone.

10

Kid Colt was now far up the canyon.

And Judith McKillian, with her artful tongue and voluptuous body, seemed as remote as the Martian moons.

What was more evident to the Kid, and much closer at hand, was the blazing afternoon sun, which baked the twisting, chaotic arroyos like an oven. What was also evident was the Kid's failure to pack sufficient water. Throughout the trip a Mex wrangler had watered the stock, and the Kid hadn't realized how much that damn horse drank, not out here in the desert. He'd been so all-fired hot to impress the McKillian woman that he hadn't grabbed much more than a half-gallon canteen, a morral of grain, and a little jerky. Now the gray was blowing white froth and was lathered from eyeballs to hocks. Without more water, the horse would not make it another day.

And the Kid's canteen was down to the last cupful, which he figured to save for himself.

He cursed the horse silently, and bitterly recalled Deacon's bullshit about how much extra mileage Slater and them heathen 'Paches got from their livestock. Hell, he'd raked his mount bloody with them big Chihuahua gut hooks, and still he couldn't get that nag to move no more. No matter how hard he kicked and spurred her, the big mare just tossed her head, blew pink foam, hung her neck and head between her legs, and stumbled along haltingly. The only movement that damn oat-burner seemed capable of was swishing her tail to chase off the flies.

Aside from the flies, not much else was stirring. Only the locusts, which continued their endless whining drone. Otherwise, nothing. Not a breath of breeze, not a hint of a cloud in the long, winding ribbon of blue overhead. A scattering of mesquite, creosote shrubs, here and there an arid stream bed which seemed to have dried up back in the Pleistocene. Occasional prickly pear, a few stunted yucca. A scattering of sage.

They rounded a long, winding bend in the gorge, and less than a hundred feet away the Kid saw a jumble of boulders big as boxcars. They were throwing off some shade, and a fairly stout mesquite bush was growing out of a crack in the canyon wall. He thought about stopping there, unsaddling, and rubbing down the gray. Then maybe he'd drink that cup of water in his canteen and roll a smoke. Hell, might as well pack it in. Hole up here and wait. He'd never catch Slater, at this rate. Torn Slater was packing too damn much water, that was the answer. Living off raw snake meat, grazing his stock on mesquite and prickly pear—bullshit! That old man Deacon spread shit like that just to rank out men who really had the stuff, men like Kid Colt. Slater had extra grain and water, that was all.

Deacon. He could hear that old man now, ribbing him about how he'd run out of water and had to wait up for the old folks to rescue him. Well, this time he wouldn't take no rawhiding. Not from Deacon, not from J.T. Cross. He'd throw down on both of them if they—

Then he saw the cat.

The cat was on top of large house-sized boulder about fifty feet to his left. The great sleek tawny tom, long of body, at least six full feet from tip of nose to crack of ass. The flanks were specked and shaded charcoal gray, and the head was surprisingly small for such a massive torso. The blazing, yellowish eyes were steady and unwavering in their stare. But the thing that struck Colt most was the tail. Long and snaky and curled, it stretched a good four feet, switching back and forth constantly, just as the amber eyes remained dead still in their studious stare, empty as void, unreadable as God.

Colt had seen the animal at all only because he had caught the blur of peripheral motion as he made a spectacular seventy-five foot leap down from a wall ledge onto the big rock. Colt also realized that something or someone had flushed him down from that vertiginous canyon outcropping onto the boulder so far below, because nothing—not even panthers—make such precipitous leaps unprovoked.

The tom apparently was not pleased at making the jump, either. From deep down in his throat came first a low, grating rumble, then a high, piercing scream. The scream seemed to Colt almost supernatural in its pitch and intensity, somehow not of this earth, but from the deepest bowels of darkest hell—an unholy howl that froze his blood and shocked his soul.

The horse heard the tom too. Which, as the Kid quickly saw, was not a good thing. The gray, who seconds ago had been incapable of a trot, was now exploding.

Arching her back with demented fury, the mare shoved her head deep between her legs and left the earth like a rocket. For a moment the Kid just hung there on the bowed back, a look of stunned horror on his face, his mind wild with fright, his body suspended in time and space high above the saddle. Then the gray came back down, inches ahead of the Kid's now-falling body, came down stiff-legged on all fours. And when the Kid's own weight hit that back, the jolt shot through his ass, slammed up his spine, all but shattered the teeth and broke the jaw, then nearly whiplashed his head clean off his shoulders.

The Kid never had a prayer. Because by then the bronc was busting him every which way but loose. The gray was already into her second buck, though by now the Kid was hardly in the saddle. Dropping the reins, clutching the horn with both hands, he was banging off the sides of the saddle and the cantle more than he was on the fork. By the second buck, both feet had also left the stirrups, which were now flying straight up in the air, slapping him in the face and the temples. By the third buck, he was off the cantle and onto the gray's rump. By the fourth buck he was on the ground.

Now the horse was rearing back on her hind legs, slashing savagely in the air with her front hoofs. The mare was snorting, blowing, and whinnying, only to the Kid the whinnying sounded more like a wrenching, echoing scream, like the screech of a train whistle.

The gray was in total panic, side-lunging, crow-hopping, jumping like a jackrabbit, fighting to get enough self-control simply to run away.

But it was too late.

To the Kid's utter astonishment, the panther leaped more than fifty feet in a perfect parabola and landed squarely on the horse's back. The horse's eyes were walled with frenzy. Her attempts to unseat the cat, which had taken Colt's place right in the saddle, were so furious that Colt could no longer distinguish between bucks and kicks, side-jumps and crow-hops. The ear-splitting whinnies, which were shrilling up and down the canyon, had taken on the hideous pitch of one blood-curdling scream, horrendous in its tone and tenor, yet somehow strangely human.

The Kid was crab-walking away from the slashing hoofs, terrified, yet unable to take his eyes off the grisly spectacle: the biggest painter he'd ever seen, close to seven feet long, astride the bucking gray. All four of the cat's paws were digging deeply into the gray's sides, and blood was spraying all over. The big tom had a much firmer seat than any rider could have had. He was welded to the gray as tightly as the saddle, and as the horse side-lunged, bucked, and kicked, it was obvious he would ride the horse to death.

It was when the horse tried to roll the cat off her back that he had his move. Opening his jaws a full eighteen inches, he clamped them down on the base of the horse's neck, and with one gut-churning crunch! snapped the gray's spine.

The mare stopped bucking, walked two steps to her right, and then the huge, walled eyes, which a second ago had been so filled with terror, went dim. The gray tried to snort, but the only thing that blew out of her nose was a huge clot of blood, then another, and another. She tried to walk one more step, then pitched forward and died, crashing to the earth with a bone-jarring thud.

But by then, with an almost effortless ease, the panther had leaped, no, danced off the back of the falling horse. Had it not been for the great gouts of blood drenching his jaws and fangs and whiskers, Colt might have said that he leaped from the gray's back with winged grace. But no—this was no gentle cherub, rather an embattled seraph, a killer angel. Moreover, he was less than twenty feet from the Kid, who stood staring at him unblinking. The Kid knew he was next, knew it with all his heart. As he stared into the eyes of the painter, he slowly slipped the split thong off the hammer of his sidearm and casually loosened the gun in its holster.

It seemed now that there were only these two creatures in the whole world. The panther staring at the Kid with blazing amber eyes, staring at him with a strange, fixed curiosity. And the Kid staring back, trying to read something in those unfathomable depths, seeking a clue in the animal's reflexes that would somehow give him an edge.

For the Kid knew now he would have to make the fastest draw and the best pistol shot of his life. There, on the canyon floor, facing down the painter—there, on his knees.

The big panther would be moving too fast for a head shot, so the Kid figured to go for the heart. He had hot-loaded rounds in his Peacemaker. Two hundred and fifty-five grains of lead backed by sixty grains of black powder. One of them through the painter's pump at twenty feet would put out any cat's lights, even one of them Bengal tigers Sutherland bragged about.

The long, serpentine tail which had been switching endlessly stopped abruptly. A deep, low-throated, bass rumble was vibrating from the cat, all around the cat, all around the canyon, *hrrrrrh! hrrrrrh! hrrrrrh!* almost as if the big cat were telling Colt that it was time to make his move.

The Kid took a deep breath and held it.

Then he went for his gun. And it was good. He could feel it, even as his hand was wrapping around the butt, the webbing of his thumb simultaneously cocking the hammer, the pistol sliding smoothly within the basket-weave holster.

And in the same instant, the panther sprang.

The gun cleared the holster, levelled, and fired.

The Kid was literally nose to nose with the springing panther. The animal's roar was now directly in his face, horrendous and deafening. The breath from the gaping, foot-and-a-half-wide jaws was unimaginably foul, and the amber eyes, which had remained calm and unblinking throughout it all, were rendered even more evil by their very coldness, as though this flawless killing mechanism, with all its majesty of motion and grace of angels, had, in fact, only the coiled strength and the same absence of heart as a big, steel bear trap.

And yet, nose to nose with the big cat, locked in the throes of his hot embrace, the Kid did not feel that way. In fact, he felt different, changed, transformed. He felt strangely at peace with the big painter with the gaping jaws, arched talons, and curled tail.

For the first time in Kid Colt's life, he was not even afraid.

11

The panther's roar, the mare's screaming whinnies, and the Kid's pistol shot did not reach Deacon's ears as individual noises, but as a chaos of sound. Even the hard, flat report of the Kid's pistol was so mangled by ten miles of twisting canyons and winding gorges that it was lost in the over-all effect, which was that of distant, high-pitched thunder, long and eerie and shrill.

But it did bring Sutherland's outfit up short.

"Deacon," Sutherland suggested, "maybe you, Cross, and some of the boys should ride up ahead."

"These here mounts is ridden 'bout as hard as we're gonna

ride them. After that Black Beauty spring, they're gonna need rest and grain. And lots of rehydration. Even if they get it, I ain't sure how much bottom they got left. Hell, half of them are wormy and diarrhetic as it is.'' He pointed to a big, buckskin packhorse, who, as if on cue, was emitting a stream of muddy manure. ''The other half is stone-bruised and saddle-galled. We'll be lucky to walk them out of this goddamn desert, let alone gallop them.''

''But Kid Colt is—''

''Pardon me for sayin' so, but we warned him about Slater. The Kid, he's a good ten or twelve miles up this pass now. That's way too far. The plain truth is it's too damn hot. Must be 120 degrees.'' He waved his hand at the stock. The horses' heads were bowed in the heat, and rifle butts angled up pommel-high. The only movement was the occasional swish of the tail, chasing off the endless, buzzing flies. ''The stock's cooked halfway to death. And right now a couple of horses is worth more to us alive than that half-baked Kid. We can *ride* them horses out of this here desert. You ain't gonna get very far climbing onto Colt's back and stickin' rowels to his sorry ass.''

Sutherland looked dismayed, recognizing the truth in Deacon's words.

''Anyway,'' Judith McKillian was saying, trying to muster some hopeful enthusiasm, ''that noise, it could have been the Kid nailing Slater.''

This time it was J.T. Cross who spoke. He'd dropped back from his lead position and was now flanking Sutherland on his right.

''Ma'am, there ain't much chance of that. Lookin' to sneak up on Torn Slater's back porch is like lookin' for cherries in a cow-camp whorehouse. You best expect the worst. That is my professional opinion. You best expect the worst.''

12

It was near twilight, and for a long time they had been expecting the worst. For several hours a swirling cloud of vultures had been gathering up-canyon. And for the last hour, the shadows of these spiraling birds had passed languidly over them, each flashing shade bringing the brief illusion of chill.

Now, the sun was sinking over the western rim of the canyon, and although the world beyond the gorge was still hours from sundown, within their own gloomy precipice it was now growing dim. A long shadow was spreading over the canyon floor, and while the winding ribbon of blue overhead continued to illumine their odyssey, the shadowy world of the canyon turned cool. Ponchos and serapes were brought out and wrapped around hunched shoulders.

It was during the last half hour that they began to catch the occasional vagrant scent of turning meat. It was then that Judith McKillian rode up between Deacon and J.T. Cross. Not that she was chagrined. The McKillian woman seemed to be enjoying this inevitable encounter with the Grim Reaper. She was smiling widely. Her emerald eyes had a mad glitter, an unnatural sheen that Deacon had not noticed before. He noticed a sort of breathlessness in her as well, a sense of eager expectation. She was jocular, amused.

And she made him thoroughly sick.

"Mr. Deacon, would you mind if I ask you a personal question?"

"If you don't mind not gettin' no answer."

"Why did you choose the noble profession of law enforcement? Your Holy Crusade for Justice, Truth, and Right?"

"That's easy. The money."

"Please, Mr. Deacon. Answer truthfully. There couldn't have been much money in that line of work."

"More'n drovin' or sod-bustin'. More'n layin' track for the Union Pacific."

"No, Mr.Deacon, you could have done other things. I think instead you enjoyed the danger and death."

"Pardon my sayin' so, ma'am," J.T. Cross interrupted, "but you sure talk a lotta shit."

Judith McKillian gave a shrill, wicked giggle which rang in Deacon's ears and made his flesh crawl. At the same time, he noticed a wheeling vulture catch a thermal, and soon the bird's wide circle was corkscrewing lazily over the rimrock, leaving his spiraling companions to hover near the earth.

"Mr. Deacon," Judith said blithely, "do you ever feel like a vulture?"

"You mean do I feed off carrion? No, ma'am. Men like Torn Slater, they ain't exactly dead meat."

Again, the shrill giggle, and again, Deacon winced.

"Oh no, not that. I mean, look at him." She pointed to the solitary vulture who was still rising on thermal gusts high above the canyon wall, far beyond the spiral cloud of buzzards which was now virtually overhead. "It must be nice, gliding and wheeling so far above. Like soaring through space in a dream. Wouldn't you really like to be a vulture? In another life?"

"Don't hardly know, ma'am."

"But they lead such a charming life."

"Yeah," J.T. Cross said in that dead-flat Panhandle drawl, "they kin eat anythin', but nuthin' eats them. Ain't that right, Deacon?"

"You got somethin' there, Cross."

Suddenly, rounds were exploding behind them. Deacon turned, and, to his dismay, Sutherland was levering his Winchester into the wheeling carrion birds overhead.

"Cut that out," Deacon yelled back. "They ain't hurtin' nuthin'. Hell, they just keepin' the land clean. Like them Denver boys what drives them gut wagons. Them birds sure ain't the ones us here got to worry about. You got Torn Fuckin' Slater up there, somewhere, somehow. Plus a shitload of Apaches. Save your biscuits for them. Load your magazines and keep one in the chamber while you're at it.''

Deacon then brought them to a halt. He took off his bandana and tied it down over his nose.

"I'm goin' on up ahead. I should be back shortly. With some news.''

He started to kick his mount up the pass when J.T. Cross grabbed his mecate and pulled his bay back on his haunches.

"Uh-uh, Deacon. The Kid and me were the top gun-hands. You be the ramrod. This one's mine.''

He pulled his own bandana, which he'd been loosening, up over his nose and mouth and headed into the cloud of carrion birds.

13

A few minutes later a shot echoed down-canyon, rolling and slapping off the walls in endless, booming replication. Now Deacon, the McKillian woman, Sutherland and then the rest of the crew were pounding leather up the pass, pulling Winchesters from their scabbards as they went. Even the jerk-line string caught the sense of excitement, and it was all Eduardo could do to keep them from galloping out from under their wobbling cross-buck packs.

But when he rounded a curve some two miles up the draw, Deacon was sorry he had been in such a rush.

A dozen vultures were fighting over the remains of the half-gutted mare, and an equal number battled over the disemboweled painter. They were big, black-feathered birds with long, snaky necks and blood-crusted beaks. They beat at each other with their massive wings, some of the flapping appendages four to five feet in length. Deacon had not seen buzzards so ferociously hungry since the last days of the great northern buffalo herds, when the birds were so famished they would swoop on living men.

A few, Deacon saw, had gotten their share. They had glutted themselves, and now wobbled and crow-hopped across the canyon floor. When these lucky ones tried to take off, they made it only a few feet off the ground before crashing back to earth, too bloated to fly.

Deacon turned to the man propped up against the base of the boulder. He had a charred bullet hole between his eyes, and there was not a vulture mark on him.

Which meant that up until a few minutes ago the man had been alive.

God only knew how he had managed to keep breathing. His clothes had virtually been slashed from his body by panther claws. His chest and stomach had been ripped open by an awful tear, the shoulders raked by a maze of claw marks. He was covered with flies, and his gaping wounds were already crawling with maggots. The maggots had eaten his shoulder wounds to the bone and were competing with a long, meandering troop of red ants over his exposed testes.

But it was the head that got you. The panther, before dying, had taken off the face with one tremendous bite. That was the only way to describe it. The massive jaws had clamped over Kid Colt's face from top of head to tip of chin.

Then had torn it off.

The bite had taken away most of the jaw and all of the nose. Apparently the puma's upper mandible was the weaker. Somehow the eyes and one of the brows had been left intact.

The eyes. Deacon had seen a lot of dead men's eyes in his time. In the wars, in the Indian campaigns, riding for Quantrill and Judge Parker. He'd found the remains of men tortured by the Apaches for days, men whose eyes spoke of unimaginable horrors and unutterable agonies. But he'd found nothing like this. The Kid's death-stare had lost any semblance of humanity. The eyes had in them the deranged look of a hydrophobic dog gone mad with feral suffering.

J.T. Cross pointed to a big mesquite bush growing out of the crack in the canyon wall.

From it were looped, fly-blown and crusted with gore, the intestines of the disemboweled painter.

Now Sutherland and Judith were standing beside Deacon. Sutherland had vomit stains on his shirt front and looked green. But Judith McKillian's eyes glittered madly, and her voice still had that breathless, expectant quality.

"Why . . . ?" she asked, pointing to the coiled intestines.

Deacon nodded to the ground beneath the hanging guts. Under them, Slater had gouged in the earth a large arrow, at least six feet in length. It pointed unmistakably back down the canyon.

But now Sutherland had his voice back.

And he was burning up.

"I'll get Slater for this! I'll get him if it's the last thing I do!"

Deacon had had it. He grabbed Sutherland by the front of the shirt and the back of the neck. He dragged him to the arrow, bent him over till his eyes were directly above it.

"You see that, Sutherland? It's sign language. Injun talk. Get it?"

"Get what?" Sutherland said, confused.

"You say you're gonna get Torn Slater? Well, he says he's gonna get your bowels. Now do you get it? He wants them wrapped around the mesquite and maguey, the yucca and the prickly pear. Here to Geronimo's stronghold. Unless you go back. Unless you follow the arrow and get your fuckin' ass back."

But Sutherland wasn't listening. He was screaming: "We got bolt-action Mausers. Double-action Remingtons. We have two dozen horses and ten pistoleros. I'll crucify his fucking—"

But now Deacon was mad. Now Sutherland had to listen. Deacon grabbed him by the front of his ruffled silk shirt, yanked him up nose to nose, and shouted into Sutherland's face.

"Mausers? Remingtons? Slater's got the panthers, Apaches, and this whole desert. He killed Colt with *a cat,* you asshole. He's got Mother Fuckin' Nature backin' him up."

Then suddenly J.T. Cross was grabbing Sutherland, wrenching

him out of Deacon's hands yelling into the Englishman's face:

"But he's still givin' you a way out. Don't you see? He's willin' to let you go."

14

They chased off the vultures and buried the remains. The smell of blood or the slightest scent of cat panics horses, and even with the panther corpse and the other bloody remains deep underground, the horses balked.

But they did it, one animal at a time. Rearing and kicking, side-lunging and crow-hopping, the horses blew and snorted their way through the pass.

By night they were camped two miles up-canyon from the scene of the slaughter.

Deacon kept a heavy guard. Not only did he fear Slater, but now they were also well into Geronimo's territory. And while Apaches seldom attacked outfits as well armed as theirs, they were hurting badly. They had sick, wormy stock, low water and rations, and the men were whip-dog tired.

The four of them—Deacon, Cross, Sutherland, and McKillian—stared at each other over the campfire. The desert night was cold, and seemed even colder after the scorching heat of the day. The firelight still flickered brilliantly, casting vivid shadows on the canyon walls. Finally Deacon spoke:

"First off, we be down to forty gallons of water. That ain't much, but it can get us back. We'll lose some stock along the way, but hell, it won't be that bad. We'll butcher the carcasses like 'Paches, and we won't have to carry much rations. Even if'n it takes us twenty days to get back, we should have water."

"I say we push on to the Black Beauty."

"Sir, I sorta figured you might say that," Deacon continued, "and I just gotta say it don't make no more sense. The only hope we ever had of catching Slater was by surprise. We ain't got that no more."

"By God, sir, he's still only one man. We have ten good hands. Three dozen horses. Scores of firearms. And you're sayin' turn back?"

"Mr. Sutherland, we can still get back. That's a sure thing. The only thing sure about headin' onto that spring and goin' after Slater is that a lotta us is goin' die. That is sure, dead-solid certain."

"Mr. Cross, is that your opinion, too?"

"Deacon's right on that count, right all the way. On the other hand, we all knew that when we signed on. Maybe a lot of us hoped we'd get lucky. Or maybe we figured we'd never catch up with him at all, never get this close. But that ain't the way it is. Deacon wants to back off now, I say fine, he's got logic on his side. But I also say I ain't never backed down from no man all my life, no matter how big or how small. And I don't like startin' now."

"But Slater could follow us back, couldn't he?" McKillian said. "He could water up at the Black Beauty, then trail us back, pick us off one by one. He could steal our horses, gear, whatever money we're carrying."

"That ain't his style. Slater'll steal from a man, but he does it up front. He don't bushwhack, and he don't lie. No, when he give us that Injun sign, he was offerin' us a way outta here. And he meant it. He give us a choice."

"Mr. Cross, what is your feeling?"

"Sir, if I was you, I'd turn around. Go back to hunting bear, tigers, and whatever else you hunt. Find yourself another Bill Cody. You got *mucho dinero* and everything to live for. Torn Slater ain't worth dyin' for."

"But what about you?"

"I'm thirty-eight years old, thirty-eight hard years. I've lived them years by my gun-hand and my reflexes. I measure it out in split seconds, on the razor's edge. One of these days some gun-punk with a skin full of pilgrim whiskey's gonna end my illustrious career over some cow-camp whore or a handful of nickel-ante cards. I'll be boot-buried in some wind-scoured boneyard, and all for nuthin'. No one'll know whether I lived or died. Or care. You? I'd say Slater give you a chance, and I'd take it. Me? If I'm gonna die by the gun, I'd just as soon it be Torn Slater put me under. Not some two-bit, back-shootin' punk. Especially considerin' the stakes. 'Cause let's face it, Sutherland, the money you been speakin' on, hell, it don't mean squat to you. You already got money. But to men like me and Deacon, that Wild West Show you spoke of, it'd be everything. It'd be *mucho dinero*." He gave Deacon a hard stare. "It'd be a whole future."

"Dyin' ain't much of a livin'," Deacon said. "And it sure ain't no future."

"Then it's settled," Sutherland said lightly.

"What's settled?" Deacon asked. "We still got forty gallons of water. That's enough to get back on. For those of us what might want to get back in one piece."

"We had forty gallons of water, Mr. Deacon."

"What?" Deacon did not like the demented grin on Judith McKillian's face.

"Show him, my dear." Judith McKillian reached into her skirt and removed a long, rubber, douche tube. "Miss McKillian discovered about two days out that by the artful strategem of inserting this tube into the top of those five gallon water cans and by syphoning out precisely one quart of water from the cans on each side of a cross-buck packsaddle, we could easily obtain a half gallon of water per night."

"You was stealin' water from the camp?" Deacon was confused.

"But it was *my* water, good man. Bought and paid for. I owned it. Really, Mr. Deacon, in point of fact I see no reason why I have to justify my actions to you. I—"

"Sir, you owned the cans, but you did not own our lives. That water *was* our lives."

"But did you really expect a woman of Miss McKillian's quality and breeding to travel this godforsaken desert without her nightly ablutions?"

"Her what?"

"Her sponge baths. Really, Mr. Deacon, you can't expect

people of our stature to cross a scorching inferno without *bathing*."

Deacon was speechless, so Cross finally asked the question: "Just how much water did you two take?"

"Not much," Judith responded. "Not much. Over twenty days, I'd guess twelve, perhaps fifteen gallons. Unless, that is, my friend filched my tube and syphoned some for himself behind my back."

Sutherland grinned sheepishly. "Only a few gallons."

"How many?" Cross asked. "Exactly."

"Four or five."

Cross looked at Deacon. The look was not pleasant. "Well, Deacon, that tears it. We done crossed the Powder River. That leaves twenty gallons of water, more or less. Hell, that ain't even enough for the stock, let alone the men."

"Sir," Sutherland was shouting, outraged, "it is not as though I was stealing. It was my water. I did buy it. Anyway, how was I to know those last three holes would turn up dry? And you said the Black Beauty Spring was 'reliable.' "

Cross and Deacon ignored him. "What do you think?" Cross asked Deacon.

"I think we got to push on to the Beauty. Slater ain't gonna like it, but if we take the water and let him know we are leavin', maybe he'll cut us some slack."

"It don't seem likely."

Now Sutherland was shouting. "I don't believe it. You men outnumber Torn Slater ten to one, you're armed to the bloody teeth, and yet you sound afraid. You sound bloody fucking afraid."

Finally Deacon was able to look at Sutherland. His gaze was baleful. Sutherland could not meet his stare, and looked away. Deacon said:

"I'd be careful who I called a coward."

Sutherland still looked away.

"And as to being afraid, Torn Slater might teach us all something on that subject, Mr. Sutherland. He may teach us a powerful lot."

"More'n you wanted to know," Cross agreed.

15

It was near midnight when Judith McKillian came to Deacon's bedroll. She was still in her Levi's and the red ruffled shirt. She sat alongside him and shook him by the shoulder.

"Hey, Deacon, you want to talk?"

"Not hardly."

"Yeah, you wouldn't dream of talking to someone who bathes more than once a week, would you?"

He ignored the gibe. His bedroll was on the southern perimeter of the camp, a significant distance from the rest of the circle of sleeping bodies. The remuda and the guards were on the northern rim of the camp, so he and Judith were pretty much alone.

"Go to hell," he finally said.

"No doubt I will. Still, I want to talk to you. You will talk with me, won't you, Mr. Deacon?"

"What for?"

"I want you to know something. I know you think me terrible, just awful, and maybe I am. But not as bad as you think. Christ, you act as though I'm as bad as him, that man there, Sutherland."

"Yeah, that's what I always liked about you. You're the lesser of two evils."

Judith McKillian grinned, and for once the grin did not have that mad glint. She took off her Stetson and let her long coil of crimson hair tumble down her back. She added a few more candlepower to the grin, and soon it was lighting up the eyes. Deacon had not had a woman since before they left Prescott. Watching Judith McKillian smile, he imagined she could be nice.

"Why do you insist on playing the dumb hick, Mr.

Deacon, the intrinsically ignorant hayseed? You're really not that way at all. I think you're really quite clever.''

"If I was really clever, I sure as shit wouldn't be out here.''

"Oh, you're always pretending to be worried and scared. Even of me. And of the Apaches. And of Torn Slater.''

"I am afraid of Slater.''

"Well, you did ride with him. You two were friends. It was probably nice being friends with Slater.''

"Like shakin' hands with the devil.''

"He was that bad?''

"Damn straight. He was about the snakiest man I ever knew.''

"And you really think things are getting tight?''

"Tight as a vise. Tight as a gnat's snatch. Air-tight.''

Judith McKillian smiled again, and against his will, Deacon felt the warmth.

"You best get back to your bunkmate,'' Deacon said.

"Maybe I like it here.''

"Sutherland's waiting.''

"Sutherland's sleeping.''

"Sutherland's dead, is what he is. He just don't know it yet.''

"You're a stubborn man, Deacon. You don't know half of what's good for you.''

"I know Torn Slater ain't good for me.''

"You really believe Slater is that bad?''

"I don't believe. I know.''

"You talk about him like he was boils, locusts, lightning bolts.''

"He is. He's more trouble'n Jehovah gave the Jews.''

Judith McKillian giggled, and the sound was actually musical. "You're really rather handsome in a craggy sort of way.''

"Whatever you say.''

"Suppose I said very handsome?''

"That's goin' some.''

"You know, Deacon, you must have made some real

money in your day. I don't see why you had to get into this. Did you hit a streak of bad luck?"

"Hell, weren't for bad luck, I wouldn't have no luck at all."

"What happened? You must have made some money over the years. How'd you lose it all?"

"Hard liquor, fast women, slow horses. It weren't difficult."

"You know, Deacon, I could really go for you. I admire all that virtue."

"Ever try it yourself?"

"Oh, the virtuous life is too hard for me. I prefer a life of sin."

"So I see."

"But I could like you, I really could."

"Look, missy, I didn't ride in here on no hay wagon. This ain't my first time at the rodeo."

"I thought we might end up friends after this."

"I don't partner up."

"Mr. Deacon, I somehow get the impression that you don't approve of me."

Deacon shrugged. "People come in all the shades of shit and most smell 'bout the same."

Now her smile had more of an edge, and the wicked glint was returning to his eyes. "And if Torn Slater killed me, say, tomorrow. Out there on the trail. You wouldn't miss me at all. You wouldn't even feel bad?"

"No ma'am, I'd just as soon see you finished off. I don't find much in you that's upliftin'."

Now McKillian was hot. "Look, Deacon, I was shanty Irish. My father followed the rail crews and laid track. He raised his family in a tent city filled with whores and pimps, card sharks, and opium peddlers."

"You don't have to explain."

"I not only don't, I can't. I can't explain wanting so badly to be free, to get out of there, to have something different that I'd sell my soul, let alone my body, not only to Sutherland but to all the others before him—to anything or anyone that'd get me out of that cesspool, that hell. But you wouldn't understand that.''

"You're right. I wouldn't.''

"I'm sorry I don't meet with your high moral standards.''

"You don't.''

"Deacon, why do you despise me?''

"No special reason. You just got this hatred in your heart, and you think that money or a night of sex or killin' Torn Slater will cleanse you of it. And you're so fuckin' wrong, it makes me sick.''

"You think you know a lot about me, don't you?''

"Like squirrels know trees.''

Her lips parted slightly. She licked them once so they were moist. "I could really like you, Deacon.''

"You'd like Slater better. He's a very thorough killer. That job he did on the Kid. That was the thoroughest job of butcherin' I ever seen. He busted that boy's bones for marrow.''

Now she had her hand under his blanket and was easing it down toward his crotch. When he tried to remove it, she grabbed his wrists with her other hand.

"Please . . . ?'' Her voice was soft, almost plaintive.

"Go back to Sutherland.''

"I like virile men.''

"That got something to do with guns?'' Deacon said with a shrug, not understanding the word.

"Sort of.''

He pulled her hand out of his pants just before it grabbed his cock.

"I still say you got a man.''

"Maybe I got a new rooster.''

"Well, I'm too old.''

"You know what they say: 'The old bull is the best bull.' ''

"Naw, you'd eat a country boy like me alive.''

"I'd try.''

Now her hand was back inside Deacon's pants, and he did nothing to stop it. And after she had his pants down, and was kicking off her own boots and skin-tight Levi's, he still did not object. The need was all over him, now—urgent, undeniable. He lay back on the bedroll, stared at the constellations ten billion miles overhead. He watched them wheel slowly around the pole star with infinite lassitude. He waited, and after a minute her clothes were off, and she was under the blanket lying beside him.

Now he had to relieve himself in a woman, any woman. The gorgeous Denver whore with the fiery hair and fantastic body—hell, she would do as well as the next.

She pulled him close to her, and at the first touch of her silken skin and velvet pussy, suddenly, startlingly, he gasped. Her naked body pressed hotly against his own, made Deacon hornier than, it seemed, he'd ever been in his life. Her mouth and tongue made a sensuous odyssey around his teeth and lips. She kissed and kissed and kissed him and then was making mock imitations of intercourse as she jammed her tongue over and over again down his throat as far as she could. At first, Deacon was confused by this tantalizing foreplay, his only real experience these last twenty-five years having been with soiled doves from upstairs saloon cribs.

And those worn-out women seldom had the energy for anything beyond a fuck.

So he was hot, hotter than he had ever been. Something about her seemed nakeder-than-naked, more female-than-female, almost scorchingly sexual. And when she pulled him onto her, grabbed his throbbing member in her fist and adroitly directed it to her wet, warm cunt, he reared back and plunged for all he was worth.

He was fucking her madly now, beating a raucous drum roll of thunderous orgasm. And she was ripe for it, too. Digging her nails into the flesh of his shoulders for leverage, reaching up with her long, lissome legs, wrapping them around his hips, she clenched him to her like a vise—pelvis against pelvis, groin against groin—in a frantic, grinding embrace.

She was going mad with her need. Pumping and straining in ecstasy, spinning out of control. One minute she was crying, the next giggling shrilly. The she was baying like some crazed, wild thing, and Deacon had to stifle her howls with frantic, deeply tongued kisses.

The genuineness of her passion touched Deacon terribly. Not since his wife died twenty-seven years ago had a woman made him feel so much need, so much a man. Not since those dim, forgotten years, long before the gang of marauding Jayhawkers had burned his farm, then killed his wife and children, had a woman made him feel so potent, so manly, so needed.

Then his cork popped, and, simultaneous with her orgasm, he was coming. Over and over, the orgasms were pumping out of them, one after another, wrenching, tearing spasms that clutched at their hearts and shocked them to their souls.

When it was finally over, Judith McKillian lay her head on Deacon's chest, and sobbed. Deacon stroked the long red tresses—almost orange in the early morning starlight—and whispered softly:

"There, there. It's all right. It really is."

But Judith McKillian only sobbed harder and said: "No, it's not all right. It's not now, and it never will be."

Staring down at her, stroking the long, red hair, she reminded him so much of his late wife, right down to the fiery hair and wonderful body, that he, too, wanted to cry. Not since Sara's death had he known the touch of a real woman.

In truth, during the last quarter-century, Deacon had felt nothing at all.

Nothing.

Nothing but cards, guns, and pilgrim whiskey.

And dollar whores.

Not until Judith McKillian.

The sensation was not entirely pleasant. The memory of Sara brought back the sense of loss at his family's massacre and the rage that had burned in him like wildfire, that forced him into the company of Bloody Bill and William Clarke Quantrill.

And Outlaw Torn Slater.

The best friend he'd ever had.

The man he'd sworn to kill.

For money.

Slowly, meticulously, she began kissing his chest, working her way down his stomach. And when Deacon felt his member rise, he was ashamed. Now she was no longer the wife he'd lost twenty-seven years ago, she was Judith McKillian, the high-priced Denver doxy, practicing her trade.

He touched her cheek and whispered: "No."

But when she looked up at him, her look was not that of the hard-nosed hooker with the glittering eyes and twisted sneer. The eyes were strangely sad, the lips parted.

"Why not?" Her voice was thick with emotion.

"You don't have to."

"I want to. Please."

He nodded, and she continued working her way down his stomach, over navel, across abdomen, plying her whore's trade with a professional delicacy which Deacon had never before known. She kissed and tongued every inch of his cock, worked her way down over his balls, which she kissed and tongued and sucked over and over and over again, down across the taint onto the tingling edge of his anus.

When she was done with the whore's tour, she took his immense member in her mouth. All of it. She sucked him off magically, with infinite tenderness, and no more did he see Judith McKillian, wanton whore, but something beautiful and idyllic. Something even beyond Sara.

Something he'd never before experienced.

And never dreamed possible.

When he came, great gouts of his semen poured into her throat, out of her mouth, and dribbled down her cheeks. Still she continued kissing and fondling and rubbing his come-drenched prick with her tongue and lips, then across her cheeks and forehead, finally wiping it clean with the long tresses of her fire-red hair.

And when she was finished, and Deacon was too weak and too shaken to resist or protest, she started in all over again.

PART II

16

They started out at first light. The Beauty was no more than fifteen miles away, and for the last two days they'd ridden into its looming blackness as if they were riding into their open graves.

During these last few hours, they rode in ghostly silence. Now the Beauty was no longer a black volcanic monolith soaring straight up out of the canyon floor. It was a dark portent, an infernal finger of doom. With each interminable mile, with each bend of the twisting canyon, the Beauty grew closer, more imposing, more ominous.

Then the sun was at zenith, and the air was hot, dry, and unmoving in the canyon. No moaning of wind or bird cries or coyote barks echoed through the draw. Only the ubiquitous drone of the locusts, which seemed to thrive in the hideous heat, the constant creaking of saddles, and the jingle of spurs, bits, and bridles.

At the very end they noticed nothing save the great ebony needle. This massive outcropping of volcanic basement rock, thrust up through the Great Sonoran Shelf, was the oldest and most awesome landmark in the desert, and by the last mile it was overshadowing everything else—heat, aridity, even exhaustion. By now the Beauty seemed more than just a rock, it symbolized life itself. Beneath it flowed the only viable spring within a radius of a hundred miles. The spring that had never been known to run dry.

During the last mile, all they could see was the monolith, and as they wearily clinked and creaked along, Sutherland and Judith McKillian rode up alongside Deacon.

"Say, Deacon," Sutherland said, "you never told me what the spring was like."

"If it's there, it's a small pond, big enough to swim in. There's a big cottonwood right alongside of it, and game from all over the desert comes there to drink. Hell, if it's runnin' we'll have mule deer, wild turkey, more jackrabbits and sage hens to eat than you can shake a stick at."

"Ummm, a bath," Judith McKillian said dreamily.

"I said 'if it's runnin'.' It's been so damn dry I ain't countin' on nuthin' no more."

"When will we see this spring?"

"It's on the far side of the needle. 'Round that needle and behind a few big boulders, and there she be."

They reached the massive monolith, and the canyon widened to several hundred feet. The tremendous rock was a hundred feet across, and Deacon slowly led his ragged-ass outfit around it, then to a confused jumble of boulders on the other side. He led them around the boulders and stopped. He took a good, hard look, let out a long breath, and swung off his horse.

Deacon stared grimly at the fallen cottonwood, leafless and barkless, bleached bone-white in the sun. Its exposed roots and its bare limbs and branches were twisted at grotesque angles. Around the gnarled remains were scattered a number of sand-scoured skulls, smooth and white as ivory. Most were mule deer. One or two looked human. A few other bones survived. Big bones. Femurs and pelvises, mostly. Any other skeletal remains had been buried, eroded, or otherwise disposed of by the desert.

There were also the usual gray clumps of prickly pear,

mesquite, and creosote surrounding the dead tree; those, too, dying from the aridity. Other than that, nothing. No mud, cracking and baking in the sun. No animals scratching for water under the hardpan. No sign of moisture anywhere.

"I had no idea," Sutherland said.

"Well, what did you think? Two weeks ago, when you tried to shave, the water dried on your fuckin' face before you could put a razor to it. It's been goddamn dry, I kept tellin' you that. Hell, I bet there ain't been three inches of rainfall in the last three years."

"What do you suggest?" Sutherland asked.

"Find some shade, rest up. Maybe shoot a horse or two. Smoke and jerk what meat we can carry. Those what can, eat it raw for the juice. Then at dark we head on out. We walk and ride by night, waterin' only, say, half the stock. The half we hope to ride most of the way out of here. If a horse breaks a leg, travelin' in the dark, it ain't such a big deal now 'cause they'll all be dead anyway 'fore we walk on out of here."

"We could continue on up the canyon," Sutherland said. "We could find another spring."

"We could. 'Course, it ain't likely. But what you will find definitely is Torn Fuckin' Slater and them heathen 'Paches. That ain't no maybe. They be a dead-solid definite. And what they'll do to you makes gettin' thirsty look like Sunday-Go-To-Meetin'."

"I don't know," Sutherland said. "We have to consider alternatives."

"Yeah, you consider them. Meanwhile, the packer and I'll slaughter a horse. They ain't gonna be survivin' no-how, and we'll need what nourishment we can find. And while you're doin' this considerin', find a shady spot to do it in. You best conserve your sweat. There ain't a whole lot left where that came from."

"Nothing else?"

"Oh, I could set some of the men to diggin' where this spring used to be. They could hit a little water. I doubt it. If'n these here dried-up prickly pear ain't found no water, don't expect we will."

"I can't believe this is happening," Judith McKillian said.

"The main thing is tighten up and don't panic. I seen men in tougher spots before. Hell, this trek'd be nuthin' to Slater or a 'Pache."

"I still don't believe it," Sutherland said gloomily. "I still don't believe it."

17

Someone else did not believe it.

His name was Torn Slater. At present, he was kneeling on a high sandstone cliff a short distance up the canyon. He was studying Deacon's outfit through his scope. The straight-line distance between Slater and the camp was about twelve hundred yards, but through the fourteen-power scope the refracted distance seemed under ninety. He could make out all the individuals and most of the details of the camp with astonishing clarity.

And he had never seen such a miserable collection of scalp-hunters. With weary disdain, he gazed down on the three cheap gunsels rolling quirlies. They looked like they'd been recruited from some cow-camp jail or scraped off a whorehouse wall. Then there was the dude in the dandified clothes and bowler. He was smoking cigarettes from a long-stemmed holder. Slater dismissed him as some sort of demented freak. Then there was a tracker, whom he knew definitely to be a freak, whom he'd personally half-killed for raping a young boy back in the days when he was riding with Quantrill.

He wished now he'd finished the job.

Then there was one man he recalled from the Texas Panhandle country who'd been a real veteran gun-hand, J.T. Cross.

Him, he'd watch out for.

The scope stopped dead, and his breath whooshed out of

him in a sudden rush. There was one hell of a red-haired hooker in the tightest Levi's and the sheerest red ruffled shirt he'd ever seen, though what on God's good earth they'd brought her for was beyond him. He gave her a closer look, caught the nipples taut against the red silk blouse and thought, Jesus, that child-raping tracker would probably kill for a crack at her, let alone those two-bit gunsels. Bringing pussy like that on a trek like this was plain fuckin' suicide.

He looked at the long, jerk-line string of horses. He caught a glimpse of the Mex packer who was obviously in charge of tending the stock. He knew the man, and knew him to be goddamn competent. From Slater's point of view, Eduardo was the most valuable man there.

Slowly, he focused on the ramrod, the man everyone else was turned to. Jesus Christ, his old buddy, John Henry Deacon. What was a trail-wise hard-case like Deacon doing leading a gaggle of geese halfway across the Sonoran Desert for? Not to catch Torn Slater. Deacon wasn't that foolish. Anyway, Deacon knew Slater, knew him well. Hell, they'd been friends, close friends, time-when. But there it was, just as plain as the balls on a tall dog. Deacon was leading that pack of lame-brained bounty-hunters right up Slater's ass.

And there was only one explanation for that kind of desperation.

Money.

Meaning, the dude was paying.

He refocused the scope on the dandy in the bowler hat who was sucking on the cigarette holder, and winced.

He figured the dude there was the money-man, paying for Slater's hide.

Then he got sore.

That they were trailing him was an inconvenience.

That they were paid by a man like the dude was an embarrassment.

And that they were led by a man like Deacon—that was an insult.

Slater put down the scope and surveyed the red cliffs around him. He did not like them. Every year at this time, all the diamondbacks in the vicinity migrated to these cliffs surrounding the Beauty. Slater was not sure why. As far as he was concerned, it was just an odd habit diamondbacks had, the desire to periodically hold a convention.

But whatever the reason, the cliffs, the crevices in the cliffs, the rocks and boulders surrounding these cliffs were now filled with hissing, buzzing rattlers.

Most rattlers didn't bother Slater that much. Copperheads and prairie rattlers were dry most of the time. As for timber rattlers, hell, they were so friendly you could tame them and keep them for pets. Rattlers, if you let them alone, would usually leave you alone.

But not diamondbacks.

Put one in a cage, and it would refuse food till it died. Take out the poison glands, and you quickly saw they packed five times as much venom as any other rattler. While most snakes holed up at night and went to sleep, not so with the diamondbacks. They had an extra heat-seeking organ that let them hunt you by the warmth you gave off.

They were very aggressive, very effective killers.

It was fair to say that Torn Slater hated diamondbacks.

Slater was not proud of his animosity. Long ago, the much-lamented Cochise had explained to Slater that hate was fear turned outward. Cochise had said that a truly brave warrior never hated an enemy, but respected him for his strength.

Nor did the true warrior hate or fear any aspect of Nature. All aspects of Nature were as arrows in the true warrior's quiver, Cochise taught, and could be used against the enemy. The desert's heat, its canyons and arroyos, even the buzzing diamondbacks were friends to the Apache. They were part of the Apaches' armament.

Only the intruders needed to fear the desert.

Slater raised the scope. To his dismay, he saw the two trackers digging up the old spring, hoping to hit water. Deacon was directing the dig. The hole looked dry, but Slater, like Deacon, thought there was a chance. After this outfit turned and headed back, Slater had planned on going down to the Beauty and digging up the water hole himself.

This changed everything. Now if they hit water, they

would continue after him. And with them having ample water—and Slater almost dry—they would have an edge.

Even worse, Slater felt outrage. That was his spring. This was his land. Land where he had been raised. And he had allowed them to drive him off it.

Even as these thoughts came to him, Slater realized that Geronimo's scouts would be out there watching his actions and sending heliographic messages back to the stronghold with signal mirrors. Geronimo would already know of the lone stranger who ventured into his land, who was followed by the band of scalp-hunters, who had been driven off the Black Beauty Spring.

And when the Apaches learned that the lone stranger was their chief's blood-brother, great shame would come to Geronimo's lodge.

Anger swept through Slater, and for this he felt great guilt. Anger, as Cochise taught, was the sign of a frightened warrior. A true warrior was calm in battle and coldly calculating; Torn Slater felt neither.

Slater took deep breaths and fought to control his mounting rage. He must make his decision in cold blood, not in blind hate.

What should he do?

What would Cochise do?

Would he run?

Or fight?

Absently, without thinking, he gripped the breech of his single-shot, .50-caliber Sharps and felt its tremendous heft. It gave him a sense of comfort, of reassurance.

18

Deacon was unable to shake himself loose from Sutherland. Wherever he walked, the dapper Englishman followed him, repeating the same lecture.

"Look, Slater is a man just like the rest of us. He puts his pants on one leg at a time, just like you and me. There are ten of us, one of him. We have bolt-action Mausers, double-action Remingtons. If those foolish savages want to get into this, I say let's deal them a hand, too. What do you say? Mr. Deacon, you aren't responding to my proposition. Are you listening to me?''

No, Deacon was not listening to him. In fact, he swore that if Sutherland made one more condescending speech, he'd kick his ass all over the canyon floor.

Finally, he walked over to the remuda. He had to talk to Eduardo about slaughtering a horse. Eduardo could decide which one.

But Deacon never made it.

Halfway to the remuda, he caught a glint of light, perhaps reflecting off metal, up on a high cliff some five or six miles up the maze of canyons. As he watched the flash of light, he estimated the straight-line distance. A good twelve hundred yards.

Then a tiny cirrus cloud of white smoke burst atop the cliff.

Deacon knew exactly what that was, and, reflexively, he dove.

The flight time of the Sharps ''Big Fifty'' slug, traveling approximately twelve hundred yards, was three seconds, so as Deacon hit the canyon floor, glancing up over his shoulder, he saw it all. The slug slammed into the mule-packer's face—seven hundred grains of soft, decelerating lead, moving by now at about nine hundred feet per second.

A man's head is a hard, heavy object, and a projectile as soft as a bullet will, at that speed, flatten it like a pancake on impact.

Which the slug did.

Deacon saw the round rip into the man's forehead, tear away the top of the skullcase, and exit above the occipital protuberance.

Deacon saw the brains go, huge coils of snaky gray matter. Dripping blood and riven with pieces of the cranium, they spilled and splattered all over the canyon floor.

The sound of the rifle shot was substantially slower than the average velocity of the decelerating bullet. So the blast did not reach them until almost a full second after the projectile actually hit.

In fact, Eduardo's brains were strewn across the canyon floor by the time they heard the shot.

And the noise, when it came, was spectacular. It reached them as a tremendous *boom!* which lasted for seconds before it was reverberated into many smaller *boom-boom-booms!* which slapped, echoed, and replicated up and down the canyon, first crashing endlessly like rolling thunder, then popping spasmodically like packets of exploding firecrackers, finally crackling, rattling, and fading away.

Slowly, Deacon pulled himself to his feet. He stepped over Eduardo's remains. He looked up at the gape-jawed Sutherland, who was staring dumbstruck at the dead mule-packer. He grabbed him by the back of the neck and pointed his face toward the cliff top from which Slater had made the shot.

The white cirrus cloud still floated eerily atop the rim.

"That's where it came from, Sutherland. How far would you guess? Nearly a mile? Well, that's what you're up against. A man who runs the mountain lions. A man who shoots you from one fuckin' mile away. Understand now? That's who you're tryin' to kill."

19

It was evening.

They were gathered around the fire. Sutherland, Deacon, Cross, and McKillian. Sutherland looked composed, confident. Under the bowler, his cigarette holder was cocked at a jaunty angle.

Deacon could see, to his chagrin, that his boss was high on drugs. Perhaps opium. Perhaps cocaine.

Before Deacon could even express his considered opinion on their situation, Sutherland was running off at the jaw:

"The way I see it, Mr. Deacon, we have only two choices. We can go after Slater. We have professional gunmen here, the latest in modern firearms, two expert trackers. Two days, tops, we should nail him."

"What you plan on doin' for water?"

"One of us stays behinds and digs. Also, Slater may have some. Maybe he's loaded his packhorse down with two hundred pounds of water bags. Or it could be there's a party of travelers up-canyon just waiting to be divested of any available *agua pura* they might be packing. There might even be another spring up-canyon. These underground steams pop up in the most surprising places, sometimes overnight. You've told me so yourself."

"What's the other alternative?"

"Give up. Turn in our traces and go limping back to Tucson. Maybe we make it. Maybe not. You will. You're rawhide-tough and border-wise. The trackers, too. Cross and those other bottle-worn gunfighters? They've spent too many years falling off of bar stools, passing out in brothels. Myself and the esteemed Miss McKillian? You have to be kidding. We'd never make it out of the desert."

"Sir, I think you would. Both of you."

But Sutherland was charging ahead. "Mr. Deacon, from my point of view, life is simply a big rock. You either climb on top. Or get under it."

"We are under it," Deacon said.

"Sir," said Sutherland, his voice raising in anger, "I do not like your attitude. It's weak and defeatist. Mr. Deacon, this life out here will eat you alive if you let it. And I can see you're prepared to do just that!"

"Okay, okay," J. T. Cross said, struggling to calm the ill temper. "Deacon's opinion is well taken, Mr. Sutherland. Let him make his point."

Sutherland looked away, still obviously hot. Quietly, Deacon continued:

"First off, Mr. Sutherland, when Slater smoked Eduardo, he killed the best man we got. That Mex packer, hell, without him we're up the creek without a paddle. Him gone, that stock ain't got a chance in hell."

"What's so hard about loading packs?"

"You load 'em onto a movin' surface. A tender surface. The weights and shapes of the loads got to balance. You pack them horses wrong, the wood sawbucks'll cut them animals clean to the bone. The cinches, breast straps, and breeching'll do the same, slash 'em bloody.

"Also, as the stock works, it sweats, gets thinner. You got to keep balancin' them packs, tightenin' them straps. You got to know exactly where and when to do it. You don't hit it right, the packs'll slip, chafe, gall. The stock'll founder."

The silence was unnervingly quiet. For once even the droning locusts and barking coyotes had stopped their cacophony.

"Mr. Deacon, I believe we'll find water," Sutherland finally said.

"Sure, you believe it. You think you continue up them gorges and arroyos you may just find a nice bubbling spring or a big seep of water tricklin' out of the canyon wall. What you'll find, though, is nuthin'. This be a slick-rock desert, red-hot canyonlands. It be full of all kinds of evil surprises."

"Deacon," Cross said.

But Deacon was adamant. "No offense meant, but how you think you're gonna catch and kill Slater while you're up there? Set out a block of salt and shoot him when he comes to lick? Like he was a fuckin' deer? Maybe with that fancy six-foot longbow with the telescopic sight? You just ain't gonna get it done."

"Mr. Deacon," Sutherland said, "I am a hunter by trade. I've shot game for their hides, for food, and for their heads. I'm shooting Slater for his head. You know that hogshead of water? Mr. Deacon, when I shoot Torn Slater—the most wanted desperado in thirteen states and territories—I'm taking more than that twenty-thousand-dollar reward. I'm taking his head. I'm bleeding it like a stuck pig, putting it in the barrel, and then mixing a large flask of concentrated formaldehyde with the water."

"What?"

"Sir, I shall put Torn Slater's head in my Wild West Show. I shall take it across the country in a clear glass crock. I shall build that show around Slater's head, and around the live, on-stage reenactment of how I impaled Slater with my bow. I shall perform for millions. I shall make tens of millions. I shall be rich. All of you—who will, of course, be actors in my Wild West Extravaganza—shall be rich. We'll be bigger than Halley's Comet!" he yelled, his eyes blazing with excitement.

"Ain't that a little extreme?" Deacon asked.

"Extreme? Mr. Deacon, that is where you and I differ. To be artistic, you must be extreme, and it is now clear that you have no aesthetic faculty, no sense of self-expression whatsoever."

"I understand murder."

"Precisely my point. You don't understand murder. Murder, sir, is an emotive art. It must be performed with style, clarity, finesse. I must say, if the truth be known, I find your attitude to be strangely crude. How would you kill Slater? Hammer him between the eyes and butcher him like a steer? No sir, my mode of expression—replete with stage plays, novels, and glass-plate camera work—will electrify audiences for a hundred years to come. This bold undertaking in this infernal desert is the stuff of myths and legends, not the tawdry working-out of crude jungle justice."

"And the Apaches?" Deacon asked.

"You mean those Stone Age hunter-gatherers?" The contempt in Sutherland's voice was total. "Those in-bred, unbathed hordes of retarded racial defectives? That's what we're paying men like Cross for. While I'm skewering Slater with my three-bladed broad-heads, Cross will pot those childish savages for you."

"The Apaches are hardly childish."

"Oh, certainly, certainly, they have their uses," Sutherland groaned dismissively. "Without these worthless redskins, there would be idleness throughout the land. As it is, however, they provide employment for syphilitic soldiers, corrupt Indian agents, and those whiskey-peddling gun-runners plaguing our war-torn border country, to say nothing of the war profiteers in Washington who apparently run this bloody country."

Deacon's face was grim. As if in an attempt to cheer him up, Sutherland said merrily, slapping Deacon on the back:

"Buck up. I see us as latter-day Prometheuses, stealing fire from the Greek gods. And giving man this divine gift."

"And you see Slater's head, displayed in a crock, as this holy fire?"

"Correct."

"And what happened to this Prometheus fellow, having robbed them gods?"

"Ah, he overreached himself. The gods, well, they impaled him on a cliff. And for all eternity vultures feed on his liver."

"Well, I seen that. I seen vultures eat men's innards. And I seen Slater nail men to trees and cliffs. I've seen him nail them by the balls."

"Well, Slater isn't any god, and by George, I'm not going to let him go free—just when we have him in our grip, just when his head is almost in that barrel of formaldehyde."

"Well, it ain't been done before, sir, Prometheus or no. And I just don't see us gettin' it done, neither. I don't see how."

20

Deacon rose at first light. He gathered up his things, loading them on his saddle, and cut a packhorse out of the remuda. He was starting back. Alone.

When he heard the disruption.

A half-mile or so up the draw, a horse was whinnying—no, screaming would be more accurate. So Deacon sent the Pima tracker up the canyon and told him to bring the animal back.

But after ten minutes Deacon heard the pistol shot and understood. The horse was not returning. When the tracker came back, he told Deacon his story.

Deacon went to the cook fire where J.T. Cross was frying a pound of bacon. Sutherland and Judith McKillian watched hungrily. He told them the story.

"Mr. Sutherland, what Mangas found up the canyon was a snorting, bucking dun. Some 'Pache raided our remuda last night, stole the dun, and led him off up-canyon. There, he carved a big piece of meat off the horses's rump. The dun was out of his mind with pain, so Mangas shot him."

"What?" Sutherland was shocked.

"That's about it, sir. A sure sign we're in 'Pache country. Slater nor any other white man I know wouldn't do nuthin' like that. Only a 'Pache. When they be hungry and have a cravin' for horse or mule meat, they don't take the time or effort to kill the beast. They just cut their steaks off the rump and turn the critter loose."

"God!" Sutherland gasped.

"I never intended to come so far into 'Pache country. Hell, we're right on Geronimo's back porch now. And they're onto us."

"Even so, they are still nothing but primitive Stone-Age savages, and we do have Mr. Cross and—"

"Yeah, I know all 'bout them modern weapons. But I'm sorry. This is as far as I go. My horse there is saddled. And I've loaded me a pack horse with exactly two gallons of water. Which is only my ration. Nothing more, nothing less. I'm clearing out. Anybody what wants to come along with me can. But I'm through."

Overhead, a spiraling cloud of vultures was already gathering up the canyon over the dead dun. Shadows of the circling carrion birds wheeled over them with excruciating lassitude. Nearly a dozen birds circled. Deacon glanced up and said quietly:

"This is mighty sudden country."

"Sudden for the weak," Sutherland responded.

"No sir, sudden for the strong as well. This here is Golgotha, the place of skulls. You are not coming out of this alive. You're lookin' into your open grave."

"I think not, old-timer." J.T. Cross pegged him with a hard stare.

"Not what?"

"I don't think you're leavin'."

"Look, Cross, these here 'Paches, that tears it. You wanna

stick around, be my guest. Them heathen savages won't kill you quick, you know. You'll get acquainted with hot coals and hot knives first. They'll skin you out like a side of beef and roast you over a long, slow fire. And that other piece of business. You think you're bottlin' Slater's head like some scientific specimen, you try it. But that ain't no man prowlin' 'round out there. That be a buzz saw. You tangle with him, he'll kick your sorry ass all over this canyon floor.''

"We have Slater now. I can feel it," Sutherland shouted, his eyes glittering with drug-induced elation. "We have him like a bull caught in a castrating chute. His head is in the yoke, the gelding knife at his flanks, and you, sir, wish to walk away?''

"And them 'Paches?" Deacon was almost speechless with disbelief.

"The Apache Indians? You wish to know what I think of them? You know there's a man in England who says we are descended from apes. I believe those Apache aborigines categorically refute Darwin's theories. The Apaches have not *evolved*. They've *devolved*. They've turned in their biological traces and retreated back down the evolutionary scale. They're not men. They're West African mandrills.''

"Yeah, and them West African mandrills are 'bout to feed you your balls for breakfast.''

"Deacon," Cross said softly, "I'm backin' Sutherland on this one. He's got a real good point about not comin' back broke and empty-handed. I'm gonna gamble on goin' after him.''

"Then you're a dead man, J.T., deader'n Lincoln's nuts. You just don't know enough to lie down yet.''

Silently, Cross slipped the thong off his hammer, loosened the gun in his holster, and began flexing the fingers of his right hand. But Deacon was undismayed. He said:

"Maybe Slater'll put you down, or maybe them 'Paches'll hang you by the hocks to cure. Either way, you're dead.''

Sutherland interrupted. "Please, Mr. Deacon, I want you around. Stay.''

"It's time to move on. This place has about it the smell of

death. You men want to go on up, fine. But you'll end up like our packer, like Kid Colt, like that fuckin' horse.''

"You're stayin','' J.T. Cross said.

"I didn't buy into this hand here. Just deal me out.''

"No way, old-timer.'' Cross was insistent. "We just may need you before this is out. You're the only one what knows this here desert, so we're goin' to war. All of us.''

Deacon ignored Cross. He looked over at Sutherland. "Mr. Sutherland, I thanked you once when you give me that money. I don't feel like thankin' you twice, so I'll just be movin' on.''

"Deacon,'' Cross said firmly.

Deacon's horse was rein-standing a dozen feet away. The packhorse was tied to a mesquite bush directly behind his roan. Deacon walked over to the packhorse, untied the mecate from the bush, and dallied it once around his horn. He carefully put his foot in the left stirrup and prepared to swing on. He heard behind him the unmistakable *click-click* of a Colt. He did not turn around, but he heard J.T. Cross say carefully:

"Old man, I'm a gunman. I make my way killin' men. I don't kill if'n I ain't got to. But if I do, I don't make excuses. You swing onto that bay, and I'll shoot you out of the saddle.''

"Whatever you say,'' Deacon said, tightening his grip on the horn, and started his swing.

The report of the big Colt was deafening in the narrow confines of the canyon. It echoed and reverberated up and down the draw.

Deacon also heard the whine of the bullet as it punched a hole through his hat brim.

"Old man, I'll shoot you down like a fuckin' dog. I swear 'fore God. I swear on my eyes. On my balls.''

"Shit,'' Deacon said tiredly.

He drew his foot out of the stirrup.

21

It was late morning before Cross and Sutherland fashioned a plan. When they came over to Deacon, who was sitting on a boulder by the side of the canyon, and explained it to him, he listened with disinterest.

"Mr. Deacon, we need you to get back, but we will not take you on up the pass against your will. By the same token, we cannot trust you with horses, equipment, and excess water. You would simply desert. So we are leaving you with half a canteen and this small shovel. Perhaps the dearth of water will encourage you to dig up what once was the spring. As you said, there may be water ten or fifteen feet down."

Cross tossed him the canteen, then threw the small collapsible spade over toward the dried-up spring. The three walked over to their horses and swung on.

The outfit was moving out. Riders in front, jerk-line string to the rear. J.T. Cross stayed behind long enough to yell to Deacon:

"Holler when you hit hell!"

Then he kicked his mount into the dust of the two dozen horses and men.

22

The tracking was easier now. One of Slater's animals had slashed himself on a big prickly pear and was leaving a blood-spoor. Small, crimson starbursts dotted the rocks and sand every hundred feet or so. Tracking Slater was now child's play.

Still they moved slowly, carefully. Mangas, the Pima tracker, had not picked up the tracks of the Apaches who had butchered the live horse that morning, and he feared an ambush.

And deep inside they all feared Slater. As much as they wanted money and water, as much as they wanted Slater dead, they all knew the fear. This was Slater's country, not theirs. And Torn Slater, armed with a Sharps "Big Fifty," had the capacity to pick them off from as far as a mile away. He had the capacity, and he had the will.

They camped in the shadow of a big cliff, the one which the Pima claimed Slater had climbed when he picked off the Mex packer. There, Sutherland announced that he had a plan.

"Whereas I would like to transfix Slater with one of those admirable Norwegian pine arrows, I do also recognize that time is of the essence. So I am willing to try a different approach. If Mangas will scale that cliff, then help me up, I could be on the rim by first light. When I spotted Torn Slater, I would shoot out his eyes with my bolt-action Mauser."

"Whatever you say," J.T. Cross said wearily, as he watched the canyon darken with sunset.

"Buck up, old boy. It could be worse," Sutherland chirped. "At least, we don't have old Deacon whining and pussyfooting around, warning us off of his old nemesis, Torn Slater."

"That be true," Cross acknowledged.

But suddenly, deep inside, he wished that Deacon were there.

23

Mangas found the climb surprisingly simple. By midnight he had finished all but the last thirty feet. Those thirty feet were straight up, and he had to hammer several peg-shaped wood chocks into the cliff face if Sutherland was to make the ascent. Especially at the very top. There, the face of the cliff jutted out at a low angle, creating a slight lip. He would have to drive in extra chocks for his boss, drop a rope, then stay by the lip to help pull him up over it. But it could be done.

He adjusted the rifle strapped diagonally across his back. It was slung cavalry-style, with the muzzle pointed down so that the heavy wood stock would not bang his kidneys.

Instead, the butt hammered at his head, and the awkward bolt, shoved into his breechclout, dug into his groin.

Criss-crossing the slung rifle was a coil of light rope from which hung an old grain sack filled with wooden chocks. Inside the bag was a small hammer.

Mangas took out two chocks, put them into his mouth, and began working his way up the face.

24

It took Mangas a full hour to scale the last thirty feet. Every two feet he had to stop, brace himself on crumbling handholds, and hammer in another chock. Mangas felt it was important that Sutherland have sufficient handholds and chocks. The man claimed to be a mountain climber, but he somehow couldn't picture it. And he did not want to pull him up by hand.

Negotiating the lip was the hardest part. At the lip's edge, there was finally only one way to do it: grab the lip, take your feet out of the footholds, and swing off.

Which Mangas did.

For a brief moment, hanging from the rim of the cliff, Mangas dangled there. He dared not look down. Mangas feared heights, and he was now clinging from the edge of the precipice.

The canyon floor was five hundred and fifty feet straight down.

Eyes squinted shut with the straining effort, Mangas painstakingly pulled himself up. Chest on the rim. A knee up. Then his stomach. Now he was crawling on hands and knees along the top of the cliff, grunting, eyes squinted tight against the fear and the pain.

Carefully, he slipped the Mauser off his back, dropped the bag of chocks, and pulled the coiled lass rope over his shoulder. He was leaning against a saddle of rock and decided he could belay the line there as well as anyplace. He looped one end over the sandstone outcropping and tossed the rest of the line over the edge of the cliff.

The Pima, who was petrified of heights, sat there and trembled. The steep ascent had unnerved him. Pulling himself up on his haunches, he shut his eyes, shook his head violently in an attempt to clear it, and crawled even further from the brink of the cliff.

Only when he was a good twenty feet from the edge of the abyss did he open his eyes. Cross-armed, he sat there and clutched his sides. He groaned softly with terror and relief.

It was then he heard the shrill, unmistakable buzzing of the first diamondback, *Crotalus atrox*, the most dreaded snake in the North American desert country.

The rattler was crawling out from behind a jumbled heap of large rocks less than a half-dozen feet to the left. The snake, thick as Mangas's forearm, moved with a flowing, languid grace, every square inch of the reptile's body writhing, squirming, and undulating. The high-pitched rattles vibrated with an almost locustlike *whirrr!* and the snake's head levitated above the irregular coils, the wild, yellow eyes stunningly bright, the dripping, five-inch fangs unfolding from the mouth's roof, the thin, forked tongue darting in and out.

The Pima was terrified, but also awed. For while it was true the Indian feared, even hated the snake for its deadly fangs, he also revered the reptile. By the Pima's lights, all rattlesnakes were emissaries from the Dead Land, spirit-things possessing potent medicine. Among the Pima's people, the killing of a rattler was one of their most heinous taboos.

For the crime of rattlesnake murder, a man could face terrible punishment, even the awful sentence of exile and abandonment.

Not that the Pima loved the snake. The Indian's reverence was born of a healthy respect for the reptile's killing ability. Anything that could murder so efficiently had to be blessed by the gods. All Pimas were willing to suffer death itself rather than risk the enmity of the serpent world and face the wrath of the dreaded Dead Land.

So the Pima spoke soothingly to the approaching diamondback, hoping to appease the snake, perhaps charm him out of his destruction. He whispered unctuously to the reptile:

"Ah. Coo. Ah-Coo. AhCoo. AhCoo." Still the snake approached. The wedge-shaped head with the humps of bone above each eye floated languorously above the writhing coils, the segmented tail flopping noisily along the cliff top. "Go away, little snake. Go back to your hole. Take your evil medicine with you," the Pima crooned.

Then it seemed as though the hissing and the racheting buzz was not the approaching diamondback's, but was a chorus of vibrating *whirrrs!* coming at him from all over the cliff. *Zig. Zig. Zig-zig. Zig-zig. Zizzz. Zizzz. Zzzzzz. Zzzzzz. Zzzzzzzzzz.*

The Pima turned his head and could see at least two dozen rattlesnakes crawling toward him, the air around him vibrating raucously with their trilling buzz.

Mangas knew in an instant that someone—namely, Torn Slater—had salted the cliff top with a bag of diamondbacks. The cliff was too inaccessible, too waterless and devoid of prey to have this many snakes on it. Yet, here it was swarming and rippling with rattlers. Slater had guessed that they would send somebody up top. The cliff was obviously climbable, and he knew that they would try to copy his own plan.

So Slater had sown the cliff with serpents.

The Pima fought panic. He was consumed now by a fear as ancient and evil as Man's first fall. But he also knew that it was important in such a moment to be brave. When emissaries from the Spirit World took your life, it was crucial that you did not show the feather, that you treated them with respect.

After all, you would meet them again in the After Life. It was all right if they took your life. But you must fight for your medicine. You must not let them steal your soul.

He felt a red-hot knife-blade of a bite slash his left arm, but he forced himself not to groan or grimace. The snake had bitten him, fine. Let them all bite him. There was no escape. He was encircled. So be it. Clear your mind and die like a man.

He squatted on his haunches and held out his arms to the rattler. Rocking on his heels, he began his monotonous intonations, *"Ei. Ya. Ei. Ya. Ei-ya. Ei-ya. Ei-ya."*

Now the buzzing was almost deafening, and the red-hot fangs were searing his arms, back, and legs. Soon, he knew, he would lose consciousness.

It was important he begin his death song now, the death song he had composed in his youth, which was his and his alone. He cried out to the night:

"Grant me time, rage, and strength.
Grant me fire, war, and blood.
Please to pardon this brave warrior's soul.
Please to pardon this fierce fighter's flesh.
Never shall I shrink from bloody death.
Never shall I cringe and groan from pain.
Now I live and die a man.
Now I live and die a man."

25

Sutherland was stuck on the ledge, thirty feet below the cliff's lip.

And he was pissed. For a full hour he'd been screaming Mangas's name over and over again. All to no avail.

Damn it, he'd been opposed from the beginning to taking on that Indian tracker. He'd explained to Deacon the absurdity of hiring a foul-smelling, submongoloid savage as a guide. Now it was obvious to Sutherland that he'd been right all along.

Just when he needed Mangas, the Indian had folded, caved in.

Then Sutherland saw the rope. It was dangling over the edge of the lip only four feet from his hand. In the black of night, he had missed it. Now, as the moon was coming up over the horizon, it was faintly visible.

Sutherland took off his belt and began swinging it in an arc toward the hanging line. On the fourth swing, he trapped the lass rope with the buckle and knocked it toward the ledge. He caught it with his empty hand.

He tested the rope. It was secure, so he knotted it under his arms. He called for Mangas again—again, no answer. Cursing silently, his hoarse throat sore from calling Mangas's name, he started up the trail of wood chocks which the Indian had left for him.

Negotiating the lip was hard. If he hadn't had the rope, he couldn't have done it. Not that he gave a damn for the Pima. If the redskin had been worth his salt, he'd have been on that lip waiting to pull him up. The brainless aborigine! He'd take it out of his hide for this one. Dock that fool, Deacon, too, for hiring the Pima against his advice.

He made it over the lip with a hard, grunting pull up, got his chest and stomach onto the rim, got one knee up, and—

Sutherland froze. The full moon was presently shining brightly up above the cliff, and in combination with the brilliant desert starlight, his vision up there was now good.

What he saw made his stomach turn.

The Pima was now blue-black, swollen beyond comprehension from the massive injections of diamondback venom. His body was literally alive, a writhing mass of buzzing, hissing rattlesnakes. The Indian's lips were pulled back taut against his teeth. His tormented eyes stared sightlessly at the night sky. He was grinning in rictus.

Then Sutherland heard it: the shrill *whirrr!* of a buzzing diamondback, and he saw the spade-shaped head circling above the undulating coils, the fangs flashing, the segmented tail vibrating angrily.

Slightly to his right and less than two feet from his face, the fork tongue darted in and out at him.

Sutherland screamed, a demented, echoing wail of a scream, and instantly lost his grip on the rim of the cliff.

He was falling, tumbling end over end. The nightmare vision of the coiled rattler, Mangas's corpse, the overhead stars, and the distant campfire five hundred fifty feet below were now spinning madly, till they merged with Sutherland's blood-curdling howls into one hideous tableau.

Then the lass rope paid out, snapped tight, and mercifully knocked Sutherland out cold.

Hanging over the edge of the cliff, he twisted slowly, slowly, in an infinite circle five hundred and twenty feet from earth. A plague of diamondbacks hissed and buzzed in the viper's nest thirty feet above, and the desert stars, a billion light-years away, stared down on him with perpetual patience and icy indifference.

Inexorably, as the rope spun, the edge of the cliff sawed away at the strands of hemp.

PART IIII

26

Cross and the gunsels spent the morning getting Sutherland down off the cliff. By the time they reached the canyon floor he was half blind with fright, and his armpits were livid from rope sling.

But he was still alive.

And to Cross's dismay, Sutherland was furious.

They rested that night, and at dusk, Sutherland's sides had stopped aching sufficiently for speech. After that he muttered repeatedly, endlessly: "I'll have that bastard's balls. I'll have them for breakfast. Seeing him die, I think I'd actually come."

27

At first light they moved out.

They'd lost a day, and Sutherland was determined to make

it up. He was not going to let Torn Slater slip through his fingers. As long as there was air left in his body, as long as he could pull a bowstring or squeeze a trigger, he was not letting Torn Slater ride away. Too many men had died. Sutherland himself had been humiliated.

Toward noon they had their first stroke of luck. For the preceding hour they had watched a horde of vultures circling up-canyon, and when they reached the kill, they discovered it was Slater's pack mule. Not only was the animal dead from the cactus tear in its side, the dryness in the mouth meant dehydration.

"He's hurting," Sutherland said. "I can feel it in my bones. He's running out of water."

"That mule sure did," Cross agreed. "'Course, that can make him more dangerous. Like a rattler with a broken back. Now he gets mean. Crazy mean."

"I don't get you."

"If he's low on water, as you think, where do you guess is his nearest supply? On our packhorses. Now there's no turnin' back, even if we want. He can hunt us from behind. And with that 'Big Fifty' Sharps, he can get the job done."

"What do you suggest?"

"We got no choice. We're goin' to war. Can't sit 'round and let him pick us off one by one. We got to take the battle to him. We send our gun-hands and that tracker on up ahead. See if they can get around him. If'n they can, they can flush him back down-trail. We can get us a good spot, plenty of cover, and maybe you can nail him with that osage longbow you're so proud of. I'll back you with a Mauser in case you miss, and a sawed-off eight-gauge goose gun for up close. Anyway, we got the fire power and the mobility. We got to use it. There just ain't time to sit on it."

"Then send those boys out," Judith McKillian said, "and let's get this over."

"It'll be over," Sutherland said, "when we nail his hide."

"When we nail it to the fuckin' barn," Cross said.

"That's right," Sutherland agreed, his eyes smoldering

with rage. "Damn him anyway. Damn him for what he did to Kid Colt, the Mex packer, to me."

"Damn him to the blackest pit of hell," said McKillian.

28

With the trackers and gun-hands gone up ahead, the three of them were left behind to pull jerk-line.

And as Deacon predicted, the jerk-line didn't make it.

The packhorses were foundering badly, and when Cross unhitched the packs he could see why. The wooden cross-bucks and leather breech straps had torn up the animals like cross-cut saws. The backs and withers were open clear to the ribs and spine. Each animal was covered with dozens of red slashes, so deep that chalk-white bone was protruding.

"What happened?" Sutherland asked, stunned.

"Guess it were what Deacon claimed," Cross said with a shrug. "As they dehydrated, they shrunk. Them leather straps and wood sawbucks started to scrape. Tore through them like knives."

The animals were wall-eyed and frenzied with pain. They were panicking from thirst and fright. When Cross tried to approach them, rub them down with an old grain sack, put liniment on the galls and the gaping cuts, they shied. In fact, they bucked, reared, and snorted.

As packhorses, they were through.

Cross took the mecate off his snaffle ring and slapped them back down the canyon with it.

"They just be crow-bait now," Cross said. "Let that old man Deacon have them."

"Yeah," McKillian said mordantly, "while he's digging for water, he can reflect on how he 'told-us-so.' "

29

The late afternoon got little better. Shortly before dusk, buzzards were circling up-canyon. When they got there, they saw that the kill was the body of the tracker, the one with the big jaw, greasy black hair, and hooked nose. He was the one reputed to be a dangerous degenerate.

The man's tongue had been ripped out, and he had been gutted from gullet to crotch. Coils of red-pink intestines, liver, kidneys, and stomach lay strewn in front of him.

Cross fired a round alongside the tracker's remains to scatter the dozen-odd vultures. However, two ravens stood fast. They crow-hopped on the ground in front of him, cawing, picking at the entrails with bloody beaks.

Cross took a closer look at the corpse. The eyes had been plucked out by carrion birds. But he could see that the tracker had suffered terribly. The face was a death mask, grotesque and hideous. The lower lip, which the man had bitten against the pain, was cleft in two. The upper lip was stretched taut above the front teeth in an insane sneer.

"Are you going to say something?" Sutherland finally asked, "or just choke on your spit?"

"I ain't gonna lie to you, sir. I ain't gonna piss in your pocket and tell you it's rainin'. He ain't makin' no effort to cover his tracks or throw us off the trail."

"Meaning what?" McKillian asked.

"Meaning he wants us to find him. Meaning when we do, we gotta be snake-fast. Meaning my eight-gauge Greener may not be enough."

Sutherland shook his head in irate disbelief. "That goose gun has bores like stovepipes. It'd knock a bull elk stiff-legged."

"Not if I ain't fast, sir, real fast. Otherwise, he'll have us skinned, smoked, and pummeled into pemmican 'fore I can cock the hammers."

"Mr. Cross," Judith McKillian said, still staring fixedly at the dead tracker, "you never told us the whole story on Slater and Mac, here."

"Ain't much to tell. Mac got to stickin' it where he shouldn't. Raped a small boy. This was up in Bloody Kansas during the War, and since Colonel Quantrill didn't hold with rape, he wanted to teach Mac a lesson. Accordin' to Deacon, Slater did the teachin'."

"Yes?" she asked, interested.

"Slater took down Mac's pants, straddled him on an old fallen tree, and nailed his scrotum to the log with a rail spike. Him and Quantrill's men left Mac there. He eventually got off that log, to safety. But his balls, they didn't. They stayed in the scrotum. On that tree."

"I find that rather drastic, Mr. Cross," McKillian said.

"So did Mac. Deacon, though, claims it improved his character."

"Is that what got him to help us track down Slater?"

"Reckon so. You might say, Slater heifer-branded him. But I guess he weren't satisfied. Torn came back to finish the job."

"That he did," Sutherland said, staring at the tracker's disemboweled corpse. "That he did."

30

They camped a few miles from the remains of the tracker, and at first light they headed out. The three of them were mounted, and J.T. Cross led Mac's roan, which carried their few supplies lashed to its McClellan saddle.

They rode well strung out. Cross was in front. Sutherland came next, a hundred behind. McKillian took up the rear.

Halfway into the morning, they came to a sharp, angling bend in the gorge, and Cross rode back, motioning them to halt. By now Judith McKillian had caught up with her friends, so all three of them were together.

"I smelled a cook fire just beyond that there ridge," he said, pointing to a sloping cliff face directly up the trail. "I plan on kind of sneakin' up there for a look." He pulled his Mauser out of the saddle sheath. The scope was already affixed. "I'd strongly recommend you two stay back and watch horses. Could be your gun-hands. Could be 'Paches. Could be Slater. Anyways, somebody's got to guard them mounts. It's a long ride back."

He wheeled his horse around and loped up the canyon, the rifle butt braced on his hip. At the bottom of the steep slope of the canyon, he tied his mount firmly to a mesquite bush, slung the rifle over one shoulder, and began scrambling up the ridge on hands and knees.

Sutherland turned to Judith McKillian and said under his breath: "I'm not letting some two-bit gunsel rob me of my one moment of glory. J.T. Cross is not about to steal my kill."

Sutherland dismounted. He walked over to the packhorse which was carrying the long metal tube which held his osage hunting bow. He pulled out the bow and removed the metal case holding the scope. He screwed the scope to the top of the contoured grip, then stepped between the bow and the string with his right foot, placing the lower end over the left arch. He reached behind and grasped the upper end with his right hand, pushed with the right hand toward the left, and slipped the loop over the end with the left-hand fingers.

He removed a second tube from the McClellan containing a quiver of Norwegian pine arrows, fletched with eagle feathers and tipped with inch-wide, tri-bladed Folsum broad-heads. The points were of razor-sharp German steel. He hung the hard rawhide moose skin quiver over his shoulder and slung the strung bow diagonally across his back.

He vaulted his mount and took off up the canyon at a high

lope. Sparks were flying from iron-shod hoofs, the clinking of the shoes ringing up and down the draw. The arrows rattled dully in the hard quiver. He made so much noise that Judith thought contemptuously he might as well be the village tinker, covered head to toe with banging pots and pans. 'Cause if Slater hadn't known we were on to him before, she thought bitterly, he sure will now.

31

As J.T. Cross clambered up the sloping sandstone ridge on hands and knees, he heard the clinking and banging down-canyon. He cursed silently. What had he done to deserve these idiots? He wished Deacon were here to see him now.

He reached the sandstone rim without scraping all the skin off both hands and knees. He carefully slipped off his Stetson and lifted the crown up over the top. When nobody shot the hat off, he put it back on and raised his head.

On the other side of the ridge, the canyon had widened to a good two hundred feet. By the west wall, alongside a chaotic heap of boulders, somebody, presumably Torn Slater, had innocently set up a hunter's camp.

With good reason.

In front of the pile of rocks was a small, clear pond.

Water.

Torn Fuckin' Slater had stumbled onto a sweetwater spring.

A brand-new water hole sprung smack in the middle of the Great Sonoran Desert.

Not only that, there were trees. On the other side of the boulders was the prettiest stand of cottonwoods Cross had ever seen. Shit, he said to himself, the bastard has every-thing. Water, trees, game. Because off to the right of the spring, using branches from the cottonwoods, Slater had set up three pole tripods. He'd bagged some mule deer—hell, they looked from two hundred yards like fair-sized antelopes—and was hanging them by the hocks over a slow-burning fire to cure. Damn, Slater had it all.

For the first time in two weeks, Cross felt a flush of enthusiasm. A good spring was in front of him, plenty of good meat, a bolt-action Mauser in his hands.

And sitting there propped up against a nice cool shade tree, under a poncho, his hat piled on top, Outlaw Torn Slater was taking a siesta.

Probably got tired after putting away a big lunch, and needed a nap. Couldn't believe that men like Cross and Sutherland had the sand to keep on his ass all the way up this gorge.

Cross looked over his shoulder. Sutherland was at the bottom of the ridge. He was waving at him furiously, pointing to the strung bow slung across his back, whispering harshly:

"Slater's mine. I say he's mine."

Like hell he is, Cross thought crankily. There ain't no way I'm letting you blow the first lucky break we've had this whole damn trip.

He raised the big Mauser to his shoulder, adjusted the trajectory for two hundred and fifty yards, and sighted in on the tan Stetson. The cross-hairs converged on the sweat-stained hat, which now looked only twenty yards away. He quietly bolted a round into the chamber, took a deep breath, and squeezed the trigger.

The big rifle boomed, then kicked against his shoulder. His vision was obscured by the whitish-black powder smoke, and he bolted another round into the chamber. Then he blew away as much of the smoke as he could. He examined his shot through the scope.

Cross was good. The Plainsman's hat lay ten yards from the tree, and he had left a large charred hole smoking in the bark.

But Cross had not killed his man.

For the force of the shot had knocked off Slater's hat and flung the poncho aside, revealing old clothes stuffed with rocks and sticks and mesquite bushes.

There was no man to kill.

The hairs on Cross's neck and arms stiffened. Fear burned inside of him. Slater was still out there, watching him, studying him, sizing him up. He could feel him out there, behind the boulders, up in the rimrocks, somewhere, everywhere.

Now Sutherland was up alongside him panting, grunting. "Did you get him?"

Cross pointed wordlessly to the shot-up saddle and Stetson and empty bedroll.

Sutherland shook his head incredulously. "God, he must hate us," he finally said.

"He ought to."

Cross put the scope back to his eye. He continued surveying the camp. It was true he was afraid of Slater, damned afraid, yet at the same time he felt the pull of the water hole, which he now slowly scanned, the cool shade of the cottonwoods, and all that smoked meat, which he scrutinized through the scope.

"Oh, no," he groaned softly, and motioned to Sutherland to point his bow-scope toward the pole tripods two hundred yards away.

Cross returned to his scope, and again, involuntarily, he groaned. Stripped naked, the three gunsels hung by the heels from the tops of the tripods. Their hands were trussed up tight behind their backs, and, as with the tracker, their tongues had been amputated to keep them from howling.

But they were still alive. Their eyes were wild with agony, as the slow, burning fires scorched and sizzled the peeling tops of their heads. Even at two hundred yards Cross could hear the raucous popping and crackling of the broiling flesh. Worse, he could see the great raw blisters on the heads and faces, now starting to char.

Then, slowly, Cross understood. Slater was up there. Watching them now. Watching them squirm. Even Sutherland understood. Sutherland, for all his drugged, insane bravado, even Sutherland understood.

Cross had felt terror before, but nothing like this. This sensation was more like panic, or hysteria. He felt fear, that was true. His stomach churned, bringing him to the brink of vomit. His neck and arm hair was bristling. He had to tighten his bladder muscles to keep from pissing in his pants.

But more than that, he felt the urge to cry, to shout for mercy, to cringe and beg. He wanted to throw down his rifle, give up.

Instead, he turned to Sutherland. "I don't think we have a chance. But if I was you, I'd slope on down this ridge, and if you can get to your horse, I'd haul ass out of here. Deacon was right. What you are looking at is no mortal man and no human place. This here's Golgotha, sir, the place of skulls."

Sutherland nodded dumbly, his eyes like saucers, huge with fright, and they began sliding down the ridge.

32

Then they were vaulting their horses and pulling leather back down the canyon. Sutherland could feel the big, deep-chested bay thrumming underneath him as he bore head-on at a hard run. He cursed and flogged the horse with the romal-end of his reins and raked his flanks repeatedly with his six-inch Mexican spurs. He squeezed the bay with his thighs and knees, hanging on for dear life, and the wind whooshed by his face, blowing the bowler off his head. Now the horse's heart was hammering between his legs, the tremendous muscles driving and pounding. Sparks jumped as the iron-shod hoofs hit stone. Sutherland could feel all one thousand pounds of horse, sixteen hands high, pounding beneath him.

He rounded a bend in the gorge and could see McKillian and Cross in front of him. He was gaining on them both. Then McKillian was suddenly bending over, her face flush against her horse's neck. She was screaming unintelligibly and reining in her mount.

Cross was leading the extra horse by the mecate and was having trouble making the animal keep up. His head was turned sideways now, and Sutherland, riding directly behind him, was close enough that he could hear him curse the saddle mount which was packing their gear.

Then Sutherland heard McKillian scream again, and saw her slouch even lower along her horse's neck. He saw Cross, who was thundering directly behind her, turn to stare, likewise confused.

When it happened.

The long, thin wire stretched across the canyon caught Cross just under the chin, above the Adam's apple and flush against the jawline. Since Cross was firmly mounted on the galloping horse, the momentum was tremendous. The thin steel strand shot through the neck like a guillotine. And Sutherland's memories of the next two seconds, hideous beyond belief, would haunt him like the devil's own spawn, each macabre image, photographed, filed, catalogued and locked away in the horror chambers of his mind.

The first image to impact itself on his retina was that of a crimson explosion. The jugular vein and carotid artery transport massive quantities of fluid, and when the steel thread sliced through these conduits, the blood pumped out of them like water out of a hose, arcing a good three feet above Cross's shoulders.

Then there was the bodily response. With the amputation of Cross's cranium from his neck, the arms, torso, and legs convulsed into violent, seismic spasms. Flailing in four directions at once, the headless body exploded in a frenzy of thrashing legs and flapping arms, until the bucking, rearing, panic-stricken dun tossed the blood-soaked body from its back.

This lurid horror paled beside what was coming at Sutherland. No, Sutherland's point of view was riveted on Cross's head.

A large, heavy, highly dense object—with a tan sweat-stained Stetson still tied tightly beneath the chin, the jawline spewing a veritable flood tide of blood—was coming directly at him.

At high speed.

Cross's cranium flipped once in the air, so when it reached

the point of impact, the two men were literally face to face, eyeball to eyeball.

When it hit Sutherland.

Exactly between the eyes.

Before he even had time to scream.

His last conscious impression was that of being lifted out of the saddle, a split second before the taut wire was to have whipped through his own neck, and dropped smack on his ass in the middle of the canyon floor, his skull aching and throbbing as though Cross had hit him between the eyes with a sixteen-pound sledge.

And then the lights went out.

And Sutherland knew no more.

PART IV

33

It was nighttime when Sutherland came to. His head hurt savagely, and his pulse pounded in his temples like a kettle drum.

The thought of sitting up made it worse.

The act of sitting up turned out to be not that tough. Only slightly harder, he decided, than fighting the Franco-Prussian War. It was all that nauseating, clotted blood in his nose, mouth, and ears that really bothered him. That, and the black eyes.

And the horrible fear that again he might run into Cross's ghostly, severed head.

He pushed those memories deep in his mind and looked around the canyon.

To his utter astonishment, he saw his horse rein-standing less than thirty feet away.

The reason, simple:

His mouth was caked with gore from having stepped on those reins and jerked on the spade bit.

Hence, the bay was standing stock still.

Slowly, Sutherland pulled himself to his feet and stumbled over to his mount. He gripped the horn with both hands and hung there awhile, wishing the pain in his head and the pounding in his ears would subside.

Clumsily, he swung onto the saddle and booted the bay down the pass and into the night.

34

He rode through the night and all the next day, praying that he would not run into Slater and that the Black Beauty spring was sweet and bubbly. The blazing sun was beating him senseless.

And as to his horse's condition, Sutherland doubted he would make it to the Beauty.

The animal didn't. Five miles from the obsidian needle, the horse began blowing red froth. During the last mile, he went down. Sutherland jumped off barely in time.

So the last mile he walked. Stumbled, actually. It was now late afternoon, and Sutherland had been ten hours without water. His tongue was swollen, and his parched throat throbbed. It was imperative that he get a drink before dealing with Deacon.

Which was not out of the question. Fifty yards up the canyon from the Beauty was a heap of boulders behind which lay a small cave. Their last night, Sutherland had secretly cached an emergency supply of water.

In the cave, under a pile of mesquite branches, was now safely hidden the cumbersome hogshead of water.

There was no more point in saving it. The trophy he'd hoped to house in it—well, Sutherland was a practical man. Slater's head would not be his. Instead, he could drink the water and discard the formaldehyde flask. As much as he hated to admit it, Deacon had been right.

Outlaw Torn Slater was too fucking tough.

He slipped into the maze of boulders and made his way between them. He followed the cave to its far wall a dozen-odd steps from the opening. Frantically, his parched, throbbing mouth and throat aching with dehydration, he began throwing the mesquite branches off the barrel.

When he got to the keg, he took out his Arkansas toothpick and began prying off the lid. When that took too much time, he simply smashed it with the blade, over and over, till the blade snapped in two. Then he smashed at it with the broken blade, out of his head, delirious, panicking for a drink.

Finally, the barrel top shattered just as the other half of the blade snapped off the haft. Crazed by thirst, he plunged his aching head into the keg's cool depths.

And yanked it out, horrified.

The water was a soft luscious pink. Clots floated on the surface. It reeked of formaldehyde.

And on the bottom, staring up at him, open-eyed and full-faced, through the blood-tinged translucence of the barrel, was J.T. Cross's severed head.

Within the closed confines of the cave, Sutherland's screams were more than demented, they were ear-cracking. For they were now inflamed by more than terror. He'd gone beyond that. He was wholly unhinged.

Then, over his shoulder, audible above the shrill screams, ringing tinnily in his own ears, he heard a soft:

"Looking for me?"

He turned around. There, standing in the cave's mouth, was a tall man with massive shoulders and an amazingly narrow waist. He wore sweat-stained frontier attire—Levi's, a collarless brown shirt, a tan, rather badly battered Plainsman's hat. On his left hip he wore a Single Action Army Colt, rechambered to take the new .44-40 rounds. But mostly it was the eyes that struck Sutherland. Even in his present agitation, he noted the eyes. They were the blackest he'd ever seen. Blacker than the black obsidian needle outside the cave. Blacker than the spaces between the stars. Blacker than the abyss.

Reptilian in their flatness.

Outlaw Torn Slater.

"You fucking bastard!" Sutherland howled.

And he put his head down and charged across the passageway at Slater, roaring like a gored bull.

He did not get far.

The first kick caught Sutherland squarely in the mouth. The heavy boot broke most of his teeth, caved in the roof of his mouth, smashed the septum.

The second kick shattered his pelvis.

Sutherland's last recollection of the cave was of Slater grabbing him by the back of the silk bandana, which was knotted around his sunburned neck, and dragging him headfirst out of the cave, toward the soaring monolith.

After that he remembered only the pain.

And the prayer that he might somehow, miraculously, die.

35

Up in the rimrock, slightly less than two hundred yards from the newly dug-out Black Beauty Spring, John Henry Deacon felt pretty good. Of course, twenty-four hours ago, he hadn't felt too well. At that point he'd been eight feet down in the ground, hoping to hit what had once been the monolith's waterhole.

Even when he hit it—mud first, then slowly but surely a big, bubbly, knee-deep slough of water—he was not exactly ecstatic. His mouth was so dry, his body so dehydrated that he knew he would have to drink at least a pint before he could be sure whether it was brackish or sweet.

And if it was brine, he knew he would be dead. As Deacon well knew, the body required prodigious amounts of water to get rid of excess salt.

Water he did not have.

But the spring was sweet, and when Cross's riderless horse

came galloping into camp, he gave the horse a good drink, too. The same with the extra mount the three had used as a packhorse. He also filled the five water bags someone had lashed to the packhorse's McClellan.

Then he led the mounts down-canyon, hid them in a cul-de-sac, rubbed them down, grained and watered them again. After that, he strapped Cross's bolt-action Mauser across his back, scaled the rimrock, and crouched behind a boulder. He stared down at the Black Beauty.

And waited.

The first to arrive was Outlaw Torn Slater. Between moonglow and starlight, visibility in the canyonlands was excellent, and through the rifle's fourteen-power scope, Deacon observed the scrupulous manner in which Slater looked after his stock.

After the Appaloosa was rubbed, watered, grained, and bedded down, Deacon watched Slater dismember the fallen cottonwood. Hacking the longest, strongest limbs off the tree, and lashing them together at the top with rawhide thong, he watched Slater erect a pole tripod, or what they'd called back in Missouri "hog poles." He watched him sling a small noose over the tripod's top and tie it off.

There were other happenings. Back behind the Beauty, Slater went exploring. Deacon couldn't guess what went on there. Toward dawn Judith McKillian stumbled into camp, horseless, exhausted, delirious with thirst. She literally flung herself into the hole he'd dug, and it was a good hour before she clambered out.

Now she lay near the edge, passed out.

Slater ignored her.

It was late afternoon when the real action occurred. Something stirred back behind the needle. Slater's Appaloosa nickered, but already Slater was halfway around the monolith. There was some distant, muted screaming, and a few minutes later Slater returned, dragging Sutherland behind him by the scruff of the neck.

Apparently, Sutherland had put up a fight. His whole face was livid, covered with blood. His jaw looked almost broken off, and his nose was terribly mangled. His eyes were black and blue, and swollen shut.

Slater dragged him over to the poles. There, he grabbed him by the pant legs and hoisted him up till his boots were in the hog noose. He stood back and studied his work. He decided he wanted the hog hung higher. He raised the noose and tied it off again. Then he lashed Sutherland's hands behind his back with more rawhide thong.

By now Judith McKillian was awake and propped up on an elbow. She watched Slater curiously, with no particular emotion on her face, her eyes containing all the cold, unwavering fixity of a bitch-cat.

Even when Slater took out his bowie and hacked off half of Sutherland's scalp, Judith McKillian's stare remained unblinking.

Even when Sutherland once again began to scream.

Then Slater turned his back on them. He walked over to the fallen cottonwood, and with his bloody bowie hacked off an armload of kindling. He returned to the hog poles, made tinder out of some dried mesquite and cottonwood shavings, and laid it under Sutherland's bleeding head. He placed sticks and twigs over the tinder, and the broken branches over those. He took a phosphorus-tipped Lucifer from his shirt pocket and scratched it with a thumbnail. He lit the tinder.

It was a low, smokeless fire, so slow-burning that it took the moaning, semiconscious Sutherland a full thirty seconds to realize what was happening. By then he was fully awake and shrieking like a banshee.

To Deacon's horror, McKillian's eyes were still impassive, expressionless.

As for himself, he struggled to fight off nausea and to focus on the positive side of Slater's actions. For one thing, the heat was cauterizing the bleeding head. In fact, if Slater were to stop the fire now, cut Sutherland down, Deacon suspected that with the bleeding stanched, the bastard might live. He was certainly mean enough.

But it was clear that this was not Slater's intention. Audible above Sutherland's howls, he could now hear the crackling and popping of the scorching skin, and through the fourteen-power scope he could see tremendous red blisters as big as a silver dollar ballooning up on the sides and bottom of the twisting, gyrating head.

Deacon had had enough.

He stood up, put down the rifle, and yelled into the canyon: "Slater. It's John Henry Deacon. I been ramrod to this little expedition."

Slater stared up at him over his shoulder. "Yeah, I knew you was up there. With that rifle from the other one's horse. It had a scope."

"I put the rifle down."

"Don't see why. You could've back-shot me with it."

"Maybe. Two hundred yards is a long shot for an old man. Might of missed."

"Naw, bushwackin' never was your style. What do you want?"

"Wanna know whether you're comin' after me. If you are, I'd just as soon settle it right now. Right here."

"I got no quarrel with you, Deacon. I was you, I'd slope on outa here."

"Just one problem. I'm takin' them two with me. Least I'm tryin'."

Slater winced. "Him too?"

"That's what he paid me for."

Slater shrugged. "You just make sure I'm long gone 'fore you do it. I'll be visitin' them 'Paches now, and some of them savages might be watching up in the rimrock. Can't let them think I let this shorthorn off scot-free. They'll think I gone soft in the head."

"I'll wait."

"You do understand my position. I got my reputation to think of."

Slater turned toward the Appaloosa and the packhorse. He crossed the canyon, took the pack animal's mecate, and started to dally it once around his saddle horn.

When suddenly Judith McKillian was up, charging across the canyon, and grabbing him with both arms around the waist.

"What do you want?" he said.

She stared up at him beseechingly. Her eyes brimmed with tears, her chin trembled.

He looked down, raised the coiled, horse-hair mecate, and

back-handed her with it across the side of the head. It sent her tumbling head over heels across the canyon floor.

Slater swung onto the big Appaloosa and trotted up the gorge, the packhorse close behind.

Deacon waited a long while, till there was no doubt Slater was gone. Then he picked up the Mauser and headed down into the canyon to cut Sutherland down.

He hoped and prayed there were no Apaches watching.

BOOK II

Little girl, you're born for the tree.
You aren't born for love but for sorrow.
Your tormented soul will never be free.
In death you lose your flower.

When will you find your white-eyes stranger?
And when will you find your dance?
When will you find that white wild stranger,
Who brings to you your blood on his hands?

—J.P. Paxton, "The Ballad of Outlaw Torn Slater,"
circa 1877

PART V

36

Eight thousand feet up in the Sierra Madre, a young woman stood on the rim of a cliff. Below her, the desert floor shimmered. A miasma of heat waves trembled over the ground, and in the distance, where the horizon loomed, receded, then dipped over the edge of the earth, mirages danced. And dance they might, the young woman thought. The sun was at zenith, and in the scorching heat, nothing else seemed to move. Not on the desert floor. So it was only fitting that heat itself should provide the desert with its only illusion of motion.

She casually brushed a buzzing deerfly away from the sleeve of her white buckskin robe, and while the move was reflexive and unthinking, it was wonderfully graceful. The woman in the elaborately beaded, spotlessly white robe was touched not only by grace but by poise and beauty. Anywhere on the Scandinavian fjords, on the banks of the Aegean, or on the languidly undulating barges of the Nile, she would have been thought striking.

By Apache standards she had the radiance of the gods.

Shiny jet hair, which was often likened to a raven's wing, a generous mouth, and a strong chin. She had wide, flaring cheekbones. Her dark, flashing, deep-set eyes were black as onyx, as glistening chunks of obsidian, and contrasted brilliantly with her flawless complexion.

Being a virgin, Ghost Owl's hair was bundled vertically at the nape and wrapped in a *nah-leen,* or hair bow, and the effect of the raven hair and nut-brown skin in contrast with the creamy-white robe was almost ethereal.

Many had commented on the sacred quality of her beauty, and it was thus that Ghost Owl was a true-seer, a tribal shaman.

She stared out over the Sonoran Desert a moment longer, then turned back toward the camp. When was Snake Woman coming? The sun was at high, Geronimo would be meeting them at the sacred lodge. Still her sister-friend was not here.

Slowly, Ghost Owl returned to camp. She thought she knew where Snake Woman was. Her friend had been approached the day before by the pregnant wife of Horse Ears to bless her baby after delivery. Snake Woman had declined because she did not approve of the midwife. Like herself, Snake Woman found Limping Dog's deliveries to be cruel and often lethal.

Instinctively, Ghost Owl found herself heading toward Horse Ear's wickiup on the other side of the rancheria. Perhaps his people could direct her to her friend.

Rounding a huge cluster of boulders, she could already smell the camp. As always, the scent of smoke pervaded everything, including the people themselves. On the other side of the boulders, there were three dozen wickiups—circular, dome-shaped brush lodges which looked like overturned bird nests—scattered across the cliff top. In front of each wickiup were cook fires.

Ghost Owl strolled past the big lodges of thatched brush, past the open-air arbors known as ramadas, past scores of children playing Bull-Roarer, past many braves and squaws. On and on she walked, heedless and undisturbed. No one stared lasciviously at her, or made lewd jokes. Apache males were trained from childhood to treat women with civility. Respect for the yet-unwed was total. After the age of eight, boys were no longer allowed to converse with their mothers. Courtship was restrained, closely regulated.

Premarital intercourse was a capital offense.

Nor did the ancient rancheria hags shriek their indecent derision as she passed. Whatever laughter or slander the other passing women provoked, the crones promptly shut up around the Owl. Some glared, a few crow-eyed her easy gait. But most lowered their eyes. Better not to excite the vengeance of this sacred shaman. The grace of the gods was a mixed blessing, at best. Those capricious wraiths could be summoned for ill, as well as for good. So no one courted the anger of the Owl. All knew that even the kindest conjurer could quickly turn wrathful witch.

Toward the middle of the camp, the smoky haze and the heat of the many fires grew intense. Venison cooked in paunches full of broth, simmered slowly, heated by hot stones. Hunks of rump steak—mule, deer, horse, and dog— and long slices of tongue turned lazily on roasting spits. Around the campfires, women in buckskin dresses and beaded, painted shawls cut moccasins, softened hides with deer brains and ashes, worked on their robes with needle, knife, and awl. To her left, a group of squaws sat alongside huge, coiled burden baskets filled with the annual harvest of maize and piñon nuts. These, they ground into meal with their slablike *manos* and *metates*.

Without a galnce, she passed them by.

Toward the far edge of the rancheria, beyond the last ring of wickiups, were clusters of women pegging out green hides. A handful of men helped with the stretching and scraping. This menial labor was usually beneath the touchy dignity of braves.

In a piñon grove beyond the rancheria, she saw the true elite of the camp. This was a large circle of warriors and hunters. They squatted on their haunches, rocked on their heels, smoked, passing gourd dippers of *tiswin,* which they got from the big *olla* in the center. A few of them worked at straightening arrows, shaping bows, and mending gear. But most only bragged and laughed.

A few raised their heads as she passed. One or two moaned

wistfully under their breath, but like those in the rancheria, all were still.

By a clump of cottonwoods was Horse Ears's cousin, Quick Bird. He was a big man in a breechclout, buckskin leggings, and thigh-high moccasins. But his shirt was calico, no doubt the plunder of a bloody *pindah* raid. He was helping his wife stretch a large, hard hide. He also lived near Horse Ears. Perhaps he could direct her to the delivery.

"Have you seen your cousin and my sister-through-choice?"

"The one who writhes and undulates like a serpent?" Quick Bird spoke instantly, but without sarcasm.

"Yes."

He pointed toward a shallow ravine. "Down the defile and under the jack pines. Limping Dog took your spirit-sister down there to help."

Ghost Owl nodded her acknowledgment and turned toward the arroyo. Her face remained calm, impassive.

She knew his cousin was in desperate trouble.

Quick Bird knew it, too.

Down in the arroyo, she walked carefully. The scrub chapparel was a dense jungle of spiny octillo, dagger-sharp yucca, spiked nopal, and the omnipresent prickly pear. Needles reached out of every creature, every plant. It was as if everything imaginable had thorns.

At last, she passed out of the gorge, and could see the stand of jack pines.

She discerned the disaster.

Horse Ears's wife, Little Flower, was sitting under the tree. Her back was propped against it, and her wrists, pulled high over her head, were cross-tied and lashed to the trunk.

Her chest was secured with a rawhide thong.

Her legs were spread and staked out in a grotesquely wide *V.*

Her head was slumped sideways on her right shoulder at a sickeningly skewed angle.

Then Ghost Owl saw Snake Woman. She was wearing a buckskin skirt and top, and her moccasins were rolled up well over her knees. Her neck and waist were festooned with the sacred cords, sashes, and medicine bags of her trade.

And while it's true Ghost Owl saw Snake Woman, "heard her" was the stronger impression. She heard her friend's singsong death chant for the mother. The echoing wails were all gibberish, with no linguistic meaning, but that was intentional. Nonsense in the Apache Spirit World was thought to possess more potent medicine than meaningful incantation.

Snake Woman's chant was a wailing chorus of trills and tremolos, during which she jumped and trembled and danced. Horse Ears, meanwhile, was wallowing in the dust, pausing only to shriek with grief, slash his arms and legs and long hair with his knife.

Still moaning and trilling, Snake Woman took two buckskin pouches from around her neck. One was a large sack of ashes which she'd procured when Horse Ears came for her. The other was her medicine pouch containing the sacred *hoddentin,* or cattail pollen.

She slowly circled the tree, strewing ashes from the first bag around the dead woman. Then she half emptied the bag onto Little Flower, the rest on a heavy, brown object hanging from the limb of the jack pine.

Which Ghost Owl recognized.

The cradleboard.

Even at that distance she could see the gruesome thing made of split sotol and an elongated hooplike frame of bent oak. The flat roof was stretched buckskin, and the foot rest was hard wood—oak or ash, she thought. The buckskin sides were colored with yellow ocher and laced together with deerskin bands.

The dead baby was inside.

The cradleboard was caked with crimson gore.

Now Ghost Owl watched as Snake Woman took out a big, trade sheath knife, and, with a hair-raising shriek, began hacking and mutilating the sides of the frame, rendering it unfit for any further use.

She scattered the sacred pollen on the dead baby and mother, cast more pollen to the sky, the earth below, and to the four cardinal directions, starting with the east.

Done.

She hurled the medicine pouches away from her and

stamped off toward Ghost Owl. When she reached her spirit-sister, she kept on walking, her face an angry grimace. Ghost Owl fell silently into step, and followed her through the thicket of thorns.

37

Then they were back on the rim of the cliff, eight thousand feet above the great desert. They stood there next to the sacred lodge and waited.

For Geronimo.

While they kept a brooding silence, Ghost Owl stood looking sideways at Snake Woman. Her sister-friend was dressed in typical Apache attire, a mid-length buckskin skirt and a top which extended well below the hips. A red lightning bolt was painted on the back. The seams were double fringed, and numerous sacred cords, bags, and sashes were festooned around her neck and waist. The entire outfit, including her thigh-length, rawhide-soled moccasins with the turned-up toes, was heavily beaded. Her hair, Ghost Owl noted, she stubbornly wore in the fashion of a man—straight, shoulder-length, a rolled-up red bandana for a headband. A sheathed trade knife hung from a belt which bristled and gleamed with conchos and brass tacks.

Ghost Owl studied Snake Woman's face. Brown as old saddle leather, fifty years of crow's feet etched along the corners of the eyes, a great scar transversing her right cheek, another down the left side of her nose.

Mutilation.

Inflicted on her by a jealous lover for sexual infidelity.

Over twenty years ago.

By Geronimo.

Still, Ghost Owl thought, the eyes were what really got to you. Great, blazing orbs that burned like emerald fire. Some said it was her eyes that first led Cochise to believe that Snake Woman was possessed of Spirit Power, who urged her to undergo the excruciating rites of fasting, scarification, prayer, and sundance. And turn shaman.

Others said it was the magical eyes which had brought Geronimo, a legion of lovers, and five husbands to her bed.

Still others said it was the secret behind her notorious name, Snake Woman. Woman who writhes and twists and trembles like a snake.

In the throes of lust.

Most believed it was this lurid gift which had transfixed Geronimo, conscripted his loins, and snared his soul.

Finally Ghost Owl broke the silence. "It went badly? The birthing?"

"As you say."

"Was it the staking or binding her to the tree that killed her?"

"Everything. That old fool, Limping Dog, pegged the girl's legs out like green hides. Her hips were too narrow, were constrained by the binds, and her stomach could not push. The baby would not pass. So the toothless old whore pulled. By the time I got there, the baby had been mangled to death."

"How did the mother die?"

"Limping Dog had lashed her neck to the tree with a rawhide thong. In her agony, she strained against it. The side of her neck finally yanked on it so hard that when the cord gave, her neck snapped all the way to the shoulder and broke."

"Knife and awl," Ghost Owl said softly, muttering the worst curse Apache women knew. "The mother and baby, both. The old hag did it this time."

"When I got there, I told her: 'I can drive the ghosts off Horse Ears. They were his family. But not off you.' I pointed to her gory hands and said: 'That's dead people's blood on your hands. Dead people's. Their spirits will follow you forever, old crone. For-all-tomorrows.' "

"Enju." Yes, Ghost Owl said under her breath.

"Of course, the old woman was furious. She denied all

guilt, and even suggested I was partly to blame, apparently thinking I am empowered to raise the dead. So I said to her: 'Listen, pig-dung, the owl will come one night and drag you off. Or maybe two owls will come. Mother *and* baby owls. Perhaps ten owls, or maybe even a hundred. But they'll come. They'll be ghosts of all the mothers and babies you've butchered. They will drag you off, not to our own Dead Land, but to the Comanche hell, the Land-Between-The-Winds, where you'll wander for all time to come. You're dead, hag. It's time to chant your death song. You're finished, over and done. You just don't know enough to start singing.' ''

''What happened then?''

''That evil face of hers turned white as old bone. She started wailing and wallowing in the dust. She was simultaneously trying to hack off three finger joints. She was pleading with me to intervene on her behalf, but I was so sickened by it all that I just kicked her ugly carcass back down the ravine. You just missed her coming up.''

Suddenly Ghost Owl was laughing uncontrollably, and Snake Woman, against her will, joined in.

''You should have seen that broken-down old wreck rolling down the defile!''

After they caught their breaths, Ghost Owl said to her friend: ''What do you think Geronimo wants now?''

''The same thing as always. He wants you to marry him, or he wants you to give him a true-vision, a vision which will destroy *pindah-lickoyee*. The white-eyes. He obviously can't have either.''

''*Enju.*'' Agreed.

''But they are the same, are they not?'' Snake Woman said. ''In his eyes? He believes you have the medicine to obtain such a vision, a vision which will drive the palefaces from our land for-all-tomorrows, again-and-always. If he cannot buy the vision from you, he hopes to marry you. After that, he feels he can force it out of you.''

''He is crazy. Medicine vision comes by instruction from those who have it, from *di-yin*, from the holy ones. We have it because we had the patience and strength to sing the exhausting chants and observe the endless rituals. Tell him he can have it, too. If he has the strength. If he has the patience."

"He wants it now."

"Giver-of-Life, who brought the Apaches up from the bowels of the earth, through the sacred caves in the sacred mountains, He gives power. Not me, not you."

"Enju."

"And Giver-of-Life requires fasting and prayer. And time. Tell that to Geronimo."

"He says he has no time, and that marriage to you will be faster. And easier."

Ghost Owl shuddered.

"Look at it this way," Snake Woman continued, mockery running through her voice. "Is, not Geronimo the most sought-after man in the tribe? Do not the young men copy his walk, grow their hair long after his fashion, imitate his every move? Do not the young boys strive and dream to be like him?"

"I am no young boy."

"What do you wish? For him to sit by a water trail? Pipe a flute as you pass? Bring horses to your wickiup? Or do you know what you want?"

"I can tell you what I do not want. I do not want a man driven only by self-pride, bloody fury, and butchery. I do not want a man like Geronimo."

"Perhaps you want a true-seer like yourself."

"Perhaps."

"Or perhaps you seek that thing the white-eyes speak of. That thing called 'love.' "

"Yes, I've heard of it, too. That, I do not understand."

Then Ghost Owl saw her friend's eyes fix on the boulders. Geronimo was coming. Slowly, Ghost Owl turned her head and took in his arrival. As she studied him from afar, Snake Woman whispered teasingly:

"Why don't you marry him?"

"I'm no scar collector. I'm not like you."

She shrugged off the gibe. "He's a good provider."

"My family doesn't need his horses or blankets or guns. I provide well enough."

Now Geronimo was alongside the two friends. Up close, whatever else Ghost Owl thought of him, he was a marvelous specimen of a man. He had a wide, dark, hawk face with fine, white teeth. He was big, deep-chested, and long of leg. He was the supreme example of Apache manhood.

But today he was afraid.

Terrified.

His body was covered with sacred charms to ward off the evil which he felt was all around him. As though he were trying to protect every square inch of skin.

First there was the buckskin medicine shirt. Feathers and fossilized clam shells were stitched into the front and back, and long double rows of specially blessed Mexican scalps had been sewn into the seams along the sides and on the shoulders. Even more striking were the shirt's paintings. Scores upon scores of multicolored drawings, piled together willy-nilly, one on top of the other, covered every bit of the shirt. Not even the area under the arms and surrounding the rows of scalps was unpainted.

Numerous medicine cords were hung from his rawhide headband and belt. They were strung with beads and shells, eagle down, diamondback rattles, lightning-charred wood, fragments of fossilized conch shell, chunks of holy green *chalchihuitl,* and hawk claws.

Around his waist was tied a medicine sash, festooned with figurines of Child-of-the-Water and his immaculate mother, White-Painted-Lady. Eagle feathers. Rosaries taken from Mexicans murdered during Geronimo's countless raids.

Wedding rings, obtained from the same bloody ventures, were stacked knuckle high on his fingers.

Around his neck was the usual assortment of medicine bags and amulets, which Ghost Owl knew to be filled with the standard charms-against-evil. Bits of crystal, petrified wood, sacred meal and pollen, more lightening-riven wood, medicine arrows, and trophies from the enemy, including crosses, medals, and the *Agnus Dei.*

Ghost Owl also took in the necklace of grizzly claws, the

longest she'd ever seen. Over half a foot, arched like scimitars, and needle-sharp. The neck-piece was interspersed with five-inch fangs. She knew that Geronimo had recently proclaimed the grizzly to be his "medicine bear."

But to Ghost Owl the most shocking of Geronimo's sacred relics was the medicine hat. It was a small shell of buckskin, which Ghost Owl instantly recognized as rare and costly. It was sitting atop Geronimo's big, square head at an angle. The hat was plain buckskin, except for the painted figures and symbols, done in yellow ocher and mountain-mahogany red. The ornaments—more lightning-blasted wood, bits of abalone shell, owl feathers, a *chalchihuitl* stone, and three diamond-back rattles at the very top. The drawings were of lightning bolts, rainbows, the black *Gan*, several butterflies, and a dazzling yellow sunburst.

Ghost Owl was about to tease Geronimo about his fears and the profusion of relics when she caught the look in his eyes.

The eyes were terrible. The pupils were dilated and out of focus. The whites were lined, and cross-lined with red.

It was clear he hadn't slept in many days.

"What is wrong?" she heard Snake Woman say.

"Ghosts," he said softly. "Every night when I shut my eyes, it is all I see. Mangas Coloradas, or 'Red Sleeves,' as the white-eyes called him because his arms dripped with blood. Cochise, who died two seasons past. My wife, Alope, who with my first three children was murdered twenty-and-five seasons past by that Mexican bastard general, Carrasco. Then I get reports of the lone white-eyes who rides these last twenty days through the canyonlands to enter my stronghold. I don't know."

"What sort of *pindah* do the scouts say?" Snake Woman asked.

Ghost Owl noticed that her sister-through-choice seemed unusually interested.

"That's what I wondered. Perhaps, I thought, that is why I dream ghosts. So I ask the scouts. They say a band of paleface scalp-hunters follow him. Maybe ten. He kills them all. He uses rattlesnakes, mountain lions. He kills one with a rifle from farther away than a man can see. With a single shot, they say. He cuts off their heads with strung cord. He hangs them over fires and roasts them to death. They say he leaves two alive—a man and a woman—no doubt to return to the other *pindahs* and then tell of the stranger's potent medicine."

"Do you think . . . ?"

"I do not know. I fear the consequences. Who knows who he is, or what?"

"Perhaps it is your brother-through-choice?" Snake Woman asked.

"That is not possible. Long ago I lost hope, and concluded he was dead. Otherwise, he would have returned. To his people. We all lost hope."

"Not Cochise."

"No, not Cochise. He always believed up to the moment of his death. Our brother would return."

"How do you feel? Ghost sickness, that is a serious thing."

"Weak, tired. I despair. I fear the night. I fear to sleep, and I fear to dream."

This was not the bragging, drunken brute she was used to. He was almost human.

Ghost Owl was impressed. "What else do the scouts say? About the man himself?"

Geronimo shrugged sadly. "They say he rides as if he owns the desert, mountains, and hills. He rides as if his enemies—even his Apache enemies—were as nothing. He rides as if the whole world, the Chiricauhuas included, belonged to him. They say this of a man who should be tired, starving, sick with thirst. This man has traveled the desert alone for thirty, perhaps forty days. He has lived on jerky, wild nuts, and cactus pulp. They say this of a man who ought to be dead."

"So? Let him come up to the stronghold. Look him over and decide."

"I don't know."

''So he's a white-eyes. You've seen them before, and they've seen you.''

''They did not see me and live.''

''He did,'' Ghost Owl pressed. ''Your blood-brother did.''

Snake Woman smiled.

''Why do you grin?'' asked her sister-through-choice.

''Yes, he gazed on Geronimo. Before you were born. And Geronimo tried to kill him.''

Now Geronimo was shaking his head gloomily.

''What happened?'' Ghost Owl asked.

''We captured him in a raid,'' Snake Woman said, ''when he was a boy of perhaps ten-and-four winters. We considered raising him as a Chiricauhua. As a test of bravery, Geronimo heated a knife blade in a camp fire and placed it in his hand. Then he closed his fist over the red-hot knife.

''He did not respond well to the test?'' Ghost Owl asked. ''You mean he was not brave? He cringed?''

''Not at all,'' Geronimo said. ''He did not even blink as the skin sizzled and smoked. When I finally opened the fist and pulled away the blade, he calmly closed it again and hit me. Hard. He broke my jaw.''

''So you tried to kill him?'' Ghost Owl asked. ''How?''

''I staked him out between two anthills. A red and a black. I started an ant war over his body.''

Ghost Owl was fascinated. ''What happened?''

''I don't know. I can't explain it. I think he may have gotten some blood from his hand onto the thongs tied to his wrist. But suddenly the red ants were going for the blood and the thongs. Before we knew it, they bit through the rawhide and freed his hand. Then he freed himself and got up.''

The hair bristled on Ghost Owl's arms and on her neck. ''You mean the ants themselves intervened on his behalf? The gods sent him to us and you tried to kill him?''

''That is what Cochise said. He tried to make up for it by raising the boy as his own, and by making me his blood-brother. I never knew if it helped. None of us did. Oh, I prayed, fasted, chanted, did all the usual things. I was never any good at those usual things. I received no sign. Then one day he went away. To fight the white-eyes' war. He said that many years ago, in a place called Kansas, blue-bellies killed his family. He went to the war to fight blue-bellies. He said he would come back. But he never did.''

"And you would risk killing this stranger? It could be him again.''

"I don't know. A man who kills ten others on his back-trail like he was slapping flies. A man who shoots what others cannot see. A man who kills with lions and rattlesnakes the way we kill with bows and knives. I don't know. I fear this man. I fear my dreams. He may come for much harm, much evil.''

"What do you want?'' Ghost Owl asked.

"I want a vision. A medicine vision. I want the true-seer to tell me what to do.'' He gave Ghost Owl a searching look. "I need you.''

PART VI

38

It was three days later.

The first day was the easiest. All Ghost Owl did was dance on the rim of the cliff next to the sacred sweat lodge. Snake Woman had supervised the ritual by sitting on a nearby rock, shouting words of encouragement whenever Ghost Owl's energy started to flag.

There was pain. Fatigue. Blurred vision. Nausea. And since Snake Woman only let Ghost Owl drink twice a day, she was overwhelmed with thirst.

But on she whirled into the night, incanting vocables she had memorized untold-seasons-past, which now, after a full day of fasting and praying, had no more meaning for her than the Martian moons. Yet still she cried them out, replete with singsong trills and vibrant tremolos.

By dawn she was almost blinded by weakness and dehydration, and when Snake Woman led her into the hide-covered wickiup which was the sacred sweat lodge, for a moment Ghost Owl felt relief.

For only a moment.

SAVAGE BLOOD

In the middle of the sweat lodge blazed a fire, and alongside it, in a shallow hole, were piled round, smooth stones, taken from an old river bed. These were heated white-hot in a fire outside, and frequently replaced by a young female acolyte. Periodically, Snake Woman dipped water from an *olla* onto the hot rocks and filled the tightly sealed wickiup with clouds of vapor.

The combination of breathless exhaustion, steam-seared skin, and burning thirst had Ghost Owl on her knees.

Snake Woman now took her medicine pipe out of a bag tied to her belt. She crushed tobacco leaves in the palms of her hands and packed them into the black obsidian bowl. She mixed in ground peyote. She removed an ember from the fire with a forked stick and lit the pipe in the ceremonial fashion, carefully avoiding the sides of the bowl.

She offered the stem to Spirit-Above, Spirit-Below, and to the four cardinal directions, beginning with the east.

Then she offered the stem to Ghost Owl.

Owl had no wish to sear her parched throat, but she knew that the sacred smoke was part of Snake Woman's ritual. She accepted the pipe.

As they smoked in silence, Ghost Owl took in her surroundings. She stared around the brush wickiup, its walls sealed off with deerskins. She smelled the age-old Indian smells of wood smoke, burning sage, and ancient hides. The lodge had few totems, since most wilted in the choking steam heat, but medicine cords festooned the walls. A large cross carved from lightning-blasted wood hung from the ceiling.

As for Snake Woman and herself, they were naked. Sweat ruins buckskin. Now they sat across the fire from each other, steamed a bright crimson.

When they finished the bowl, Snake Woman said: "Tell me, Little-One-Who-Hoots-and-Shrieks-Through-The-Night, does the holy heat teach you true-humility? Does it bring you true-learning?"

"I learn that steam scorches and sears my naked breasts. I learn that heat chokes and blisters the skin. I learn that old women with skin like rawhide are less sensitive to the pain than young girls such as I."

Snake Woman laughed heartily and called out the flap over the crawl-hole: "More hot rocks! The hottest rocks! Hurry! My little friend grows cold!"

The young girl came in with more large, smooth, white-hot stones on forked sticks. It took her several trips to pile them up in the shallow hole. When she was done, Snake Woman poured four gourdfuls of water onto them. Soon steam was sizzling and billowing so thickly through the lodge that Ghost Owl was blinded by it.

"Now do you feel true humility?" her sister-through-choice asked again.

"Now I feel hot."

"That is good, very good. It would be bad indeed if you now felt cold." Snake Woman laughed hackingly.

Ghost Owl ignored the gibe. "Tell me, old woman, why does Geronimo not dance and chant and come to the sacred-sweat? Why does he require that women do his seeing?"

"You mean why does he not confront his true-soul? Many dare not peer into the fiery abyss of their spirit. They know not what they will find."

"But if a young girl and an old woman can face this true-soul, why not a brave chief? Is not Geronimo brave?"

"Yes, he is physically brave. But he lacks the spiritual strength for the visionary path."

"Some say Geronimo will one day become a great man."

"Little One, it is through mystic communion with the Spirit World that one becomes great."

"Perhaps he has never tried."

"He has tried. I have seen him try. I have seen him pray day and night for a holy dream, a sacred vision."

"But it never comes?"

"Never."

"Why?"

"Cochise said that Geronimo had stained his birthright with blood, that his true-soul had been divided time-when and was now only reunited by violence. Once in a moment of rare anger he told Geronimo that his true-soul was created only by violence."

"Why would Cochise say such a thing?"

"Because Geronimo argued unceasingly for war with the white-eyes. He believed such a conflict to be a holy war. He said that when the Apaches were gone and an enormous emptiness once again filled the land, we would have vanished without a trace, leaving no graven images, no awesome cliff dwellings. All we would leave behind us would be vestiges of violence in the hearts of our gods and in the bones of our dead, which would lie bleaching in our canyons and deserts. Cochise told Geronimo that would be a sad thing. Cochise argued that such a war would be too costly, too bloody, and would spell extinction. Geronimo said that this conflict with the white-eyes would be a sacred war."

"What did Cochise say to that?"

"He said it would be a black stain."

Now the wet, rising steam was all around Ghost Owl, and despite her scorched skin and burning throat, she found herself sinking into the sweltering heat. Part of her wished to sink into it, all the way into it, and die forever.

Slowly, as if from a great distance, she heard Snake Woman's voice bringing her back to her spirit-task.

"Remember the stranger. You must find and recognize the white-eyes who rides toward the camp. Who is he? What does he want? Good or ill? Friend or foe?"

Then Ghost Owl was falling, falling, falling.

39

Was it really a medicine dream? Perhaps. But to Ghost Owl it seemed more like the old recurring nightmare from her childhood. There she was: captured by a band of Mexican scalp-hunters. They had massacred the village, raped and killed and scalped the women and children, had taken her alive. No doubt she would be sold into sexual slavery in one of the border-town brothels.

The stink of the scalp-hunters was all around her, as were the ubiquitous scalps—sewn into shirts, hanging from rifle scabbards, draped from their saddles. Those which they did not keep for their own decoration, they sold to the governors of Chihuahua, Sonora, and the American territories, for the bounty.

One hundred dollars for a male Apache.

Fifty for a female.

Twenty-five for a child.

In the dream, Ghost Owl was perhaps four, but a precocious child. Apache children were taught virtually from infancy to hate Mexicans because of the unspeakable scalp-hunting bounty, and in the dream, despite her lack of years, there was no doubt in her mind what was happening, what her fate would be.

In her dream, she rode across the neck of a big roan mare, clutching the mane for safety. The big *bandido* who rode behind her wore a tan felt sombrero with a diamondback hatband, the rattles still on, a dirty red shirt, black *charro* pants, and black boots which came up over the knees. His rowels were six-inch cartwheels, and across his chest the cartridge belts were criss-crossed. The webbing gleamed with brass cartridges for his new Henry repeating rifle. The man had a nose which had been broken and badly set many times, jagged teeth, and very bad breath. When he smiled, Ghost Owl shuddered.

There were another ten like him in the band, plus extra saddle mounts and pack animals.

In the dream, Ghost Owl was overcome with fright. The earlier scene of the massacre and the scalpings had filled her with dread.

The long line of scalp-hunting bandits was plodding through a long, twisting arroyo toward the setting sun. She was half blinded by the light.

Then it happened.

They rounded a bend in the gorge, and he was at the other end of the pass, less than thirty yards up-canyon. The man was tanned brown as an Indian, and his raven hair, held in place by a rawhide headband, hung down to his shoulders,

Apache style. He was dressed in breechclout and was naked above the waist.

Ghost Owl had difficulty making out his face. It was obscured by an ancient Sharp & Hankins .69 caliber buffalo gun with the long heavy barrel. The butt was braced on his hip.

The *pindah* had covered his face with warpaint—zig-zag streaks of yellow, red, and black. And when occasionally the flag flapped to the side, and she could glimpse the face more fully, she never really got beyond the eyes. They compelled her utter attention. They were dark and dazzling, and she could not stop staring into them.

If she was taken aback by the appearance of this stranger, the scalp-hunters were even more stunned, and talked rapidly in Spanish.

Finally, they organized a reception committee for the lone rider. Four *bandidos* rode to meet him, slowly fanning out. At the same time, he cantered toward them.

But something odd happened as he rode. He came on a slight downhill slope. And since it was westering, the sun was at his back and hung just above his shoulder.

A big fireball of a sun, blood-red and blindingly incandescent.

Suddenly, the big rifle lowered, right into the belly of the closest Mexican. The gun roared, and the far end of the canyon filled with a cloud of black powder smoke. The roar was deafening in the enclosed arroyo, and the whitish smoke obscured Ghost Owl's vision. But still she stared on in compulsive fright.

Now the man had dropped the rifle and snatched revolvers from his saddlebag. An ear-shattering roar from the handguns did not sound like three individual shots that killed the three other bandits before him, but more like one protracted, echoing blast. The end of the pass was so filled with smoke that Ghost Owl barely saw the three other Mexicans tumble from their mounts.

The lone white-eyes with the brace of pistols charged out of the gunsmoke, reins in his teeth, his two guns spewing fire and smoke and death. Scalp-hunters left and right fell from their horses. When the man with whom she rode attempted to wheel his mount, she heard one of the stranger's bullets strike him in the side of his turning head and knock him out of the saddle.

The Mexican's horse was spinning madly. The gelding was bucking, kicking, snorting, and all the other horses around her—most of them now riderless—had gone berserk, their hoofs and teeth slashing at the air. Somehow Ghost Owl managed to cling to her mount's neck. If she hadn't, she would have died under the scores of bloody hoofs.

But more terrifying than the thrashing horses was the white-eyes who cut in and out of the rearing animals, his guns hammering in every direction. Every second or third buck, Ghost Owl caught a glimpse of this marauding *pindah* with the Apache war paint, and heard the blazing roar of his heavy guns.

Finally, she could no longer cling to the horse's mane, and the mount was shaking her loose.

She did not know that the gunshots had stopped. She was thoroughly deafened by the blasts. But she was aware of the gun-butt hammering the roan between the eyes, and an arm sweeping under her belly, pulling her onto the neck of his own horse, and taking her back down the canyon.

Toward another Chiricauhua rancheria.

Toward Cochise's rancheria.

Toward her new home.

And with the *pindah's* arm around her waist, she passed out.

40

When she came to, she related the medicine dream to Snake Woman. Then she slept the day and most of the night. Periodically, she'd recall or reexperience snatches of the vision, would call to Snake Woman and tell her, but still she could not identify the face. It was always obscured by the white truce flag, or the blazing guns, or the streaked war paint.

It was toward dawn of the third night that Snake Woman brought her the news.

"Unless you can identify the face. Unless you can connect this white-eyes to your dream, and this stranger is a friend, Geronimo will send out a dozen scouts to ambush and kill him."

"Do you think that's wise?"

"It does not matter if it's wise. It is what they will do."

"Suppose it is Geronimo's blood-brother."

"He thinks he is dead. No, he thinks it is a *pindah-lickoyee* come to do us harm."

"What do you think?"

"If the White-Painted-Lady wanted us to know the stranger's identity, she would have told us. So now we never know. He is just another *pindah*. A dead *pindah*."

"I want one more day."

"You've had three. Nothing happened. Sometimes no vision comes. Or an incomplete one. It is no disgrace. Swallow your pride and forget it."

"I will try again."

"What else can you do?" Snake Woman asked. "You've chanted, danced, sung. You've suffered hunger, heat, and thirst. There is nothing else. Let it go."

"I can't let go. It's there. I can feel it. I have to know."

"You've tried everything. There is nothing else you can do."

"There is one thing else. I can do the thing you did."

Snake Woman looked at her spirit-sister in horror. "You don't mean it."

"Yes, I do. You will help me. I will dance at the pole. I will perform the ritual of our brothers in the north. I will dance for the sun."

41

Sundancing was indigenous to the northern brothers of the Plains, not to the Apaches. Only one shaman in their history had dared to put skewers under the back muscles and hang from the pole, where the wise-one might gaze on the sun, and achieve a glimpse of the wisdom of the gods.

Snake Woman.

She was not pleased that Ghost Owl had chosen to follow her path. While it was true that great wisdom could be learned at the pole, Snake Woman also felt the experience to be evil. Whenever she touched the humped ridges of livid scar tissue along her back, she felt that no amount of wisdom could be worth that much sacrifice. Only pride, a staggering, monumental, wicked sort of pride, could provoke one to accept the ordeal of the pole.

Pride.

The exact opposite of true-humility.

True humility: the only spiritual-good.

The end-goal of all mystical communion.

I had been motivated by such pride, Snake Woman thought bitterly. That was what drove me to the pole and the sundance.

And to other things.

Especially to other things.

42

The pole was erected on a cliff face above and beyond sight of the camp. If Ghost Owl was going to endure the agony of the sundance, let her do it without showing off. Let her endure it alone.

With only Snake Woman to watch and, if need be, cut her down.

Geronimo had been informed. He'd agreed to the ceremony and promised to postpone the decision on the *pindah*.

Then he'd sent out men to find an adequate pole, and, under Snake Woman's supervision, it was erected on the cliff.

Then she sent them away.

She and her sister-through-choice were by themselves. She stood alongside Ghost Owl, a long, thin knife in her hands, as well as two sharp skewers and two rawhide thongs.

Implements of the pole.

This was no Mandan sun-gazing ceremony with piles of gifts heaped high for Those-Who-Danced-At-The-Pole. No women would thrill for this celebrant. No men would dance. No kill-stories would be told. In future days, no children would think back on the awesome spectacle and dream of the courage and respect that such things bring.

There would be Ghost Owl and her sister-through-choice, Snake Woman.

That was all.

Alone.

Two of them on a high cliff, the main beam erected, the cross-beam securely lashed. Two heavy rawhide thongs hanging from the cross-piece.

Snake Woman fixed her friend with a searching stare. "They say that when a person suffers at the pole, more than flesh and blood suffers. Something dies inside."

"I know. But they also say that to whomever dances at the pole, the truth will be told. Sister-friend, that is what I need now. The truth."

"Truth is a harrowing experience. Most of us spend all our lives preparing to learn this thing you call truth. And when we learn it, we are still unprepared. We are mutilated."

"Who can gaze upon the gods? Who can gaze upon the sun? Such truth is blinding."

Again, Snake Woman fixed her with a stare. "How much self-awareness can *your* spirit bear?"

"We shall see."

Snake Woman began the ceremony by sprinkling the *hoddentin,* the sacred pollen, to Spirit-Above, Spirit-Below, and to the four cardinal directions, starting in the east.

Meanwhile, Ghost Owl unceremoniously slipped out of her buckskin medicine shirt and skirt. And moccasins. By the time Snake Mother had finished sprinkling pollen and incanting, Ghost Owl was stripped naked.

A small block of wood was resting under the two dangling thongs, and Snake Woman motioned her friend over to it. The naked girl stood up on the log, facing the sun rising in the east. Snake Woman got behind her and glared unhappily at the knife in her hand.

Then she began kneading and pressing the flesh around the trapezius muscles in the upper portions of Ghost Owl's back. When she was finally sure of their position, she began pinching around them as hard as she could. This was meant to numb the flesh, to diminish the shock of pain when she inserted the knife.

When the area was livid and inflamed, Snake Woman began to probe with the long, thin knife blade.

Ghost Owl stood motionless, impassive as a stone.

Slowly, Snake Woman began working the knife under the muscle. Finally, the blade poked out the other side. Ghost Owl's back and neck were drenched in blood.

Still Ghost Owl had not moved. Nor trembled. Snake Woman could not see the young girl's face, but she guessed that it was calm, the eyes open and clear.

She worked the first skewer under the muscle through the canal opened by the knife. She worked the second skewer under the other trapezius in precisely the same way.

Still Ghost Owl did not move.

Snake Woman quickly tied the ends of the thong to the ends of the skewers, then lashed each to the hanging rawhide thongs.

Snake Woman took a deep breath. She tried to prepare herself for the torrent that would pour forth when she removed the wood block from under Ghost Owl's feet. Then she squatted on her haunches, got a shoulder under the bend in Ghost Owl's knees, and pushed up. When she felt the body rise, she pushed the block away with her free hand. Slowly, ever so slowly, she lowered her friend's body till the ropes pulled taut and the body hung suspended.

Which it did.

The toes dragged softly on the ground as the body swung gently back and forth in the breeze.

Snake Woman rose, stood back to stare upon her work. Involuntarily, she winced. The flesh on Ghost Owl's back was wrenched up grotesquely, high as the back of her head.

But her chin was still up, strong and unwavering.

And her eyes were angled at the elevation of the sun.

For now Ghost Owl's back was to her, but the body was slowly spinning. In a few seconds she would circle face to face. What would she be like? Would the eyes be calm and expressionless? Or would her face be contorted in pain, a silent prayer on her lips?

The head came around.

The eyes were rolled back, the face empty of expression. Ghost Owl was already into her trance.

43

There was little that was coherent about Ghost Owl's vision. This struck her as odd, since the pole was supposed to produce absolute truth, utterly accurate prophesy.

But there was little of that today.

The vision was marked by a total absence of clarity.

That, and the pain.

The pain had begun with the kneading and pinching of the tender upper back. Which had, of course, been unpleasant. But, then, Ghost Owl was, even at that early age, an experienced shaman. The excruciating rituals of incantation and dancing, fasting and sweating, prayer and self-immolation involved extensive pain, and so to some extent she was prepared for what lay in store. She knew pain, understood it, accepted the bargains one made with it and with one's self, as one endured it.

But as Snake Woman had pointed out, no one could ever be prepared for the agony of the pole, for what their Mandan brothers of the north had called the *O-kee-pa*.

The most hideous self-immolation in human history.

When Snake Woman slipped the knife under Ghost Owl's back muscles, and then pushed the skewers through the hollowed-out pathway, the pain was so staggering that Ghost Owl felt only disbelief.

That this was happening to her.

And when Snake Woman slipped the thongs over the skewers and tied them to the rawhide ropes, Ghost Owl did not believe she could endure what was to follow.

In a sense, she did not endure the rest. For when Snake Woman kicked the block out from under her, and eased her down till her toes barely dangled on the ground, the pain transcended anything Ghost Owl knew about pain, and she passed to a different level of consciousness. It was not that the pain ceased. It hurt more than anything she'd ever felt, heard of, dreamed or divined. But it was different. All the other trials she'd borne in her life had been relegated to a fixed portion of her being. But this torture was total. Her entire self—mental, physical, and spiritual—was focused and transfixed by a blinding, searing fire-ball. Now she understood why they called the ritual the sundance, because that was all she saw: a white-hot blaze of flame.

Which she in no way attributed to the sun.

No, this was a different state of being, a plane of awareness which she was either ascending or descending to, a ritual journey she was not sure she could make.

She did not trust the white-hot field of fire on which her mystic vision seemed so fixed. It was slowly changing color and form. The field was contracting into a fire-storm. It gave off bursts of crimson, plumes of red-hot flame which crackled and roared. Soon the whole focus was that of a sphere, a perfectly round sphere, orange-red in color like the sun at dusk, like the sun as it stood over the stranger's shoulder in the dream. A great, blood-red beast of a sun, almost a living entity, a creature apart but still throbbing, vital, and alive. Then this, too, began to change, evolve, transform. It grew a trunk of red fire under its bottom—no, it was as though the ball were growing out of the trunk, that was it, growing, rising, and swelling, swelling so fast that her consciousness had to expand to contain it, swelling so fast it seemed to consume everything—earth, sky, stars, the void. Reduce it, reduce it, a voice was saying, reduce it back to the throbbing, living sun. Put it over the stranger's shoulder. Put it there. Bring back the stranger. Let me see his face.

She stared searchingly into the mushrooming cloud of fire, threw all her spiritual strength into the task of containing it, shrinking, and bringing back the stranger.

But nothing happened.

Except that the cloud continued to grow and that her consciousness, too, seemed to grow, rise, expand to encompass this monstrous fiend of fire.

She held on grimly. Despite the intense, unrelenting, incomprehensible pain, she wrestled with the exploding ball of brimstone, struggling to bring it down to its sunlike size. It felt, in those moments, as though Ghost Owl was taking on all the pain in the world, all the pain that the entire Apache nation had endured in their wars with the Comanche, the Spaniards, the Mexican scum, and now the white-eyes. All the pain that the white-eyes had endured in their own war, which Cochise believed to have been horrible beyond description. All the pain these white-eyes claimed that their own God, the one the Mexicans called *Hesu* or sometimes *Chucho*, had endured when he took the form of a man and walked on earth, and breathed and loved and suffered and died on a cross, tortured and killed by these Christians, a people he thereafter swore to redeem (though why a god would want to save a people who spat on him when he walked among them, who obviously did not love him or even want him, that part these Christian believers never did explain). Maybe that was her fate, the calling each person had, the particular unique destiny which Cochise claimed each of us did not live but suffer, maybe it was her lot to take on the agonies of the

Apache people and thereby lead them into a better world, a more whole world, a world based on the mystic communion Snake Woman spoke of, not the greed and blood-lust and pillage and war which had characterized their life for all-their-yesterdays, for all-their-seasons-past, since time-when. But had not Cochise said that was the blood-brother's lot, the strange *pindah* who was brother-by-choice to Geronimo? Ah, that was a contradiction. Here at the pole where all was said to be clear and true and absolute she gets a vision—Ghost Owl, as the savior of her people—only to have it contradicted by the words of her late *hunka* father, the great Cochise himself.

But as she meditated the implications of this paradox, the crimson fire-ball swelled monstrously, and again the still, small voice repeated, reduce it, reduce it.

So be it. Slowly putting every ounce of spiritual strength into the labor, repeating over and over to herself, *Fire-ball, you are of my mind, I can do with you as I wish,* she worked on shrinking the magical sphere.

It seemed as though it took forever. Fire, water, earth, sky were born. The gods reigned. The Great-White-Painted-Lady immaculately conceived Child-of-the-Water. They, in turn, saved the Apaches from death, eternal darkness, eternal woe; and the Apache people walked the land, proud and noble and free, fighting Comanche, Spaniard, Mexican scum, and *pindah-lickoyee*. She was born and—

Slowly the ball began to shrink.

The trunk of fire disappeared.

It reduced to a beautiful red globe, sinking into the dusk of a distant desert arroyo, the heat rising out of the gorge met by the sudden, settling cool of the night.

When the stranger appeared.

Stripped to the waist on a big bay horse, a rifle butt-braced on his hip.

Still she could not glimpse the face truce banner, but saw only the eyes, which she now could see filled with hate, implacable, unforgiving.

The recurring nightmare passed before her as it always did, again and again. But this time, through the pistol shots and the rearing of horses, she struggled to fix on the face of the stranger. Even when the Mexican was shot off his horse, and she was clinging to the mount's neck and the stranger swept her off, put her on the neck of his own horse—even then she was twisting her head to see his face, twisting again on the horse's neck, writhing to glimpse the face of the dark-eyed *pindah*.

The field of white-hot fire returned, but now the flames did not scorch. They lapped gently at her body-spirit like the foaming ripples of water in a stream. She felt serenity, and in this fiery vision she saw a speck—first a black speck, but growing larger, larger, as though approaching her from the end of a tunnel. Larger, larger, until it was a face—not a face, but a head tilted down so that the face was angled. She could not make out much, only the eyes which blazed like balefire and which she now knew to be the eyes of the strange *pindah* who in the dream saved her from the evil Mexicans, the strange *pindah* whom she did not fear.

Fear was the last thing on her mind. For now she saw that it was not the languid, fiery pool which was lapping, so gently licking at her body; it was the *pindah* stranger with the obsidian eyes who was caressing her knees and thighs and loins with his dazzling mouth. More, more, deeper, deeper, till his face was buried in her, licking thighs and vulva with infinite caresses.

She could not believe his touch. She a *nah-leen,* not only pure, untouched virgin, but a sacred virgin.

But it was true. It had to be true. At the pole all was just—fair and just and wise.

Now the stranger's face was down in her, and his magic, flickering tongue was perfect, whirling round and round, a sacred sundance spiraling around the-thing-of-joy, till the sun over the stranger's shoulder was no longer a sun, but a red, throbbing button of flesh, human flesh, her flesh, quivering with jolts of pleasure which she could not control, had not experienced, never before dreamed possible.

Again the vision began to expand, only this time her consciousness did not grow to match it. Cracks appeared in the clear, crystalline surface. The central core of her pleasure was erupting in a volcanic frenzy over and over, gasps tearing out of her throat, her body shuddering and sobbing with ecstatic fury.

The cracks in the crystal were growing larger, larger, till half of the vision was breaking up, a great, wrenching coming apart, a tortuous odyssey she was not prepared to make. She was coming, over and over now, violent, shattering climaxes.

And the crystal across the man's face cracked, and the cracks grew wider, wider.

Don't leave, she pleaded with him, his head still down, still circling the source of her joy.

The cracks widened further, and, combined with the angling slope of his face and head, still buried in her pleasure, they were now barely discernible.

Please, I must— See you— I— Must—

Then he was moving up her body, kissing her stomach, probing her navel, carefully caressing her breasts, doing the thing the *pindahs* call the kiss, and which the Apaches find disgusting but somehow was not unpleasing to her.

I— Must—

Then he was kissing her neck, and grasping her cheeks in both hands, stared at her open-eyed, full in the face, kissed her frankly as she opened her mouth, accepted the touch of his tongue on her lips and teeth, returned hers to him.

And then the crystal cracked, shattered, fell apart.

And her body was racked by choking, convulsive spasms.

Come back, please, come back, she was sobbing.

And then there was darkness.

And that was all she knew.

44

It was dark in the wickiup when Ghost Owl came to.

Her body was racked with pain, but that was not what bothered her.

"The stranger, I saw the stranger."

"I know," Snake Woman said gently, placing a poultice of herbs, salt, and ashes on her slashed, swollen back.

"I saw the face. It was his face. The face of the *pindah*. Our blood-brother."

Suddenly, in violation of tribal custom, Geronimo, who had been waiting by the crawl-hole, was crawling into the sacred lodge.

"It could not be him. It could not. You never saw him."

But again she was breaking up, crying uncontrollably, her chin trembling. "But I did. I saw the face, the eyes. I saw him."

"You do not know his face."

"But I know the scars," she said, sobbing convulsively. "On his hands. He put them on my face. I felt the stigmata. The blood-brother stigmata. On my face."

PART VII

45

The stranger with the flat, black eyes worked his way up a steep mountain trail. The going was hard; he was dusty and tired. And above all, hot.

He was doubtful as to how much more his clothes could take before they simply gave out. His collarless tan shirt, threadbare Levi's, and brown Plainsman's hat were heavy with sweat and alkali dust. His square-toed, calfskin boots were run down at the heels. His red bandana had long since rotted away.

The trip had been hard on his stock. The dun-colored packhorse, which he had appropriated from the scalp-hunters, hadn't made it. The big gelding had been a thoroughbred Morgan, used to soft grain and plenty of water. It hadn't done well on mesquite and prickly pear.

The man's Appaloosa, on the other hand, which was bred on forage, was still going. The horse was gaunt and stove up, and the man was not pushing him. For the last five days he'd spent most of his traveling time walking his mount. The big, deep-chested horse with the brown front quarters, white mottled rump, and strangely streaked hoofs had been good to him, damn good. As much as the man was capable of loving anything, he loved that freckled pony. He was not about to ride him into the ground.

The mountain trail gave way to a succession of stone benches, giant irregular steps of shelf rock. With a little encouragement, the Appaloosa headed up the steep incline.

Above the towering stairway the creosote and sagebrush gave way to clumps of bear grass, which yielded in turn to small forests of brush and occasional stands of piñon. The first fingers of the vast pine forests reached down into these foothills, but nopal, prickly pear, and yucca were still as plentiful as in the desert below.

It was an afternoon of agony for the man and his horse. They were both fighting for every breath. Against his will, the man finally had to hang onto the pony's tail, and let the Appaloosa haul him up the rocky incline.

The broken path wound precipitously around deep canyons and twisted through chaotic mazes of massive boulders. The spotted pony clung to the edges of rock-falls, scraped through brush that clawed at the empty saddle and at the man clutching his tail.

Always they climbed, always they squirmed and twisted.

Till the man lost all sense of time, distance, and direction.

46

Then he was climbing up out of the boulders and brush, out of the rock-falls and canyons. He was on a long, even, sloping trail.

He was near Geronimo's stronghold.

Very near.

Great rises of rock with scattered jack pine and juniper jutted against the sky, and Apache sentries were coming out of the cliffs and boulders to stare at him. Stocky, bare-chested men with ebony-black, shoulder-length hair, breechclouts, leggings, and thigh-length moccasins. A few had buckskin shirts, and one wore a blue cavalry blouse with a charred, blood-stained bullet hole through the chest, obviously taken off a dead trooper.

The rise gave way to a fairly level cliff top. The stranger now swung onto the Appaloosa and rode around a cluster of boulders into the rancheria. He was going to see his blood-brother.

He was going to see Geronimo.

He made his way through the legions of curious children, hostile squaws, and yapping camp dogs. The smell of wood smoke, burning sage, and old hides was almost overpowering, and he remembered how much he missed old times and his Apache brothers.

From across the camp, approaching him at an acute angle, was an Indian on a gaudy paint. The Apache rode bareback, clutching only a handful of mane, his presence and poise immense. He rode as though man and horse were one spirit, one flesh. He rode as if the desert were his private domain. As he drew closer, he impressed the stranger as one who knew neither fear nor mercy.

The Indian was Geronimo.

The stranger wheeled his mount around and rode up to meet him.

As he approached, the stranger observed that the Indian had a big head, almost too big for his square, stocky frame. That was the first thing that struck anyone about Geronimo. Then there was the face. It was brown as a hide and had wide, flaring cheekbones. It was deeply marked with planes and angles, and time had furrowed the forehead and gouged crow's feet around the corners of the eyes.

The *pindah* stranger knew his friend's appraisal of himself would be even more severe. The Civil War, eight years on the owl-hoot, three years on the Yuma rock-pile—all those years had taken their bitter toll, left their lines.

The two men were now close enough so that their horses

nuzzled. The Apache bristled and pulled back on the jaw-cord. His paint threw back his head and snorted.

The chief was irate. With the broad-brimmed Plainsman's hat pulled down over the eyes, the *pindah* clothes, and the week's growth on his face, Geronimo could not recognize the pale-skinned stranger before him.

Then the white-eyes hooked a knee around his saddle horn, leaned back against his cantle, and smiled.

There was something in the paleface's smile. Recognition flickered in Geronimo's eyes. But still he scowled, still the hawk-faced countenance was grave.

So the stranger broke the deadlock. Unexpectedly. Unceremoniously. Shockingly. He broke the inviolable taboo of naming names.

And he named his own name.

"It's me. Your old friend, Blood Ant." Geronimo's face gaped in horror, so the stranger quickly added: "Your blood-brother." Geronimo's face still reflected his disbelief, so the stranger raised his right hand and slowly opened it, the inside of the hand turned out.

The palm was transversed by a long, white scar.

The blood-brother stigmata.

Suddenly, a middle-aged woman with a scarred nose and a long, ancient knife wound slashing one cheek rushed out of the crowd. "You're here," she said, crying. "Cochise was right. You've come home."

"Enju." Yes. And then, ruffling the woman's long hair, he said: "I've come home."

47

Then there were four of them—Ghost Owl, Snake Woman, Geronimo, and the white-eyes called Blood Ant. They were sitting around Geronimo's brush wickiup, a big, dome-shaped lodge twenty feet across and fifteen feet high. They sat on deerskin robes and passed the calumet.

Ghost Owl smoked in silence, while Snake Woman rubbed salt, ashes, and herbs into the dark scar tissue of her sundance cicatrices. The healing process was proceeding rapidly. Ghost Owl's only discomfort was mild itching. Her back was improving.

As they passed the ceremonial pipe, Ghost Owl took in Geronimo's home. The wickiup was supported by light mesquite poles, bent and bound together at the top, then thatched with bundles of bear grass. The ground was covered with deerskins, and an old heavy hide hung over the crawl-hole. She glanced casually at the random disarray of his weapons and gear: colorful buckskin blankets, horsehair halters, several three-foot cane arrows fletched with vulture feathers and decorated with red and black bands. Two double-bent bows of oak and mulberry painted black with yellow lightning bolts zig-zagging the twin curves. Wrist quirts, saddle bags, quivers, and bow covers of mountain-lion skin with the fur and tails still on, adorned with sun signs and the wheel-of-life. Several trade knives, a double-barreled shotgun, two repeating Winchesters, a bow drill, flints, and pyrite.

By Apache standards, he was a wealthy man.

At last, Geronimo broke the silence: "My brother, you return. It is good to have you back."

"All rivers return to the sea. I too return."

"But it is so-many-winters you are gone. We wait many seasons. Cochise, especially. He is dead now, you know?"

"I have heard. It shadows my heart," Blood Ant said, emphasizing the words by sign language as well as speaking them.

"It shadowed his heart that you stayed away so long."

"I have made many mistakes. The worst was leaving my people."

"Well, you are here now. Will you tell us of your plans? What it is you wish to do with the-seasons-that-remain, with the rest of your tomorrows? What is it you want?"

"The same thing as always. The same thing as you. Revenge on the blue-bellies."

"Perhaps you would rather revenge yourself on the infidel," Geronimo said with a short, mirthless laugh. "The Apache infidel?"

"No, only the blue-bellies." He fixed Geronimo with a tight stare. "But I see you laugh. Perhaps you lose your stomach for war with the *pindah*."

"*Ha!*" Geronimo shouted sharply. "*Pindah-lickoyee?* Your white-eyed friends? The ones who try to poison, shoot, starve, and imprison us? The governors who pay your *hideputa* scalp-hunters one hundred American dollars for every male scalp? Fifty and twenty-five, they say, for our women and children? Who invite us to feasts, hide their wagon guns behind bushes and rocks, then fire on us?"

"I know."

"Do you remember how they invited Mangas Coloradas and your *hunka* father Cochise to sign the peace paper, then tried to murder them? How they spread-eagled Mangas to a tree and almost flogged him to death with a blacksnake whip? Do you forget the massacre at their Camp Grant? Or their attempts to squeeze and imprison us into reservation-prisons?"

"I remember."

"Then remember this: We are Apache. We live for war. It is our reason for being. To raid, fall back and ambush, torture, loot, and burn. We have always warred. Always. We hunt our enemies just as our northern cousins hunt their buffalo. We harvest the stupid peons of the south just as our Hopi brothers reap their maize. No one remembers a time when the Apache did not raid and plunder and make war. It was always thus."

"*Enju.*" Agreed.

"*Pindah-lickoyee!*" Geronimo spat the words out. "Your white-eyed brothers left during your Great War. They left our land, and again it was ours. Our deserts, mountains, and streams. But the pull of the yellow and white metal was too great. Was that not so? Your people returned."

"I returned, brother."

Geronimo shook with racking laughter. "Yes, but you we understand. You come not for the worthless metal in the ground. Like the Apache, you come for blood."

"Not always, old friend."

"Always!" Geronimo shouted, now angry as though Blood Ant had doubted his word. "Was it not always so? Even as a boy it was thus. That was why your medicine as a warrior was so great. You cared nothing for plunder or valor. Only blood."

"Time-when."

"Time-when? Ten men lie dead on your back-trail, and you say 'Time-when'? Time-now. Time still the same as before."

"Those men, they gave me no choice."

"No *pindah* choice."

"People change. I changed."

"No. Never. Blood is blood. Blood does not change. Or tell me: Are you here to pick mesquite berries and to grind maize on *mano* and *metate* with the old women?"

"One man. I want just one man. The blue-belly that runs the prison just over the border. They call the prison Yuma."

"Why?" The question was Snake Woman's.

"He killed a friend. He beat him to death with a bullwhip, as the *pindah* miners beat Mangas. I was in that prison. The man who died—he was a shaman, a great shaman—he tried to help me. The blue-belly warden killed him for it."

"Your friend is dead? That is nothing. All men die. Forget it, my friend."

"Never."

"Never?"

"Not while I breathe."

Geronimo looked perplexed. "The blue-belly warden is hard to kill. The prison has walls. He stays behind those walls. Always."

"He needs you. You can get him out. He needs you to hunt escaped prisoners. Your cousins did it before, only the ones who did it are dead."

Geronimo's face was an ugly scowl. "They were *mansa* traitors. They deserved that death."

"Yes, but now this warden needs you. No one else will hunt his *escapados*. They fear Geronimo. They fear his wrath."

"With good reason."

"Make a meeting with this man. He'll come to see you."

"Perhaps. But why should I?"

"You say you fight the *pindah*. What you fight are the deadly wagon guns, white-eye soldiers more numerous than the grains of the desert sand. And you fight them with bows and arrows."

"We will fight."

"Not for long. Not without rifles. Many rifles."

"Rifles? Why not speak of wings? Then we could fly. Or lightning bolts. With those we could split the earth."

"I could get you lightning bolts, my friend. I could get you rifles. Repeating rifles."

Geronimo appraised him coolly. "Many rifles?" Slater nodded. "If I set up the meeting with this warden?"

"*Enju.*"

"He will want only me. He fears my *broncos*. He will want only me and my translator." Geronimo pointed at Ghost Owl.

"And your trusty bodyguard." Slater indicated himself.

"He will bring many men. Many blue-bellies."

"I will bring my bullets." Slater fingered the turned-out butts of his holstered Colt and the second one in his belt.

"I don't know."

"You have seen me do it before."

"But what if you fail?"

Slater shrugged elaborately. "It is a good day to die."

"I do not think he will do it."

"Send a man. Ask him. Or contact him on the singing wire."

"I don't know."

"Try it. He'll come. I know he will."

Geronimo looked away, his face anxious. Finally he shook his head no.

Slater hesitated, and then he said it: "*Go-yath-khla,*" calling Geronimo by his childhood name, He-Who-Yawns, and, in doing so, evoking an ancient custom, making his request a matter of Apache honor, sacred duty, tribal trust. "Do it for our people, for the rifles." Then Slater said, his voice harsh: "Do it for me."

PART VIII

48

Then there were two of them, Ghost Owl and Geronimo.

They'd received the return message from Warden Stark, confirming the meeting by the Gila River mouth. And three weeks later, Geronimo and Ghost Owl were riding up a small, arid canyon adjacent to the Gila. Stark and his men had to come through that pass, since the gorge was the major leg of their route between Yuma and the Gila's mouth, and when they did, they would meet Geronimo and the girl head-on.

But the two also had a friend. Blood Ant, dressed only in a breechclout and war paint, had gone up ahead. With four horse pistols holstered to his McClellan and a fully loaded Winchester angling over the pommel, he was prepared to face Stark and his dozen troopers.

It was, indeed, a good day to die.

The night before, Geronimo had asked Ghost Owl for a vision, or at least a sign, presaging the outcome of the inevitable battle. So the Owl had chanted, prayed, and sung.

When no vision came, he asked her for a dream. When no dream appeared, a portent.

And the gods gave her nothing.

So that morning, as they rode up the canyon, she asked her companion: "Tell me, do men like you and your brother-through-choice fear death? Seeing so much? Dealing out so much?"

As their horses picked their way through the stands of prickly pear and the scrub chaparral, Geronimo said:

"I am not sure. I sometimes think we are partly dead already. Each night I hear the owl. Each day I look upon the dead and dying. We see so much death, men like the *pindah* and I, if we'd stopped to hesitate, to ask our fear what to do, we would both be dead already. Many-seasons-past. Time-when."

"But is it not a fearful thing to die?"

"No, but it is bad to be fearful in the face of death. To die badly, to surrender your medicine to your foe, that is not to be borne. Death itself? Nothing. Years ago, Cochise said I would finish up a wrinkled, wizened old man, that I would live for-many-seasons, for-many-tomorrows. Anymore, I find the thought repellent. I have often prayed for the bullet or the blade that would prove Cochise false."

"We have not proved him wrong. Not ever."

"I know. It bothers me. Warriors make poor dotards."

"Do not fear, my friend. 'Only the desert wind blows for-all-tomorrows.' "

Completing the verse, Geronimo said: " 'And only the drifting sands endured time-when.' "

Then, rounding a sharp bend in the canyon wall, they saw them. A line of a dozen troopers riding high-stepping bays. They were hard-looking men, wearing dark blue military blouses with shiny brass buttons flashing brilliantly in the sun. Their sky-blue trousers with the bright yellow stripes running down the outer seams were stuffed into their black, knee-length riding boots. They packed sabers and pistols. Springfield rifles were strapped to their backs, muzzles down.

They were all seasoned veterans. Even Ghost Owl could see that. Above the shoulders, they all looked the same. Long drooping mustaches, battered campaign hats, and the thousand-yard stare.

Only their leader was out of uniform. Like General George Crook, Colonel Stark was dressed in a frock coat, black twill pants, and a white boiled shirt. He wore a black silk plug hat. And a long beard. He was grinning.

He ordered his men to halt and then rode up alone to meet Geronimo and the girl. He leaned against his pommel and looked them over.

"You the translator?" he asked. She nodded. "Geronimo?" he said, motioning to the chief. She nodded again. "Then tell this bronco bastard I'm bringing him in. He jumped the reservation at San Carlo. So did you. You two are celling in Yuma till the Indian agent picks you up. Then it's the reservation guard house, I expect."

"You lied about the job?" Ghost Owl asked matter-of-factly.

The back of his hand whipped against her mouth, and his West Point ring cut her lip.

"I don't need no flat-back, blanket-headed whore tellin' me to—"

"Sir!" a voice barked out behind him.

Colonel Stark raked her up and down with an angry stare, then turned his head to investigate the commotion.

Up the pass was a tall white-eyes dressed only in a breechclout. He was mounted on a big, deep-chested Appaloosa. Red and yellow war paint streaked his cheeks and forehead, and a dazzling yellow sunburst was painted on his bare chest. His hard eyes were black as the grave, flat as a diamondback's. Slowly, his horse began walking toward the queue of troopers.

The last four soldiers wheeled their horses around and rode up to meet him, cautiously fanning out.

Just as in the dream.

Only cavalry, not Mexican, Ghost Owl thought.

When the four were no less than ten feet away, they halted. So did the stranger.

"Yes?" the trooper on the far left asked. *"Enju?"*

"Enju?" the white-eyes repeated.

Then he pulled two Colts from his saddle holsters, and in a burst of gunfire that boomed up and down the canyon as one protracted, echoing roar, he shot the four troopers dead.

Pandemonium reigned.

The eight remaining riders wheeled around to charge the lone stranger, while simultaneously Geronimo leaped off his gray. Reaching under his mount and lifting up the far, rear hock, he put a shoulder into the gray's hind quarters, hard. With a bone-jarring *thud!* one thousand pounds of horse crashed onto the canyon floor. And Geronimo, after whipping his Winchester out of the saddle sheath, was crouching behind the fallen pony, already levering rounds into the melee up-canyon.

Simultaneously, Ghost Owl was in motion. Along her thigh, in the rolled-up portion of her long buckskin moccasin, she had secreted a hide-out pistol. Snaking the .41-caliber Derringer out of the leather, she jumped off her mount straight onto the neck of Stark's roan. Sitting there, nose-to-nose with Stark, one hand on the pommel, the other shoving the pistol into his crotch, she said in perfect English, her voice audible above the thunderous gunshots:

"Don't blink. Don't even breathe. Or I'll blow your *cojones* to Kingdom Come."

Still, out of one corner of the other eye, she watched the battle. Again, it was just as in the dream, only this time it was cavalry, not Mexicans, and now Geronimo was present, crouched behind the fallen gray, levering rounds into the roiling mass of blue-coats. Otherwise, it was the same. The violent white-eyes with the reins in his teeth, and his pistols spitting death, was charging and swerving through the soldiers, who dropped like flies. After one hellish charge through the blue-bellies, he wheeled around, drew two more pistols, and thundered back up the canyon. Ten soldiers lay dead or dying, but two others had continued past him straight up the pass in full rout.

With a spine-chilling war whoop, he galloped after them. Within seconds gunshots roared, and he cantered back.

Meanwhile, Geronimo was up and scrambling over his gray. A dying sergeant with red-orange hair lay a dozen feet to his left. The wound in his chest bubbled sickeningly, and death rattled in his throat.

Geronimo stood over him and stared coolly. Finally, the light went out in the man's eyes, the body settled, and he gazed sightlessly into the late-morning desert sky. Flies were already buzzing over the man's face.

Geronimo bent over him and carefully studied his pate. The red-orange tresses would go well on his scalp shirt.

He decided to take his hair.

He took out his knife and commenced the scalping.

Ghost Owl averted her eyes.

PART IX

49

Nighttime in the rancheria.

For two full moons the people had waited—waited for word of the raiders' success.

Or of their death.

The word was good. The stronghold's scouts reported far in advance of their arrival that the raid had been successful. The two Apaches, the *pindah* Blood Ant, and a captured *pindah* were on their way home, picking their way through the long maze of canyons.

However, no feast was declared. Celebrations were held only when warriors returned victorious—meaning when they returned loaded with booty. Stolen horses and mules, rifles and ammunition, cloth and saddles and bridles, these were cause for days and nights of revelry—for dancing, singing, fornicating, and the drinking of much *tiswin*.

The capture of the lone *pindah* with the beard, the funny hat, and black coat, these were cause only for derision.

Still it was good to have them home, safe and sound.

And when they arrived, and when Geronimo told a few

trusted friends of the battle fought in which many white-eyes died, all were excited. He showed his trusted friends the red-orange scalp he planned to sew into his medicine shirt. Then someone divulged that they had recently cooked a tremendous batch of *tiswin,* or corn beer. Indeed, he had prepared a vast, fifty-gallon *olla* of it, and since *tiswin* rapidly went bad, it was decided perhaps that a feast be held after all. Horses should be slaughtered, huge fires built, the travelers should refresh themselves, and all others should prepare for the dance.

50

By sunset, three great feast fires were blazing in the stronghold. Vast circles of men, women, and children crowded around them. The men danced the kill-tales of past raids and wars, while the women trilled their high-pitched, piercing applause. Other warriors danced out the stories of their bloody battles, danced of the plunder won and the captives taken. The shrill applause to these plunder-tales was deafening, almost ear-cracking.

It was clear that plunder-tales were preferred to those of slaughter.

Even so, Geronimo danced to thunderous trills and tremolos the kill-tale of their latest triumph over *pindah-lickoyee.* He danced out the saga of Blood Ant roaring through the troopers. He told the story of knocking down his horse and of slaying six white-eyes with his many-shot rifle.

And when he told the story of Ghost Owl vaulting the warden's horse and threatening to shoot off his *cojones,* the tribe became hysterical. Everyone leaped and danced. Danced and chanted and sang and laughed. Men took the divorced women—who on such nights were granted tribal dispensation for acts of lewdness—into the bushes. Great gourdfuls of *tiswin* were passed among young and old, male and female, even among the babies strapped to their cradleboards.

The evening became wilder, more licentious, till only the two medicine women, their captive, and their friend Blood Ant hung back. They sat along the far edge of the festivities with Warden Stark, whom they kept bound and gagged.

They talked.

"The party is good, is it not, *pindah*?" Ghost Owl asked.

Blood Ant allowed that it was.

"Among your white-eyed friends there must be many such parties."

"Not really."

"Why?" She was surprised.

"Ain't got many friends. A few scattered here and there. Mostly they be dead."

"Hmmmm," Ghost Owl said with great seriousness, "it is bad to be so alone."

Blood Ant knew that exile was the Apaches' single worst punishment, and he quickly added:

"I'm alone by choice."

"No man is alone by choice," Snake Woman said bluntly. Then, giving Blood Ant a searching look, she continued: "There is much pain in your face, my friend. Much more than when you left us so many-seasons-past."

"I lost much in the white-eyes war," Blood Ant said, revealing more of himself to those two women than he had to all the friends he'd made over all the years since the war. "Maybe I lost everything."

"When you were here, you had everything. You were complete."

"No more. I lost too much to be complete, ever again."

"Ah, my white-eyed friend," Snake Woman said pleasantly, "most men shrink from despair, but not you, yes? What is it? In despair you find your secret strength, your hidden courage? In despair, you have nothing left to lose. Or gain. Or love. Is it not so?"

Blood Ant shrugged. "At least, you are still free."

"No, freedom does not matter to you. For you, it is only

war that counts. You live for blood, only blood. Not this freedom you speak of."

"I used to think so. Then I was in the white-eyes' jail. Oddly enough, I had freedom, or thought I had it for a while. Even with the whips and chains and bars. There was an old man there, a shaman. He taught me about freedom. He taught me I was free."

"In this jail?"

"Yes, in the jail. He said each of us is free, and each of us suffers his freedom."

"This freedom cannot be a very good thing if men must suffer it."

"Perhaps you're right. Freedom is not a gift, he said. He even said that it is bled over on countless battlefields. He said that I myself would endure hunger, fire, even death for my freedom, but that in the end I would find it. He said it was my destiny."

"You must have respected this man very much to have remembered all these things he said."

"He was like a *hunka* father to me, like Cochise. All them years I was rotting in that prison. He kept me alive. He kept me well. And he gave me hope."

"He sounds like a great and wise man," Ghost Owl said. "What did you say happened to him?"

"He's dead. They killed him with a blacksnake whip." Blood Ant pointed at Warden Stark, who lay slumped on the ground. "He beat him to death."

"What will you do to him?" Ghost Owl asked.

"Kill him."

Snake Woman allowed herself a small, ironic smile. "That won't do your friend any good."

"It'll do me some good."

"Will it make you free?" Ghost Owl asked.

"I don't know. This freedom thing is very rare."

"Perhaps," Ghost Owl said, "because it does not exist."

"It exists. That old man showed it to me."

"The freedom to kill?"

"Yes."

"How will you kill this man? Will you hurt him a great

deal? Will that make you feel better? Perhaps you will use a blacksnake whip, as he used on your friend."

"No." And now Blood Ant allowed himself a small smile, the black-fire eyes terrible in their vengeance, the teeth flashing like the steel of knives.

"It will be worse?" Ghost Owl asked, somehow disturbed.

"Much worse."

51

Then it was dawn.

Blood Ant, Ghost Owl, Snake Woman, and Geronimo had taken the warden on horseback into a box canyon several miles below the stronghold. In the gorge there was good, deep sand, and on the floor grew a scattering of creosote, cholla, and prickly pear. They continued on up the canyon until Geronimo pointed out a spot among the boulders.

There were two large conical mounds, perhaps six feet high.

Anthills.

Geronimo dismounted and dragged Stark off his dun. The warden still had his hands tied behind his back and was gagged. But he'd seen the anthills, knew what they were about to do. His eyes were like saucers, rolling wildly. He was jumping up and down and shaking his head. Blood Ant found his behavior a serious embarrassment.

"Are all white-eyes this brave in the face of death?" Geronimo mocked derisively.

"Not all," Blood Ant said.

And he hit Stark in the side of the neck with a looping left hook, knocking him to his knees.

Without further discussion, Geronimo got a rawhide *parfleche* full of two-foot stakes from his horse. He slanted one on each side of Stark's ankles, so that the tops of the pegs crossed, forming an *X*. With rawhide thong, he securely lashed the *X*'s together, then lashed the ankle to the stakes. He continued this procedure with the other ankle, while Blood Ant did the same thing with Stark's wrists and neck.

When they were done, Stark was coming around. Only now he was spread-eagled and immobilized. He could not even raise his head.

Blood Ant took out his sheath knife, slit Stark's befouled long-johns down the arms, legs, and torso, and ripped them off his body.

He then slit the gag and ripped it out of his mouth.

At first, Stark couldn't talk. His throat was parched from the gag, and his vocal cords were still. But finally he choked out the words.

"Jesus, mercy. You're a white man. Please."

But now Geronimo was calling to them, and Blood Ant and the women went to him. He pointed to a crevice in the canyon wall. A big, brown hive around which buzzed hundreds of bees was lodged in there.

"I think your friend would like some honey, no?"

"*Enju.*"

Geronimo took a rawhide sling out of the *parfleche* slung over his shoulder. "I thought we'd need one of these. If we wanted honey."

The sling was a small square of rawhide. The leather was worked soft, and slit near each of the corners to make it more flexible; around two opposite corners rawhide thongs were attached. One thong had a loop at the free end, which was slipped over his middle finger. The other thong was unlooped, and Geronimo held it between his index finger and his thumb.

Geronimo was now glancing around the canyon floor, selecting small rocks the size of eggs. "I haven't done this since I was a boy," he said.

After selecting a dozen small stones, he began slinging them at the hive from fifty feet away. The rocks hit with unbelievable force, and at such a short distance the sling was an accurate weapon. Every one of the rocks hit, and after the dozenth stone smashed into the hive, it shattered.

Of course, this was not the smartest way in the world to

raid a hive. Ordinarily, one would have built a fire under it and smoked the bees out, then taken the honey. This way, one got the honey out, but the bees would still be around and would let you know.

Not that Geronimo seemed to mind. Perhaps he was eager to demonstrate for all those present how a real man stands up to pain. Or perhaps after two straight days and nights of drinking *tiswin*, he no longer cared. In any event, he took the *parfleche* and walked into the middle of the hundreds of buzzing bees. He scooped big handfuls of honey into the bag while the bees buzzed and screamed and whined angrily.

And stung him.

But he kept right on grinning, and returned to the staked-out Stark with a big bag of honey dripping in his hands.

Ghost Owl was absorbed by the spectacle, but when Geronimo began dripping honey into Stark's mouth, nose, and over his genitals, she was sickened.

Then Blood Ant took a gourd dipper out of his saddle bag.

He began scooping holes in the side of the great conical ant mounds. When he got a big dipper full of black ants, he took it over to Stark and poured it across his stomach. Then he went over to the other anthill and did the same thing, only this time he brought back dippers full of red ants.

In a matter of minutes a full-scale ant war joined the two massive hills. Soon it seemed to Ghost Owl as though all the ants in the world were swarming over that patch of earth.

The ants fought as if they were insane, tearing off legs, feelers. They ran in circles half the time, as if they were blind—gnawing, ripping, rending everything in their path.

Their stench was appalling.

As for Stark, Ghost Owl could no longer look at him, or she would have gagged. His body was a writhing, pulsating, squirming mass of red and black ants.

The ones who had gotten into the honey were the worst. They were biting their way through anything to get to it. They were biting through lips, tongue, bone, gums, nose, cheeks, throat. As were the ones who had gotten into the honey-drenched genitals. Scrotum, balls, penis, anus, prostate, and pelvis were slowly eroding before a swarm of crazed ants.

In the end, the only reality enveloping Stark was the ants. No portion of his body was even visible, and all movement, all signs of life, emanated from that one throbbing, writhing reality. Stark had become a living body of warring insects. That was all.

How close he was to death was hard to say. Although he was sustaining enormous pain, the overwhelming violence was being done ant-on-ant, not ant-on-Stark. Though it was not exactly feasible to sit down alongside him and put a mirror to his mouth or check his pulse, it seemed to Blood Ant that after two full hours of torture, the Yuma warden was still alive.

Despite numerous suggestions from Ghost Owl that they leave, Blood Ant hung on, watching. It was almost as though he were waiting for a sign.

The sign came.

It came after two hours of watching the pile of ants vibrate and tremble. It came with a suddenness that horrified the women, amused Geronimo, and amazed Blood Ant.

One eye blinked open.

The act seemed to have affected even the ants. They instantly backed off from the open orb and did not try to devour it. Furthermore, the eye blinked at periodic intervals. Light shined from it. The body was not only alive, the mind was cognizant of what was happening. *Everything* that was happening.

Blood Ant went over to Stark. He bent over the man's body. The eye began blinking rapidly. Recognition. Blood Ant stared at him and shrugged.

"What do you want?"

With infinite, excruciating lassitude, the gnawed remains of the bloody jaw moved. The mouth opened. The interior was hideous to see. Tongue, gums, lips, roof of mouth, anything, everything that had been touched by honey, had been chewed to pieces. The rest of the mouth was filled, literally packed with ants, black and red in equal numbers, most of them dead.

Then the mouth closed.

Slowly, interminably, it proceeded to open again.

Close.

Blood Ant did not have to ask him to repeat the words. Stark had said: "Kill me." He'd asked for mercy, for surcease from suffering.

Geronimo laughed raucously, and his grinning teeth glinted in the desert sun like pearls. "You have done well, my brother, very well," he said. "I am proud of you. You are more Apache than the Apache."

Blood Ant moved away from Warden Stark and continued his pitiless death watch.

Finally Ghost Owl stepped up alongside. "So this is freedom? The thing you spoke so glowingly about? I do not think I like this freedom of yours."

"The *pindah* gods preach an eye for an eye."

"So what is this you preach? A *head* for an eye?"

Blood Ant looked down at the young woman by his side. She was clearly revolted by this savagery. He looked over at Snake Woman as though to study her reaction, but she quickly averted her eyes.

"*Enju*. Maybe so."

He went to the Appaloosa, took his saddlebags off the pommel. He walked back to Stark's spread-eagled, ant-covered body. He bent over him and said:

"Stark? You still there?"

The eye opened and blinked several times rapidly.

He was still there.

"Remember Doc Harper, the man you blacksnaked to death?"

Again, the eye blinked rapidly.

"Okay. Now listen good. Remember Outlaw Torn Slater?"

Again, the eye blinked rapidly.

Blood Ant pulled the saddlebag off his shoulder, lifted the flap, took out a big .45, and cocked it. The eye blinked rapidly several times, then remained open, pleading for the stroke of mercy.

Geronimo saw what was happening, and now he was hot. "No," he shouted from the other side of Stark. "Don't do it!"

But Blood Ant was bending over the spread-eagled, ant-swarming remains. "Remember me," he said, "remember me, Stark." He placed the muzzle carefully over the open eye. "Remember me when the lights go out."

Within the narrow enclosure of the tight box canyon, the roar was ear-shattering.

The bullet entered the man's brain, the body settled, the lights went out.

52

That evening in Ghost Owl's wickiup, she lay on her stomach on a soft deerskin robe, while Snake Woman rubbed herb ointment into her hard, tight, back scars. Then she slowly massaged the muscles around Ghost Owl's neck. When she was done, Ghost Owl rolled over onto her side. She looked up at her friend and said:

"Tell me."

"Tell you what?"

"About the *pindah*. About why you and Cochise never spoke of him."

"Perhaps we thought the *pindah* was dead. It is not our custom to spin lengthy tales of those spirits who have crossed over to the Other Side."

"All right. But now he is alive, and you still never speak of him. What was he like? I want to know."

Snake Woman shrugged. "When the *pindah* was young, he was brave and strong and wise beyond his years. He was the sort of youth that old men listened to. At a very early age, Cochise put him on all the councils, even the war councils. Long before any of the elders listened to Geronimo, long before Geronimo was allowed to sit in, they listened to this white-eyes."

"Is that why Geronimo hates the *pindah*?"

"You have observed that?"

"Yes. Hates and fears him."

Snake Woman looked away. "He always did. Always. Cochise expected great things from the *pindah*. In fact, after Jeffers told him the story of the *pindah* Christ, Cochise became convinced that the young white-eyes would be the Apache messiah. He placed great store in him. This, Geronimo could not stand."

"But the *pindah* left."

"Yes, and it broke Cochise's heart."

"But still Cochise believed that the young man would return."

"No, he *knew* he would. But he also feared it would be too late."

"Is it?"

"Who knows? He comes with the promise of many rifles. With enough of the many-shot rifles we could hold out a long time, a very long time."

Snake Woman rubbed tobacco between her palms, then filled the black obsidian bowl of her ceremonial calumet with it. She picked an ember out of the lodge fire with a forked stick, and in the proper manner, careful not to touch the sides of the bowl, she lit the pipe. She offered smoke to Spirit-Above, Spirit-Below, and to the four cardinal directions, starting in the east.

She offered the smoke to Ghost Owl, who sat up and graciously accepted. When she returned the smoke to Snake Woman, she said:

"A question."

Snake Woman nodded.

"The recurring fear-dream. The one in which I am a captive of the Mexicans, and I am saved by the terrifying stranger. You know the dream."

"It was your youth-dream."

"Was it? Was it a dream?"

Snake Woman looked away and said nothing.

"I had the dream at the pole. Not as a vision, but not as a dream. I believe I saw truth at the pole."

"Perhaps it is yet to be."

"No, I experienced something similar, though it was not with Mexican bastards, but with the blue-coat soldiers. But the man in the dream was the same. He looked the same, fought the same. The man was the *pindah*. I believe this thing is no dream. I believe it happened before.''

Slowly, Snake Woman met her stare. ''Cochise felt it wise not to tell you. I concurred.''

''Then tell me now. I am not a babe strapped to my cradleboard.'' Ghost Owl's voice was tinged with anger.

Snake Woman nodded her agreement. ''When you were little more than a babe, perhaps four seasons, scalp-hunters raided your village. They massacred almost everyone. Scalped them for the money. You, they took captive.

''The *pindah* would have been only a boy. Ten-and-six winters. No more. He and Geronimo were hunting, scouting around, and learned from a survivor that you were taken captive. They agreed to go after you. He had only a pair of saddle guns, but he knew how to use them. Geronimo had his rifle.''

''Why was I never told?''

''Geronimo behaved badly. The *pindah* cut the scalp-hunters off in a canyon, while Geronimo kept to the high rimrock with his rifle.''

''Yes?''

''Geronimo never fired a shot. Fear, hatred for the *pindah* who now was taking on the eleven armed scalp-hunters alone—we never knew. Perhaps he wanted the *pindah* to die in the canyon, just as he'd wanted the ants to kill him the time they freed him instead.''

''How do you know all this?''

''I was with Geronimo on the rimrock. I saw. I also saw that there was one surviving scalp-hunter with a gun, and the *pindah*'s were empty. Geronimo was going to let his brother-friend die. So I hit Geronimo with a rock, wrestled the rifle from him, and killed the scalp-hunter. When the *pindah* looked up, he saw it was me with the rifle.''

''Why was no one ever told?''

''The *pindah* and I went to Cochise. We said it was not safe to send Geronimo out on further war parties. We no longer trusted him. Cochise said something different. He said that now Geronimo would become a truly great warrior. He would run from this act of cowardice by fighting more fiercely than any Apache alive. If we did not destroy him first by denouncing him as a coward. So we spoke with him and gave him another chance. Cochise was right. Geronimo became a fierce warrior. The fiercest warrior."

"After the *pindah* left?"

"After the *pindah* left."

They were silent. Ghost Owl finished the smoke and emptied the ashes into the lodge fire. Finally, she broke the silence.

"Sister-friend, another question. Why did Geronimo scar your face?"

"I'd had five husbands before I met Geronimo. I'd buried them all. I'd had many lovers. Geronimo was one of them. He wanted something more. He wanted marriage. I did not."

"So?"

"I went to the wickiup of another man one night. He found out and cut me."

"Geronimo had not the right. You were no wife to him."

"*Enju.* Cochise made him do a hard penance. Geronimo gashed his arms and legs many times. He went out in the desert and wallowed in the dust. He chanted, sang, prayed. Cochise had once again told him he had offended the gods."

"But Geronimo did not gash his face?"

"No, only mine."

Ghost Owl gave her sister-friend a searching look. "Tell me, did the *pindah* ever take a wife?"

"No, he was quite young."

"Did he ever take a woman?" Ghost Owl could see irritation on her sister-friend's face.

"You ask too many questions. I return to my lodge. I am older than you. My bones need rest."

"Then I ask you by your name. You cannot refuse me then. It then becomes a sacred honor you would not violate."

"Watch me."

"Snake Woman, I ask you by your sacred name. Did he ever take a woman?"

"Yes. A *bi-zhahn*. It is legal and proper for a single man to take a *bi-zhahn*, a formerly-married-woman."

"Who?"

"It was I. I admired the *pindah* for what he did for you. And I despised Geronimo. That night I went to the *pindah*'s wickiup."

"And Geronimo cut you for it? How did the *pindah* respond?"

"He wanted to kill Geronimo, but Cochise forbade it. So the *pindah* ripped Geronimo's quirt from his wrist, dragged him into the center of the rancheria, and nearly beat him to death with it. He beat him till he whimpered and sobbed." Snake Woman was glaring at Ghost Owl, her eyes angry at having been forced to reveal these ancient feuds.

"One more question."

Snake Woman shrugged.

"Was he any good? The *pindah*?"

Snake Woman stared at her young friend a long, hard minute, then nodded once. Slowly.

Ghost Owl reached out and touched her sister-friend's arm affectionately. "My closest friend, you are still a desirable woman and could have other men. Apaches do not mind scars. Yet you have told me that you have not had a man for many winters, for many-seasons-past. Not since Geronimo cut you?"

"*Enju.*"

"That was long ago."

"So? I have had my pleasure. Many times. For me the earth has shaken six times. Six full times. How many other Apache women can say that?"

Again, Ghost Owl touched her friend's arm, a rare expression of affection. "Tell me," she said, "just between friends. What were the men like? What were the occasions?"

"There was only one occasion, one man."

"What?" Ghost Owl was confused.

"They were all that night. All with him."

Ghost Owl stared at her friend in stunned silence. "And after *that* the *pindah* left?"

"*Enju.* He went off to fight the white-eyes war." Snake Woman gave her young friend a gentle smile. "Now I've answered enough of your prying questions. It is time for me to rest. Let me go. Do not call me by my name again." She began moving toward the crawl-hole.

But Ghost Owl stopped her. "Sister-friend, these men you had, they are too-many-seasons-past. You could still have other men. Just because of one night?"

"It was enough. I have had my pleasure."

"It was time-when," Ghost Owl said, indicating time long-gone and out-of-mind.

"*Enju.* Time-when. And for-all-tomorrows."

Slowly, Snake Woman pushed the hanging hide away from the hole and went out into the night.

53

Lost in thought, Ghost Owl strolled through the rancheria. By now all that was left of the three-day party were a few bitter-enders, passing gourd dippers of *tiswin,* their attempts at laughter cracked and tired, their speech slurred. The rest of the tribe, women and children, too, were sleeping off their hangovers.

Without thinking, she found herself drawn toward the *pindah*'s lodge. The deerskin over the crawl-hole was skewed and half open. She was a dozen feet away, and she dropped to her knees and looked in. She could see him in the dim, flickering light of the lodge fire. He was sitting on a robe at the far end of the wickiup, his back to the door. Slowly, she stood. She walked over to the crawl-hole and said:

"*Pindah*? May I enter?"

He turned, looked at her, and waved her in.

She sat across the fire from him on a buckskin blanket. He was sitting with his side to her now, reading a paper. As he looked over the writing, she took the opportunity to examine him more closely. He was wearing only a breechclout and leggings, and was naked from the waist up. She had seen him that way before, but only from a distance. Now she studied him closely.

First, she noted his muscles. They were not of smooth, rolling tissue like an Apache's. His back muscles were massive and bunched, the shoulders huge, blocklike, the biceps heavy and large-veined. He had the legs of a runner, true, but even there the calf and thigh muscles strained against the buckskin leggings. This was the strongest man she'd ever seen.

Then there were the scars. A long, diagonal knife scar, reddish-brown, transversing his torso from shoulder to hip. And above the right clavicle, the big, puckered bullet hole which seemed to exit and erupt laterally below the shoulder blades in a spectacular starburst of brilliant, bone-white scar tissue. It must have passed within an inch of the heart, she thought. And it was impossible to miss the heavy shackle scars on the wrists and ankles. Or the long, white blood-brother stigmata on his palms. Or the broad, white stripes of Yuma prison which he wore on his back. It seemed as though not a square inch of his body had escaped.

He finally looked up from the paper and fixed her with a level, but not unfriendly, stare. "Yes?"

"*Pindah*, I do not understand you. I do not understand this thing you speak of, freedom."

"I do not understand it either."

"Is it truly a gift? Are we born with it?"

"Perhaps."

"If so, then why are so many of us, *pindah* and Apache alike, in chains? Why are the black-skins bought and sold like beasts of burden? Why do you wear the shackle and whip-marks of prison on your ankles, wrists, and back?"

"That one's easy," he said. He tossed her the piece of paper.

She looked at it and gasped. At the top of the paper was an extremely accurate portrait.

Of the *pindah*.

"They have stolen your medicine," she said fearfully.

"No," the *pindah* laughed, "the drawing has no magic. If it did, I would not be here. If it did, I, not Stark, would be feeding the ants."

Still she stared at the portrait, dumbstruck.

"Read the writing aloud," the *pindah* said. "The name included. Read."

She looked up, and he was smiling widely. She shook her head and read:

WANTED: TORN SLATER
FOR TRAIN ROBBERY, BANK ROBBERY, AND MURDER.
FAST, ACCURATE PISTOL SHOT
AND NOTORIOUS KNIFE SPECIALIST.
THIS MAN KILLS WITHOUT HESITATION AND
IS EXTREMELY DANGEROUS.
TORN SLATER,
WANTED IN 13 STATES AND
TERRITORIES.

$20,000 REWARD
WANTED—DEAD!

She finished the reading and handed him back the paper.

"That's what's called a 'dodger,' or a 'wanted' poster," he said.

"Are there many of them?"

"Thousands. A lot of them are in Spanish, too. Seems I'm also wanted in Mexico. All of which is by way of explanation. I'll be pullin' out at first light. You people've done enough to help me. I don't want to be bringin' no more trouble down on your heads."

"But we will see you again, no?"

"Next time you see me, it should be with freight wagons full of rifles. Otherwise, you can just figure I'm dead."

"You bring us no trouble. I do not believe that."

"Some might differ," he said, indicating the "wanted" poster.

"You must be a very great man to be so feared by the entire *pindah* people."

"Scarin' people don't make a man great."

"Yes, but look at them. They try to steal your soul by printing your name and drawing your face. And they do not succeed. You must have very great medicine."

"That's goin' some."

Ghost Owl looked at the *pindah*. She could grow to like this face. And the modesty. The other men she'd known would have preened and puffed at the slightest hint of a compliment, but not the *pindah*. She had not expected this.

"White-eyes, I understand you saved my life when I was a little girl. I'd been captured by scalp-hunters. You came after me."

"The memory escapes me." He was watching her closely.

"You killed them all. Or almost all. Anyway, you brought me back. To Cochise. You gave me life."

"Anything you say."

"So I wanted to thank you. Thank. That is a *pindah* word, is it not? I know no Apache equivalent."

"Look, assumin' that was true and assumin' you wanted to thank me, you done that by the Gila. You done more than that."

"No, you gave me life. I only helped you get revenge."

"I don't see it that way."

"Perhaps life to you is revenge. Perhaps men like you know only revenge."

"No doubt. Anyway, I got some hard travelin' tomorrow and need my rest. If you don't mind, you'll be leavin' now and I'll be turnin' in."

Ghost Owl stood up, but, instead of leaving, crossed over to Slater's side of the fire.

"First, I want you to show me something."

Slater looked skeptical.

"It is what the white-eyes call the kiss."

"Now look—"

"You saved my life. I only want to thank you in the fashion of your own kind."

"Not likely. You be a *nah-leen,* a fuckin' hair-bow virgin. I am not about to—"

Then she was on him, in his lap, her mouth on his, her hands behind his neck. Then, as in the dream, their mouths were opening, and when his tongue did not respond, she moved hers into his mouth, rimmed his lips and gums and teeth with it, probed in and out back and forth, tasting the sweetness therein.

At first, he attempted resistance, so she reached a hand inside his breechclout, grabbed his member, and squeezed as hard as she could. He groaned unbearably and whispered:

"Damn, I hope you ain't threatening to shoot it off like you did Stark."

But he was falling backward, and all resistance was gone. "Show me," she was whispering, "show me this *pindah* kiss."

He showed her. He showed her how to kiss languidly, delicately; he showed her kisses of infinite tenderness alternating with kisses of terrifying passion on the mouth, eyes, in the ears, and along the throat and neck.

Then his kisses worked down her body, along the arms and chest, down the stomach, probing her navel, working their way along the inside of her thighs—wet, licking kisses. Then back up the thighs, and slowly, tenderly as in the dream, he gradually encircled the vulva.

But now it was more than a dream, it was a vivid reality which no hallucination, even at the pole, could match. Sharp jolts were shooting through her vulva like tremendous shocks, and the hard nub of pleasure which he tongued was on fire. This little button, this most intimate ally, this secret sharer to whom Ghost Owl had confided her most private fantasies—it was as though her little friend were now telling them all to the *pindah*. For there seemed to be nothing about her he did not know. Every square inch of her seemed to be crying out to him that she was his, all his, that all he would ever have to know of her, he knew already, and the truth was being proven right now, even as he kissed and caressed the wondrous thing between her legs.

She started to groan, and she cursed herself for it. She, the woman who had borne the agonies of the pole without a whimper, was now being rendered a mewling babe by this man. She could not bear the humiliation, and gathering up all the courage and will power in her, she clenched her teeth and bit off her groans and squeals. She swore to be brave, as brave as the day when Snake Woman drove the skewers through her back and hoisted her over the ground.

Only now he was crossing the bar, making brief *X*'s and

dashes across her hidden islet, that forbidden no-man's-lan
which she'd always believed to be inviolable and sacrosanct
So there was no help for it. She was worked up to a feve
pitch. Now she was ready, and he was all over the button
molding it expertly with both tongue and lips, sucking
squeezing, kneading, cajoling.

Then she was off.

A wagon-load of gunpowder, a warehouse full of dyna
mite, all the volcanos in Mexico were going off between he
legs. And maybe she could be brave and strong and true a
the pole, but not now. The groans and squeals and sobs wer
tearing out of her throat repeatedly. Slater had to clamp
hand over her mouth, and when she tasted the salt sweat o
his palm and felt the long line of the blood-brother stigmatum
it only served to heighten her ecstasy. She struggled t
wrench his hand away and scream out her desire till the sob
were choking out of her over and over and over, and she wa
falling down a black, bottomless abyss.

Mother, Son, and Holy Ghost.

Holy Ghost Owl.

Owl.

Slowly, she pulled out of the abyss. She felt alive, free
That was it, free. What the *pindah* had told her of freedom
She thought she understood it now. Yes, this was it. This ha
to be it. If this wasn't freedom, what was?

She was lying on her back on the soft buckskin robes
looking up at the white-eyes. She was smiling.

"What's so funny?" he asked.

"You, me, everything."

"You know I really have to go."

"Not till I tell you to," she said.

"What do you want?"

"Everything. I want you to do everything to me. Show m
everything. Teach me everything. Then teach me to d
everything to you."

"That's a tall order for a little girl."

"Then you will make me a big girl overnight."

"You are *nah-leen*." Virgin. "I've left you that way."

"I am shaman. The silly customs of this tribe do not apply

I am immaculately conceived by the lightning. My mother is the White-Painted-Lady, and I frolic with the Water-Child. My playthings are the *gans,* and I have power over grizzlies, snakes, and the owl. I am the Owl."

"I don't know."

"You have no choice."

"Why?"

"The Owl even has power over you. Witch power."

"Are you sure?"

"Just watch."

Slowly, she rolled down his leggings. With gentle respect, she took off his breechclout. Then she commenced kissing his mouth and eyes and ears and neck.

With infinite care, infinite cunning, she began working her way down his chest.

54

Geronimo sat alone in a dark wickiup. And drank. For three days and nights Geronimo had stayed drunk on *tiswin.* The last several months had been hard on him, harder than anything he'd ever known. The bad dreams, the return of Blood Ant, the capture of the *pindah* warden. Now the painful bee stings.

And worst of all was Ghost Owl.

She was really at the bottom of it. He had to save her. She had total control over his heart, head, and balls. He had to have her—had to. He had to have her, even if he hung for it. It meant that much. He'd have sold his soul to the foulest fiends of the underworld for just one night.

It was worth everything to him.

Everything.

He knew now there was only one strategy. Complete surrender. He would go to her. Lay bare his chest. He would tell her that he was hers and hers alone. All that he had, even his life, was hers. His horses, his rifles, his wealth. All the rifles that the white-eyes promised to bring. They would be hers. He would worship at her feet, be her servant, her slave.

The sun was up. He stumbled drunkenly out of his wickiup. Crossing the rancheria, staggering and weaving, he finally made his way to her wickiup, and, without even calling out, pushed aside the deerskin and entered.

It was empty.

He crawled back out and stood up. The deer bladder of *twisin* was still clenched in his fist, and he felt an uncontrollable need to talk and to drink with someone. If not the Owl, someone else. His eyes scanned the tops of the wickiups for smoke, for someone awake. Someone important like himself. Someone who would understand.

In this terribly hungover Apache dawn, smoke curled from the dome of only one lodge.

The *pindah's.*

So much the better. He would talk to his brother-friend. The *pindah* would understand. He would understand the despair of being separated from the one you loved. The *pindah* a man lost between two worlds—the one dead to him, the other incapable of being born. The *pindah* would understand the anguish in Geronimo's heart. He would make him understand.

Stumbling drunkenly across the rancheria, he made his way to the *pindah's* lodge. Pushing the deerskin aside, he crawled halfway through the hole.

Then froze.

There, on a deerskin robe lay the Owl. Her long, beautiful hair, black as a raven's wing, was disheveled.

And encrusted with the *pindah's* glistening lust.

His eyes continued down her half-exposed, heavily used body, and he instantly recognized the tell-tale signs. Breast and neck, red from sucking and kissing. Cheeks streaked with the smeared tracks of *pindah* passion. And worst of all, between her legs.

The clotted blood of her lost *nah-leen* virginity caked with his white, dried-up come.

And all the *pindah's* possessions, gone.

Geronimo quickly left the wickiup. He had to catch up to the *pindah*. After such an affront, he had to kill him. Kill him, or kill himself. He raced across the rancheria, down into the valley, to the pony herd. He would catch the *pindah* as he saddled his Appaloosa.

But from the top of the hill overlooking the valley, he could already see that in the remuda there was no beautiful spotted pony with the brown forequarters and the white, freckled rump.

Gone.

The *pindah* was gone.

There on the hill, Geronimo fell to his knees and sobbed. He did not care who saw him. He could not stand it any longer. He could not endure it any longer.

Because he knew deep inside that it did not matter if he caught the *pindah*. He could not take him. He'd tried before. And failed. It would do no good. He could never kill the white-eyes.

He never could.

He never could.

The *pindah* was gone.

Gone.

BOOK III

My friend, will you never understand? I do not want my enemies' respect. Nor do I trust to the loyalty of my men. I trust fear. By Christ's bones, by His bloody nails, will you never see? This "human dignity" and "freedom of man" you so glowingly expound on, does not apply to these Aztec aborigines. Without my violent intervention, they would once again be choking on human blood, devouring each others' flesh, sacrificing their daughters' vaginas to barbaric priests and pagan gods. Free these people, you say? I do not want them free. I want them branded, shackled, and ruled by the whip. I want them laboring in our mines and factories and fields until they drop. And when they can work no more, even then, I do not want them living in this *liberté, egalité, fraternité* you speak so luminously of. I want them dead.

—Porfirio Diaz, President of Mexico from 1877 to 1910

Pity poor Mexico: so far from God, so close to the United States.

—Porfirio Diaz

PART X

55

A man and his horse stood at the edge of a dense colony of prickly pear and stared out over a hot desert flat at the fortified hacienda beyond. He was tall, angular, with a brown hawk face, a hooked nose, lines deeply etched around the eyes. His name was Immanuel Carpenter, and while the name and and the nationality were technically *gringo*, he was half Mexican—that is, one-half *indio puro*.

The mount was a beautiful roan war-horse. The animal had been trained not to spook at a cannon's concussion or the Gatling gun's hammering roar. He was the epitome of patience. As the man quietly surveyed the scorching plain and the distant hacienda, pausing only to boot the cinch up another notch, the horse never flinched. The big gelding stared ahead blankly, interrupting his unblinking gaze only to crop a nearby mesquite bush occasionally.

The man let out a long, slow sigh. He took off his red felt sombrero with the fancy gold embroidery. He beat the dust out of his black *charro*-style pants—loose around the thighs, tight around the knees and ankles. He slapped the dust out of his white peasant's shirt of bleached homespun cotton. The black gun belt with the cross-draw holster and the knee-high riding boots, both of imported French calfskin, he did not bother with. Nor did he touch his big, blue-steel .45 with the ebony grips. He'd checked the heavy Colt before getting up.

The blood-red ball of sun was rising just above Diaz's sprawling hacienda, the most lavish in all of Mexico. By the end of the year Diaz was expected to be *El Presidente,* not merely *Generalissimo* or *Excelencia.* While he awaited this ascension to the Presidency, his personal safety was of no small concern. The high, white corner walls of the great estate were surmounted by Gatling guns, ringed by sandbags and embrasures with firing steps. A battery of nine Napoleon cannons—aging but still effective relics of the War Between the States—was concentrated behind elaborately reinforced breastworks directly in back of the main wall. These were the big guns that at Tejada had blasted the army of Sebastian Lerdo to bits, establishing Porfirio Diaz as the premier military leader of Mexico. These were the cannons which would defend Don Porfirio against all adversaries. Here at *El Alacrán.* The Scorpion.

Carpenter stared out over the sweltering plain. It was hardly dawn, and already the desert floor was shimmering with heat waves, the big hacienda across the blistering flat now wavering in and out of focus.

Yes, with its remote location, its high ramparts, and precipitous four-thousand-foot drop-off behind its rear wall, with its Gatlings and battery of Napoleons, *El Alacrán* seemed impregnable.

Then why did Diaz want Immanuel Carpenter, *gringo* gun-runner and arms specialist? Why did Diaz send for him, asking for more big guns? Why summon a radical revolutionary such as Carpenter, who had supported Lerdo, opposed Diaz, and, indeed, supplied all his enemies with the guns which had nearly destroyed Don Porfirio?

Immanuel Carpenter would soon find out.

He swung onto the big roan, headed him down the rise, and out across the hot, red plain.

By dusk he hoped to make *El Alacrán*.

56

By nightfall, the man and the big roan were close to the massive hacienda. Scouts and sentries had been stopping him for the last several miles, but, seeing his letter of transit, they not only let him pass but sent back word informing others to let this half-*gringo* through. All knew the price for deviating from his *Excelencia's* wishes. All knew of the dark, windowless rooms under the hacienda, rooms soaked with blood and resonant with the howls of tortured *soldados*. And of the *flagellente* Franciscans before them. And, some said, of the ancient Aztecs before them. All knew the penalty for violating his *Excelencia's* express commands.

El Alacrán was known to the men as *El Palacio del Miedo*, or the Palace of Fear.

Carpenter knew the stories and saw the fear on the faces of the sentries when they noted the Diaz seal on his letter of transit. Don Porfirio's ruthlessness had always been legendary, but, seeing the terror in his men, the Gatlings on their high gun platforms, and the long line of Napoleons, the force of his reputation was driven home hard.

His roan trudged wearily toward the redoubt, the saddle creaked, the bits clinked, and the hoofs thudded dully on the hard, dry sand as Immanuel Carpenter reflected on Diaz and his erstwhile mentor, Juarez.

Juarez. At the very thought of the man, Carpenter smiled. There was a man who would reign in *la gloria*. He caused peoples of all colors, of all languages, of low and high birth to throng the public squares screaming with one voice: *"Viva la Libertad! Viva la Revolución! Viva Mejico! Viva Juarez!"*

He told these throngs—and made them believe—that when the freedom of Mexico and her people was at stake, they had only two choices: Victory, or the sanctity of death. He routed France, shot Maximilian, liberated the people, fought the vast power of the church, and reformed the land. He had more than a talent for making men fight. He had a faith that touched men's souls, and made men brothers. His statues stood in a thousand *zocales,* while none stood for Maximilian. For if Juarez had been the soul of Mexico, Maximilian was the boot. If Juarez had stood for the dignity of man and opposed the ruthless tyrannies of the *buena gente* and the hacienda system, Maximilian had stood for the shackle and the whip. And when Juarez died, his passing left more than a break in Mexico's leadership, it left a void in her people's heart.

Diaz? Thinking of Don Porfirio made Carpenter strangely uneasy. Diaz had been the most ferocious and successful of Juarez's generals. Juarez had referred to him as my *culebra de cascabel,* or "my rattlesnake," and my *bastardo.* After Juarez's ascension to the Presidency, he retired Diaz, confiding the reasons to his closest associates: "The man is a complete animal. Do not let him near political power. Ever. He sees men as tearing, rending, and clawing for the top of a hill, with himself at the summit. In his heart there is a vast darkness, a gaping nothing. He was once useful because he liked to watch men die, and with so much killing we needed him. But those times are over."

But Diaz's time was not past. France again threatened to invade Mexico's shores. The United States gazed fondly at Sonora and Chihuahua provinces. Mexico's own politicians wrangled like schoolchildren. Generals raised armies in the name of *"la Revolución"* and waged bloody civil war. The country teetered on the brink of dissolution.

Now only one man had the brains and strength and determination to put Mexico back on her feet. Diaz. Whether he had the grace to raise her people up and make them brothers, whether he had the vision to grant them dignity and peace, Carpenter did not know. That Diaz loved his country, of that the gun-runner was sure. But whether Don Porfirio loved her people, of that Carpenter could not say.

Only one thing was certain: If Diaz did not take the reins of state, anarchy would soon engulf the land.

And if he did not get his guns, he would never come to power.

57

Now Carpenter was only a few hundred yards from the square white walls of the hacienda, riding through the camp of the *peon* foot soldiers. These men were the guts of Diaz's private army, a rugged infantry of peasants. Their uniform was the same as those tilling the soil. White, loose-fitting trousers and blouses woven from coarse, homespun *maguey*. Their heads were covered with wide, straw sombreros, and their feet with rope-soled sandals. For weapons, they carried ancient, smooth-bore, muzzle-loading muskets of a dozen calibers . . . Sharps, Spencers, Springfields, Starrs, Gallaghers, Maynards, Ballards, one ancient Remington Joslyn, he noted, a Smith, a Burnside, Sharps & Hankins, and an occasional Enfield. They were commanded by officers in crude uniforms of dusty green.

On and on his horse trudged, through the long rows of whitewashed adobe barracks, past stables and corrals, through the drill field, and around the cook fires. On all sides, the *peon* soldiers were busy. They shingled roofs, repaired the telegraph, dug new breastworks around the camp, and drilled in the hot westering sun.

Carpenter observed the signs of Diaz's stern discipline. Here by the cook tent, a soldier was forced to stand "on the chimes"—barefoot on the rim of a barrel. Over by the stables, two soldiers were spread-eagled on wagon wheels. Another trudged across the parade ground, bent under an eighty-pound log. Another was strung up by the thumbs from a barracks beam, his face ashen, contorted with pain.

The Don's touch was everywhere.

Now Carpenter was approaching the fortified breastworks.

These rows of trenches extended a good hundred yards in front of the wall. Each was nine feet deep, the same across, and every dozen or so feet, firing steps were embrasured. Sally ports were built up for counterattacks by Diaz's own mounted cavalry. Carpenter understood that Diaz had over two hundred crack *cuirassiers*, Spaniards who'd fought with Maximilian. These troopers were battle-tested, as good as any who had served under Mosby, Stuart, or General Jo Shelby. They rode like Comanches, thought like Apaches, and fought like Quantrill's Raiders.

Carpenter took the roan over a small, wooden bridge spanning the first of the long rows of breastworks, and nodded casually to the Spanish cavalry men lounging in the trenches. They stared back at him with dark, empty, battle-weary eyes, pulled down the ancient, battered campaign hats, and looked away.

If the *peon* foot soldiers were the guts of Diaz's army, these *cuirassiers* were the shock troops, the hard, sharp point of Diaz's lance.

Carpenter made his way till he reached the last breastwork, beyond which was the wall. It was twenty feet high, six feet thick, built of heavy adobe blocks, whitewashed to a glistening alabaster.

The wall had no gate, and could be breached only by a covered passageway that went partly under and partly through it. This tunnellike entrance was as wide and deep as a Conestoga, and sealed at both ends by massive oak doors, secured at night by massive crossbars.

He waved his letter of transit to a guard high up on the wall, who signaled the other side. Slowly, the oak door groaned, opened, and Carpenter passed through.

Inside sprawled the *plazuela*. This great courtyard was four hundred feet across and equally wide. Huge cottonwoods and piñon pines were scattered across the square and loomed over the walls and the main house. The grounds were of packed earth, flat and hard as stone.

Carpenter crossed the *plazuela* and tied up the roan at an ornate brass hitch rack. He swung off his mount slowly, loosened the cinch, and tossed a stirrup over the horn. He gave the hacienda a careful scrutiny.

Four stories, white adobe, it was surmounted by a massive red tile roof. In the front of the building, under the broad overhang, was a great veranda, replete with huge white Corinthian columns and hand-carved, scroll-pattern corbels. Carpenter climbed up the front steps, and when he reached the top, the door was opened by a *majordomo*.

The man was in red livery, and his nervousness, along with his pipestem neck and protuberant teeth, made him look even thinner than he was. *"Señor Car-pen-tor?"*

Immanuel Carpenter nodded, and the fidgeting, angular servant held the door wide.

Carpenter entered directly into the grand hall. The *sala* was a vast, sprawling room filled with light which filtered through leaded stained glass in bright, iridescent patterns on the high, thick ceiling beams and the polished mahogany floors.

But more than the windows, more than the gleaming floors, the high ceilings, the ornate furnishings, the thing that struck Carpenter was the walls. They were so incredibly white. Every vertical surface, from the *plazuela* to the interior of the main house, truly shone. The whole hacienda sparkled with white *gesso*, the gypsum deposited along the nearby rivers. Dwellings all over Mexico, from those of the richest *grandees* to those of the lowest *peons*, scintillated with this glowing alabaster. The *gesso* was crushed and powdered, mixed with water, and applied with woolly sheepskins in the style which their forebears had brought from Spain and which the Moors had practiced a thousand years before Christ.

Now, in a land of so much dirt, bloodshed, and darkness, dazzlingly white dwellings stood in stark, ironic contrast to the reality of Mexico's existence.

Carpenter stared out over the room, and studied its furnishings. A half-dozen chairs were grouped in the center of the *sala*. Tall, narrow, ramrod straight, with the arms and legs uncomfortably high. They were of intricately carved wood, teak and mahogany, draped with colorful leathers, rich Valencian velvets, golden laces, and gaily festooned with silken fringe. Beside the chairs were teak tables, intricately carved, and the ubiquitous *vargueños*. These ornate Castilian chests with many tiny drawers and hidden compartments were heavily inlaid with silver and gold and ivory.

At the far end of the room was a wall-sized fireplace of black Carrara marble threaded with fine, golden veins. Its hearth was granite, and heavy, smoke-blackened fire tools hung in its massive aperture. Before the fireplace stood a long, narrow table set with silver salvers and goblets, with antique silver decanters in its center. A dozen high-backed chairs with long, stiff arms were set about the table.

Turning his head, Carpenter noted that the room was empty of all religious artifacts. A curious anomaly in fanatically Catholic Mexico. No statutes of saints, no crucifixes, no religious paintings. The only wall decorations were gilt-framed mirrors.

He heard a man shout: *"Señor* Carpenter." When he turned, he saw Porfirio Diaz crossing the room toward him.

Big, with a stocky frame, a square head. Under the drooping mustache, wide, white teeth. He wore tan twill pants, heavy boots, and a light green campaign jacket. A short sword hung from one side of the belt, a holstered double-action Adams revolver from the other.

Both men quickly closed the distance between them. Folding one another in their arms, with two quick slaps apiece on the shoulders, they gave each other the *abrazo*. Then Diaz backed off, and said softly: *"Compadre."*

Compadre. In Mexican, meaning "co-father"—a sacred bond of friendship which remains whole unto death and is breached only by the most violent of passions.

Diaz said with animation: "Ah, my friend, when did we meet last? Face to face? It was *Cinco de Mayo,* was it not? Do you remember it?"

"I am not likely to forget it."

"You remember how you and I rode through the dust and

smoke, surrounded by the wretched screams, the howls and groans, the piles of corpses and shattered trees, and the earth itself smoking like it was on fire?''

"And then that shell hit?"

"Yes, *amigo,* it detonated less than a dozen feet to your right. Your body saved me from the impact, but you were deaf and mute for days, drifting through the battle in that blasted void like a broken spar in a bloody sea, with death blowing through us like a hot, black wind.''

"You pulled me through that battle, Don Porfirio. You saved my life.''

Diaz threw his head back and laughed. "But of course, *compadre.* You were supplying me with my guns. I could not afford to lose my arms and munitions. Just as I cannot afford to lose them now. Just as you will supply them to me again. Now.''

Diaz's smile was magnificent. Carpenter could not recall ever having seen such perfect teeth. He let Diaz smile a little longer, and then said deliberately: "I supplied those arms to Juarez, not to you.''

The smile faded, and Diaz's face grew ominous. "Do not play with me, *gringo.* Under this jovial exterior there is no sense of humor. Yes, you sold arms to Juarez. But it was I who used them, and it was I who defeated the French. Not Juarez. You supplied the arms to me then, and you will supply them again to me.''

"I have supplied guns to many men, for many causes, *Excelencia.* I could just as easily have run guns to the French at *Cinco de Mayo.*''

"Yes, you could have. For more money. But you supplied them to Juarez. Just as most recently you could have supplied them to me to use against Lerdo. For more money. Instead of the other way around.''

Carpenter had to grin. "For more money, *Excelencia*? Most assuredly. By Lerdo, I was not paid at all.''

Again, Diaz threw his head back and laughed. "See, *amigo.* I said you were on the wrong side. Not since *Cinco de Mayo* have you backed the winner. But we are in a forgiving mood. And I feel this shall be a lucky day. For us both. I shall once again get the guns I need, and you shall be paid. For this time you shall return to the ranks of the victors. Here, *amigo*, this is indeed something to drink to.''

Diaz motioned Carpenter into a narrow, straight-backed chair and clapped his hands. Instantly, a servant appeared with a crystal decanter and two goblets of hammered silver. After Carpenter sat down, Diaz poured him a goblet of red wine, then one for himself, and sat in the chair next to him.

"A rare *Chateau Lafite*. The year was 1855, my friend. This is a bonafide *premier cru classé*. A wine of truly great *sêve*. You know that year the French vintners voted this wine the finest Bordeaux of all time. Some are predicting that the 1877 casks will surpass this vintage, but I somehow doubt it. Here, drink. *Salud y pesetas*.'' Health and wealth. Diaz sipped the great Bordeaux tenderly.

'*Salud y cojones*.'' Health and balls. Carpenter tossed his wine back in one big gulp.

Diaz fixed Carpenter with a cold, searching look. "Why are you so hard, my friend? I do not hold it against you that you conspired with my enemy, Lerdo, to destroy me. I am willing to let bygones be bygones, and remember instead how it was on the battlefields of *Cinco de Mayo* when you and I fought as comrades, shoulder to shoulder. And yet you mock me. You abuse me as though I were a child, knowing full well that no one baits Diaz with impunity. What is it that goads you to taunt me? Perhaps it is all the blood and death these guns bring. Is that it?''

Carpenter averted his eyes. No, it wasn't the blood and death. He'd witnessed their destructive power many times, and it no longer bothered him. Death came to all, some soon, some late. How you died, and when, was nothing. He returned his gaze to Diaz. The man was still staring at him, awaiting his answer. But how could he tell him?

"You are losing faith, *compadre*,'' Diaz said.

"Or interest,'' Carpenter acknowledged.

"Ah, but then you are only half Mexican, is that not so? The other half is *gringo*, *yanqui*-born, and that half has so much trouble relating to our backward *peons* with their dark, grave faces and sad, obsidian eyes.'' Carpenter started to speak, but Diaz cut him off. "Yes, I know. In *norteamerica* no woman suffers, and your *gringo* men live forever. Up there, all problems can be solved, but here life is more hard. Here you find nothing is as you thought, and nothing turns out right in the end. So your *gringo* pride rebels, you walk away and leave these insoluble problems to men like me. And when we fail at the solution, just as you did before us, you call our methods questionable and blame us for the fiascos. Just as France did before you, and Spain before her, and no doubt Columbus before them. Yes, you *gringos* are all the same. It isn't Mexico you come to. It is some passionate pilgrimage through the Outer Dark, across the foul gulf of hell, through the blackness and the silence of time unborn. In the end you hope to find heaven, and when you discover you have merely found Mexico—life as it is, the very definition of *gringo* hell—you turn your back on her and say, ah, it is all the fault of Diaz. Blame it on Porfirio."

"That's not the way it is."

"Is it not? I've seen *gringo* nations come to our land. Each in their turn hangs Mexico from her hocks, guts her like a hog, and when she bleeds, they blame it on men like Diaz, on those poor relentless realists like myself who must see life as it is and who are forced to act on it. The *gringos* blame us, and say if Juarez had only lived, if Juarez had power today, it would be different. And they talk of Juarez as though he did not die, but had entered into heaven by immaculate ascension, like he was of the Holy Family."

"That is still not the way it is."

"Then how is it, *yanqui*?"

Carpenter took a deep breath and let it out slowly. "*Excelencia*, from the Rio Grande to Tierra del Fuego there are four million white men and forty million Indians. They cry out for freedom, for honor, for dignity. *Generalissimo*, you and I come from a long line of *revolucionarios*. It is laid to our charge: We must not let the flame die. We must not let our hopes and dreams vanish unseen, as in a dream, without a trace. That is all I say."

Diaz looked at him carefully. Before, he'd thought of Carpenter as just another *gringo* gun-runner. A few foolish illusions about *Viva la Revolución!*, but after the fighting they were all the same. Gold shoved into their sweaty hands, and they were gone. But not this one. This one was different.

"You believe all this, *amigo*? Freedom, honor, the dignity of man?"

"Yes."

"Then come here." He led Carpenter out onto the porch. He pointed to the hacienda's high white adobe wall. Standing against it were a man and a woman. Both were in torn, soiled clothes, which Carpenter realized had once been elaborate finery. "What you see there is my *majordomo* of twenty-five years. He is the most trusted friend and confidant I have ever had. The other was, let us say, my *mujer*." My woman. "She gave me more satisfaction than all the women I have known in all my life. And I have known many. Now they wait for me to step out into the *plazuela* and give the order for their execution. The line of soldiers with the muskets will blast them into bloody eternity."

"What for?"

"Not much. Some Indians in these hills have refused to come down to the hacienda and work my mines and fields. These two were sympathetic to the plight of poor, long-suffering people and were no doubt critical of my harsh treatment of our noble savages. So they saw that certain stores of food made their way to the renegades up there in the *cordillera*. I also suspect them of supplying information to the runaways, but on that score I have no evidence. In any event, I am now about to have my closest friend and the best piece of ass I have ever encountered in all my days as a *muy macho caballero* shot to pieces against that wall."

"For giving food to the poor?"

"No, for betraying the honor and freedom and dignity of man. My friend, these things are not won up there in your *norteamericano* drawing rooms. Down here, they are won at the point of a gun. And to keep my *soldados* in the battle-field, I need *peons* in the cornfield and men in my mines. Without them, the *revolución* you speak of so beautifully is lost. If I allow my friends to subvert that cause, all is lost."

"I understand."

"Then since your half-*gringo* understanding is so acute, would you like to give the order?"

"No, but since my understanding is so acute, and since we are about to embark on such a propitious business venture, I would ask that you set them free."

"I do not understand."

"*Por favor.*" As a favor.

"My friend, you are either soft-headed or soft-hearted. Or both." He trotted down the steps and shouted the commands. "*Listos! Apunten!*" The green-clad officers leveled their weapons.

"*Por favor,*" Carpenter said softly, "*y por la revolución!*"

"*Viva la revolución,*" Diaz said under his breath. Then he bellowed: "*Paraden!*" Stop. He dismissed the firing squad abruptly and beckoned the man and woman toward the hacienda.

59

There were four of them at the table—Diaz, Carpenter, and the two he had saved from execution. The man and woman sat there washed, scrubbed, attired in new clothes, and struggling for composure. They were back in the Don's good graces, and obviously shaken. As for Diaz, he seemed to harbor no shadow of ill will.

He wanted them all to enjoy a pleasant evening.

But the afternoon's events had done little to stimulate appetite or conversation. So after the dishes had been cleared, and the brandy and Havana cigars offered, Diaz got down to brass tacks.

"My friend, you received my message. I need big guns, heavy artillery, and I presume by now you have looked around. You are aware no power wishes to sell such weaponry to an erstwhile *bandido* of dubious political persuasion. Yet I also presume you have found something. Otherwise you would not be here. What do you have?"

"Three-inch Rodman wagon guns," Carpenter said slowly. "The kind the Indians call a *boom-boom!* because it makes two explosions—one when it fires, another when its cannister detonates, unleashing one hundred and forty-eight minie balls. You can drag each of them behind a span of mules."

"How many can you get?"

"Six."

Diaz nodded, impressed.

"Maybe a dozen 'Bottle Dahlgrens.'"

"What are those?"

"Rifled naval pieces that were converted and bolted onto flatbed wagons during the Civil War. They're old, but don't let that fool you. They're murderously accurate. Then there's thirteen Cohorns. Mortars made of bronze. With a half-pound powder charge, they'll lob a seventeen-pound shell twelve hundred yards. The bore is 5.82 inches, and the piece only weighs one hundred and sixty-four pounds. Which means you can break it down and pack it on a mule. Also figure nineteen Hotchkiss two-pounder Mountain Guns. They have a 1.65-inch bore, a forty-six-inch barrel, and weigh one hundred and twenty-one pounds. Breech loaded, bolt operated. They'll lob a two-pound shell two-and-a-third miles. You determine the range by the amount of powder. If you want, you can fill the shells with lead shot and they'll explode and shatter on impact. Black powder and carriages for the heavy guns come with the package. Also figure two hundred repeating Winchesters, plus ammunition."

Diaz's jaw went slack. "How will you deliver all this?"

"A troop-munitions train is hauling it to El Paso. I've made arrangements to bring the train on through the Mexican border, through Ciudad Juarez, and south into the Chihuahua desert. Your Mexican railroad runs out of track down there, so you'll have to meet me en route with mule teams, freight wagons, and mule-whackers. You can take the guns to wherever you want to store them. Mexico City, I presume."

"No, *señor*. That much armament, if it ever fell into the

wrong hands, would end my illustrious career. I'd store them right here, behind these very walls. Until I needed them."

"Yes, and with all that weaponry, no one would dare oppose you, not even for the Presidency. You'll be a sure thing."

"*Precisamente,*" Diaz said. "But tell me, how did you arrange with the United States to make such a hazardous deal? Why would they agree to sell so many guns to a neighbor on their border, a neighbor with whom they have not had particularly good relations?"

"They haven't agreed to it."

"Then how are you going to do this thing?" Diaz's face was suddenly hard.

"*Excelencia,*" Carpenter said, leaning forward, fixing Diaz with a tight stare, "I am going to take that train."

60

Diaz had to convince himself that Carpenter was not deranged. When the evenness of Carpenter's manner and the reasonableness of his tone continued into the evening, Diaz still had doubts.

"How, precisely, are you going to capture this train, which is armed to the teeth and manned by over one hundred troopers and their mounts?"

"*Excelencia,* gun-running is no trade for an old man. If I ever hope to put some money away for myself, and at the same time do something for Mexico, it has to be now. Same with your Presidency. You want to gain office, put down these endless rebellions, and stabilize this country—well, you're going to need guns. You just aren't going to do it with nine Napoleons and two Gatlings."

"What does all this cost, given the risks and expenses?"

"One hundred and fifty thousand dollars. In gold. Firm and final. It's worth it."

"And more. But how will you accomplish it?"

"In this line of work, you need experts. I will recruit one. I will get the most expert outlaw ever to rob a train on either side of the border. I will recruit a man who was raised by the Apaches, who rode with Quantrill's Raiders and the James-Younger Gang. A man wanted by both the United States and Mexico. A man with a total price on his head of over twenty thousand dollars. I will explain the deal, join his gang, and stay with him. When we stop the train, take it over the border, and present the guns to you down in Chihuahua, I will be there."

Diaz's face flushed with exasperation. "You don't really think you are going to—"

"*Excelencia*, yes, I do. I am going to recruit Outlaw Torn Slater to stop the train and steal your guns."

PART XI

61

When Immanuel Carpenter strode up to the Horseman's Club in El Paso, Texas, he looked very *gringo*. No *peon* shirt or *charro* pants or wide-brimmed sombrero this time. El Paso was not a good town for Mexicans. The Horseman's Club was not an establishment that let them in.

And to meet with Torn Slater, Carpenter had to get through that door.

Carpenter stared at the big oak portals with the ostentatious brass knobs a good hard minute. Several thoughts spun through his head. He could not help recalling the stunning blond hooker he had balled there six weeks before. She was the best fuck he'd ever had.

She was also the one who had assured him that she could set up a meeting with Outlaw Torn Slater for this evening.

While under most circumstances he would never have taken a whore's word on anything, Cimarron Rose was a very unusual lady, a woman with a strong personal code and a special kind of hard-edged integrity.

If Cimarron said she could introduce him to Torn Slater, she could.

The next thing that flashed through Carpenter's head was the realization that he was horny and needed Rose again. Tonight. Now. This was not a good sign. Sex to Carpenter was not a pastime of pure, unmitigated pleasure, something to be prolonged, savored. It was a libidinous itch. When a hard scratch was needed, Carpenter became irritable, hostile, drank too much, sometimes became downright violent. Worse, he became irrational and dangerously impulsive.

He must relieve the feverish tingling in his groin, or he would hopelessly fuck up his negotiation with Slater.

He knew he would.

He knocked on the door. When a black butler in a red frock coat and matching stovepipe hat answered, Carpenter announced himself, pushed the door open the rest of the way, and entered.

The main hall was a large, square room, one hundred feet on edge. Since the middle of the second floor had been knocked out, the center portion of the room extended up to the vaulted ceiling, twenty-four feet in all. The area surrounding the gaping hole had been turned into a balcony, and along its four edges stood black iron railings over which hung the club's two dozen soiled doves. Each had a leg propped up on the lower iron bars, their bare bosoms dangling provocatively over the railings. They all called down to the gentlemen below to come up and sample their wares.

And if whole brigades were called, many regiments were chosen. For the staircase leading to the second floor was continually filled with prosperous northern cattle buyers, high-ranking army officers, big-time bankers, and ambitious gamblers, here to try their luck with whiskey, women, and the many green-baize gaming tables scattered across the grand hall.

For gambling was here a-plenty. Numerous faro tables with shoes full of cards, dealers with black silk elbow garters, calling the play and riding the tiger. A dozen eight-handed poker games at huge octagonal tables, with stacks of blue chips piling high. Countless blackjack, keno, and roulette layouts, the walls echoing with the constant *whir!* of spinning wheels, cries of "Ante's a buck," "Five on the Lady," and "Jack of Clubs on the Diamond Queen."

Gambling, however, was the last thing on Carpenter's mind. His eyes searched the overhead gallery for Cimarron Rose, the blond-haired beauty who had set up this meeting, and with whom, for the moment, he would like to arrange a private pre-Slater conference.

His eyes scanned the array of women lined up at the balcony rail. Raven-haired doxies, red-headed vixens, an interesting assortment of brunettes, all with a leg propped up on the rail, their cleavage hung well over the crowd, a sultry come-hither look in their eager eyes. He studied them slowly, while in the background a piano dude in a red derby, a boiled shirt, and crimson elbow garters pounded out "A Cowboy's Lament" on the keyboard, banging the loud pedal on the refrain. Carpenter's eyes swept the balcony two more times. Still no Cimarron Rose.

He lowered his search to the main floor and studied the edges and corners of the crowd. Majors, colonels, and even two generals in the blue dress uniforms of the U.S. Army. Numerous gentlemen in black frock coats, several waist-length jackets. A few in expensive linen shirts with lavish French cuffs and silk bow ties. One man sported a satin evening cape and a mahogany walking stick with a solid gold handle.

A few of the more liberal townswomen took in the action. Ladies in tightly buttoned shirtwaists, long, floor-sweeping dresses with bustles and petticoats. Their high-buttoned shoes peeked out from under the jouncing ruffles and underskirts.

No Cimarron Rose there.

He glared at the far red walls papered luridly in close-napped velour, almost blood-red in hue. Nothing. Raising his eyes, he stared at ten massive curlicue chandeliers, each ablaze with four dozen guttering, sputtering candles, the crystal prisms of the chandeliers flashing brilliantly.

Still no Cimarron.

He turned to the far end of the hall, toward the sweeping teak bar with its polished brass foot rail and its vast assortment of rums, brandies, bourbons, vodkas, and gins stacked on glass tiers behind the dandified bartender.

A hand touched his shoulder and turned him around.

Long, blond, flouncing hair, a wide generous mouth, sky-blue eyes, a tight, low-cut dress of red satin.

Cimarron Rose.

"Here kind of early, aren't you, cowboy?"

"I have to see you in private."

"Look, I gotta keep busy. And I don't want you gettin' drunk or fuckin' around. This is a big night, and you gotta keep your wits about you."

"And I said I have to see you. Privately."

Her face was suddenly grave. "Is it about our friend?"

"It's about tonight."

She nodded. "Okay. Upstairs."

He followed her up a long, winding staircase amid hoots and cheers from the gallery courtesans. Down the hall past whores who amused themselves by pinching his ass and yelling: "How 'bout twosies?"

"Twosies, baby? I'll settle for threesies," a raucous contralto voice called out amid female horselaughs.

Cimarron led him into a small private room with a roll-top desk, two straight chairs, and no bed. She locked the door.

"Okay, Carpenter. This is the office. What's the deal? And you better not shit me."

"This is the deal," he said coldly, indicating his crotch.

"You asshole."

She started to move around him toward the door. He caught her by the shoulder and flung her back across the room into the wall. Hard. She glanced off the wall, caught herself on the curve of the roll-top, and pulled herself up.

"Fuck you," she snarled.

He grinned at her lewdly.

She hammered the grin with a hard right, cutting his lip.

She started around him again, and this time Carpenter pivoted to his right, brought his hand all the way behind his body, and, swinging off the pivot, struck her open-handed across the side of the head, every ounce of his one hundred and ninety pounds behind the blow. He felt the palm connect just in front of the temple, felt the force of the slap turn her head and whip painfully across her cheek, chin, jaw, and mouth. He felt the lips bruise and brush between his palm and her teeth. He watched anger flare in her eyes, and then, a microsecond later, he saw those same eyes dim and grow vague. He saw the jaw go slack, the eyes water as the crimson swathe along her cheek and chin and the instantly swelling lips were overrun with involuntary tears. Then her knees buckled, Cimarron grew limp, and she was falling.

He caught her under the arms a few feet from the floor and lifted her up. Leaning her up on the roll-top desk, he grabbed her under the chin and cheeks with one hand and began unbuckling and unbuttoning his pants with the other. When he was done, her eyes opened, still unfocused, but semi-conscious.

"You were saying?"

"I was saying," she slurred groggily, "that you're a bastard."

"So?"

"So on one hand, I think maybe I'll have you killed."

"And on the other hand?"

"On the other hand, fuck it."

She took his hands and guided them under her incredibly ripe rump. When she was firmly supported by his big hands and the roll-top, she reached behind the back of his head and gave him a murderously harsh stare.

She let him inspect the damages. Her left cheek was a scarlet smear from side of ear lobe to tip of chin. The crushed lips were ballooning to over twice their former size, which had already been quite puffy and pouty. Worse, the mouth was now bloody, the swelling lips livid. Both eyes were tearing uncontrollably, her face streaked and wet.

Slowly she eased her head forward. When her mouth was pressed against his, she began circling his lips, gums, and teeth with her tongue till he opened his mouth and probed hers in turn. Now the briny redolence of her blood was rich in both their mouths, and he was frantically french-kissing her distended lips. To even out the pain, she bit at his cut lip savagely, feeling the teeth sink in once, twice, three times.

Pulling away, she smiled to see three sharp tooth marks, bubbling with blood, on the inside of the lip, and a stinging grimace on his face.

Now they were both kissing, sucking, and biting at each other, oblivious to the pain, a teeth-scraping, tongue-grappling orgy, half agony, half ecstasy. He was ripping the front of her shirtwaist away, roughly cupping the breasts, rudely squeezing the nipples till she was squealing with unashamed desire.

He lifted her up higher on the roll-top, braced her against it with a hip, and removed his left hand from under her buttocks. He pulled up her dress with two ferocious motions, and, as he reached for her crotch, she was already pumping her hips and moaning a soft prurient dirge of frantic anticipation. Then the dress was up, the hand was ready, and when he pulled back from her to look, her eyes were rolled back, her chin trembling, her whole body breathless with lust.

Suddenly, he spun her around and flopped her belly down on the curving face of the desk. Reaching around with his right hand, he dexterously massaged her clitoris, and, simultaneously reaching under with his left, he deftly fingered her cunt. As her body convulsed, he shoved his massive member into her snatch.

She was writhing wildly on his cock with pain, anger, and pleasure, and he responded wildly by grinding furiously on her clitoris, kissing her nape, tonguing her ear, and mumbling obscenities. She was spinning and thrusting and pumping out her hunger, and his orgasms were thundering riotously, great heaving spasms pounding out of him, inflaming them, ravaging them, consuming them both.

He rutted at her, and she at him, for a full half hour. Orgasm after orgasm convulsed them, but they remained insatiable. In and out, round and round, they stroked. Languidly, without thought or purpose, they rocked to and fro in a soothing, slow fuck of diminishing desire. Even in the end when he, at last, tried to disengage, Rose still moaned: "No, baby, don't stop."

"Don't worry," he said. "I'm not stopping."

He turned her around, hoisted her butt up till one cheek was back on the roll-top. Slipping his right hand underneath the elevated globe, he commenced to finger-fuck her ass while he massaged her clitoris with his thumb. Her body trembled with his touch, and it was then he entered her vagina.

As he entered, his mind felt that it was drifting into space. It was as though his cock and balls, his body and soul were separate entities, things-unto-themselves, beings and worlds apart. It seemed to be the same for her. Impaled against the roll-top desk, her eyes glazed and fixed on the ceiling, her head swinging giddily back and forth, up and down, the same eerie prurient dirge again groaning, deep and low-throated, she seemed adrift, her mooring stripped, lashed drowning to a sinking spar, tossed and turned in a nether sea.

How long they fucked he could not say. Sometimes they exploded in violent frenzies—in biting, scratching, and slapping. Just as often they fucked like lovers—indolently, peacefully, tenderly—in a dreamy, slow dance of time-stopped and infinite, immeasurable desire.

Even after the last throbbing of passion, after Carpenter's drooping cock slid out of her slack, pleasure-weary cunt, they still hung on in a clinging, murmuring embrace. Their swollen, salty mouths were still locked lovingly. After a seeming eternity of tangled tongues, of lips rubbed raw from too much kissing, biting, and slapping, of teeth scraping and mouths sucking, they pulled away.

"Ah, honey," Rose moaned, falling forward into Carpenter's arms, weak-kneed and shaking. "No more."

"One more," he said urgently. "I need it."

"But I can't, baby. You can't. You're too soft."

"You can use your mouth."

"No, please, baby. I'm too tired. I'm all fucked out. And it's time to go. Slater could be here any minute."

"Fuck that. I need it. Now."

Then he had her by the back of her hair and was easing her down onto her knees. Carefully, he worked his half-limp dick into her open mouth.

She stopped her whimpering and began to suck him off. Head gyrating giddily, tongue half in, half out of her mouth, the sucking and gasping of her labored breath filling the room. Now Carpenter's eyes were rolling back, and the eerie, prurient dirge was rumbling deep and low-throated out of his own trembling soul.

His cock got hard so fast it made his balls ache with the sudden tension.

Halfway through the blow job, he thought absently how Diaz had claimed Maria, the girl he almost ordered shot, was the greatest piece of ass in the world. It was obvious that the best piece of ass, best everything, everywhere, every time was going down on him at this very moment in the business office of the Horseman's Club in El Paso, Texas.

Yet somehow the seed of doubt was planted. Maybe Diaz was right. Maybe his mistress could do magical things neither he nor Rose had ever heard of. If so, he, Immanuel Jose Carpenter, would have to find out. For the good of women everywhere, he would have to find out and teach them. For the good of all the men who would ball those women. For the good of Immanuel Carpenter's own insatiable, inexhaustible passion.

At the thought of such spectacular fucking, Carpenter began to come. Tremendous gouts of lust, gushing down Cimarron's throat, pouring into her mouth, spilling out onto her cheeks, as she choked and sputtered and coughed, unable to contain the colossal quantities of sperm.

When she finally pulled away, Carpenter was still coming into her honey-hued hair.

"Oh God," she gasped, falling to the floor, struggling to wipe the insane amounts of jism from her face. "I'm going to get you. I swear by all that's holy, no man has ever used me like this before."

"You mean because I haven't paid you?"

"You bastard," she said, looking up at him from the floor. "I swear before God I'll have you killed. Laugh if you want, but Carpenter, I swear to Christ, you're a dead man."

"Okay, okay." He knelt down beside her, pulled out his roll, and peeled off twenty dollars. "That enough?"

She stared at him slack-jawed, unbelieving. "You're finished, *amigo*. You're boxed and tagged."

He stood and carefully pulled up his pants. He buttoned his fly, buckled his belt, took off his Stetson, and smoothed back his hair.

"Now where do I meet Torn Slater?"

Cimarron Rose shook her head incredulously, stared down at the floor, and let out a long slow, feral groan.

"You'll meet him in hell, you half-spick sonofabitch."

62

Carpenter was downstairs at the long teak bar, heel hooked on the brass rail, a double shot of Old Crow in his hand when Cimarron approached him with the girl. Cimarron was now in a new shirtwaist of red shantung silk and tight vest of black crushed velvet. Her hair was freshly combed and fluffed. Her mouth and cheeks were carefully made up. She once again looked dazzling, unscathed.

However, if Cimarron impressed Carpenter with her resiliency, he was utterly taken aback by her young friend. A girl of perhaps fifteen, in a long calico dress, a frilly bonnet, and a black lace shawl. She stared at the floor with scared, downcast eyes.

"Take her to a room," Cimarron said.

"She isn't my type."

"Doesn't matter. She's new trade. A virgin. People here want some kind, gentle man like yourself to show her the ropes, break her in. You being such a stud, we thought you could get it done."

"Ain't up to it."

"I don't care. You got time. We want you to kill it with her. You two can sing psalms and read the Bible for all I care. But we can't have men hanging around here all night, sipping whiskey, ogling women, and not spending money."

"You mean . . ." Carpenter gave her a questioning look.

"That's right, cowboy. Part of the job. Comes with the territory. And don't come down till it's time."

Rose left him.

Carpenter shrugged and turned toward the young girl. She looked away.

"Well, I guess we better get it on," Carpenter said wearily.

He headed her toward the steps, wondering what all this had to do with Torn Slater.

63

Carpenter had no intention of getting it on with the frightened, underage virgin. Aside from the fact that she was not his style, he was fucked out. The only thing Carpenter wanted to get it on with was the bottle of Old Crow, which he carried up to the room. And maybe, later, a financial transaction with Outlaw Torn Slater, if he could convince the man to deal.

Mostly he waited in the whore's bedroom. He relaxed, the bottle of bourbon resting in his lap, the room's only chair tipped back, his feet propped up on the wall. Behind him, the timid, unblooded whore shuddered with dread. She was apparently terrified that Carpenter would put down the bottle and take her by force.

An hour passed. Two more. Three.

Carpenter was just starting to doze, chair tipped back precariously, boot heels slowly slipping down the wall, when the first shots rang out. Carpenter bolted to his feet, bottle crashing on the floor, hand snaking toward his holster.

Actually, the first shots did not ring out as much as they crashed through the grand hall in one ear-cracking, protracted echoless roar.

Then they could be heard as individual sounds.

And, indeed, Carpenter, for all his sudden movement, was very much aware of this fact. Being an expert in weapons, he intuited that the first fusillade was the simultaneous rapid-firing of Winchesters, .45's, and at least three scatter guns. He estimated their number to be over a dozen, and, in that first ten seconds, he calculated that they had gotten off a good hundred rounds. That meant ten rounds per second. That meant the men downstairs were also experts. Which meant that Immanuel Jose Carpenter was in trouble.

Carpenter went for his Colt with complete confidence, knowing that it would be there. It was then that the gravity of his situation was brought home. For Carpenter was a man attuned to small movements, pressures, and touches whenever they occurred in the vicinity of his guns. He was a man who measured his life out in grains of lead, in the size of powder loads, and in rounds per minute. Any flicker of motion occurring around his pistol, and he was instantly alert.

But his gun was gone.

"Lookin' for *this*?" The ominous *click-click* behind him was unmistakable.

He wheeled around and faced the bed. The girl was standing, Carpenter's Peacemaker in her fist, the barrel leveled at his stomach. The girl was pulling off the frilly bonnet and letting her hair tumble out. The hair was shaggy, cut just above the shoulders. A little short, Carpenter thought, considering it was an age when men and women alike wore their hair long. Shears were still crude and not a standard item in everybody's saddlebags.

However, it wasn't the muzzle of the gun or the length of the hair or even the tone of the voice that got to Carpenter. It was more the set of the jaw, which jutted belligerently, and the lips, which curled back over the teeth—teeth which now flashed like two long rows of brightly polished knives.

Then it hit him, just like that.

The bitch was a man.

Furthermore, this newly recognized male was moving toward him, a twisted sneer on his lips. His pale eyes were filled with malice, and only now was Carpenter aware of the telltale signs of his gender—the broad shoulders, the six-foot frame, the big hands, and the hairy, raw-boned wrists protruding from under the dress and shawl.

"Well, *amigo,* I heard you were pretty rough on my girl," the guy said, his voice thick with slow, soft menace. "Maybe it's time to try a man on for size."

"It ain't what you think."

"How do you know what I think?"

"I'm just sayin' it was different."

"Different 'cause my girl's a whore? That way you can do any damn dirty thing you want to her? Slap her around, cut her mouth, butt-fuck her till she can hardly walk?"

"I didn't mean it like—"

The gunman in the calico dress brought the barrel of the .45 across Carpenter's mouth with a downward, slashing swing, the filed tip of the front sight laying his cheek wide open. The blow knocked Carpenter to his knees.

"You don't understand," Carpenter said, pulling himself back up, blood bubbling in his mouth. "I'm here on business. I think you're part of it. You don't know what—"

"No, *amigo,* you're the one who don't seem to know what. You don't seem to know I'm gonna shoot your *cojones* off a quarter-inch at a time."

"But I'm here to see a man. You really don't—"

The gunman cold-cocked him, just like that. And when Carpenter flew backward and crashed into the wall, the man stepped forward and hit him again and again and again.

Carpenter was on the floor, his mouth a bloody mess, filled with very wobbly teeth. With clouded vision, he looked up into the gunman's eyes, and suddenly it came to him.

"You're Sam Bass, the train robber," Carpenter said.

"Good for you, friend. You can go to heaven happy." He leaned forward and placed the muzzle of the .45 directly over Carpenter's crotch.

It was his last chance, and Carpenter blurted it out. "I'm here to see Torn Slater. It's been set up in advance. I got a train job for you and him. And me."

Sam Bass paused, and a look of genuine bemusement

crossed his face. Finally he said: "Nice try, *hombre*, but it won't work."

"Check it with Slater."

"Why?"

"You can always kill me later, but if Torn finds out you shot me now and cost him a lot of sweet scratch, he won't be happy. It generally ain't wise makin' Torn unhappy."

Bass stared at him for a full thirty seconds, saying nothing. Finally, he motioned Carpenter to his feet.

"Okay, we'll talk. But you better be holdin' somethin' in your hand. Somethin' besides your dick."

"Just get me to Slater."

"That ain't hard. But you may curse the day I done it."

64

Walking out onto the balcony was like descending into the inferno. The upper ceiling, where they were standing, was thick with rolling, swirling clouds of whitish smoke. The stench wrenched at Carpenter's gut, and as he and Bass walked the gallery, it took every ounce of strength he had to force himself toward the winding staircase.

Carpenter's reluctance was out of character. He was a man who had spent his life peddling the engines of destruction, a man who had been to every major combat field of the last twenty years, who'd seen countless battles, any one of which could have made this brothel shoot-out look like a convent at vespers.

Yet he was afraid.

And when, at last, he looked over the railing, he knew why.

It wasn't that there were so many dead. Carpenter had seen battlefields littered with corpses and never even blinked. It was that these people were so intimately dead. This was a group of men and women at their pleasure, at their very wealthy, safe, and secure pleasure, who had suddenly been invaded. When they resisted, and the Reaper came to take them, they were caught totally unprepared. When the blow came, it took them in the fullness of their years, or in the flower of their youth. It caught them in their love, and it caught them in their lies.

Men armed with Winchester repeaters were already trotting up and down the gallery, kicking in doors, levering rounds into the room, and screaming for money. Glancing into the boudoirs, Carpenter saw that more than a few gentlemen had died in the act, either from congestive heart failure or a charred bullet hole through the head. Those who'd survived the assault were lying face down on the bedroom floors, trembling, the pockets of their pants turned out. The naked whores sat shaking and blubbering on the beds, no less afraid.

Finally, Carpenter forced himself to glance over the railing again, down through the choking fog of black powder smoke into the main hall. It was like staring into the Pit. Of the forty or fifty card and roulette tables scattered across the big floor, at least a dozen had bloodied bodies strewn across them. Some face down, some on their backs and sides, feet hanging over the tables' edges, eyes staring sightlessly at the glittering crystal chandeliers overhead, or into the bloody baize, almost all the victims lying there with bullet holes through their faces and temples, the entrance wounds gaping, fuming pits, the exit wounds starburst patterns of brainpan, scalp, and skull.

If Carpenter saw twelve men spread-eagled on the gambling tables, and six more gunned down in the rooms, he saw twice that many either crumpled on the floor or slumped against the walls. Wherever these men had crawled or slid or dragged themselves, they'd left in their wake smeared mopstreaks of blood. He noted that among those who died with their red-hot pistols still smoking in their fists, bullet holes were numerous, as many as eight or ten, and concentrated in the face and chest. Most of these casualties were the uniformed soldiers.

Hold-up men were still trotting up and down the gallery,

ducking in and out of rooms, nodding to Bass. A few chuckled at his costume, though Carpenter recognized the cleverness of it. Up in the balcony, armed with a Winchester, what better sniper and back-up man than an outlaw disguised as a hooker?

Quickly, Carpenter counted the ones he'd seen robbing the balcony rooms, then estimated the number in the main *salle*. By his count, only five men were robbing nearly two hundred people.

No wonder they wanted someone on the inside.

Rounding a corner, he and Bass descended the winding oak staircase, a trip he did not wish to make. He felt that tying up with Outlaw Torn Slater was the worst idea he'd ever had. His life with Juarez, his years on the battlefields of Shiloh, Cold Harbor, the Wilderness, Fredricksburg, Antietam, Pittsburg Landing, Vicksburg, Spotsylvania Court House, Chancellorsville, Gettysburg, right up to Appomattox Court House, had been as nothing. His gun-running forays into embattled Paris during the Franco-Prussian War had been a breeze. Fortifying Lerdo for his main drive against Diaz had been simple. His whole life, compared to what was waiting for him down those steps, was a cakewalk. It was at the foot of the staircase that he would find hell.

At the very bottom he was greeted by an Army colonel in dress blues bent belly-down over the bannister. He, too, was shot through the head. His Single-Action Colt, still hooked to his lanyard, was smoking in his fist, held there by his clenched, rigored fingers. His neck was twisted at a skewed angle, and he was looking straight up the stairs at Carpenter, his face a frozen death mask, his shot-off jaw accentuating the ghoulish grin, a starburst pattern of blood and bone fragment exiting his right temple.

As Carpenter rounded the colonel, it was easy to make out the outlaws. The people still alive were standing face to the wall or were prone on the floors. The robbers had now moved to the middle of the room, where they could watch survivors more carefully. The hold-up men were dressed in linsey-woolsey shirts, leather vests, heavy canvas pants, and wide-brimmed hats—either slouch, Stetson, or Plainsman's. None were masked, and all wore some remnant of the butternut-gray, the Lost Confederate Cause, either a hat, a shirt, or pants. Each had at least six pistols, as far as Carpenter could count. All had shotguns—usually a sawed-off eight-gauge Greener—or a Winchester braced on their hips. Most had longish hair and sweeping mustaches.

They were the toughest-looking bunch of hard-cases Carpenter had ever seen.

At the far end of the room, there was an outlaw with a whore. He had dropped his pants and backed her up against the bar. He was fucking her standing up, one hand under her ass, the other clutching the shotgun still braced on his hip. The hostess was rutting at him feverishly, almost dementedly, her body arock with frenzied passion. The look on her face was one of stone horror, and her eyes, crazed with fright, as huge as saucers, kept sweeping the room, taking in one violent death after another. And when the man started coming, and his body was pumping furiously into hers, she detonated into an equally powerful orgasm. Her hips ground savagely against his. Her fist unconsciously pounded on his shoulders. Her fingernails scratched at his back and neck. The groans ripped out of her throat and lungs so shrill in their intensity that even the most duplicitous whore in the world could never have successfully mimicked those feral cries. Still, her eyes maintained the same lost look of absolute horror. Her tear-streaked face had contorted into a hideous mask of raw, animal fear. And in between the multiple orgasms—induced by hysterical terror and the prayerful anticipation of release and escape—her body shook with sobs.

Carpenter kept walking. Around the bar, off to one side, Sam Bass was directing him to a big, octagonal poker layout covered with green baize. On the table were eight canvas bags filled with loot and a big strongbox filled with double-eagles and hundred-dollar gold certificates. It was obviously the till. There was a big man bending over the table in a white duster and a tan, sweat-stained Plainsman's hat. He was casually counting the take.

Cimarron Rose stood directly behind him.

Not a good sign.

"Hey, Boss," Sam Bass called out as they approached, "this pilgrim wants a meet, says he's lookin' for you."

The big man straightened, and Carpenter saw he was well over six feet, and a good two hundred pounds. And when he caught Carpenter with a cold, tight look, the gun-runner found himself pinned by the hardest, flattest, blackest eyes he'd ever looked into.

"Well, *honcho,* I guess you found me," Torn. Slater said. And he held out his hand.

65

They rode all that night, and the next two days. At dusk they camped near the Nueces River in an arroyo filled with prickly pear and thorny ocotillo. No deps would come charging in through there.

They built a good fire of piñon and greasewood, which cracked and popped and cast grotesque shadows on the walls of the wash. Now there was only the glow of the fire beating back the dark, the pickets dim, ghostly silhouettes.

Slater, Bass, Cimarron, and Carpenter sat around the flames, squatting on their haunches, drinking grog from a passed bottle. Overhead, the sickle moon sliced through a sparkling carpet of stars, while Orion loomed over the northern rim of the gulch.

"I don't know," Slater said to Carpenter. "This plan you have for robbing a troop-munitions train. You think you're being heroic or something? You think this is a damn dime novel? In case you ain't heard, that Yuma rock-pile ain't no Ned Buntline paperback book. It be for real."

"Yeah, that's what I keep thinking. But men like you and me, we live by the gun, by the hair-trigger's touch. We never live except by fits and starts, in the cracks, somewhere between the hammer's snap and the muzzle's roar. We live and we take and we never put anything back. Sure, I want to make some money. I always want to make money. But this time I want to give something back. We get these arms for Mexico, we'd be giving something back.''

"Yeah," Cimarron said, "but you be leavin' something out."

"What?"

"Them blue-bellies. You fuck this up, they'll tear your sorry ass seven ways from sundown."

Bass had to laugh at that one. "Speakin' of sorry ass," he said, pointing to Cimarron. "You see my girl back at the Horseman's Club. Danger, bloodshed, almost gettin' her butt shot off.''

"And lookin' beautiful," Torn said, nodding.

"Well," Carpenter said glumly, "if I can't inspire you with love of man, there is always money."

"Yeah, you did mention something 'bout that awhile back. How much did you say?"

"It would be a hundred and fifty thousand dollars. Split how many ways? Let's say five ways. That's thirty thousand dollars apiece. A lot better that what you pulled out of the Horseman's.''

"I count eight of us."

"Some won't make it."

"Some never do."

"Them troopers come through, none of us will."

"They're in the last five cars," Carpenter explained. "When the first troop car crosses that big gorge south of the Brazos, we blow the train. They'll be dead on and gone to heaven by the time we jump the engineer."

Cimarron's face contorted with displeasure.

"What's the matter?" Slater said. "You pissed at his program? I hate to say it, but it ain't half bad. It's risky, but we don't hardly live in a world of careful decisions."

"Might as well be hung for a sheep," Carpenter put in.

"Hey, gun-runner," Cimarron said, "tell us some more about how we're doin' this for the good of mankind, how history will redeem us."

"History's a mighty cold bitch," said Slater.

"Say, *amigo,*" said Bass, "suppose them blue-bellies knew that eight bold fuckers was thinkin' of jumpin' that train. What do you think they'd be doin' right now?"

"Who knows?" Carpenter said.

"Weavin' our shrouds," Cimarron decided.

"Now, don't be so hard on him," said Slater, shaking his head.

Bass rolled a quirly, flicked a phosphorus-tipped Lucifer with his thumb. He inhaled deeply and blew the smoke upward. "Ain't worried 'bout our risks. I'm just concerned with us hijackin' that train, high-ballin' it over the border, and handin' it over to them greasers. I can't help worryin' 'bout what it will do to U.S.–Mexico trade relations."

Slater nodded wisely. "It will surely damage our country's import-export balance."

Laughter throbbed in Cimarron's throat. "Torn, when I hear you talk like that, I sometimes feel I'm standin' eyeball-deep in hell."

"We rob that train, you may be," Bass said.

"That's what bothers me," Cimarron continued, " 'cause I get the feelin' that under all that bullshit laughter, that is precisely what you men plan to do."

"Don't let nuthin' hold you back but fear," Slater said evenly.

"Torn," said Sam Bass.

"No," Cimarron said, "really, I want to hear some more from the Great Redemptor here. I want to hear how he plans to use them guns to deliver all them spicks from evil. How he wants to give something back to mankind, and all that."

" 'From the bottomless pit and eternal damnation, from the lion's mouth and the darkness therein, I shall deliver them,' " Carpenter quoted mockingly.

"Torn," Cimarron said hotly, "we should have killed this fucker in that whorehouse. You're gonna regret not doin' it. I promise you."

Slater just shook his head. "Damn girl, you can't decide whether to kill him or fuck him, can you?"

"Torn," Bass said again.

Slater smiled widely. "Ease off, little bro, you got a

hard-on big enough to murder the world. It's what you deserve for gettin' sweet on a whore. But this here's business, and our business is a matter of hard, fine lines. So don't go jumpin' salty on me. There's too much crazy violence in this gang already. The kind that softens the brain, till we can't think straight. I don't like it.''

"Torn," Cimarron said, "them's mighty fancy words. Must be all them books you read in Yuma. 'Cause I don't unnerstand a damn thing you're sayin'.''

"I think he's talkin' 'bout how Hardy fucked that other whore," Bass said.

"Yeah, you're right. I didn't like it. I was gonna call Hardy out tonight and throw down on him. Till Carpenter told me 'bout his plan. Figured then I could do it after the train job. Maybe send his share to the whore.''

"If he survives the heist itself.''

"Yeah, if any of us survives it.''

"Sounds like you got your mind made up.''

"Sort of. Just one question. Carpenter, why you trust Diaz to pay you all this *dinero*? He could hold out. Or bushwhack us.''

"I've been dealing with him and his people for twenty years. Never had a problem yet. And they need me. They'll need me again, too. They always have. Diaz knows that.''

"Yeah, maybe so. But that part, I still don't like it.''

"You like it less than the blue-bellies?" Cimarron asked incredulously.

"Damn straight. They be the enemy. Them we just fight. Can't be betrayed by them, by the opposition. Only by them we're supposed to trust. Like Diaz.''

"We could hit another whorehouse," Bass said.

"Three thou. Three fuckin' thou apiece.''

"For a lotta risk," Carpenter pointed out.

"And that don't feed the bear," Bass grudgingly agreed.

"Say, gun-runner," Slater said, "if five of us cut up the pile, and my share comes out to thirty, suppose I just take it out in trade?''

"How do you mean?''

"Them two hundred repeating Winchesters and cartridges. Thirty's a fair price."

"That's what you want, that's what you'll get. I'll stipulate that with Diaz."

"What you want with two hundred rifles?" said Bass. "Gonna sell them to the 'Paches?"

"Naw, gonna give them away."

"No shit?" Carpenter said.

"Like I said."

Now it was Carpenter's turn to smile. "You know, Slater, you're gonna like Mexico a lot. You could even learn to love her. *Viva la Revolución*. The spirit. Mexico, I mean."

"Well, I've sure loved some of her banks and trains."

"That's a lock-cinch," Bass said, laughing.

"Viva pesetas?" Long live wealth? Carpenter asked.

"Damn straight," Slater said. Taking out his Colt, he spun the racheting cylinder for emphasis. Carpenter noted the blackness in Slater's eyes grow murkier, darker. A blackness akin to the grave, as Bill Hickok once described those eyes. Then Carpenter looked and saw that Slater was staring off into the distance at the dim silhouette of Hardy, the man who'd fucked the whore, who was still standing guard at the far end of the arroyo. "Goddamn straight. *Viva* the fuckin' *pesetas*, and ask questions later."

Carpenter knew Hardy would never survive the job.

PART XII

66

Two men crouched behind boulders. They both wore Plainsman's hats, broadcloth shirts, and canvas pants. And a lot of pistols. They carried six apiece. The pistols were 45's and the lighter Navy Colts, rechambered to take the new .38-caliber cartridges. Their mounts, a sturdy Appaloosa and a big roan war pony, were staked out behind them. Each of these also packed a brace of revolvers, heavy Walker horse pistols, the most powerful and accurate handguns made.

The larger of the men, well over six feet, was studying a massive railroad trestle which spanned a huge, almost impossibly deep chasm. He studied the trestle with its network of X-shaped underpinnings, its endless array of criss-crossed planks and beams. It seemed impregnable, substantial enough to endure anything—freight trains, earthquakes, even outlaws like themselves.

Carpenter turned to the big man and said: "Here, let me have a look."

Torn Slater handed him the spyglass. "See where we put the charges?"

Carpenter nodded. Yes, he could see them. A hundred feet from the eastern wall of the chasm, fifty-two separate charges were packed, braced, and jammed into numerous junctures of heavy wood cross-beams. Fifty-two charges that were laid approximately fifteen to twenty-five feet below the track. These blocks of explosive each contained between five and fifty sticks of sweaty dynamite. The task of planting them at strategic intervals between those cross-crossed pine planks was something that Carpenter would like to forget—he and Slater with haversacks of wet dynamite, packed in sawdust and strapped to their backs. Climbing hand over hand amid that endless, labyrinthine maze of beams and crossbars, forming what seemed to be an intricate matrix of infinite X's, stretching from the top of the trestle to the bottom of the gorge some fifteen hundred feet below. He and Slater wedging the tightly wrapped dynamite bundles into the X-shaped cross-beams, lashing them to the underpinnings with wire, then twisting the ends tight with pliers. Periodically, they went up top and loaded their packs with more blocks of dynamite, more caps, more wire. Into the abyss they returned, set the charges, lashed them secure, hoping that the bridge did not blow up in their faces then and there.

Finally the last charge was laid. A whopper—fifty sticks of dynamite in all. A giant square of explosive three feet on the edge, wired a stick at a time, flush around the south face of the trestle. This was to be Slater's target and detonator. He would blast it with his Sharps "Big Fifty" rifle when the train was almost over the chasm, blowing to high hell the second half—the one with the two hundred blue-bellies on it. The other fifty-one wired-up charges were so placed that when the big sheet of dynamite went, it would set off a chain reaction.

Carpenter peered through the spyglass at their handiwork. He was able to make out the big three-foot square of explosive, but it wasn't easy. The other charges were virtually invisible.

"Goddamn, Slater, can't we get closer? How on God's good earth are you going to hit that postage stamp from here, six hundred yards away?"

Slater just grinned.

Cimarron Rose was up behind them. "Hell, Torn here can shoot the balls off a runnin' buck at six hundred yards. Ain't that right, baby?"

"Don't know about that, but Carpenter, you see that bend in the track where the train, after leavin' its back half in the chasm, takes almost a right-angle turn and comes barrelin' down the desert straight at us? Right where we be sittin' now?"

"I follow."

"Well, don't worry about me hittin' the charge. You just worry about that Gatling gun on the flatcar, the one they be pushin' out in front of the locomotive. 'Cause, boy, they got a one hundred-caliber Gatling *leadin'* that fuckin' train. You know the effective range on a Gatling?"

"Of course."

"A thousand yards. A thousand fuckin' yards. And don't say they'll be shootin' it off a movin' flatcar so it won't be that accurate. 'Cause what they'll be shootin' is one thousand rounds per minute. Hell, if this here 'Big Fifty' fired a thousand rounds per minute, I could up alongside the bridge, blow the trestle, and still nail them Gatling-gunners even though the train was high-ballin' *away* from me at sixty miles per hour, that is, one mile per minute, that is, thirty fuckin' yards per second. No, this way they still be high-ballin' but they be high-ballin' right into my sights."

"Aren't you forgetting something?" Carpenter said.

Slater shrugged.

"You'll be starin' right into their sights, too. Into the sights of a hundred-caliber Gatling. That's one inch in diameter, in case you forgot. When they come high-ballin' up that track, they're gonna cut you down like they were choppin' cotton."

"That's why I have you." Slater was smiling. The smile wasn't pretty.

"To do what?"

"To draw their fire. See that long line of boulders on the other side of the track?" The southbound section of track was about fifty feet from them. On the other side was a string of wagon-sized boulders. "You're gonna set up ten or fifteen powder charges on top of them boulders. Get yourself a red-hot stogie, and when the action starts, run up and down them rocks, settin' off the diversion. Hell, you'll get so much smoke explodin', them Gatlin'-gunners'll think it's fuckin Shiloh.''

"I'm gonna draw their fire? Uh, they be firin' one-inch rounds, about a thousand per minute. Range on those rocks will quickly reach point-blank, or pretty close to.''

Cimarron Rose was grinning widely. Slater merely nodded

"I could get killed,'' Carpenter said. "I mean, have you ever seen one of those Gatling guns in action?'' Slater nodded. "Each of those rounds is four times bigger than your Sharps 'Big Fifty' bullets. And those 'Big Fifties' are consid ered goddamn big. I don't like it. I don't like goin' head-to head with Gatlings.''

"Like fightin' a grain thresher with kid gloves.''

"I don't like this. I don't like it at all.''

"Yeah, but if I don't get two clean shots at them Gatling gunners, we ain't never stoppin' that train. And I just don' shoot well dodgin' rapid-fire artillery.''

"So it's my turn in the barrel?''

"We each get a turn.''

"I don't like it.''

"Well, I do,'' Rose blurted out. "I like you settin' of charges and dodgin' hundred-caliber, thousand-round-per-minute bullets. I like it just fine.''

67

It was dawn the next day, and Carpenter stood by the boulders watching the red sun blaze over the rimrock, throwing of shafts of red and purple and bright orange. Overhead a buzzard wheeled, keeping his patient, solitary vigil. For personal company, a mosquito, left over from the night keened, waiting for a chance to strike.

Carpenter was developing a strange identification with this desperate beast.

It was then that Slater whistled to him, and, turning toward the trestle, Carpenter saw a big eight-wheeler Baldwin locomotive materialize out of nowhere. It was grinding toward the trestle like a black, hulking monster, an endless explosion of embers, smoke, and sparks belching out of its diamond-shaped stack. Its profusion of bright, polished brass glinted and flashed in the early dawn. Steam rose from under the wheels like fumes floating up from the pit of hell. As it inched onto the trestle, its whistle shrilled and wailed, chilling Carpenter to his soul.

But if the Baldwin chilled Carpenter, it was nothing compared to the thing on the flatbed that the Baldwin was pushing. For the lead car carried the bolted-down Gatling, ringed by sandbags. The big gun's muzzle, sweeping back and forth across the rails, was capable of cutting down anything in its way.

The two soldiers manning the Gatling waved the engineer forward, and slowly the locomotive moved across the bridge. First the Gatling. Then the locomotive, with its firebox and stack. The tender, stacked with cords of wood, the mail car. And then a whole succession of freight cars loaded with Rodmans, Bottle Dahlgrens, Mountain Mortars, Hotchkiss Guns, crates of Winchesters, shells, shot, powder, carriages, and accessories.

One, two, three, four, five, six, the freight cars rolled. When the sixth reached the other side, Carpenter knew it would be time. Slater would attempt to set off the square-shaped charge. The charge which, from Carpenter's vantage point, wasn't even postage-stamp-size.

It couldn't be seen at all.

Shoot the balls off a running buck at six hundred yards? Bullshit! Six hundred yards was over a third of a mile, and at that distance, scope or no scope, it couldn't be done. They should have gotten closer, that was all. Carpenter should have insisted. That way, at least they would have blown the train. At least, they would have had a shot at the two Gatlings. This way Slater would take his shot, inevitably miss, and then—

The roar of the "Big Fifty" caught Carpenter by surprise. His first reaction was to stare at the source of the noise, the detonation of the hundred and seventy grains of black powder which had sent the seven hundred-grain cylindrical lead slug rocketing toward the trestle six hundred yards away. The next blast, a full second and a half later, startled Carpenter even more.

He was so stunned that he'd forgotten the plan to blow the trestle was based on chain detonation, not one big bang. So when the next fifty-one blasts followed, first singly, then merging into one horrendous, echoing, ear-cracking roar, his bowels almost released.

Carpenter had been to the wars, and had seen a lot of work with explosives. But nothing seemed to him so—so—beautifully, that was it, so beautifully executed as the way Slater had mined and charged and then set off that trestle.

First there had been the timing. Slater had done something here which Carpenter hadn't believed possible. He'd coordinated the explosion with a moving object—down to the last millimeter, down to the last second. And the bridge blew at the exact moment that the sixth freight car crossed over. Bang. Right on the button. Just like that. Then there were the fifty-two separate, then suddenly merging, blasts culminating in the most horrific, ear-shattering sound Carpenter had ever heard.

Then came the catastrophic results. Most explosions were routine. Due to problems in timing of the detonation systems, these blasts had to be limited to stationary objects like buildings. Hence, half the burst was absorbed by the ground, or dramatically slowed down by walls and ceiling and floors.

Not so with the trestle. The thousand pounds of dynamite was packed near its top, so the only things above the explosive were criss-crossed beams and planks, train rails, and, above those, six or eight freight cars. The only thing below the explosive was a quarter mile of timbers and planks.

And, indeed, Carpenter had never seen or heard one like it. It didn't simply blow. It blew and blew and blew. It began with a *ka-ka-ka* which quickly merged into a steady protracted *kaaaaaaa* which then merged into a *kaaaa-whummmmp-kaaa-*

whummmmppp! which then finally blew into a numbing, rumbling, deafening, gut-churning *KA!WHUMP!WHUMP!WHUMP!WHUMMPPP!*

Then the trestle began to move. If it seemed to move slowly, that may have been because Carpenter was so far away. The burst was also going in four directions at once—down into the gorge, which was visible from Carpenter's vantage point, to each side of the gorge, and high above the gorge.

First there was a lot of smoke, a great billowing ball of it which obscured much of the view. Nonetheless, it was possible to see through and around enough of the cover to realize that the freight cars were literally breaking into a myriad of fragments, and simultaneously levitating. At the same time, the trestle beneath and around the blast was dissolving.

Then the ball of smoke slowly metamorphosed into fire. The ball grew bigger and bigger, burning off the white smoke, bigger, bigger, till the top of the ball simply exploded with a deafening *KA-WHUMPPP!* and quickly outswelled the smaller fiery globe six to eight times, until the red-orange fire-cloud took on the shape of a mushroom.

The blast was no longer fragmenting the trestle and the cars. The hellish heat was so intense everything simply evaporated in its path. Only the fragments from the initial blow-up survived somewhat intact. Many were pelting and showering Carpenter in a sooty, smoke-blackened hail of charred splinters and dirt.

After a veritable eternity the fireball receded—slowly, ever so slowly, and as it did, a surprising quantity of debris came back down after it, debris that had been blown thousands of feet into the air. It almost seemed to Carpenter as if the bits and pieces of wood and steel were returning to what had once been the trestle to take their exact, same, rightful place, precisely where they'd been before, and once again to keep right on spanning the chasm. Only, when these bits and pieces returned they did not stop, but kept right on falling, because now that the fire and smoke had receded, Carpenter could clearly see that there was no more trestle. It was simply gone, dispersed, as if it had never been. It was almost as though it had vanished unseen, as in a dream. There were only shards and slivers, dust and ashes, falling back from the sky and into the canyon. Nothing remained of the-thing-that-was.

Except the first half of the train.

Miraculously, the train had survived. It stood there on the track in that blasted, voided silence, its engine still chugging, steam rising up from under the wheels, sparks and smoke pouring out of the diamond-shaped stack. Then the whistle wailed and the drive wheels turned, and the next thing Carpenter knew the train was hauling ass, peeling around the bend, barreling down the south-bound track toward him and Slater.

In case Carpenter had wondered when to start setting off the powder charges atop the row of boulders, the Gatling-gunners made up his mind. Obviously scared out of their wits by the explosion, they were simply spraying everything in front of and around the track with hundred-caliber bullets just as fast as they could crank.

And the gunners were good. One man loaded fresh drums into the gun's breech as soon as the previous drum ran out, and Carpenter doubted that they lost ten seconds in rearming.

So he began setting off the charges.

As soon as the gunners spotted his smoke, they began laying it on with everything they had. The boulders shook as if they'd been kicked by the gods, and rock shards were flying over him like shrapnel. With every charge he touched off, he risked an arm.

Then he heard Slater's gun, and the Gatling was still. Risking a look, he peered from behind a rock. The gunner was blown clean off the car, lying a dozen feet from the track. Then the feeder grabbed the Gatling and was on him once more.

The train was near, ominously near, when the Sharps spoke again. The racheting Gatling was abruptly stilled. This time he jumped straight up in time to see the gunner get one all to himself.

He turned to look at Slater. He was already mounted. the Appaloosa bolted from a jack-rabbit start, and in an instant

Slater was galloping parallel to the track. He was going to board the train.

68

Carpenter was on his horse, following his fellow outlaws. Slater had stationed them all well in front, and they were in full gallop as the train came alongside them.

Carpenter scarcely believed anyone would have the guts to swing on.

It was then that he saw Slater, silhouetted atop the mountainous pile of cordwood, towering over the tender. Bigger than Beelzebub, he stood there with his sawed-off eight-gauge Greener braced on his hip. He was looking down into the locomotive. And when Carpenter saw the shotgun swing off his hip, point down into the engine car, when he saw the flash and the scattergun's kick, he slowed down the roan.

He knew this train was coming to a stop.

69

Cimarron Rose did not particularly like her job as firewoman. After they had successfully commandeered the Baldwin locomotive, Torn wisecracked that if "she couldn't turn a Gatling any better than her two-dollar tricks, she'd better stoke the firebox."

But while she didn't care for the tone, she recognized his point: Crashing through the border at El Paso–Ciudad Juarez would be hell with the hide off. She wouldn't want to handle the Gatling or the eight-gauge or try fighting hand to hand.

And if the border crossing was jammed with *turistas*, a lot of innocent people could get killed.

Also, her job was important. As important as any on the train. They all knew the El Paso–Ciudad Juarez set-up, and to get through those barricades they'd have to high-ball. Which meant someone would have to keep that boiler hot.

That was Cimarron. She was stoking the engine. Cord after cord of wood she threw into the firebox. Every half hour she raked the box, then fed in more fuel. When she wasn't doing that, she was back in the tender, moving more cord-wood to the front so she could get at it faster. She had to check the pressure gauge constantly. The needle must split the blue and the red. If it fell back into the blue, they were losing compression. If it hit the red, she had to pull the steam release valve.

She looked over her shoulder. Hardy, Bass, and Langford were up on the stack of cordwood at the rear of the tender. Abbey and Logan were on the mail car behind them. All were armed with Winchesters and shotguns. When she motioned to them for more wood, they kicked cords of pine down. Otherwise, they just passed a bottle of Old Crow and waited for the border.

On the flatbed car, encircled by stacked-up sandbags, Slater and Carpenter manned the Gatling. Periodically, Slater looked back at Cimarron and raised his fist over his head and pumped it up and down. This meant he wanted more wood, more steam, more speed. He seemed oblivious to the gauge's red line.

Rose threw in more cords of wood. Sweat streamed down her face and arms. She was filthy from the dirty cordwood, the smoke and soot. By the time they reached El Paso, she would be bone-tired and black as a navvy.

Still she grinned and threw on more wood. She began to whistle "Yellow Rose of Texas."

She could not remember ever having been so happy.

70

Now they were five miles from El Paso and the border, high-balling to beat hell. The track edged precipitously around long washes. Steep mountains rose abruptly to the south.

Mostly the land was hot, flat desert—yucca and creosote, sage and prickly pear. Balls of weed tumbled in the dust-laden wind, and a lone, perennial vulture wheeled overhead. Abandoned adobe shacks and unplastered *jacales* began dotting the sides of the roadbed. And then, in the distance, she could see the town.

They were barreling into the city, full-bore. She wanted to shrill the whistle, but Slater had warned her off, saying they needed all the surprise at the border they could get.

She glanced over her shoulder once to check the men behind her. They didn't look happy. The firebox was cooking just as hard as it knew how, and the diamond stack was ablaze with embers and ashes. The men on the woodpile and atop the freight cars were getting it bad. Soot and red-hot cinders were stinging them like angry hornets.

Worse, she didn't like the looks of the steam gauge. The needle had fallen hopelessly off the dial and lay in the red zone as though it were dead. Every time Slater glanced back at her, she gestured toward the needle, but he just shook his head, raised his fist in the air, and pumped it up and down, meaning more cords of wood, which she faithfully threw in the box.

Now they were in El Paso. Horses and wagons, adobe huts, and people were all just a high-speed blur. The telegraph poles whipped by like pickets in a fence. The noise in the cab was a constant, ear-shattering roar. And hot? In the El Paso shade it was a good hundred and eleven degrees, and in front of that hellacious firebox, Rose figured a hundred and forty.

When she first heard the howling inside the boiler, she imagined the bone-breaking labor, the desert sun, and the cab's hell-furnace had brought on hallucinations. Because the shrill, banshee shriek echoing through that engine car was like nothing she had ever heard before. The throbbing, wailing scream was now literally exploding out of the depths of the boiler, like the supernatural screeching of some infernal monster, raging dementedly from the farthest reaches of hell.

Then the rivets started to go. They were blowing out of the boiler at a rate of one every five seconds, and in Rose's mind, she thought she heard the popping accelerate. Then it did. Next, they were popping simultaneously, with an irregular, staccato beat, banging, whining, and ricocheting around the cab like bullets. She cringed behind the tied-down throttle, her hand reaching instinctively for the steam-release valve, when Slater, as if anticipating her move, turned abruptly, raised his fist, pumped it up and down, and mouthed the words, *More steam! More steam!*

Frantically, almost involuntarily, she threw more cords into the firebox.

When the last cord was in, while the boiler screamed and rivets clanged, she looked down the line and saw it: the American border crossing.

It was empty.

Slater was looking back at her and motioning toward the screech whistle. She opened up. It shrilled and wailed and howled up and down the tracks, letting everyone know they were coming through. As a further warning, Slater cut loose with the Gatling, shattering telegraph transformers, conductors, and insulators as the big locomotive screamed through town.

Through the American border they hauled ass, without a sign of resistance. Over the Rio Grande train trestle they continued to race, and Rose was giddy with excitement. She forgot the red gauge, forgot the banging rivets. She looked instead at the water below, and laughed. The river was perhaps two hundred yards across, and from the looks of the

vaders, maybe three feet deep in the middle. Rose saluted it
as they roared on by.

She turned her head back down the track toward the empty
Mexican border crossing, which she had assumed they would
just whip on through.

Then it happened.

With an infinite, torturous lassitude, a seeming inch at a
time, a burro pulling a two-wheeled ox cart piled high with
hay, which was obviously far too heavy for the puny creature,
crept up over the train bed, turned, saw the screeching,
smoking train, panicked, got twisted up in the harness, lost
his temper, sat down obstinately, and brayed.

It was not the biggest ox cart in the world, but it was big
enough to derail a Baldwin engine, hauling ass at eighty
miles per.

Rose wanted to cry, scream, throw herself on the floor of
the cab and beat it with her fists, when Torn Slater turned and
froze her with a look. Pumping his fist up and down, he
ordered her to pour on more wood.

Which she did.

Carpenter dived to the floor of the flatbed car, put his hands
over his head, and, no doubt, prayed.

It was then that Slater went to work. Slamming a fresh
drum into the Gatling, he started cranking hundred-caliber,
high-speed rounds into the cart. Closer and closer, they
moved toward the obstruction. Harder and harder he cranked.
One hundred, two hundred, three hundred rounds. Three
hundred and fifty. Three hundred sixty.

Smoke and fire poured out of the overheated muzzle.
Slowly, with excruciating torpor, hay fluttering in all directions, the cart began to shake, break up, fall apart, shatter.

Then Slater was firing into the cart at point-blank range.
Rose dived to the bottom of the cab, even as she saw the first
pieces of the cart slam into the flatcar, the muzzle of the
Gatling nose to nose with the wreck. Slater, still bolt upright,
still hammered away.

Now the interior of the cab was simply one deafening
protracted howl—shrieking boiler, popping, banging rivets,
the remains of the cart crashing into the Baldwin, metal

screaming against metal as the train fought to hold the rails
When she could stand it no longer, she stood up in the car fu
of whirling splinters, straw, and sawdust, and pulled th
whistle cord. Now the screech whistle, shrilling and wailin
up and down the track, merged with the rest of the roa
YIP-YIP-YIPPPINGGG! the news that Outlaw Torn Slater ha
hijacked an arms train, killed all its two hundred troopers
barreled over the border, the Yankees be damned!

When the sawdust cleared and she looked into the flatca
Torn was slumped over the Gatling, his head skewed gro
tesquely, bleeding from the ears and mouth.

71

The train pulled over at a siding a considerable distance sout!
of Ciudad Juarez. It was unlikely that any troops were in th
area except those of Diaz. Carpenter had telegraphed hin
with a portable transmitter, then cut the wire. For the tim
being, he, Cimarron, and Bass, and Slater were safe from
federales.

Their other friends had not been so lucky. Three had gotter
shot or knocked off the top of the freight cars and tender back
in El Paso. As for Hardy, he did not make it past the las
water and fuel depot. Standing by the siding, still bleeding
slowly from the ears and mouth, Slater had reminded him o
how he'd fucked that whore against standing orders during
the Horseman heist.

"So what if I did?" Hardy had said with a shrug.

"Fine," Slater had said. "Then pull that hog-leg."

"Suppose I ain't gonna?"

Now it was Slater's turn to shrug. He shot Hardy between
the eyes.

But that was then. Now they were on a different siding

waiting out the night. For Diaz to come. With their gold and fresh horses.

Carpenter felt a sense of relief.

He'd held up his end.

72

The bright crimson ball of the sun blazed over the eastern rimrock when they saw Diaz and his men riding up from the south. Through his spyglass, Carpenter recognized Don Porfirio at once. He was riding a massive, deep-chested white mare. Instead of a simple McClellan, he had a huge Spanish saddle of black leather, inlaid with turquoise and ivory with a sterling silver riding horn the size of a small melon. Instead of observing battlefield caution and removing insignia of rank, his entire chest was festooned with medals and campaign ribbons.

The hair on the back of Carpenter's neck began to bristle.

Diaz had with him two hundred crack *cuirassiers*. Foreign-trained, blooded by fifteen years of civil war, these were some of the best cavalry in the Western Hemisphere. Carpenter was also sure that Diaz's personal army of *peon* infantry was not far behind.

Diaz halted his men, then rode on ahead, perhaps a dozen feet. He smiled widely at Carpenter and dismounted. With a hearty laugh, he gave Carpenter the *abrazo*, which was returned with misgivings.

Diaz stepped back. "I hear you have been successful, very successful."

"*Excelencia*, you shall be most pleased."

"*Amigo*, seeing you well, I am already joyful."

To the rear of the *cuirassiers* were a dozen freight wagons, each one drawn by three spans of mules. Diaz gestured to his adjutant, who quickly ordered the freight haulers to unload the cars.

"*Don Porfirio*, we have everything plus a Gatling, which we throw in free. With our compliments."

"*Gracias, gracias amigos*," Diaz said warmly. "You four are patriots of the *revolución*, is that not so?"

Cimarron nodded agreeably. Bass stared at him and shrugged. Slater, who now had a soiled, bloody bandage around his head, looked away, unable to conceal his disgust.

But Diaz continued to grin. "Say, *compadre*, which one of these is the *gringo*, Slater?"

Slater turned to Diaz and fixed him with a stare. Diaz caught his glance. "*Hola, hombre*," he said pleasantly. "I have looked forward to meeting you."

"You say so."

"Men like you and me, we have so much in common, is that not so?"

"Like what?"

"Like death, *señor*. I see it on you plainly as if it were sitting on your shoulders. First living and fighting with the Apaches, then fighting for your Lost Confederate Cause in your *puta* Civil War. Then your life as a robber and marauder, here and in your own country, feuding, fighting, on and on, as through this *puta* war of yours can never have an end."

"Maybe it don't."

"Your country burned? Your capital sacked? And you say this war, it has no end. *Amigo*, there is no war. The war is in you. In only you. *Hay que tomar la muerte como si fuera amante*." You have taken death as a lover. "That is the truth. For I know you, *señor*. I know you. I have groaned each time your much-abused face, she jumps out at me from newspapers, magazines, off post office walls. I, too, have read those 'wanted' bills. What is your job description? Bank robber, train robber, murderer? My friend, what kind of life is this?"

"Somebody's gotta do it."

"You make light. That is good. And, yes, you are right. Somebody does, indeed, have to do it. I have had to do it, too. Men like you and me, we have that in common, no? We bring the gift of death. We bring it with us like a plague.

Juarez, he used to say: 'That Diaz, he kills more men than cholera.' And you know what I used to say? That Juarez, *me cago en su puta madre.* I piss in the milk of his mother. He did not understand. For the *revolución* is like a woman, no? Sometimes you want the *chingo,* sometimes you want to fuck, you gotta kick her in the ass. Is it not so?''

"Never liked them kind much.''

Diaz's face darkened with anger, but then he turned his head. Most of the big guns were loaded into freight wagons, and when he saw them, his grin returned instantly, wider than ever.

"But no, *señor,* I am not here to argue. I am here to thank you. A compliment on your *caza. Buena caza!''* Good hunting! "For my *soldados,* they are not like your starry-eyed *confederados, Señor Slater.* Sixty years of the *revolución* are behind these *amigos. Revoluciones* which had promised freedom and glory and reform, and which have ended in blood and tyranny, each worse than the last. No glory here, my friend. No romance, no longer even hope.'' He waved to his *cuirassiers.* "Did you ever look into their eyes? Eyes ancient in their cynicism, depthless in their despair. The eyes of the oldest *putas* in the worst cantina cribs in the world.''

"They are good men, *Excelencia,''* Carpenter said. "They've been to the wars, they've smelled the smoke, and they've heard the guns. They've seen the enemy die, and they've sometimes died themselves. They know what it is to fight.''

"Yes, and they will fight again. Now that they have the guns. And you have given me them.''

"We've sold you them,'' Slater reminded him.

"But, of course, *amigos.* For a price. Always for a price. The *gringo,* Carpenter, has finally sold me for a price his *gringo* guns. All the guns he should have sold me instead of giving them away to Lerdo. But I am not bitter. I have lived too long among you *Americanos* to be bitter. I understand your *norteamericano* morality. I have learned it from you and your Golden Rule. You know the *gringo* Golden Rule?''

"I think I'm about to know it,'' Slater said.

"He, who has the gold, rules. I learned it from you *yanquis.* It is a good rule, no? So here is your price, *amigos.*'' Diaz walked over to his horse and took a small leather sack out of a saddlebag. He tossed it to Carpenter. Carpenter looked in it and tossed it over to Slater. Slater took out the paper money and examined it. Scrip. A valueless currency substitute, barely negotiable, hardly worth the parchment it was printed on.

"Not exactly the gold we agreed on."

"Oh, I have the gold, my friends. Back at *El Alacrán*. And someday I might give it to you."

"What do we have to do to get it?" Carpenter asked, glancing wearily at the two hundred *cuirassiers*, his face darkening with slow, smoldering rage.

"I'm afraid you can do nothing, *amigo*. As a *soldado* your talents are modest, and as a gun-runner you're through. That last *buena caza*, that the *Americanos* will not forgive. They will hound you to the ends of the earth. They will harrow hell for your lost soul. They will never give up or let go. So you see, you are no longer of use to the *revolución*. You, though," he turned abruptly to Slater, "I would like you to work for me. I have followed your career, and all I can say is *magnifico*! That last piece of business I have followed especially—from the Horseman's heist to that mountain trestle demolition to the arms train's hijacking and that *muy macho* border crossing. A man like you I could use. Anywhere, anytime. You could be my personal adjutant. You could lead special operations. Anything you wish."

"For a price?"

Diaz's grin was splendid. "Always for a price."

"We struck that bargain once already. And all I got was an assful of scrip."

"Ah, *amigo*, what is gold? Tell me, if you lived down here, what would you be doing for a living?"

"Same thing I do up there. Rob trains."

"Why?"

"It's what I do."

"And what do you do with your gold? Whore yourself into a stupor? Cauterize your brain with tequila?"

"Just as fast as I know how."

"Is that a life for you?"

"Long as I got me a good horse and a good gun, that's all he life I need."

"Then that is a shame. We could have done much together, ou and me."

"For the people of Mexico, I suppose," Carpenter said, is voice rising with anger. "You will lead them into grace nd light. With these guns."

Diaz kept his eyes fixed on Slater. "Your friend, Carpen-er, he does not understand. Life here is *muy* hard, *muy* loody. It is not comprehensible to half-*yanqui gringos,* such s himself. We can expect no more help from him or from em. At least, for the time being. They do not understand. What we need is time and money and guns. When we have ese things, we will get help."

"That's awfully trusting of you, Don Porfirio," Carpenter aid hotly, shrugging off Slater's sign to cut it out, to back ff. "Next you will tell us that Our Redeemer liveth, and that eacemakers are divinely blessed."

Diaz turned to him. His eyes were hard and cold. "Will ou never understand? The *revolución* in Mexico is not like *p there.* Life here is not like *up there.* Our Redeemer liveth? Our Redeemer in Mexico is dead. The peacemakers in Mexico, ey are forever cursed. By Christ's bones, by his bloody ails, will you never see? I do not want your *gringo* indepen-ence. I do not trust your *gringo* independence. I trust fear. his human dignity and freedom of man you so glowingly peak of does not apply here, to our stupid Aztec aborigines. Without my intervention, these savages once again would hoke on human blood, devour each other's flesh, sacrifice eir daughters' cunts to barbaric priests and pagan gods. Free ese people, you say? I do not want them free. I want them randed, shackled, and ruled by the whip. I want them boring in my mines and fields until they drop. And when ey can work no more, I don't want them living idly off the and, basking in this *muy buena libertad* you speak so ovingly of. I want them dead."

"And our money?" Carpenter said.

"Be happy I leave you with your lives. Be happy I offer

your friend employment. Perhaps he will even reconsider th
offer at some later point.''

Carpenter shrugged off Slater's sign to cool it and pinne
Diaz with a stare. ''There's always Lerdo.''

Diaz waved at the distant *cordillera*. ''Yes, I leave hir
there alive. I want him alive. I like to think of him ther
waiting, hating.''

''Maybe Lerdo will deal?'' Bass piped up.

''Lerdo is finished,'' Diaz said with a broad smile. ''You
guns finished him.''

''We'll get you,'' Rose suddenly shouted.

''Listen, you stupid *puta,* you'll get *nada.* You four ar
nada. You're dust, debris. You're in the wind.''

Diaz approached the white mare with the hand-carve
black Spanish saddle, inlaid with ivory and turquoise. H
grabbed the big, ornate silver pommel and swung on.

''Then pity poor Mexico,'' Carpenter said slowly.

''Yes, pity poor Mexico,'' Diaz agreed. Then he waved hi
hand north and shouted: ''So far from God, so close to th
United States!''

He swung the big mare around and kicked the horse into
canter, on up the tracks, the freight wagons with their bi
mule teams and his two hundred *cuirassiers* following clos
behind.

73

Two men and a woman sat in the dining room of Delmonico's
the most expensive hotel in Denver. The man reading th
newspaper wore a beige derby and kept a cigarette holder i
his teeth cocked at a jaunty angle. His knee-length ridin
boots had sharp silver rowels which played havoc with th
surface of the dining room table, on which he kept ther
propped. It rankled the headwaiter to the bone, but the ma

ipped so well and spent so lavishly that management concluded discretion to be the better part of continuing remuneration.

The man's soft, white shirt of finest doeskin was tucked
neatly into his red twill jodhpurs which in turn were tucked
tightly into the brightly polished boots. His mouth was
twisted in a habitual sneer. He seemed the most insolent man
who ever walked the earth. The only flaw was the bald, no,
the scarred swath of flesh dipping below the derby on the
back of his head to the left of and just above the eye.

The other man, who was hoeing into his second order of
steak and eggs, was worn and gnarled, hard-used from
spending most of his years as a law enforcement officer. He
had the tough, weathered tan of a man who has spent too
much of his life in the desert country squinting and grimacing
into the burning, cutting wind and sun. Under the black dress
Stetson, his eyes were pale gray. They were opaque, uncaring
eyes, eyes that suggested that something behind the retinas
had given up. No one who knew him would have disagreed.
Something had died. Years ago.

Inside the black frock coat, the man carried two hard-
traveled .45's, scarred and worn smooth around the walnut
grips. The pistol on his left hip he wore butt turned out. His
right hand was presently on his lap, resting near that gun. It
was always near that gun. Even while he fucked.

But the few patrons, still seated in the luxurious dining
room with its many tables, its spotless linen, its sterling silver
settings, and massive overhead chandeliers of scroll-pattern
crystal and myriads of bright, flickering candles, did not
notice the two men so deeply immersed in their reading and
breakfasting. They looked at the woman.

She had a long mane of flame-red hair flowing casually
over her shoulders, down her upper torso, almost to the small
of her back. She had wide-set, emerald eyes, the sort of skin,
sometimes called buttermilk, that stretches tightly over the
wide, flaring cheekbones and yet leaves the large, generous
lips looking soft and sensual.

She wore a ruffled silk blouse, which, like her eyes, was
emerald in hue, and her whipcord Levi's were skin-tight and

black as the underside of a raven's breast. She was staring blankly into space, smoking a cigarillo.

The man with the beige bowler spread the newspaper on the table. Slapping his hands together excitedly he said: "Ah, boyo, this is news to warm the cockles of my foolish heart."

The woman's expressionless eyes continued to stare into space while the older man worried his overdone piece of beef with a bone-handled, poorly-honed steak knife. The man in the bowler slapped the front page of the paper.

"I say, you two, don't bust a gut with enthusiasm. Just because a gang of murdering outlaws robs the biggest casino-brothel in this godforsaken country, kill half the patrons, rape one of the doxies, run off with a cash box, blow a gigantic trestle with a big, fucking troop train on it halfway to Holy Hell, commandeer a train full of munitions and full-throttle it straight over the Mexican border where they sell it to an unnamed horde of kill-crazy Mexican revolutionaries—don't bother showing any interest. Not on my behalf. Please. My skin is thick. I can take a lot."

"Mr. Sutherland, you pay me to protect your sorry ass and to occasionally satisfy hers. The deal don't say nuthin' 'bout tossin' hats in the air nor doin' handsprings over no newspaper stories."

Miss McKillian came alive. "Speaking of satisfaction, duck, I could use a little of that even as we speak. Perhaps a little mid-morning gratification—a little head, let's say, is in order as soon as Suthie here gets the check."

"Not quite, you two," Sutherland said heatedly. "Stop and think about it. A major whorehouse-casino is hit. A mountain trestle plus troop train is blown to Hades. Its freight of munitions is hijacked, high-balled over the border, sold to *revolucionarios*. What does that mean to you?"

Judith McKillian massaged her crotch frankly. John Henry Deacon started in on his eggs.

"God in fire," Sutherland groaned, "the one has her brains between her legs. The other keeps them in his tapeworm. Don't either of you care?"

"I'm all ears." The voice was Deacon's.

"Yeah? Then listen up, buckos. Both of you. TORN FUCKING SLATER!" he yelled. "That's what I'm talking about. Now do you get me?"

"Yeah, I get it," McKillian said. "You want Slater to part your hair the other way."

"His ass is ours. I know it."

"Give it up, friend," Deacon said simply.

"Not while I'm above ground."

"Take him on again, that won't be long."

"We'll do it different this time."

"Different, how? Put salt on his tail? Snap him with wet towels?"

"We'll go to my old business associate, the one with whom I own that silver mine. The one that's making so much profit on so little overhead. I tell you, this fellow Porfirio is a genius with mining. Agriculture, too. Americans could learn something from him. Wouldn't be surprised what kind of technological breakthroughs he's stumbled on. He also has a real gift for labor management."

"What's this guy's name?"

"Diaz. Porfirio Diaz. Some of the experts are predicting he'll be the new *Presidente*. In any event, he has his own private army and one hell of a lot of know-how. I'm sure we could strike some sort of deal."

"How do you want your epitaph? 'In the fullness of his youth'? Or just 'Shot dead'?"

"Don't make me negative. I can feel this one. We got Slater cold. We got him by the balls."

"Don't tell me. *'And now we start to pull,'*" McKillian said in a mock limey accent.

"His ass is ours."

74

Cimarron Rose sat in the shadowy lee of a chaotic heap of rocks. She ignored her sleeping friends, sprawled out in their own splotches of shade, and stood up.

SAVAGE BLOOD

The bloody sun was sinking over the bloody mountains along the distant rim of the horizon. In the other direction, there was the rail spur which they'd put well behind them. Across that hot desert flat there were also sage and yucca, octillo and prickly pear. There were also rocks and rattlers, Gila monsters and scorpions. Overhead, there were the ubiquitous vultures wheeling effortlessly on the rising thermal drafts. Otherwise, nothing. No unplastered adobe huts, no mud and *maguey* corrals full of horses with their tails switching and heads bowed in the heat, no stovepipes or chimneys curling smoke into the cloudless sky, no long checkerboard rows of corn and beans. Nothing. Not a tree. Not a hint of a stream. Not a breath of breeze anywhere in all that emptiness.

She stood there and, once again, watched the same bloody sun sink below the same bloody mountains. She watched it sink slowly, a fraction at a time, then vanish. With stunning rapidity, the stars came out. First one at a time, then two or three at once, then by the dozen, then the score, then by the hundreds and thousands. Soon the sky became a virtual carpet of winking lights, bright enough for her to trudge around the boulders, leaving Carpenter and Bass with their first real sleep in several days.

On the other side of the boulders, she found him. Torn Slater. He was sitting up, staring into the east.

"Far enough from the spur?"

"Ain't possible to get much farther. Not without no water."

"You ready to lay down and die?"

That one made him smile. "I got a thought or two."

"Figure on sharin' them?"

"Sure." He waved at the distant sierras. "See them mountains, the ones that Diaz pointed to, when he said that Lerdo was up there?"

"Yeah?"

"Well, did you also notice all the colonies of prickly pear around these parts? Whole forests of the stuff. I bet it runs clear to them mountains."

"You ain't thinkin' to—"

"Beats sittin' 'round here waitin' to feed them vultures."

"Torn, them mountains must be forever."

"An Apache'd make it."

"You ain't wearin' no breechclout I can see."

"I did once."

"This ain't no time to talk on what we all could do once. You ain't no Apache, and you sure ain't seventeen. Hell, you wouldn't make it twenty miles out there before you'd dehydrate to death."

"How long you think you'll last here?"

"We gotta water bag."

"I'm takin' it with me."

Rose shrugged. "I ain't never won no debates off you yet. Just tell me, suppose Lerdo ain't there. What then?"

"The body shakes. Feet thump once or twice on the hardpan. And there's a surprised new face in hell."

Slater stood up. He took off his Plainsman's hat, ripped the blood-clotted bandage from his head, put the hat back on. He slung the water bag over his shoulder and started off. Rose grabbed his arm and stopped him.

"I said I'm goin', girl."

"Jus' wanted to ask you something."

"Well," he said.

"I wanna give you a kiss."

"Rose."

"Well, you fucked me lots of times. And you always said I was a great blow. Why won't you let me kiss you? Maybe I'd be real good."

"I told you before, girl—"

"I know, you don't kiss whores. But since we might...since this might be the last time we see—"

The realization that they would all no doubt die had not sunk in before, and suddenly she was fighting to choke back the tears and to stifle the sobs. Chin quivering, hands pressed to face, she struggled with her emotions. In the end, all that was left were hard, brittle sobs, dry and silent as heat lightning, scorching the back of her throat. Then she was grabbing at Slater, burying her head in his chest, and he had her cheeks in his hands, and he was kissing her all over, all over her eyes, nose, chin, mouth, which she opened and drew him into—great sucking, rapacious kisses, lips rubbed raw from the man's seven-day growth and the woman's wild exuberance.

There was nothing for it but to get down in the sand and do it. And with murderous precision Rose had Torn's fly open, had plucked out his member, and there in the starlight of the Chihuahua desert, lost, alone, and on the brink of certain death, she backed him up against the boulder, slipped down to her knees, and with all her heart and soul and mind began frenching the bottom of his dick, lapping at the sides, kissing and caressing and sucking on its head. By now his cock was going crazy, burning with desire, and coming in short, staccato bursts which only increased her voluptuously loving soul-kisses. She was still smoke-blackened from the firebox, and the black powder smoke had fouled him even worse. They were also gamey from their march through the desert, from more than a week without a wet bandana's worth of washing.

But at death's door such things are minor.

Now he was starting to come, flat-out and full-tilt, so she accepted as much of it as she could take, almost every inch of his gargantuan member. Pounding up and down, keeping the head of his dick deep in her throat beyond the uvula and away from the gag centers, she was able to pump and pump and pump even as the tremendous orgasms were roaring out of him. Harder and harder she worked, faster and faster her tongue and lips stroked, till she was so horny herself the hot, hard button between her legs was burning up.

She couldn't stand it anymore.

She reached down into her pants and began to masturbate.

Then Slater took matters into his own hands.

He shucked off her boots and Levi's and flipped her belly down on the desert sand. Then, spreading her legs, slipping his right hand around her hip and under her crotch, he kneaded the fiery clitoris. Her crotch and butt were pumping and revolving frantically. He couldn't resist taking the little nub and rolling it between his thumb and index finger.

She simply turned into a bomb and blew.

It took considerable effort to get his cock into her vulva. He had to keep one hand over her mouth to mute the wailing groans, and one hand on her clitoris to control pumping of the orgasms. So urgent were her needs, so deliriously hysterical her desires, she was no help at all. His cock was slipping off her ass, crashing into her taint, as he found to steady her and direct his massive member into her snatch.

Slater knew he had plenty of bullets left, knew he would enjoy it, would not delude himself into pretending that this was somehow good for her soul. No, he knew who he was, what he was, and precisely what he was doing. He was about to give both of them a goddamn good time. Nonetheless, it was also true that he had just had a perfectly satisfying orgasm; he had not slept in close to four days. What lay before him was racking thirst, scorching heat, a good case of third-degree sunburn, and probable death. Lastly, Sam Bass was a friend, but an insanely jealous lover. If he woke up and stumbled onto them, he was capable of putting a couple of rounds into the back of Slater's head.

Yes, Torn Slater had reservations.

But if this was their last night together and possibly the last fuck either of them would have, hell, he had to do it right.

So for one last moment, while he still possessed that lucid detachment, he gave his dick a tentative pump, took stock of his sorry life, and said to himself: Well, boy, time to go to work.

He held her tightly in his arms, raised her rear end, and then they began the long, bouncing bobsled of their passion.

75

The next day Carpenter and Bass sat in the shade of a rock. Rose was sleeping alongside them, snoring hoarsely. Periodically, they tried to wake her to ask what had happened, but she just smiled insensibly and moaned. In any event, it did not matter, because they knew what had happened.

Slater had reamed out every throbbing orifice of Rose's insatiable body.

He'd also taken off across the desert with the water bag, leaving them to weather it out on mesquite nuts and prickly pear pulp.

His footprints, which he made no attempt to conceal, indicated he was going after Lerdo.

"Hell, I don't mind him goin' after Lerdo with our water bag," Bass finally said. "Slater's the only one with a Chinaman's chance of gettin' through, and frankly, we got no alternatives. I don't mind him not tellin' us, neither. I ain't long on teary farewells myself. What I don't understand is what it is with you and him and my girl. Why is it you guys always got to fuck her brains out every time things get rough? I mean, just 'cause she's a whore, does that give you guys the right to fuck her deaf, dumb, stupid, and blind? Like every time you get a little nervous? Can't you and Slater find some other way of steadyin' your nerves? I mean, she is my girl, you know."

PART XIII

76

The man sitting in the narrow, straight-backed chair behind the massive oak desk was confused. He rubbed his large, hawklike nose and shook his head.

A *gringo* who says he can sack *El Alacrán*?

Madre mia, Sebastian Lerdo said to himself, you've been in the hills too long. He glanced distastefully at his white *peon* shirt, his old khaki army pants, and his last good pair of leather boots. The battered campaign hat he pushed to the back of his head, and leaned forward on his elbows.

El Alacrán with its nine Napoleons, double Gatlings, and now, he was told on good authority, an arsenal of American artillery.

And some crazy, heat-sick *gringo* out wandering the desert claims he can conquer it.

Lerdo turned and stared out the rear glassless window behind him. The village *zocale* was littered with Indians in clothes similar to his, taking their midday siestas. Scrub cactus grew randomly across the square, and the huts surrounding the *plazuela* were a motley assemblage. Shacks of adobe, sheds of stone and mud, lean-tos of *maguey* leaves and stalks, one-room *jacales*. The larger, more prosperous of the houses were fenced in by hedges of organ cactus.

His own two-story colonial palace was not that bad. It had a nice, flowering patio in the back, high ceilings, the molding of which was garishly tortured with scroll-work and rosebuds. The black ironwork balconies were charming.

He called out to his secretary: "Did the *gringo* identify any of his *compadres*?"

A young, barefoot *peon* wearing what appeared to be white pajamas and clutching a straw sombrero to his chest rushed in and said: "*Si, Excelencia*, I forgot. The other *gringo*'s name is Car-pen-tor."

Lerdo shut his eyes. "Please bring the *gringo* in. *Pronto. Muy pronto*."

The *gringo* was brought in, *peons* holding each of his arms. He was eased into a narrow, straight-backed chair.

Lerdo looked him over closely. This was the most horribly sunburned man he'd ever seen. The facial blisters had merged into one bloody sore, and his nose and mouth were no longer cracked, but gouged with massive lesions which would possibly have to be stitched.

His clothes were rags, ravaged by heat and dust and thorny chaparral.

But the Indians who found him wandering the perimeter of the *cordillera* had done their best. They had daubed his burns with mule-deer fat, rehydrated him, and, when he had talked of attacking Diaz and taking his guns, they had brought him to their leader.

And now that imbecilic secretary tells me he is compadre *of my good friend, Carpenter.*

"Where is Carpenter?"

The man signaled for pen and paper, and slowly, with burned fingers, drew Lerdo a map. Lerdo summoned his Captain of the Guard, who quickly identified the huge heap of boulders on the map.

The man held up three fingers.

"Three *hombres*?" the Captain said.

The man nodded.

After the Captain left, Lerdo asked, "Can you talk?"

The man nodded. "A little."

"Then talk a little. Why do you know so much about Diaz?"

"I brought him the *gringo* guns. From over the border. In the arms train."

Lerdo studied him closely. "Why do you think you can take *El Alacrán*?"

"I can take it from the rear, capture Diaz in his bed, commandeer the Gatlings."

"There is a four-thousand-foot cliff and a twenty-foot wall behind *El Alacrán*. It cannot be scaled. You are mad."

Then the man let it out. Slowly. Two words. "Apaches can."

Lerdo paused. It was true that Apaches were trained virtually from birth to scale cliffs that no white man could ever imagine climbing. The way they lived, it was necessary for their survival.

"The Apaches are all confined to reservations. San Carlos, for the most part."

"The *broncos* aren't."

"A band of *broncos,* renegades, will capture Diaz for their white-eyes enemies and for a Mexican? *Señor,* the sun has damaged your brain."

"Geronimo will," the *gringo* whispered.

At this point Lerdo started to laugh. The hilarity of the situation was truly overwhelming. He started to call his secretary to have the *gringo* taken out.

"He will do it for me," the *gringo* rasped.

"And why, may I ask?" said Sebastian Lerdo with a sneer.

The man held up his hands. Long, jagged scars transversed the palms.

Blood-brother stigmata.

"He is my brother."

Doubt fell from Lerdo's face. "You're Blood Ant," he said. It was now his turn to whisper. "The one the *gringos* call Slater. Cochise told me of you, years and years back. You're the one he called the Apache Messiah."

Slater nodded.

"*Madre mia,* with Geronimo's *broncos* and with my *rurales*, yes, we just might do it. We just might surprise *El Alacrán.* We might just catch Diaz right in his bed. *Por amor de Dios*"—for the love of God—"if you take me to Geronimo, I swear we'll try. Hell, we'll do more than try. We'll nail that bastard."

"We'll nail him to that fuckin' 'dobe wall," the *gringo* rasped.

PART XIV

77

Six men and a woman squatted along the rim of the cliff. It was near midnight, but in the lucid glow of the stars, they could still make out the precipices of the slickrock canyon.

Torn Slater tossed a small rock over the canyon's edge. Silence. As though he'd dropped it into a bottomless well.

Geronimo peered over the rim, then glanced at the hacienda wall some three hundred yards away. He hefted his bag of pitons, liked the weight, and secured it to his belt. He slung two coils of light rope onto his shoulders, criss-crossing them over his chest. He felt calm. He was prepared for the climb.

The ropes and pitons were not for him. He, his three *bronco* braves, and his female war shaman, Ghost Owl, were carrying these pitons, ropes, wooden mallets, and even guns, just to help the white-eyes. The men called Bass and Carpenter would never survive the cliff climb without ropes and hand-holds. In fact, Geronimo doubted whether his brother, Blood Ant, could make the ascent without assistance.

He looked over at his men. Horse Ears was carrying the powerful longbow with the telescopic sight which Blood Ant had brought him. Carpenter held the lion-skin quiver containing the hard, strong arrows of ancient, shipwrecked wood and tipped with the tri-bladed broad-heads of steel. The other two braves carried Winchesters, Ghost Owl a bag with extra pistols and cartridges. The white-eyes carried only themselves.

Geronimo looked forward to the climb. He had not enjoyed any strenuous exertion for many moons. Too much time in the stronghold, too much *tiswin*. He was glad to get out.

He lowered himself over the abyss, and, looking up, flashed a broad, bright grin.

Carpenter handed him the lion-skin quiver.

Which contained more than arrows.

It also held dynamite packed in sawdust. A dozen short fuses were attached to each stick, and each was lashed to an arrow. It also held a big, fat cigar.

Geronimo could not understand why the white-eyes looked so queasy.

78

Lerdo waited with his fifty *cuirassiers* behind a small, sloping hill. In another hour, he would order them to tighten cinches and mount up. If and when Slater and Geronimo breached the rear wall, if and when they took the twin Gatlings and captured Diaz, if and when they blew up the barracks buildings, then Lerdo would order his men to attack. *En echelon*.

With the Gatlings blasting Diaz's troops from the rear, and a charge of *cuirassiers* from the flank, he might just rout the enemy.

If . . .

He glanced at his troops. They were without a single vestige of a uniform. His captain wore a tan felt sombrero embroidered in gold, with black ribbons hanging down the back. Red jacket, tight black trousers, and criss-crossed andoliers. the rest of the troops wore white shirts of home-pun *maguey*, white pajamalike trousers rolled to the knees, lack, white, and red *serapes* over the shoulders. Hemp bags lung across the back, carrying pistols, bullets, accessories. Many, even those on horseback, were barefoot.

But all had repeating rifles, eighteen of which the Chiricauhuas ad donated.

And all had *machetes*.

In these weapons lay Lerdo's hope for success.

Sabe rezar? he said to himself.

Do you remember how to pray?

79

A single-pronged grappling hook swung over the top of the acienda's rear wall, and Geronimo quickly pulled himself up. The top of the twenty-foot barricade was six feet across, o he had plenty of room to spread out, to make himself as mall as possible to the rest of the house. There he perched nd watched the other five men and the woman clamber up he rope.

The *gringo*, Carpenter, came last. He had been a big disappointment. He was drenched with sweat, and his face was ashen. Once he froze on the cliff and refused to move. At hat point Blood Ant had taken out the knife sheathed across his back, the one the white-eyes called an "Arkansas tooth-pick." He put it to Carpenter's neck and threatened to gut im throat to balls if he didn't get moving.

Carpenter believed Blood Ant, and continued climbing.

Looking back on it, Geronimo believed Blood Ant, too.

The plan was simple: Geronimo would circle around the op of the hacienda wall with his knife out, and Horse Ears would do the same. Since the sentries and the Gatling-gunners were ordered to face the front, the stealthy *bronco* would have surprise on their side.

Meanwhile Carpenter, Slater, and Ghost Owl would ente the hacienda from the rear, looking to capture Diaz. The tw other *broncos* would drop down inside the square and elimi nate any inside guards who might try to shoot the othe Apaches off the hacienda wall.

Geronimo crept noiselessly along the wall's top. In th brilliant starlight, creeping upon the whitewashed adobe Geronimo felt terribly exposed.

For the first time during this entire operation, Geronim knew something resembling fear.

Then he grabbed the first sentry from behind, had hir belly down on the wall, shoved a knee into his back. On hand around the man's mouth, another under his chin, Geronim pulled sharply. With a loud sickening *crack!* the man's nec snapped.

The sentry's body convulsed in jerking, racking spasms and his feet thumped twice on the wall with astonishin force.

No one moved.

No one looked.

Quickly, Geronimo began slipping into the *soldado*'s ligh green uniform. He had nothing to take off but his breechclout

80

Slater, Carpenter, and Ghost Owl slipped barefooted into th back door of the hacienda. The house was still as death. No even star-glow filtered through the windows; the interior wa pitch black.

They tried to stick to the middle of the rooms where all th furniture was crammed, Spanish-style. It was better tha being spotted, silhouetted against the walls.

It took them a seeming eternity to feel their way through kitchen, hallways, drawing rooms, and the grand *sala*. Finally they were at Diaz's bedroom.

The squatted in front of the doorway, knives out. Carpenter held a slip-hammered .45. He'd wired back the trigger and filed down the hammer notch and sear, so he could thumb back without the telltale *click-click*. This was their in-house piece. He stared blankly at Slater. Both men were confused by the absence of guards, but dared not question blessings. Slater nodded, and Carpenter eased open the door. He quietly slipped into Diaz's bedroom.

Suddenly the early morning darkness beyond was ripped apart by a bone-jarring explosion. Moments later, a second blast.

Slater cursed silently. Geronimo was not to dynamite the barracks until Slater signaled him. What was happening? Slater had to find out. Possession of the Gatlings was too important. If they lost those guns to Diaz's men, the game was up.

He motioned Carpenter on into the bedroom after Diaz, but grabbed Ghost Owl by the arm. She and Slater moved quickly toward the front door, leaving Carpenter to face Diaz alone.

81

Geronimo was now upright, walking along the top of the wall in the sentry's green uniform. Indistinguishable from the other guards, he silently thanked the Child-of-the-Water and the White-Painted-Lady for giving him such wonderful luck. He promised them a special offering when he got back to the stronghold. He would have Snake Woman and Ghost Owl perform ceremonies full of chants and songs and dances and magic pollen, expensive ceremonies which would demonstrate the sincerity of his—

Then, perhaps a hundred and fifty yards beyond the front wall, he saw the two barracks buildings.

Soldados in straw sombreros and white *peon* clothes were pouring out of the infantry barracks.

Geronimo's next move was purely instinctive. He strung the high-powered, osage-orange longbow, lit the Havana cigar with a Lucifer, and nocked a dynamite arrow. Amid confused shouts of: *"Ey, que pasa, compadre?"* he lit the fuse and thrilled the arrow in a high arc toward the crowd outside the barracks.

The arrow flew high and far, and just a little in front of the crowd. Even as it left the bow, Geronimo knew this to be the trajectory, and was pleased. And even before it could hit the ground, the next dynamite-arrow was lit, nocked, and thrilling through space, only this one was aimed at the roof.

Several things happened. The first arrow landed directly in front of the two-hundred-man mob and went off with a tremendous, ear-cracking *ka-whumppp!* and a red-orange ball of fire.

For which the *soldados* were totally unprepared.

They had left the barracks expecting a boring evening of night maneuvers out on the drill field and in the desert. Their guns were not even loaded.

They panicked—charging pell-mell back into the barracks which contained all their powder and ammunition.

When the second arrow hit.

The second blast was spectacular. It blew the sun-baked, dried-out, termite-ridden adobe building and its kegs of black powder into a hundred thousand pieces of dirt and straw and mud and brick and timber. When the ear-splitting, stomach-wrenching concussion was over, and the blazing, blood-red fire-ball was levitating along with most of the roof, every eye was on the conflagration.

Including those of the Gatling-gunners.

Which was Geronimo's big chance.

When Geronimo was loosing the arrows, the Gatlings had spun around on their turrets to search out their target. But so dramatic had been the blasts that the gunners turned toward the new threat.

Geronimo was too far from the nearest gunner to hazard a shot. And even if he had got him, he never could have reached the Gatling. The one on the far wall two hundred yards away would have killed him first.

So he did the only thing possible.

He pulled his Colt from his belt, put his head down, and, barefoot and silent, ran just as hard as he knew how for the Gatling, hoping and praying the gunners would not turn.

82

The interior of Diaz's lavish bedroom was utterly lightless. Carpenter inched forward, a knife in his teeth, the slip-hammered Colt in his right hand.

It was a full forty-five seconds after the two gut-churning blasts, and at last he heard the dull rattle of gunshots from the courtyard. They were almost a welcome relief. Anything was better than the unnerving silence.

Then it happened.

Bang.

He hit his head on the bed post.

He heard someone sit up.

He gritted his teeth on the knife blade, tightened his grip on the Colt, coiled his muscles like steel springs, and leaped onto the bed.

Someone was beating his face with a pillow, and, when it caught on the knife clenched in his teeth, it ripped open, filling the air with goose down and feathers. He kept on charging, swinging, fighting. If the knife hadn't ripped out of his teeth, he would have started slashing. He didn't give a fuck anymore what Slater said about taking Diaz alive. He not only hated the bastard; Diaz was personally dangerous. He would have a loaded pistol under his pillow. Christ, with all that gunfire in the *plazuela*, Diaz would probably start spraying shots around the room any second.

Charging through the floating snowstorm of feathers, he was swinging with fist and gun, but his opponent was fast—too fast. Even worse was the lack of light. That damn bedroom was darker than seven yards up a chimney.

Then something hit his head. A rock? A lamp? Whatever it was, it hurt like hell, and then it seemed as though all the lights in the world were coming on at once. Then slowly, in a vertiginous blur, they were going out, one by one by one.

Until, at last, that final, flickering, dimly lit candle was snuffed.

And all was darkness.

83

Slater did not even bother slipping quietly out the front door. He knew that if Geronimo was using dynamite without first capturing a Gatling, they were all in serious trouble. So he charged out into the courtyard, the cocked .45 in his fist.

It didn't take long to see what was amiss. A blood-red fire-ball, which had once been the infantry barracks, was roaring, rising, and crackling like a blast furnace. And while the Gatling-gunners turned to watch, Geronimo, in a sentry's uniform, with his head down and pistol drawn, was charging the right-hand gunner.

The gunner to the left was the first to turn back, and when he saw Geronimo's silent charge, he turreted the Gatling around. Without even thinking, Slater raised his Colt. At a hundred yards, it was a tough shot, but he emptied all six rounds into the gunner, cocking with his left hand, firing with his right. Then he raced out into the maelstrom of gunfire, Ghost Owl right behind.

84

When Carpenter came to, his first reaction was that his head hurt like hell, and he couldn't move. However, there was some light in the room, which was something. But not much. His vision blurred.

He tried to move his hands and feet. Finally he realized that he was stripped buck-naked, spread-eagled, bound, and gagged. He had the terrible suspicion that he was lying on Diaz's big double-canopied bed, his wrists, ankles, and neck lashed to the corner posts.

Guns were going off in the courtyard.

His asshole felt as if it was on fire.

And somewhere in the dim, distant dark, he heard the *YIP-YIP-YIP!* of an insane rebel yell.

The room was illuminated by a single candle on the bedside table. He blinked his eyes rapidly, then peered into the face of the person on the bed bending over him.

His vision was blurred over with pain, and it took some time to make out the face, partly because he kept trying to discern Diaz's features somewhere in the unfocused chaos. But he couldn't. And it wasn't till she spoke that he recognized her.

Maria.

The girl he had saved from the firing squad.

The one Diaz called "the greatest piece of ass in the world."

She said: "I'm sorry. I'm so sorry. You saved my life, and now you are going to die."

The face came into focus. Long, black hair, parted down the middle. Sloe, almond eyes, almost oriental in their slant and sheen. Small nose, cupid's-bow mouth, white, perfect

teeth. Wide, flaring cheekbones now stained with tears o
remorse.

"I'm so sorry we had to tie and gag you," she went or
"The *majordomo* hit you. He is convinced that Diaz i
coming back tonight with his *cuirassiers*. There are tw
hundred battle-hardened infantry out there *también*. So you'r
trapped, *amigo*. If you run, they'll track you down. If yo
hole up here, they'll starve you out. There is no escape."

Carpenter bit frantically into the gag.

"So you see, there is no hope. *Majordomo* also say it is
tragedy, seeing as how we both owe you our lives, and w
both cried in each other's arms for a long time. Finall
he brushed my hair carefully and said he knew I woul
do the right thing. He locked the shutters and door from th
outside and left us alone. So I am to make you as comfortabl
as possible until Diaz returns. After which you will be line
up against the wall and shot."

She stared sadly into his eyes, her lips slightly parted. Sh
slowly removed her red silk dressing gown. She climbed ove
him.

He stared at her in disbelief as she lowered herself onto hi
member. Her vaginal muscles were strong as a vise. An
when she began fucking, jerking, and gyrating on his dic
with those big powerful clamps, he became delirious wit
desire.

It was when she brought him to the brink of orgasm tha
she raised the question. She looked him in the eye with tha
sensuous stare and said: "Did you ever hear of the Vera Cru
Love Rope?"

He had. Everybody had. Vera Cruz whorehouses ha
offered them during the Juarez Revolution until they wer
outlawed. These were knotted cords, shoved up the rear end
which, when dragged out a knot at a time, could stimulate th
man into an infinity of orgasms. Until, that is, the hear
busted or the prostate was slashed by the harsh, bloody knots

Rumor had it that a strong, healthy man could take no mor
than six.

One or two men had endured twelve inches, or twelv
knots, it was said.

No man survived beyond twelve knots.

Now Maria was riding him wildly, and he was floating off into the wonderful sea of orgasm when she did it.

His whole being was focused and transfixed by blinding, searing pain, and it was as though he were tumbling down a long, black, bottomless abyss of orgasm. No wondrous oceanic drift here. His was a hard, tough, painful, wrenching come. It felt as if a grenade had gone off in his balls, and a cannister shell was blowing up in his prostate.

Oh, he did come. That was there, too. And there was no denying that he felt pleasure in that awful ordeal. But he certainly did not want to repeat it. He could not wait for his prick to go back down and for Maria to get off.

But she was speaking again. "The *Majordomo* and I decided to use the Love Rope because it does not let you get soft. You can just go on and on forever."

He tried to shake his head no, but then she pumped up and down three times really hard, bringing him again to the point of orgasm.

And the little rope jerked again.

This time the agony was unendurable, a searing torture that wrenched his whole body being into a reality that burned like hellfire. It was true that part of it felt good—there was no denying that. But it was something he could not survive again.

By now it felt as if someone had stuck a red-hot poker up his groin, ass, and abdomen, and he was sobbing from scorching pain and humiliation. Tears were running down his cheeks, and Maria was kissing and licking the tears away.

"Oh, *guapo*, oh little rabbit, I know it feels good. You cannot stand it, no? You wonder what on earth you did to deserve such ecstasy. You are crying now because you think it will end. Well, it won't, *guapo*. I have thirty-six inches in there. Thirty-six knots. And if Diaz is not here when we are done, I will put them all up there again."

He was sobbing, shaking his head, groaning.

"*Si*, I know. You are afraid that I am not getting as much pleasure as you. That I am giving, but not receiving. That is not true, *señor*. You are *un muy macho caballero*," she whispered hoarsely.

Now she was on him again, pumping violently up and down, bringing him to the point of ejaculation with a pain that was truly stupendous, as though someone had set his bowels, prick, and balls afire.

"ARRRRRGGGHHHH!" he was groaning.

"I know. You are glad to have the gag. Otherwise, your cries of pleasure would alert the *soldados*, no? Yes, I will leave it in."

"ARRRRRGGGHHH!"

"I know what you want, *amigo*. Okay, I do not think it is wise, but if you insist, this time we do three knots."

"ARRRRRRRRRRGGGGGGGGGGGGGHHHHHHHHHH! ARRRRRRRRRRRRRRRRRRGGGGGGGHHHH! AAAAAAAA AAAAARRRRRRRRRRRRRRRRRRRRRRRRRRRGGGGGGG-GGGGGGGGGGGGGGGHHHHHHHHHHHHHHHH!"

When he came to, she was kissing away the salt tears which were stopping his nose, flooding his mouth, scorching his throat. "There, there, *guapo*. There, there. I promise you, when they line you up against the wall, you will not feel a thing."

Then her warm, pouty sensuous lips were wrapping themselves around the base of Carpenter's massive member. His eyes were rolling back. His teeth were gnawing savagely at the gag. And the last lucid vision he had was of the long length of knotted rope wrapped rightly around her hand, her white-knuckled fist squeezing it with a death grip.

And then with a shudder of horror, dread, and most frightening of all, perverse anticipation, he saw the wrist start to move.

85

It was dawn.

Slater sat up on the left-hand corner of the hacienda wall, slumped over his Gatling. Ghost Owl lay beside him, her head in his lap. Both were grimy with black powder smoke. And exhausted.

Horse Ears, who had manned the Gatling most of the night, lay at the bottom of the wall. Two hours into the fighting, he'd been shot off the wall by *Diazistas*. His arms and legs were flung about at odd angles, and flies collected around his bloodied face in a buzzing cloud.

Slater stared out across the battlefield. Vultures rode the early morning thermals, floating on massive, eight-foot wing spans above the killing ground. The gathering buzzards began their gradual descent in slow spirals, ending a patient if hungry vigil over their new-found feast.

There was an awesome power to it all that was not lost on Slater: the great black gyre of carrion birds, the blood-red ball of the sun suspended over the rimrock, throwing its reds and purples and yellows and oranges into the half-dark dawn sky, snuffing out the last stars of morning like candles, the long, deepening shadows, the scorched flats of yucca and sage, mesquite, and prickly pear, the eerie deathscape with its rising pillar of smoke, slanting up over the ashes of the infantry barracks, the scores of fallen mounts, the hundreds of *soldados* scattered across the field with twisted arms and skewed heads, half of them hacked to pieces by *machetes*, others killed by repeating rifles and Gatlings, fragments of others—heads, arms, legs and torsos—charred and tossed and dispersed across the flat by the dynamite's reverberating blast. Great clouds of smoke rolling back and forth over the waterless wastes, a vast, swelling stillness everywhere, as though something more had died on that field that night, something more than men and horses and the bloody death of their bloody dreams. Staring out across that field, Slater felt a hot, black wind blowing through him, winnowing what was left of his heart, savaging the tortured remains of his long-forgotten soul, and leaving in its doomed and luckless wake a lost and blasted void, empty as prayer.

Horse Ears dead. Half of Lerdo's men killed by the Napoleons. So many of Diaz's *peon* infantry annihilated by dynamite as they walked out the barracks door into the calm desert night, the rest cut down by Lerdo's cavalry. The artillery officers manning the Napoleons mowed down by the Gatlings. And for what? Not to get Diaz. He and his own elite corps of *cuirassiers* were gone, as was most of his gold. According to the *majordomo,* he was off with a wealthy *gringo* inspecting one of his silver mines.

Slater rested his chin on the Gatling's hot breech. His assault would never have gotten even this far, not if Diaz had put the Napoleons on mobile mounts. Then he could have turned the guns around and blown Slater's people to hell and gone. They succeeded not because they were better or tougher than the *Diazistas,* but only because Diaz believed his own artillery officers might fire on the hacienda itself.

And the guns they'd hijacked? The Rodmans, the Bottle Dahlgrens, the Mountain Mortars and Hotchkisses? They could not even take them. Lerdo was down to twenty cavalry, and what he needed was not more big guns, but speed and mobility to flee Diaz's counterattack.

The gold? There was none. Diaz's boasts were lies. If the Don had any money, it was not in *El Alacrán.* No jewels, no rare art, nothing worth stealing. He vast estate was a sham.

It was true that Geronimo would reap nearly a hundred and fifty rifles and much ammunition. At least that debt, in part, was paid. A hundred and fifty rifles would not keep the white-eyes at bay forever, but it was a start.

Absently, he stroked Ghost Owl's long raven hair. He felt a stirring for her he had never known. A sense of kinship and closeness, something born of battle and bonded in blood. Coming out of that hacienda, there had been *Diazistas* manning the wall Gatlings, armed with repeating rifles, but she was there, all the way, never flinching. Sometimes loading his guns, sometimes covering his flank. There was no doubt that in a tight spot she could be trusted.

She was now a factor he did not know how to deal with.

Then there was the other thing. An hour ago he had gone back into the hacienda looking for Carpenter. He finally found him just where he had left him. In Diaz's bedroom. There, the sonofabitch was flat on his back in the shadowy darkness of the boudoir, Diaz's personal *mujer* on top, fucking the gun-runner's nuts off, Carpenter moaning like a stuck pig.

Slater had not said anything to his friends. And would not. Partly because he did not understand the incident himself. In the middle of a pitched battle, when Carpenter's life and the lives of his friends were all on the line.

So Slater looked on quietly. He knew that the others would be furious if they found out, but what the hell? You had to admit that fucking Diaz's mistress during a fire-fight showed a certain kind of guts.

The truth be known, Slater admired him for it.

One thing was for sure, the way the man was wailing and groaning, that Maria must be some piece of ass.

He continued to lean on the Gatling as he stared into space. The events of the last few months were spinning through his head. Again, he glanced down at Ghost Owl.

He did not know what to do about *that*.

She was something he did not know how to handle.

86

Early that morning they began spiking the guns. They packed all nine of the big Napoleons, one at a time, with mud and black powder, then blew them up where they stood. They spiked the wall Gatlings the same way. Then they turned to the U.S. ordnance which so many men had died for: the Gatling from the flatcar, the Mountain Mortars, the Bottle Dahlgrens, and the Hotchkiss Guns.

These they did not have time to spike. By now it was pushing noon, and they had to be off. So these went over the cliffs. Slowly. One at a time. Till they were nothing. Till they were *nada*. Till all Carpenter had hoped for was *nada*.

When the last one tumbled over the edge of the four-thousand-foot precipice, Slater heard Carpenter mumble to himself: "The end of dreams."

They turned back to their wagons.

87

Geronimo had his crates of rifles loaded into mule-drawn freight wagons, and Carpenter, despite crushing fatigue and a ferocious limp, had packed up the most valuable piece of merchandise he could find and loaded it onto an extra wagon. They were ready to decamp.

Carpenter's companions were horrified.

"Look," Carpenter reasoned, "observation balloons have been standard issue since the Civil war. And they're expensive. They go for about twenty grand. And I know a man in Chihuahua who will take it off our hands. That's five thousand dollars apiece."

"What about Diaz?" Bass finally asked. "We'd be moving kind of slow, hauling a big freight wagon across a hundred miles of desert. He might just catch up to us.

"Fuck him. He's two hundred miles from here up in the sierras. He's showing his damn silver mine to some *gringo*. Anyway, he wouldn't be going after us. He'd hit on Lerdo or Geronimo here if he was going to go riding all over Hell's Creation."

"Sam," Rose said shaking her head, "he catches us, we get the whole fuckin' drill."

"Yeah, but I hate goin' home broke," Bass said.

"Stone-broke," Slater agreed.

"I don't like it," Rose continued.

"That fuckin' *majordomo* I saved from gettin' executed, he told me Diaz is a million fuckin' miles from here," Carpenter said.

"I don't see no other way," Slater agreed grudgingly. "We

lost everything between hijackin' that train and crossin' this here desert, and I ain't goin' back busted out. Hell, you can get shot just as dead stealin' money from banks and whorehouses as stealin' balloons.''

"I still don't like it," Cimarron grumbled. "I don't like anything this gun-runnin' fuck cooks up.''

"Rose," said Slater, "let's do it.''

"Yeah, and ask fuckin' questions later," said Bass.

88

They met with Geronimo, Ghost Owl, and Lerdo after they were loaded up. They stood by their wagons near the gate.

Slater said: "We be headin' east, Lerdo. You taggin' along?''

"No, I go north.'' His men were already mounted. "To your *yanquiland*. Mexico is not safe for me anymore.''

"Not for any of us," Bass agreed.

There was an awkward silence.

"Say, *compadre*," Slater finally said to Lerdo, "back by them train tracks, Diaz told me that the *revolución* was like a woman. What's he mean by that?''

"He meant that when you first meet her, the *revolución*, she is *muy bien, muy mujer*. All she wanna do is *chingar*— fuck. All the time. Day in, day out. And you say, this *revolución*, she is one hot *señorita*. I could come to like this *mujer*. Then just when you think you have her, she go with another *compadre*. And so you kick her ass, and drag her back, and then again all she wanna do is *chingar*—all day, all night. And you think, 'I got her now, I dominate her *muy bien*.' But the years go by, and you never dominate her. She dominates you. She is not your *mujer*, she is nobody's *mujer*.

And you, you become only her *cabrio,* her cuckold, her goat never her *hombre*."

"Will Diaz dominate her?"

"No. At least, not forever."

"When I last saw him here," Carpenter said, "he told me that one day we would return to *norteamerica* and leave the *revolución* to men like him. We would complain about him later, but it would be us that abandoned her, not Diaz and his kind. He then said *gringos* could not understand her. Mexico or *la revolución*."

"I am Mexican," Lerdo said, "and I do not understand her. And I, too, shall leave her for your *yanquiland*."

Lerdo swung on his horse and started to depart with his remaining *cuirassiers* when Carpenter grabbed his mount's cheek strap. "But he was right. Diaz, I mean?"

"Yes, he was always right. She was always a *puta*. And who should know better than a pimp like Diaz? Men like him, they sold her ass in the marketplace. They made her what she is."

He booted his horse north, away from the hacienda, he and his men waving their farewells.

Slater turned to Ghost Owl. "Seems like I'm always leavin' them's I like on my back trail, and bumpin' into them that I don't."

"You could come back with me to the stronghold. You were happy there once. You said you were complete. You could be again."

He shook his head. "Not no more."

"Then what will you do?"

"Another bank, another train. If I get low enough, another whorehouse."

"You could take me with you."

"It ain't no life for a woman."

"Neither is picking lice from your hair, scraping hides, living on lizards in a brush wickiup. Or dying of dysentery from wormy reservation beef in San Carlos."

He walked her back to Geronimo. "She says she wants to come with me. It ain't my idea. But she wants to."

"She is free." Geronimo's face was impassive.

"Nobody's free."

"What of that *revolución* you speak of? Does that not make you free?"

"The *revolución* is free to *chingar* you. That is what Diaz said."

Geronimo smiled. "I know women like that."

"That's also what Diaz said."

"I think he is a smart man."

"I hope not. I pray to God he is not."

He helped Ghost Owl into the double freight wagon. Bass, Carpenter, and Cimarron Rose jumped in back with their gear. Slater stood up and released the brake. He took the blacksnake in both hands and cracked it with a deafening *thwack!* while Bass pelted the mule rumps with rocks.

"Haw! Gee up!"

Six spans of mules hit their collars, and, with a jerk, the wagons were moving. Geronimo and *El Alacrán* faded into the distance.

89

Up in the mountains, under a grassy *ramada,* Porfirio Diaz entertained three guests. Diaz was at his best. Wearing a new, light tan dress uniform, heavy with braid, garish campaign ribbons, and festooned with ornate medals, he looked and felt the part of Mexico's potent and distinguished *Generalissimo*.

It was indicated. The three guests were of great importance to him. He wanted them to be properly impressed.

The *gringo* gunman, Deacon, he was not so concerned about. He was a good man, in his own way. Border-wise, battle-hardened, moral, responsible, with the sort of rock-bottom integrity that one instantly recognized. Diaz could no doubt use the services of this veteran gun-hand in either Sonora or Chihuahua on some of his more desperate operations.

Diaz made a mental note.

Sutherland? That was another story. Already he had struck one business deal with the man, a partnership in this Chihuahua silver mine. Diaz had known that the ore was there; his best man had told him so. However, the operation had been undercapitalized, and what he'd needed was a backer who had the guts to put up the funding and the brains to give Diaz a free hand in the operation. To get the money was easy enough. *Norteamerica* and Europe were filled with rich businessmen looking for a return on their investments. But few would grant him the loose rein that Sutherland had given him.

Then the third person. Diaz could barely glance at her without his heart stopping. Judith McKillian, the crimson-haired, green-eyed *bruja* with the silken skin and sensual mouth, with the lustrous, flaming hair rolling in waves over her beautiful back and shimmering shoulders, with the sheer violet top tautly encasing those incredible breasts, with the tantalizing trousers of blackest buckskin straining tightly against her rump and legs, tucked snugly into thigh-high spike-heeled, riding boots of mirror-bright ebony leather with silver rowels.

Diaz wanted her so badly he ached with it.

He tried to force his mind away from such thoughts. Sutherland was talking. "*Excelencia,* you will never know how stimulating I find our visit here, how delighted I am with this trip. And let me assure you I am utterly attuned to what you are attempting in this poor, benighted country. When I speak to my political friends in Washington, they will hear from me about how things have changed in Mexico and how successful is this fellow Diaz. Sir, you really understand the fundamentals of *making business work.* You understand the science of exploiting resources, employing technology, and managing labor."

Diaz produced a wide, warm smile. "And you, *señor,* will never know how *muy bien* that makes me feel. You are the only *norteamericano* I ever meet to understand Mexico. My friend, we are men of the same stripe. If you lived in this country, you would be a *gachupín* like myself, a wearer of the spurs. You would see the way of things, the way things are, the way things work."

To emphasize how impressed he was, Sutherland waved toward the opposite mountainside, directly across the gorge. Diaz handed him the 9X binoculars. Sutherland smiled his thanks, eager for a closer look.

A quarter of a mile across the canyon, there was a spectacular view of the thirty-mile trail winding between the entrance to the mine at the mountain's top to the silver-smelting operation at the bottom. Too narrow and steep and twisting for trains, the trail was traveled by at least a thousand *peons*. They trudged up and down the path in two lanes—one going, one coming—bent under colossal burden-baskets piled high with silver ore, rawhide tumplines stretched tautly across their foreheads. They were dressed in dirty white *peon* clothes, pants rolled up and worn through around the knees, wearing crownless straw sombreros. Through the binoculars, Sutherland could see they were all barefooted.

"Splendid," Sutherland whispered.

"*Señor,*" Diaz said slowly, a hint of sorrow touching the deep bass voice, "most men will never appreciate the courage, strength, and determination it takes to run such a thing as this."

"Indeed, *Excelencia,* my American friends have never once been able to set the Indian to useful labor. We have finally stopped trying. We keep our aborigines in luxury on reservations, feed them free beef, and watch them grow fat off the white man's sweat and toil. And American business-men seem able to do nothing about it."

"*Señor* Sutherland, I am sad to say that you *norteamericanos* have failed to develop this vast labor market because you are not ruthless."

"But our friends up north say that the Indian is not equal to hard manual labor, no matter how stern the employers' methods."

Diaz shook his head. "Look around you, sir. I am living proof that the aborigine is perfectly suited for the most exhaustive labor imaginable."

"Even their warriors?" Miss McKillian asked. "Some of

these tribes, I am told, have braves who are so *macho* that they can never be broken.''

Diaz's eyes blazed. "*Señorita*, the fiercest warriors in all the Western Hemisphere are our own Yaqui. The Comanches the Apaches, the Spanish, and French before me all feared the Yaqui, retreated before the Yaqui. So what did I do? I simply applied the principle of sufficient force. *Señorita*, I broke them. I conquered them with cannons, Gatling guns, and repeating rifles. I enslaved them and segregated their men. beat, branded, castrated, shackled, and transported them two thousand miles to work these mines. Half the men you see before you are Yaqui."

"But the Sioux, the Cheyenne, our North American Indians of the Plains, I'm sure they cannot be subjugated."

Diaz cut Judith McKillian off. "*Señorita*, please. With your pardon. In truth, the man does not live whom I cannot break. What you are describing is not the aborigines' strength, but the white man's failure of nerve, his lack of will. I tell you, *señorita*, before I am through, I shall not only break these so-called aborigines as individuals, I shall break them as a race. I will reduce them to beasts of burden, hewers of wood, and drawers of water. They will not grow fat on reservation beef like their American cousins. They will instead learn to serve *Mejico*, to serve God—and to serve me."

"I must say, sir," Sutherland blurted enthusiastically, still studying the miners through his binoculars, "we *do* speak the same language. These brainless yammering jackdaws of the northern climes, sermonizing about all this dignity-of-man rot. They're like religious hysterics, but without religion."

"*Señor*, I could not have said it better. They infect our shores, too. They come down here saying how they love the *Mejican* people—our sad, brown eyes, our blood-stained past, our long-suffering fatalism. It's so much goat dung."

Finally Sutherland put the binoculars down and gave Diaz an appraising look. He smiled and said slowly: "*Excelencia*, as you were saying before about men who cannot be broken. Do you remember the man I told you about? The one who took a piece of my hair, and, had it not been for Mr. Deacon, would have cost me my life?"

Diaz nodded.

"Suppose I told you this man was in *Mejico*? What would you say to that? Do you think even a man like this could be broken?"

"But of course."

"He would have to be tracked down first."

"That is no problem."

"You act as if that were no small thing. Let me assure you, sir, we followed him through the Sonoran canyonlands for two full months with a crack team of trackers, scouts, and professional guns. That expedition seemed simple, too—a small thing. I had viewed the operation as a sport, an ultimate big-game hunt. I learned better."

"Look, *Señor Sutherland, por favor.* Let us speak *de veras,* of truth. I know the man, too. He did a piece of work for me once. The nature of this work is not important. The point is that he repaid my generosity by sneaking into one of my haciendas and doing some small damage. Not much. It is the sort of thing I would ordinarily let pass. I am a busy man and revenge is a luxury I can no longer afford. But in truth, I, too, would like to meet him again."

"Let me assure you, this is not something to take lightly," Sutherland said carefully.

"*Señor,* let me be frank. Torn Slater. You want that *puta* sonofabitch? Fine. I shall arrange it. You have him. You shall watched him piss in the milk of his mother. You will make him curse the bitch for giving him birth. Believe me, this is *verdad. Señor Sutherland,* I personally guarantee it. This Torn Slater, he will die in Mexico before your very eyes, slow and hard."

Involuntarily, Sutherland slavered.

"Of course, I know what you are thinking. You are thinking, now, what can I now do for my good friend, Diaz? For the time being, *compadre,* there is nothing you can do. There may come a time when I might ask you to help arrange for certain arms shipments, but perhaps not. For the moment there is nothing."

"Are you sure it is as simple as all this? I hate to say it, but I did try him once."

"My friend, you are a brilliant businessman, a skilled

hunter, and a spectacular impresario. But there are certain things, which, although you do them well, I do better."

"Then, Don Porfirio, you are, indeed, an extraordinary man."

Diaz smiled. "You know the *peons* have a description of me, one in which I used to find offense. No more. Now when I hear of it, I merely say, Don Porfirio? A compliment on your *machismo*! You know what these superstitious savages actually believe? They maintain that I am God's own scourge on earth. They call me the *puma* pacing the rimrock, the *culebra de cascabel*, or the rattlesnake in his den. They call me the vulture circling over Mexico, waiting to feed on *peons* who perish. Those in need of surcease? They say, 'Come to Diaz.' You know what? When this morning, I get these heliograph messages, transmitted from my *majordomo* to our mine, saying that this Slater, who was foolish enough to trust my man, has vandalized my hacienda this very day, and is now heading by wagon in my direction, you know what I say? I say to myself? Ah, you poor *huaquero* bastard, you poor miserable outlaw. You, too, are in need of surcease. So come to me. Come to Diaz. Please, *compadre,* fear not. This Slater? He is *chingado*. He is fucked. He is dust, debris in the wind. This thing I do for you as a favor. So please, *señor,* a toast." They raised hammered-silver goblets of *Chateau Lafite*, 1855. "*Salud y pesetas y buena caza.*" Health and wealth and good hunting.

"*Gracias, Excelencia. Muchas gracias.*"

"*Por favor,*" Diaz said, smiling. "Your long vigil has come to an end."

90

They camped on the face of a brush mesa. They dared not risk a fire, so they shared a cold supper of hardtack, jerky, and a bottle of Diaz's best brandy.

Carpenter stumbled up into the freight wagon and was sleep within seconds, snoring and groaning loudly.

Bass and Cimarron were off in the mesquite shortly after upper, and soon fell asleep. They would get the watch after later's and Owl's. Carpenter was to get the last watch, but, istening to the groans and snores, Slater doubted the gununner would be up to it.

Slater and Owl moved to the edge of the camp. Reclining n saddle blankets, dark wool *serapes* over their shoulders gainst the night chill, they stared at the welter of desert tars, scattered garishly across the pitch-black sky, Orion and he Dipper blazing ferociously.

"Do you think I will like it there?" Ghost Owl asked, ointing a finger north.

Slater gazed on her pretty, guileless face and wondered ow to answer. Up there, she would not be a shaman, blessed vith magic and honor and dignity, but just a flat-faced, lanket Indian, hunted, hounded, perhaps shot or jailed for he outlaw-lover she rode with. How could he answer her, *de eras*? In truth?

"Probably not."

"But why?"

"The people. They want you to live your life a certain vay. Men, they're supposed to settle down, farm, punch attle, lay track, work claims or mines, or labor in their actories back east. The women are supposed to stay ome and breed kids. Man or a woman who ain't cut out or layin' track or diggin' post holes or punchin' beef, hey don't fit in. Nowhere. In my case, it's worse. I rob rains. People don't like that much. In your case, it'll be vorse."

"Because I'm Apache?"

"That. Also 'cause you be a woman. Not bastard-breedin', ome-sittin' type woman, neither. You been raised to say and lo what you want. And sometimes take what you want. It von't go easy on you. You answer only to spirit-above or to riend-through-choice. That ain't the way they play it up here."

"What will they do to me?"

"You asked me once where all my friends were, and I sai
scattered or dead. You said it was hard to be alone. That'
you. You'll be alone, abandoned, exiled."

"You'll be there."

"Yes, I'll be there."

"Then I won't be alone. I will have you."

"Some say that's worse than being alone. A damn sigh
worse."

"Never, *pindah*."

"I don't know. You asked and I tell you: Up there it b
different."

"Perhaps. But I do know this. This one thing. Until I me
you, I was nothing. I asked for nothing. I wanted nothing
Cochise once said that there was the owl in me, the creatur
that lives only in the night and then travels in the air, on th
wing. I do not know. But now I feel this thing the white-eye
call love, *pindah*. I feel it with all my heart. I feel it for you
I love you as much as I love the Apache people, as much as
love spirit-above, as much as I love and revere the spirit o
my dead father-through-choice, Cochise."

She touched Slater's cheek gently.

"I will make you the best *mujer* I can. I know that I do no
understand the ways of the *pindah*, but I will work hard, and
I will learn. And I will bring to you the ways of the Apaches
which are good and which you will like. I will make you a
mujer who is wise in the ways of the Apaches and is skilled
in the ways of the *pindah* women, too. You will never want a
second or third wife as some Apache men do. I will see to
that. I will be everything."

"*Pindah* men got no second or third wives. Only the
first."

"What happens when the men tire of the one wife, and the
wife of the one man?"

"That's where a man like me comes in. I take up the
slack."

"With me around, you will take up this slack no more
You will be too tired."

Through the stillness of the desert night, a long, snoring

groan wailed and echoed out of the freight wagon where Carpenter slumped in his bedroll. "Like Carpenter?"

"More tired than Carpenter. Tired like the grave."

She came to him, then, helping him out of his clothes even as her own were falling from her body. Then they were on the blankets, under their *serapes* in the cool desert night. He was watching the winking myriads of stars, endlessly spread across the vast, black sky, even as he wondered what it would be like with this magical girl with the obsidian eyes and strange, sad grace, where she would lead him in this weird and senseless coming and going that was life.

Then, even as he paused and pondered, she was on him. Locked onto his cock, her slender but powerful thighs clenching and squeezing and twisting, bringing him quickly to orgasm, but then stopping him, holding him, letting him release only in bursts, in tiny, infinitesimal flashes and flutters and fragments and segments, prolonging the spasm through an eternity of orgasms, as though every one was a tiny star in the coal-black sky of the desert night. Inch by inch by inch by inch, she led him, till he was breathless and deaf and dizzy and faint and falling, and a bright starburst of light exploded behind his eyes, blinding his brain, and he knew that one more wrenching, convulsing climax and he would not faint dead away, but die.

Then she released him, and he was coming, totally, all at once. Over and over and over, the flood—not of lust, but of real passion, something he had never felt before—was pouring out of him, and she was going into her own spasm. Pumping and pumping, over and over the electric shocks were shooting through her till she collapsed on him, sobbing.

He held her a long time. Finally he said to her: "Why did you cry?"

She was half asleep, but she answered haltingly, dreamily: "A vision of my youth. It came to me as I was in pleasure."

"What was it?"

"A great ball of smoke and dust and wind and fire. The owl is in it shrieking my name. Owl! Owl! Owl! It was after this youth-dream Cochise gave me my name."

"What does it mean?"

She opened her fluttering black eyes, eyes depthless and despairing, yet somehow sensual, even in their sadness. "It means I am the Owl. And I shriek of my death. In the fire, the dust, the wind."

91

They were loaded up and on the freight wagon when Slater came down from the rise, his spyglass in hand.

"Bad news. One of our tight buddies at the ranch heliographed Diaz, it seems. In any event, Porfirio and his men are coming back from the mines. They seem to know where we are headed, and they're closing a pincer movement. With military precision. One prong will hit us from in front, one from behind."

"What do we do?" Cimarron asked, her voice cracking with panic.

"Carpenter, let's find out how much this goddamn balloon of yours is really worth."

92

The massive muslin balloon lay collapsed alongside the hydrogen generator wagon. The cordage, rigging, pulleys, ballast bags, extra valves, and shutters were strewn carelessly about. The rattan basket, designed for only three people, looked frightfully small. The purifier boxes and cooler were placed a few feet from each other just in front of the enerator. Hoses, couplers, and a hand-force pump were ooked up and in operation.

In the heart of the generator were barrels filled with iron ilings and water which had been dumped into its tank. 'wenty-two carboys of sulphuric acid had then been syphoned ver them.

After three hours, the balloon hovered mightily, big as a arn, volatile as a boxcar full of dynamite, lashed to the two reight wagons with rope cables.

Bass, Rose, Ghost Owl, and Slater squeezed themselves nto the undersized basket.

Carpenter resealed the generator, and jumped in with them. 'hen he severed the cables and cut loose all the ballast.

93

Slater had seen balloons launched before, but it was never ike this. Usually they shot so quickly into the sky that the assengers almost blacked out from cranial blood loss.

Not so in this basket.

The balloon inched upward with excruciating lassitude, as hough it were still anchored to the generator car. Then, at a eight of four hundred feet, it stopped. Slowly, slowly, the asket swayed in the dead, hot air while the balloon remained notionless.

At first Slater felt genuine horror at dangling in a flimsy attan basket above the ground from a bag which was more xplosively volatile than a boxcar full of dynamite. Every ime the basket swayed to one side, and Slater was dipped recariously over the edge, he felt airsick, and his gorge rose. When he looked at his companions, even Carpenter, who'd een so eager to steal the balloon, was green with vertigo. Cimarron was ready to faint.

Then the two flanks of Díaz's *cuirassiers* converged on the generator, and their fears of height instantly vanished. Now both their lack of altitude and horizontal movement were maddening. The slightest breeze was sufficient to move balloon over many miles, and they did not have even that The air was gustless and still, with not a hint of wind stirring The balloon hung over the generator as if it were cursed, like a ship adrift in doldrums, lost and rudderless in a nether sea

Then Diaz and his men closed in from two directions. I was incredibly quiet, and those in the basket could hear the voices and clinking bridles below with perfect clarity. In the crowd Slater was able to make out Sutherland, whom he'd half scalped by the Black Beauty, the red-headed whore McKillian, and Deacon.

Now he wished he'd killed them all.

"Carpenter, you ever get anything right?" Slater said.

"If we throw him out of this basket, we'd gain a little more altitude," Rose grumbled.

"Yes, but this might help us more," said Carpenter. He raised his Winchester.

"You gonna fight the whole Mexican army?" said San Bass.

"No, I'm gonna blow it up. I sealed off that generator before we launched. It's full of explosive hydrogen. If I can hit that tank, I'll blow those bastards to Kingdom Come."

Down below, people had other ideas. Diaz gave Sutherland a rifle, motioning him away from the tank, more at an angle to the balloon.

So he could get a better shot.

But when Sutherland fired, so did Carpenter. And when Carpenter missed, Sutherland hit. The bullet smacked into Ghost Owl's neck. Blood splattered all over the basket.

She was on her knees. Slater was holding her, and above the tremendous roar from Diaz and his men below, he could hear her whisper. "Throw me out. It'll lift you out of range."

"That's right. Throw her out," Bass yelled, as Sutherland's bullets whined around the basket.

Slater shouted, "You touch her, you bastard, and it's you I'll give to the Mexicans."

But the next thing he felt was the barrel of Cimarron's .45

laid across his left temple, and then he, too, was on his knees. The basket tipped sideways as Bass pushed out Ghost Owl's dying body. Through blurred, swimming eyes, Slater saw the only thing he'd ever loved dropped over the side.

Just as Carpenter hit the hydrogen generator in the wagon below.

It was hard to get a fair look at Ghost Owl's tumbling remains because of the explosion. The blinding flash was brighter than a thousand suns, and next, erupting out of the blast, roared a swirling, red-orange maelstrom of flame—clear, clean, and strangely smokeless in its incandescence. Then the gyre swelled into a boiling fire-ball, as intensely and instantaneously hot against Slater's face as the opening of a blast-furnace door.

Still, Slater saw it. Ghost Owl's buckskin-clad body spinning into the maw of the conflagration. A violent rush of dust swept up into his eyes. The generator's ear-cracking concussion, the basket's sudden weight loss drove the balloon up with dizzy celerity. Slater grew faint from the blow to his head and the rapid increase in altitude. The prophecy fulfilled of how his love would die. *In the fire, the dust, the wind*.

Then the blackness plucked at him, and mercifully he, too, was falling, falling into the abyss of his own wracked, tormented brain.

He was touched by the brutal grace of black oblivion.

BOOK IV

We thank with brief thanksgiving
　　Whatever gods may be
That no life lives forever;
That dead men rise up never;
That even the weariest river;
　　Winds somewhere safe to sea.

—Algernon Charles Swinburne, *The Garden of Proserpine*

PART XV

94

A tall man with a black frock coat, a black Stetson, and flat, black eyes got out of a carriage at the Mark Hopkins Hotel in San Francisco. When a bellboy rushed up to take his single carpetbag, he brushed the frock coat accidentally. It flew open, exposing the pearl handle of a big Navy Colt.

The bellboy could not know that three months before, the pistol had taken the lives of three tellers during a bank hold-up in San Antonio, Texas. Actually, the three men had been Pinkerton agents. The man in the frock coat had blasted all three even as their hands were snaking toward Colts placed discreetly under the cage windows.

It was about that time that the man's hold-up partner, a desperado named Sam Bass, got the wind up.

"It's tightenin', Torn. It's tightening like hell. You're just too damn hot. Jesus, you've burned the Great State of Texas for a good forty thousand dollars in two months. *Honcho,* I'm tellin' you, it be time to take that *dinero* and enjoy it. Come back next year."

The man had not wanted to take the money and enjoy it,

but since he no longer had a partner, he did his best. As a crude disguise, he grew a beard and then proceeded to drink, whore, and gamble his ass off in every good-sized town from St. Louis to Denver to Virginia City. He played his cards loose, his women fast, and took his whiskey hard. The result was that after two months of endless gambling, his forty-thousand-dollar stake was up to nearly a hundred thousand dollars, carried under his white ruffled silk shirt in two oiled-silk money belts, criss-crossing his chest and back.

Try as he would, he couldn't lose.

Not that he didn't do his best to blow it. He called men cheats and liars. He fucked their girls and wives, then boasted of it to their faces. He threw down on two marshals in Abilene, Kansas, and planted them both. A tinhorn's widow in Tucson had ample cause to curse the outlaw's name.

He went to the desk and registered. The red-clad bellboy showed him up the stairs to his second-floor room.

There was an adjoining bath, and the man knew what he would do with it. Fill it to the brim with champagne and two of the highest-priced doxies the town had to offer.

He would join them, let them drink their fill while they dived for his tool.

The room had a black iron balcony overlooking a handsome park, a double-sized canopied bed, and massive mahogany furniture.

The bellboy cleared his throat. Oh, yes, the tip. The man reached into his pocket, took out the first thing his fingers closed on. He absently tossed the Double Eagle across the room.

"Jesus, mister, you must be an awful rich man," the kid blurted.

The man stared blankly at the boy and shrugged. Suddenly inside his heart the darkness plucked again, and he prayed that tonight he would find the bullets or the cards that would bring an end to this long roll. He'd had a good run, but it was time to get back. To the high lines, the owl-hoot trail. Or his death. It was how he wanted it. That was who he was, what he did. The alternative was to think about her endlessly, what they might have had, and what he'd lost.

He walked casually to the door. "Yes, I'm a very rich man." And let the kid out of the room.

PART XVI

Don't look back, boy, on the trail back there,
For the women that loved you or them that care.
There's a wailin' train whistle through your soul it's throbbed
For the men that you killed and the trains that you robbed,
For the banks that you hit and the women that sobbed.
It's followin' you, boy, up your backtrail.
Don't look back, boy, just listen to it wail,
Back in Yuma Jail.

—J.P. Paxton, "The Ballad of Outlaw Torn Slater," 1877

95

The tall man in a brown, collarless, sweat-stained shirt, a tan Stetson, and worn-out Levi's had a weathered face with deep lines around the edges of the eyes. He sat in the front box of a double freight wagon and scowled. He pitched a rock at the rump of the lead mule and yelled: *"Haw! Gee up!"*

Mules are the most cantankerous creatures on God's Green Earth, and ordinarily it takes two men to handle a double-wagon rig and twelve spans of jackasses. But the man did it single-handed, and without apparent effort. It was almost as if the mules, when they looked into his eyes—hard and black as anthracite—sensed that this was a drover they'd best not fuck with. Of course, no one knew what, if anything, went on inside a mule's skull. The man cared even less. Yet they never seemed to give him any shit.

Behind the man were stacked crates on top of crates. They were filled with Winchesters and .44-caliber shells. The man was taking them to Geronimo in the Sonoran Mountains.

This was, of course, utterly illegal. If the *federales* of the newly elected *Presidente,* Porfirio Diaz, caught him, he would enjoy a long stay in the sulphur mines of Sonora Prison.

But the man was not concerned. When he got the idea of purchasing the rig and the rifles with a money belt filled with nearly a hundred thousand dollars, he told himself he was discharging a debt of honor.

However, he did not really believe that.

He slapped at the mule rumps with the reins and glanced absently at his calloused palms with the jagged, blood-brother stigmata, the bonds which locked him eternally to the Chiricauhua tribe and his brother-through-choice, Geronimo.

He threw another rock at the rump of the lead mule and yelled: "Head 'em on out! Haw! Gee up!" The man was in a hurry.

With good reason.

Outlaw Torn Slater was going home.

That morning by the remuda there was trouble. Kelsey had just started to rope out the saddle horses, when Larson, the big man with the apelike arms, tangled with Slater.

"Mr. Slater, us boys been thinking. And, well, we know you're tight with the Mex there, and that maybe he was a good man once. But, Sir, he just don't have it. And he ain't ever gonna have it again. We say send him on out of here."

"Done any more thinking?" Slater asked.

Larson glanced around at the others, as if to get their approval. Then he said it. "Yes Sir, we don't quite hardly know why you and Marquez are each getting that two-split. You boys make more than *all* the rest of us put together. And that ain't fair. So, yeah, we got a couple more ideas, *Sir*." His pronunciation of "Sir" was obviously insulting. "We think it's time that you started treating us like grown-ups, starting with the way you pay us. And in the way you fire the spick." The only emotion flickering in Slater's eyes was amusement. "Otherwise it just ain't worth our while to do no bank robbing. Hot day, low pay. Hell, you might just as well

piss on the generals and call in the troops 'cause this war'
over.''

Slater said nothing.

"Well, Sir"—Larson gritted his teeth—"we're waiting fo
your answer."

"Let's see." Slater shrugged. "You want equal shares al
around plus one less gun to divide it between. Right?"

"Ri——" Larson started to concur but he never got it out
Slater's right hand was a blur as a slip-hammer Colt snake
out of his belt. He drove the muzzle up and under Larson'
rib cage so hard it punched the heart.

And the heart stopped.

For five full beats.

And Larson was on his knees, puking, choking, fac
purple.

But all eyes were on Slater. At last, he spoke: "Smitty
Kelsey, get him on his horse and keep him on it. He's goin' i
with us to take that bank. Into the bank. With me. Also don'
try anything smart. If there's one thing I can't stand, it's a
man who claims to side with you, then back-alleys you fo
money. Someone tries that again, I'll kill him."

While the men finished cinching up their horses, Slate
motioned Hawkins away from the gang. He took him aroun
and up the side of the hill.

"You're staying with the remuda."

Hawkins' face reddened. "Like hell I am."

"Old man, we been friends a long time."

"That's what I say. A long time. And just like always I'm
riding into that town with you. You and me together."

"Last night you said you had the fear."

"So what?"

"So maybe I do, too."

"Then you play stable boy."

"Samuel, I ain't got time to argue. You hold the horses.
Right here. This is the way we'll be riding back. Keep them
loose and warmed up."

"Torn, how many years we been on the owlhoot?"

Slater shrugged.

"Since before Lawrence?"

"I s'pose."

"And I never disobeyed an order?"

"Never."

"Well, you're gonna need me in there. Them punks ain't worth spit. You know it. It gets tight you'll need this old man. I respectfully refuse to follow your order, Sir."

Slowly, Slater smiled. "Aw, fuck it. What am I supposed to do now? Cold-cock an old-timer like you, tie you up and *make* you stay? That'd look real good to old Frank and Jess, wouldn't it? Torn Slater reduced to punching out old men."

Hawkins laughed.

"Okay," Slater said. "Order rescinded. Smitty will hold the mounts. Let's head back."

Hawkins started down the hill. As he did, Slater turned and hit him off the pivot in the back of the neck, every ounce of his 200 pounds behind the punch. He hit him so hard his shoulder hurt. The old man went down like a hammered steer.

Slater continued on down the hill without looking back. Everyone was mounted at the remuda. Marquez had saddled his bay for him. As Slater booted the cinch up two more notches, Marquez asked; "Where's the old man?"

"He just retired from the owlhoot."

"That old fire-eater? Don't sound like his style."

"Maybe not, but he's playin' stable boy now."

" 'Bout time. Who needs that old man anyway?" said Smitty.

"Right," Kelsey agreed. "We'll take this bank like Lee took Chancellorsville."

Yeah, but the Yanks got it now, Slater thought to himself. And they headed off down the hill.

They rode into town six abreast, and while such flamboyance automatically drew attention, that was the point. It was paramount that Brownsville know that there was heavy artillery cantering up their dirt streets: Six silent, hardcase strangers packing five to six guns apiece and wearing the gray linen dusters of their trade.

They pulled up in front of the bank's hitchrack. Slater Marquez and Larson went in to transact their business, while the other three watched the street and horses.

The inside of the Brownsville Guarantee and Trust wasn unimpressive. Tellers in three cages wearing white boiler shirts, celluloid collars and black elbow garters stood attention. Behind them a spacious office for the president. In the bull pen, a clerk with a green eye-shade was working on the books. An unlit coal oil lamp hung from the ceiling. A cuspidor stood by the door. On the wall was a sepia portrait of Ulysses Simpson Grant.

The first thing Torn Slater did was fire two rounds into the ceiling and scream; "Everybody on the fucking floor!" Next he vaulted the railing between the president's office and the bank lobby.

As he went through the door, to his undying horror, he was looking into the double-barrels of a sawed-off eight gauge Greener. He hit the floor hollering: "Pinkertons!" just as the Greener exploded over his right shoulder, taking out half the bank wall. Then he came up under the flaming, smoke billowing sawed-off, his leveled pistol pumping round after round into the Pinkerton's mouth and chest.

The man dropped the Greener. Slater could see that only one of the double hammers was down. Grabbing the Greener in his right hand, using the acrid screen of gunsmoke for cover, he slipped up alongside the door. His ears were ringing violently from the eight-gauge blast. He'd been unaware of what happened in the front of the bank.

Now he could see it all. The clerks and tellers were disguised Pinks and armed with double-action Remingtons. Inside the bank, they'd already scored. Larson, their first victim, was lying on the bank floor, face down in a gathering pool of blood. Marquez had been driven back into the outdoors gunfire.

And outdoors was hell.

The main street looked like a Civil War battlefield. Windows were smashed and the street seemed almost as choked by black powder smoke as the inside of the bank. Riderless orses were tearing up and down the street, one of them ulling a dead man with a spur caught under the latigo.

As the ringing in Slater's ears diminished, he was able to ick up sounds from the street and inside the bank. The guns ounded like howitzers. With all the blood and smoke and unfire, Slater could only think of Shiloh.

Then he noticed something peculiar. The Pinks were not urning to face him. While it was obvious that they thought e'd succumbed to the Greener's blast, it was also apparent hat they were otherwise occupied.

Then he saw the head bobbing up above the bank windows, uns throwing lead at the Pinks.

Marquez.

He was drawing their fire.

Quickly, Slater went back to the fallen Pink. He rifled the nan's pockets and came up with five more shells. He breeched he shotgun, jerked out the spent smoking shell, and shoved n another.

He returned to the door, and with the first barrel took off he nearest Pink at the waist. The second barrel ripped hrough the room and tore apart the next two cages. imultaneously, Slater's left-hand Navy Colt was hammering ounds into the third Pink in the last cage. Shoving two more ounds into the Greener's breech, pausing only to give Marquez thumb's up thanks, Slater kicked open the bank door and hit he street, firing.

When he reached the plank sidewalk, Slater realized just now bad a spot they were in. At least a dozen men lined the oof-tops, armed with shotguns and Winchesters. And they vere cutting his men to pieces. Smitty lay face-down, the back of his head blown away, snaky coils of bloody gray natter spilled across his back and neck and the dusty street.

Kelsey was the one with his rowels locked under the latigo. His mount, a big deep-chested gray, dragged him up and down the main street, face-first in the dust, blowing and snorting pink foam, eyes walled, mad beyond comprehension with the noise and smoke and smell of blood.

With Larson dead in the bank, that left only Marquez and

Durango. Pinned down behind a water barrel, Durango wa
screaming at him. Audible above the din of the battle, Slate
could make out the words: "The horses! Get the horses!"

It made sense. He waved to Marquez on the other side o
the plank sidewalk and nodded toward their mounts, four c
them still tied to the hitchrack. It was a slim chance, an
they'd take some rounds, but there was no choice.

He vaulted the rack at full run, pulling loose two sets o
reins as he jumped. One hand clutching the pommel, th
other the Greener, he swung on.

The first bullet went whining through the cantle, and th
second round, coming a split-second after the first, took th
bay squarely between the eyes. Even before the horse wen
down, Slater saw Marquez's roan take slugs in the chest, th
belly and the side of the head. Now both mounts rocke
forward onto their knees, blowing crimson foam from thei
nostrils, crashing into the hitching post and shattering it. Th
mustang he'd grabbed for Durango went down a half-secon
after them, shot through the neck, blowing great gouts o
blood. Slater dived over the bay's bent neck to keep fron
being crushed between the bay and the mustang.

Quickly, he and Marquez scrambled back into the bank
rifle bullets peppering the storefront and the walk. The bank
was billowing smoke and the street was filled with acrid fog
The rifle fire on the outside walls sounded like sledge hammers.

"Hey, *amigo*, how come no one's asking us to surrender?"

"Ain't you seen them dodgers? Can't you read English?"

"What you mean?"

"Them dodgers read **Wanted Dead!** Ain't no money in
taking us alive."

Marquez nodded. "But why they shoot the horses?"

"Cole Younger took eleven rounds in Northfield and still
rode away. The Pinks learned then, you kill the mounts.
Shooting a man don't guarantee you nothing."

Marquez said, "I think we are going to die here."

"Nothin' wrong with dyin'," said Slater, reloading his
pistols and the Greener.

"*Si, amigo*. But death, she's better between the legs of a
good woman."

"Then let's make them bastards pay."

"*Es verdad.*"

"*Por la Revolución?*" Slater asked with a mocking grin.

"*Viva la Revolución!*"

They turned to the shot-out windows and began throwing lead at the roof tops with such fatal effect that the hammering on the bank walls was cut by two-thirds.

Then to their astonishment it stopped altogether.

Slowly, languidly, drifting up the street came the melodic refrain of a mouth organ playing "Dixie."

Risking a look, they peered through the shot-out windows. There, frock coat and Stetson exchanged for a Confederate cavalry uniform, a jerkline string of remuda ponies dallied around his pommel, a harmonica pressed to his lips with one hand, the other waving the Stars and Bars above his head, rode Captain Samuel Hawkins, formerly of Quantrill's Raiders.

The YIP-YIP-YIP!!! of thirty rebel yells shrilled up and down the street. Men tossed hats in the air and broke into cheers. The butternut-gray, their defeated flag, the strains of the grand old song, turned back the clock.

It was a Texas town, populated by the most Yankee-hating rebels south of the Mason-Dixon. For five full seconds, as the townful of rebel veterans cheered the old soldier, it seemed they were transported body and soul back to the days when Bobbie Lee and Jeff Davis led the land.

It was only the sight of Torn Slater and Rafael Marquez leaping over the dead horse lying atop the smashed hitchrack, and cutting out mounts from the Captain's jerkline that brought them to their senses.

Mounting his mare, Durango was torn to pieces by rifle slugs. The other three, however, were in the saddle and beating it out of town.

It was a long gauntlet, a good 150 feet, and none should have escaped. But now it seemed as if the town's collective wrath was focused on the old man who had conned them.

Almost two dozen rounds hit him. For a moment it did not seem as though he was shot but that he exploded. His skullcase, ribcage, stomach, seemed to burst apart simultaneously, a balloon full of blood detonating across the town's streets, and Samuel Hawkins was no more.

Torn Slater was already at the end of the gauntlet, almost out of range. So those who still had the presence of mind to fire again, went for the closer, easier mark.

Marquez was blasted off his horse.

Slater was beyond their guns, when he heard the second round of shots. He glanced around to see Marquez fall. He rode another fifty yards, feeling odd. It bothered him that the old man had ridden in like that with the Confederate gray and that damn flag. He couldn't forget Marquez drawing the fire of those other four Pinks. He wasn't used to having his life saved twice in one day.

He stopped again to give that damn town one more look.

To his stunned surprise Marquez was sitting up, leaning on his dead horse, looking about the street foolishly.

His friend was still alive.

And Slater knew what was going on in his mind.

Extradition.

And Diaz.

Torn Slater went galloping back into the town, his saddle pistols fully loaded and the reins in his teeth. Throwing rounds at the roof tops, he felt good, better than he'd felt in years. In was like Shiloh, like Lawrence, like his days with Quantrill and Bloody Bill, with Frank and Jess and Coleman Younger. Yes, he thought, he'd forgotten *that*. The good feeling, the clean feeling, the sense of belonging and commitment to a cause.

The roof tops were blazing but not as potently as before. Many of the men had already come down, but damn, in his present keyed-up state it seemed he couldn't miss. His mind was working neatly, his hands were sure, his aim swift, the mount was perfection between his knees. He did not even care that his belt and horse pistols were now empty. He felt so good that he made a wide circle around the grinning Marquez, sitting there by his fallen horse in the blood-soaked streets of Brownsville. For a second even the rifle fire came to a dead halt and—

Then he saw it.

And he came to a stop.

James Sutherland was standing alongside Judith McKillian on the brothel balcony, the one he had visited the night before. He was leaning out over the edge, a scoped, bolt-action Mauser held jauntily over his shoulder by the barrel. He was waving a red rebozo at him, one with fancy gold and silver embroidery.

Dolores's red rebozo.

"Don't worry, old man," Sutherland said cheerily. "I'm not going to shoot you just yet. You have a small but pleasant grace period. For one thing, I know your pistols are empty. For another, I have a few anecdotes to relate before retiring you from this mortal coil. Interested?"

Slater shrugged.

"First of all the rebozo and your friend, Dolores. Through the usual series of both willing and unwilling informants, we learned that she had been seen lugging two wounded men home on a mule. Our investigations took time, and as a result, she still might have made it out of there. In fact, but for a little piece of avarice on her part, it would be Dolores greeting you here instead of me. Like it so far?"

Slater was silent, his eyes empty of expression.

"You see, she still had this thing about mining Diaz's placer streams. Rather impractical if you ask me. Something about avenging her late husband and making money for you. She went back. And made a haul! Close to $8,000. Unfortunately, all that placer panning took extra time. When she stopped off back home to pick up a few things, I'd gotten there just an hour or two before. And found this." He held up a small charred piece of paper. "Not much to go on except it was her writing and your name was clearly inscribed on it. Seems you threw it into the cook fire where it failed to totally ignite.

"Ah well, I know what you're thinking now. Betrayed by a woman. Under the duress of my hot coals and knives, she ratted you out to your sworn enemy. I wish it were so. During the delirium of pain all I got out of her was the word *Texas*, which is a pretty big place. And after that, well, I left the poor girl alone for a few minutes and when I got back she'd hanged herself from an overhead joist. Right above that little sleeping pallet, where you and she no doubt made wondrous love.

"But I know what you're thinking. Who did rat you out? Well, I knew you were heading toward Texas. And, Diaz did tell Marquez, after that little lashing, that he'd stashed his bitch in a bordertown brothel. Which meant you and Marquez would stick to the Texas border.

"So here's the jackpot: Who ratted you out? The same one who ratted out Marquez and his fellow *revolucionarios* to Diaz. The same one who's been on Diaz's payroll as well as in his bedroll since she was ten years old. Marquez's wife. So rest assured, Marquez," Sutherland shouted, waving down the street to the still-sitting and wounded man, "your wife is fine. Just a little joke. In fact, we had her set up in this brothel, plying her trade, business as usual. You would have stumbled onto her. And she'd hold you there long enough to get word to me. It was really quite simple."

Sutherland took the rifle off his shoulder and jacked a round into the chamber.

A young Mexican woman drifted out onto the balcony. She was wearing a tight, black lace dress. She put an arm around Sutherland and canted her hips whorishly.

Sutherland put the rifle down a moment and smiled. "Just a minute more?"

Slater shrugged again and leaned back on his cantle.

"You still with us Marquez?" he shouted down the street. "Say, old man, isn't it wonderful the thing she does with her mouth, tonguing your dick all up and down that tender underside till the top of your cock feels like it's on fire? Then when she gives you that great big blowjob?" Sutherland wrapped both arms around his chest and shouted: "Ummmm-ummmmphhh!"

To which Maria closed her large doelike eyes, pouted her lips into a seductive, sensuous *O,* and blew the sinful circular kiss first at Marquez up the street, then at Slater just below the balcony.

Slater drew the slip-hammered Navy colt from the belt behind his back. He fired the first round between her pouted lips, jolting her sideways, off and over the balcony's edge. The second round he pumped into Sutherland's chest, driving him backward through the balcony window in an explosion of broken glass.

The street was now erupting in gunfire, and swinging down low along his horse's neck, he pounded leather up the dusty smoky street in an S-curving pattern, while bullets kicked up dust on all sides of him.

Nearing Marquez on the upward sweep of one of his S's, he kicked his right foot out of the stirrup, grabbed Marquez's outstretched arms and swung him up behind as Marquez simultaneously found the ox-bow.

Then under a withering rain of high-powered gunfire, they galloped out of town.

Slater's mount had a Big Fifty Sharps in its saddle sheath and a twelve-power scope, and that had bought them a little time. The sight of a comrade being blown out of the saddle from 1,200 yards away by a 700-grain slug backed by 170 grains of black powder, a round designed to kill a 4,000 pound bison at the same distance will slow down even the most determined posses.

Still, they were now in the hills, less than twenty miles out of Brownsville, with the posse finally closing in. Their lone mount was half-dead from carrying double.

Slater staked the big buckskin out by a mesquite bush, rubbed him down with dried sagebrush and watered him. He then looked to Marquez's wounds.

They were bad. The first one had gone through his shoulder,

but had gone through clean. The next two had fragmented and lodged in his lungs. Now his breath was wet, rattled in his throat, and his lungs sounded as if they were filled with double-O buck.

He would not last the night.

Slater propped his friend's head up under his warbag and dressed the wounds as best he could. Marquez's saliva was now pink, and a thin sheen of blood coated his lips.

Slater bent over him. "You take it easy, *amigo*. The horse, unlike us, needs some rest, but afterward we mount up and ride."

Marquez took his friend's arm. Blood was bubbling in the corner of his mouth. As Slater wiped it away, Marquez said quietly: "You carry me away from the law twice. Both times across your back."

"This time you caught two slugs meant for me."

"Yes, but you came back. You did not have to do that, you know?"

"And if I had reconnoitered properly, I might have learned about the Englishman. Instead I—"

Slater put his finger over Marquez's lips. "Be quiet. There is no blame. She was your wife. You could not know what she had done."

"She was Diaz's *puta*."

"Shhh. We have far to ride."

Marquez shook his head. "No, you have far to ride."

"Not without you, my friend."

Now Marquez grinned. "Ah, where have I heard that before? I remember. Back by the cave in. The miner who was crushed. 'Don't worry, amigo. We will not leave without you. My friend here will remove the rock from your balls, and we will drag you out. This is your lucky day to have such fine *amigos* as ourselves. You will not die in the dark and the dust, alone.'"

"Shhh."

"No, my friend, for *I* am not lucky today. And I, too, do not wish to die in the dark and the dust, alone. Nor do I wish like that miner, to have my throat cut by a grinning *gringo*, who jokes with his friends."

"You are my *compadre*. I tell you in an hour's time I shall put you back on the horse and get you to a doctor. *Amigo*, I wear this on my eyes, on my balls."

With his right hand Slater lowered Marquez's eyelids, then placed his hat over his face to protect it from mosquitos and moonlight. Then he sighed.

It was all true. This was the best friend he'd ever had, an *amigo* without whom he would have died a dozen times over in the Sonoran Pit. And here Marquez was: Shot to pieces, a chest full of bullets, a mouth full of blood, the eyes dim and blank with the pain of death. And nothing Slater could do.

Here was a man who had more guts than you could hang on a forty-mile line fence, who feared nothing that walked on less than three legs. You knew who he was, what his word was worth, and things that counted. You didn't ride the river with him—he rode the river with you. And there were times down there in the Pit he almost *was* the river.

And still there was nothing Slater could do.

He'd given his word.

Carefully, deliberately, he drew the slip-hammered Navy Colt from the belt behind his back. Since the sear was filed down, the trigger wired back against the guard, and the action oiled slippery as glass, the hammer went back in silence. With his left hand he took the red felt sombrero by the crown and raised it minutely. He quickly slipped the pistol under the three-foot brim, pressed it against his friend's temple and let the hammer down.

Under the big hat the pistol shot was a muted cough.

He rose to avoid the uprush of acrid smoke. He walked back to the horse and cinched up. He swung on, spun the big buckskin around and headed toward the other side of the hill.

It was dark, and for a long moment he studied the downward twisting trail. It looked rough, and for awhile he thought about hand-leading the horse. Then he figured, fuck it.

He headed down the dark, narrow path alone, without looking back.